DOVES
and
THUNDER
GODS

ISBN-10: 098456165X

EAN-13: 9780984561650

Disclaimer: This is a work of fiction. While, as in fiction, the literary perceptions and insights are based on experience, all names, characters, places, and incidents are either products of the author's imagination or are used fictitiously. No reference to any real person is intended or should be inferred.

Cover: Lee Nielsen

DOVES
and
THUNDER
GODS

In remembrance of all who gave their lives
With special thanks to
Colonel Harold Kahlor
And
Lieutenant Colonel Herbert Maynard Carr

CHAPTER ONE

Wichita Falls, Texas. July 1967.

Sandy O'Connell removed her sunglasses to better see the military policeman. She had driven through Oklahoma and part of Texas in oppressive July heat. Now her head throbbed and her voice seized up for lack of moisture. "I'm sorry." She tried again. "What did you say?"

"I said I need four copies of your orders," he repeated.

She counted out the pages from a box on the car floor.

He studied his clipboard. "You've been assigned a BOQ, Lieutenant. Check in at the housing office, ma'am."

She pressed both hands to her temples. "BOQ?"

"Bachelor Officers' Quarters, ma'am."

"How do I find the office?"

He tossed her a map. "Building Six." As she put the car in gear, he snapped a salute.

Flustered, she pressed the accelerator and nearly ran through the entrance gate. She caught his smug smile in her rearview mirror.

❦

Large stenciled numbers identified each sun-cured building. At number six she joined a line of men hugging a thread of shade in the building's shadow. Several cast a glance at her, but most appeared too wilted to care that a young woman had joined them.

The line moved quickly. Stepping through the open door was like stepping into an oven. Texans, or maybe just the military, apparently didn't believe in air conditioning.

One soldier sat behind a long counter covered with clipboards. "Ten copies of your orders," he said without looking up.

She counted off the sheets and waited as he selected a clipboard and added her orders to the already thick stack. "Is there somewhere I can get a drink?"

He shrugged one shoulder toward the window. "The bar at the Officers' Club is always open, Lieutenant."

"Oh. No." She shook her head. "I mean a real drink—water or a soda."

"Outta luck." He shoved a packet of papers and a key across the desk. "Building Nineteen, Apartment Five. You'll have two roommates. Welcome to the United States Air Force, ma'am."

৵

An empty parking area lay across the narrow street from number nineteen. As she crossed the pavement, lugging her suitcase and box of orders, her sandals made a sucking sound in the softened asphalt. Each step up the open wooden staircase sent overheated blood pounding through her temples. She leaned forward to fit her key into the lock. The door flew open.

A girl with a dazzling smile, punctuated on each end with deep dimples, held out a beer. "Welcome to Texas," she drawled. She wore white Bermuda shorts and a silk shirt as blue as the cornflowers that lined every Texas road. Her eyes were as vibrant as the shirt. "You look like you're in need of a tall cool one." She lifted the box of orders and purse from Sandy's arm and placed the cold beer into her hand.

"Thank you. Oh, thank you. I'm dying of thirst." Sandy tipped the can to her parched lips and drank.

"Well, come on in out of the sun!" The girl's pink-pearl toenails peeked from sandals of twisted leather.

Sandy took a deep breath and dragged her suitcase into the refreshing coolness of an air-conditioned room.

"Are you Sandy or Penny?" the girl asked.

"Sandy."

"I'm Kate. I was here early so I took the bedroom on the left. You get to choose between the other two. Last one in gets the dregs."

The living room was furnished with a couch, a coffee table, and an ancient refrigerator that stood next to an open bathroom door.

Sandy carried her suitcase to a bedroom and dropped it next to the narrow bed.

"It's not much to write home about," Kate said as she placed the box of orders on a small dresser that clung to the wall below a scarred mirror.

Actually, it was more than Sandy had expected. She had pictured lines of tight-sheeted cots footed with low green lockers. She lifted her ponytail and pressed the cold can of beer to the back of her neck. Its coolness slowed the throbbing in her head.

They returned to the living room and sank onto the couch.

"Sure was nice of you to think of beer," Sandy said. "I'm not used to this heat."

"In a few days, you won't even notice. I've lived with it all my life. Arizona. Family has a ranch. Daddy's in politics."

The pedal pushers, cotton shirt, and plastic sandals Sandy had worn for the day's long drive suddenly seemed tacky. "I'm from Maine. Mostly farms and logging companies. I sure do miss the trees."

Kate curled a strand of frosted hair through the fingers of one hand as she drank deeply from her beer. Her skin was tanned to a fine golden color. "Nice car you're driving."

"I bought it this spring."

"I left mine at home. Didn't think I'd need one until Wichita. Did you know we're both assigned to Meridian?"

"Really? Gosh, that's great. If you want, we can drive up together."

They sat up late waiting for their last roommate to arrive. Nearly a six-pack of beer and a carton of powdered-sugar donuts disappeared as they discussed their printed schedules. Laughter punctuated each vain attempt to decipher acronyms created by military minds.

At midnight, when Penny still hadn't shown, Kate stuck a note on the refrigerator door: *Welcome roommate. We saved you a beer.* They called it a night.

ം

The roar of aircraft shook Sandy awake. White light told her she had overslept. She hurried past the empty middle bedroom to pound on Kate's door. They dressed quickly before dashing into an oppressive wall of heat scented with an odd mixture of aircraft fuel and sweet sage.

Kate bounced lightly down the rickety stairs. She carried a shoulder-strapped briefcase over one shoulder, a white leather purse over the other. In one hand, she held a powdered-sugar donut; in the other, the last can of beer. She alternately nibbled and drank as she moved lightly across the street to the parking area.

Sandy ran behind in fits and starts. She juggled a stack of loose papers, the hard straw purse that had been a farewell gift from her hospital coworkers, and the crumpled base map she attempted to read as she negotiated the stairs. She dropped her keys to the pavement. When she bent to retrieve them, she lost her papers. Her sandals left black prints on her orders as she saved them from drifting away.

Kate doubled over with laughter, tossed the remainder of her donut under the car, hopped in, tucked the can of beer between her knees, and began to line up cosmetics on the dash.

Sandy tossed her things into the back and started the engine.

"Hey!" A girl with copper-colored hair bounced across the lot. "You going to the Medical Service School?" Her short plaid shift, cut by the straps of a full-sized backpack, emphasized the fullness of her breasts and her sturdy legs.

"Is that OBMTM?" Sandy asked.

"Yes," the girl answered. "Officers' Basic Military Training Medical."

"That's us. Hop in."

"I missed the damned bus." She threw her pack into the back and squeezed in behind Kate's seat. "We're late, you know."

"Almost." Sandy pulled into a deserted street. "It doesn't look far on the map."

"If we're late we're dead meat. The T.O. will cream us."

"T.O.?" Kate asked without looking away from her mascara brush.

"Training Officer. Major Kharkins. And let me tell you, he's a case, if you get my drift."

"A case?" Sandy asked.

"A real ball breaker. Rumor has it he got the job because no one else could handle the gawd-egos of the docs. He despises women in the military." As the girl rolled her eyes, they showed bright green in the rearview mirror.

They approached a wide avenue, indicated on the map by several broken lines. The training building was just across the way. Sandy stepped on the gas.

"Hey!" the girl screamed. "Holy crow! Turn around!"

"We've got a direct shot. Look." Sandy flipped the map over her shoulder and continued across alternating strips of dirt and pavement.

"Stop!"

Sandy slammed on the brakes. "What?"

"We're on the flight line!"

"The what?"

"The runway! Oh my gosh, here come the A.P.s." Before anyone could ask, she added, "A.P.s—Air Policemen."

Two blue cars with flashing lights pulled nose to nose with the car. Four uniformed cops came at them with hands on their guns.

"I.D.s," one demanded. "Come on, give me your I.D.s."

The new girl handed over a card.

Sandy's hands and knees shook as she found her driver's license and handed it out the window.

"I said I.D.s."

"Your military I.D.," the girl prompted.

Sandy felt foolish and completely out of sync. "I don't have one."

"We're FNGs," the girl offered out the window as the A.P. studied her card. "We'll get new I.D.s today."

"Well, wouldn't you know? Some of our bright new officers. Out for a morning drive, were you, ladies?"

"Just trying to find our way …"The new girl's voice contained a warning as she added, "Sergeant."

"Did you know you missed colliding with a T-38 by about twenty seconds?" the man asked.

Kate pushed her empty beer can under the seat, leaned over, and smiled coyly up at him, "Can we apologize? Meekly say 'Sorry'?"

"You can each give me a copy of your orders."

Sandy turned on her knees, leaned into the back, found one of the footprinted sheets, and handed it to the cop. "I'm sorry, Officer. I'm lost."

He turned to Kate. "What about you. You got orders?"

"Yes," she said. "In my case. One minute."

Sandy stared after him as he strode to his car and began to read their names into his radio. The other cops stood in a half circle, snickering.

"What's an FNG?" Sandy asked.

"Effing New Guy," the girl answered. "Listen, you don't call A.P.s 'Officer.' We're the officers. And you don't ever apologize to an enlisted man. Officers never apologize. That's a rule."

"Are we in big trouble?" Sandy asked.

"Yes. I think we are. I'm Penny, by the way. Who are you?"

"Sandy O'Connell, and this is Kate Kiley."

"Just my luck," she said. "My new roommates."

The A.P. returned and handed Penny her card. "Thank you, Sergeant," she said.

"Yes, ma'am, Lieutenant Patterson."

"Can you get us on our way?"

"Well, ma'am, you've riled Major Kharkins. He says we should double-time your pretty little asses over there. If you'll follow me, we'll go in the back way."

Sandy stared down the black line of runway that cut through the sparse brown landscape and seemed to go on forever. Rising heat waves promised another intolerable day. This was a god-awful place. She wanted to turn around and go home.

Penny tapped her shoulder. "Go," she said. "Hurry up."

The second vehicle pulled in behind them.

"Great. Just great," Penny said. "A police escort on our first day."

Kate groaned. "You'd think they'd give us some orientation instead of letting us loose like this."

Penny laughed. "This *is* orientation. You're an officer. You're expected to manage. Sink or swim."

"I don't speak their language. Yesterday the guy at the gate had to tell me what a BOQ was," Sandy wailed. "And God help me if I'll ever learn to salute."

Penny sat forward. "Kharkins will get some good mileage out of this one."

"So what if he does?" Kate shrugged as she put her kit away. "How long are we going to be here? Six weeks. We can take a little grief for six weeks."

"That's not how it works. The officer corps is a closed clique. Our reputations will follow us wherever we go."

Sandy pulled into the parking space next to the A.P. as a small jet roared down the runway.

"That's what they're so upset about," Penny offered as they exited the car. "That's a T-38. T is for *Trainer* and 38 the model number. Two-seater, one instructor, one student." Then, as if revealing a big secret, she whispered, "All the little rich boys train here: Saudi Arabian princes, Thai royalty, and Americans with blue blood running through their veins."

"How do you know so much when this is your first day too?" Kate asked.

"I've been enlisted for six years. I just got my BSN through Operation Bootstrap and earned me a regular commission. Now I'm a second lieutenant, same as you."

"Weren't you supposed to report in yesterday?" Sandy asked.

She smiled. "I was saying good-bye to my boyfriend. It took a little longer than I expected. If you get my drift." She looked ahead to the open door of the building. "Brace yourselves. Be prepared for a dressing down. And for gosh sakes, whatever you do, don't cry."

They stepped into the front of a silent auditorium. "How's my makeup?" Kate whispered.

Sandy half-turned to answer and bumped into Penny, who had stopped moving. A sea of faces looked down on them from elevated seats. She felt tears welling up. Don't cry, she remembered. Whatever you do, don't cry.

One man, whose crisp uniform jacket didn't quite cover the slight paunch over his drooping belt, hurried toward them. His stride was oddly birdlike. His eyes darted brightly above chubby cheeks. His balding head glowed under the fluorescent lighting. This couldn't be the fierce Kharkins, Sandy thought. But a nametag over his breast pocket said that indeed he was. Colorful medals climbed his chest toward his shoulder.

"Well. Well. What have we here?" His voice reverberated against the concrete walls. "Good morning, ladies."

"Good morning, sir," Penny said.

"I'm so glad you feminine feather merchants could join us on this beautiful July day in the Year of Our Lord nineteen hundred and sixty-seven." He stepped up to Sandy, ran his eyes over her, then turned his back and faced his audience. The crowd reacted with a cheer followed by a chorus of laughter. He had made some kind of gesture.

Sandy felt small and powerless. She forced herself to look into the grinning faces. Most of them were male: the doctors, dentists, veterinarians, and pharmacists who made up the medical corps.

"Are you the driver of the red convertible?" the major thundered.

"Yes," she answered. But her throat was as tight and dry as it had been in the heat of the previous day, and when he didn't respond she thought he hadn't heard. "I am," she added.

He mimicked her tone perfectly. "I am—what?"

She struggled to control her quavering voice. "I am the driver."

"I am the driver—what?" he mocked.

If only she could go back and start again. "I am the driver of the red convertible."

The audience again responded with raucous laughter.

There was no getting out of it. She was going to cry. She made fists of her hands and pulled herself taller.

Kharkins turned and moved so close she could smell the coffee he'd had for breakfast. "Your name and rank, please."

"Sandra O'Connell, lieutenant."

"Sandra O'Connell, lieutenant, what?"

"Sandra O'Connell, lieutenant, nurse."

He half turned and gave his audience an exasperated look. "Lieutenant." His voice rose as he threw his hands in the air and nearly struck her with his fingertips. "I need you to follow military protocol when you address me."

As Sandy stepped sideways, Penny whispered, "Sir."

"Lieutenant O'Connell, do you know what I'm asking of you?"

"Yes, sir."

He placed his hands on her shoulders and turned her fully toward his audience. "Absolutely correct, Lieutenant!" He opened his hands wide and wagged his fingers for applause.

Whoops and whistles cut the morning air.

"Isn't she smart?" he staged whispered. "Isn't she wise? Sir. The magic word … sir." He pointed to the gold leaves on his epaulets. "What rank am I, Lieutenant O'Connell? Do you know?"

"Major."

He wagged his hands to her, waiting again for the magic *sir*.

She heard Penny's deep intake of breath, yet she couldn't bring herself to say it.

His eyes met hers. He stepped closer. "Say the magic word, Lieutenant. I would like to hear the magic word."

She stood mute.

He squared his shoulders and commanded her, "Address me properly, Lieutenant!"

She smiled, as Kate so charmingly smiled, and relented. In her loudest voice she shouted, "Sir. Major, sir!"

Applause filled the room.

He turned immediately to Kate. His voice took on a sultry quality. "And who are you?"

Perfectly relaxed in a belted sundress that fell wrinkle-free from her tiny waist, she turned and allowed her gaze to fall warmly on the audience. Every eye fixed on her. "Lieutenant Kathryn Kiley, sir." She dimpled.

With exaggerated slowness, Kharkins looked her up and down. He turned to his audience, opened his eyes wide, grinned lecherously, then raised his eyebrows high, Groucho Marx style, just once.

The crowd tittered. Behind his back, Kate executed a perfect curtsy that brought a roar of laughter and foot-stomping cheers.

Kharkins turned instantly, but missed Kate's performance. He paced a bit, as if pondering his next move, before he turned his full attention to Penny.

"Lieutenant Patterson, let me see if I've got you pegged. Lieutenant Penny Patterson, formerly Sergeant Patterson, daughter of Master Sergeant Patterson, which makes you a military brat. Am I correct so far?"

"Yes, sir."

"And you've very recently taken advantage of our generous education opportunities and received a coveted commission as a regular Air Force officer?"

"Yes, sir."

Sandy made a mental note to ask Penny what the term *regular* meant.

"May I ask you a question, Lieutenant Patterson?"

"Certainly, sir."

He stood beside her, but directed his voice to the audience. "Lieutenant Patterson, can you tell me why, at 0700 hours this morning, when you should have been in your seat in this classroom, you were instead out on the flight line interfering with the mission of this Air Force facility and endangering the lives of our highly—and I might add, expensively—trained pilots?" He raised his hand to stop her from answering and added, with a perfect sense of timing, "Looking for feathers, were you?"

The room quivered with controlled laughter.

Penny raised her head and answered. "No excuses, sir."

"No excuses, sir," he mocked. "No excuses? Is that all you have to say for your act of stupidity?"

"Yes, sir."

His face reddened.

Sandy decided it was time to tell him she was the stupid one. That she had never been near an Air Force base before, she had been driving, and everything was her fault.

Before she could speak, he continued, "And why, may I ask, have you no excuse, Lieutenant?"

"Because I am an officer in the United States Air Force, sir. As such, I will never offer an excuse to anyone, sir."

"Thank you, Lieutenant. If you ladies will please find a seat, I will commence to transform all of you useless feather merchants into officers of the United States Air Force."

❦

Sandy wrote to her best friend, Rita, near the end of training.

15 August 1967

Hi Rita,

I can't tell you what a wonderful time I'm having. Everything is so new and interesting. I have two roommates: Kate, who is assigned to Meridian same as me, and Penny, who is going to become a flight nurse and has already volunteered for Southeast Asia (that's what they call Vietnam here). Penny was an enlisted sergeant until the Air Force paid for her to get a degree and made her an officer. She has been a godsend. She knew all the best places to get tailored uniforms and taught us how to be officers. That was pretty overwhelming at first.

I don't know how to explain Kate. She's used to having a lot of money and not much responsibility. Her Dad is a U.S. Senator. Can you believe that? She has a fashion sense that kills and she can charm the pants off any man who lays eyes on her.

We drink and dance at the O club every night and go to Fort Worth every weekend to shop. I have spent every last penny of the money I'd saved for my wedding on new clothes.

Guess what? I can finally return a perfect salute—but I'm not so good at marching. We practice on the parade ground in the hottest part of the afternoon (temperature 104 degrees). The FTO (Field Training Officer) made Kate the point man. He says we'll pass muster because every eye on the reviewing stand will be focused on Kate's rear and won't see the mistakes our "feather merchant squad" makes. I would be mortified to march like her, but she loves being in front. Every time the FTO yells, "Wiggle it, Lieutenant Kiley," she grins and does just that.

I'm almost climatized but also happy we officers get air-conditioned training buildings and living quarters. The enlisted guys are not so lucky.

I miss Maine trees and fresh seafood and drinking water that isn't warm and full of chlorine.

We did have a few trees when we bivouacked on the Red River. The first day there, the FTO made us girls carry all our cots and equipment across the camp while the guys laid in the shade like male lions. Penny told us not to complain and it's a good thing we didn't. A really nice doctor tried to help us, but that got him daily latrine duty. That meant he had to roll steel drums of excrement out of the latrine tents, pour jet fuel in them and set them on fire. Kharkins called him "Fire-in-the-Hole" from then on.

After three days we girls were finally allowed to take night showers in a fenced area near the river. Just as we started getting wet, a flight of helicopters flew over and shined big lights on us. I was so happy to get clean, I kept rinsing. Kate stepped away from the showers, stretched both arms above her head, and shouted, "Come look all you want, yokels!" And then she did a little dance and turned in a circle.

The next day a southern belle Kharkins called "Baby Doll," because she wouldn't give up the pink ribbons for her hair or a mess of makeup, was making a dash to the latrine to use our only mirror. She fell and broke her ankle. She had to be airlifted out. Kate went with her to the helicopter and whispered to a crewman that Baby Doll was the girl who had danced in the shower.

Okay, so here's the scoop on the pictures of me in uniform. The black and white one with the stupid cummerbund is called a "mess dress." It's for formal occasions usually held in the Officers' Mess. Tonight we get to wear those to graduation. Kate and I will be starting out early in the morning for the drive to Meridian. Penny will be going to flight school in Texas and then on to Japan. She says it took some maneuvering by her congressman to get the assignments. She didn't tell him it was so she can be close to her boyfriend who is already there and flying B-52s. (The B is for Bomber. Penny will be flying in Medevacs that have a C for Cargo before the number).

I can hardly wait to get to Meridian. It's a training base for pilots who will be flying in the F-105 Thunderchief (F is for Fighter).

I'll write more when I get settled at Meridian.

Luv,

Sandy

CHAPTER TWO

Meridian Air Force Base, Kansas. August 1967.

The cessation of the rhythmic click from the bed in the adjacent room told Sandy she'd have to hurry if she was to use the bathroom. As she stepped into the hall, though, a man flashed a grin and scooted through the bathroom door. She changed course and tapped on Kate's door. It opened slowly.

"Morning," Kate smiled.

"Morning," Sandy whispered. "I need to talk to you."

Kate stretched and yawned. "It's a little early for conversation, don't you think?"

"Not for me. I have to be at work at seven and I can't get in the bathroom."

"Oh, my. You certainly woke up on the wrong side of the bed."

The sound of the running shower came through the wall.

"I've been late every day this week, Kate. Can you keep your guys under the covers until you hear me in the bathroom?"

"Sure I can. I wasn't aware it was a problem. I'll take care of it." She smiled, slid past without bothering to pull on a robe, and tapped on the bathroom door. "You'll have to hurry, hon," she called. "You're going to make my roomie late."

The water stopped. Five minutes later Sandy stood aside as the man skirted past wearing her last clean towel.

❧

As she hurried into the ward office, the night nurse slammed the patient Kardex closed. "We waited as long as we could," the nurse said. The white crowd broke and headed to their assignments.

Sandy ducked into the nurses' lounge, pulled her cap from its cubicle, twisted her hair into a tighter knot, and pinned the cap over it. When she turned to go back, the charge nurse blocked her way.

"You've got recovery room," he said.

"Recovery room? But Captain, I've never …"

"No excuses. Orientation is over." He turned and walked away.

She hurried into the darkened room and flipped on the overheads. Bright light glared off polished floor tiles, stainless steel countertops, and white-sheeted recovery beds. Snake nests of suction, oxygen, and blood pressure tubes dangled from pale green walls. She could not afford to hesitate. This would be her competency test. She moved quickly to identify equipment in the cabinets and at each bedside, made a list of supplies she couldn't locate, and returned to the captain's desk.

He didn't raise his eyes from his paperwork. "Yes, Lieutenant?"

"There are a few supplies I can't find, sir." She placed the list on his desk.

He studied it over steel-rimmed glasses. "What do you think we're doing? Cracking chests? Repairing hearts?" He removed his feet from an open desk drawer and jabbed the note back to her. "Ask the ward master."

"Do you have an O.R. schedule, sir?"

He rummaged through his in basket and tossed her a printed sheet. "If you were here on time you wouldn't need a schedule."

"Roommate problems," she started, but caught herself. An officer never offered an excuse.

He didn't notice. "Only one case is on. It will be an easy day." He turned away and swung his feet back into the drawer.

"Thank you, sir." She studied the schedule as she returned to the unit. Colonel Meyer Cobb would be her sole patient. He was to have multiple abdominal masses resected and some lymph node biopsies. She could handle that.

She had begun culling outdated medications from the emergency cart when the ward master came into the room with her supplies. "Can I give you some advice, Lieutenant?" he asked.

"Sure."

"Go slow. Do a little one day, a little more the next. You get too gung ho and you'll be tagged a troublemaker."

"Gung ho?"

"Means hot to trot. You know, like, too enthusiastic?"

∽

An hour later a male nurse anesthetist guided a green-sheeted cart into the room. Sandy helped lift the patient into a recovery bed.

"He's on his second unit of blood," the anesthetist said. "Two more in the lab if you need them. Big mess in his belly. Cancer. Doc opened and closed. He's a goner."

Sandy turned the patient's head to one side. A waxy sheen covered his face. An endotracheal tube dangled from his mouth.

"He has an interesting history," the anesthetist continued. "Read it when you get a chance."

"I will," she said.

Colonel Meyer Cobb's blond hair and unlined face made him appear younger than his forty-two years. Even as he slept, there was something patrician about his handsome features and square shoulders. She checked the rates of his intravenous fluids and his vital signs. His hands were cold. She covered him with a warmed blanket before she moved with his chart to her desk five feet away. She was soon mesmerized by his history.

The rustle of linen caused her to look up. His hand came above the bed and swung in a tight circle before he flung the endotracheal tube against the green wall.

She hurried to him.

Laugh lines creased the edges of his eyes and mouth. "God damn," he muttered.

"Colonel?" She laid her fingers on his wrist. "It's all done, Colonel."

Azure eyes stared into hers.

"Hi," she said.

The faded edges of his face brightened. "Am I in heaven?"

"You're in the recovery room."

"Who are you?"

"Lieutenant O'Connell, sir."

He dug his elbows into the bed and tried to raise himself.

"You shouldn't do that, sir. Just lay back."

His eyes focused on her face. "You're not a lieutenant. You're an angel."

She steeled her words with a practiced nurse tone that warned off patients who made passes. "Just lie still until I've checked your blood pressure, sir. Then I'll help you sit up."

He threw one arm over his head. The taut lines caused the hanging bottles to rattle together.

She reached up, settled the bottles, and guided his arm to his side. "You're still connected," she warned.

He studied her as she again checked his blood pressure.

"Doing great," she said. "I'll raise your head a bit." She hand-cranked the head of the bed. "Any pain?'

"No."

She plumped his pillow and pulled the blankets loose across his chest. "There," she said. "How do you feel now?"

"Wonderful."

"Don't play with me," she warned.

He grinned. "Honest, Lieutenant Angel, I'm a great feeler."

They stared silently at one another, each sizing the other up.

She liked him. She relaxed and smiled.

"That's better," he said. "Nothing in life is so serious a little humor can't fix it."

You haven't read your chart, she thought.

He seemed to read her mind. "What did he do?"

"Who?" She turned away so he couldn't read her face.

"The surgeon."

"Just what he planned—laparotomy and biopsies." She busied herself writing numbers in his chart.

"And what did they find?"

She couldn't look at him. "Your doc has the answer to that. I'm just the flunky here."

"Come on. What did they find?" His voice held a teasing quality.

"Lumps." She poured ice chips from a pitcher into a cup.

"Funny."

"True." She pulled a spoon from the bedside drawer.

"On your honor?"

She turned back, crossed her heart. "Did biopsies. Sent specimens."

"Are there any speculations?"

"I haven't seen your surgeon and neither have you. Maybe we could ask him together."

He winked. "Well then, enough about me. Tell me about you."

She laughed, dipped ice chips from the cup, and placed the spoon to his lips. "Have some ice," she said. "If you can tolerate this, I'll give you some liquids."

"Yes, ma'am." He crunched the ice between his teeth. "You have anything stronger?"

"Later."

"Promises, promises."

He started to fold his arms behind his head again, but caught himself and turned his eyes to the hanging bag of blood. "I hope to hell that's a Bloody Mary."

She laughed. "Yes. You were a quart low."

"Turn it up a notch, would you?"

"Are you always this flippant?" She held out another spoonful of ice.

"Are you?"

"Yes."

He chewed and swallowed. "Good. I like a woman with some sass. Life is too short for coyness."

"I never learned coy."

He began to laugh, but grabbed his abdomen, and stopped. "I haven't seen you around. You new on base?"

She nodded. She could feel him studying her again. She lifted his sheet.

"Careful now," he teased.

She ran a hand over the warm edges of his bandages to check for bleeding and then gentled the cover back into place.

"Want to try that again?" He seemed determined to make her blush.

"Have some more ice," she said.

He accepted another spoonful. "So, what do you think of Meridian?"

"I haven't been here long enough to form an opinion."

He lifted his arms into the air and pointed to the bottles. "Why don't you take those things out? I think I've had enough."

"Too soon," she answered.

This time he managed to fold his arms behind his head without pulling the tubing. "Living in the BOQ?"

"Yes. My roommate was in the same O.T. class at Waverly Falls. We drove up together."

"Is she as pretty as you?"

"Kate is beautiful."

He took the cup of ice from her hands and emptied it into his mouth. Between crunches he said, "When I get out of here, I'll introduce you to my squadron. There's nothing they like better than beautiful girls."

"I just might take you up on that," she said. She knew it would never happen. This guy would not be walking out of the hospital.

❧

Kate was waiting in the living room when Sandy got off duty. "I'm sorry about the bathroom stuff, Sandy," she said. "I didn't think."

Sandy moved to the window to watch a flight of fighters taking off. The noise drowned out their conversation. As the F-105s disappeared, she turned and smiled. "It's a moot point anyway. Major Roberts wants to meet with us for new assignments. I'm hoping she'll put me in the clinic too."

"Good. We can both bring men home," Kate teased.

Sandy took off her starched belt and loosened a few buttons of her white uniform before she settled onto the couch. "Fat chance," she answered. It was pretty hard to have a first time when you were already past the prime time. She glanced toward her friend. "Don't you worry about getting pregnant?"

"Heavens, no."

"How can you be so sure?"

"Are you going to tell me you haven't heard about the pill?" Another flight of four roared off. Kate stood and moved to the kitchen. "Want a beer?" she called.

"No thanks."

She came back, settled on the couch, popped the top of her beer, and expertly caught a torrent of exploding foam. "I guess a good Catholic girl like you," she said, "wouldn't be interested in the pill."

"It's not that."

"What is it, then? You're not weird or anything, are you?"

"Definitely not! But you're almost right about the Catholic part. We're only allowed to use the rhythm method. Try anything else and we'll burn in hell. But that's not it either."

"What then?"

"I was madly in love with my high school steady. He went to Catholic school too. We were waiting. You know, not doing anything until we got married. We were going to do the whole thing right— banns read, full mass, me in white."

"And?"

"They didn't allow married girls in my nursing school. Then Sam got drafted and went to Vietnam. When he came back, he was not the same boy. He'd become pretty wild. He was drinking. He lost his job and started chasing other women."

"So you ran away?"

"Not exactly. I used the money I'd saved for our wedding to buy the car, but then I didn't know where to drive it. So I signed up."

"And here you are."

"Yep. Here I am."

"And still a virgin."

"Yep."

"Hell, why not just change that?" Kate dropped her empty can on the coffee table.

Sandy went into the kitchen and brought back two full ones.

"So, Sandy, the entire time we were at Waverly Falls and you had Fire-in-the-Hole following you around like a puppy dog, you two never once hopped into bed?"

"No, we didn't."

"Man, it's been a long time since I could pull off something like that."

"Not every man is on the make."

"Bet me! They don't push you because you're such a nice kid. Don't you wonder what you're missing?"

That made Sandy laugh. "It's so personal."

"What's personal about sex? Everybody does it." Kate stood by the window as one flight of F-105s touched down. When the scream of their air brakes subsided, she turned. "What a waste. Here you are—perfect skin, big gray eyes, boobs that make even me envious, and not having great sex."

"The problem is," Sandy sipped her beer, "even with all these guys around, I haven't found one who can make me feel the way Sam made me feel. My friend Rita says it's too soon and I need time to get over him."

"Oh, please! It's a new age, kid. We women are finally on equal turf with men. No more condoms. No more diaphragms. No more worries about ending up pregnant and alone. God, if I had known, I would have given Fire-in-the-Hole a go."

Sandy shook her head. "He was married."

"Better yet." Kate took a gulp of beer and wiped her mouth with the back of her hand. "It could have been a perfect fling."

"Is there such a thing?"

"Every now and then I have one."

"One out of how many?"

"Oh, maybe one out of every seventy or so."

Sandy smiled.

"You need to loosen up, Sand. Before you know it, your glands will atrophy and you'll be a shriveled old prune."

That caused them to fall into a fit of giggles.

∽

Sandy could feel autumn in the air as they strolled toward the Officers' Club for dinner. For the first time in her life she would miss Maine's brilliant fall. She could not allow herself to become homesick. She had to think of something else.

"I had the most interesting patient today," she said.

"Oh?" Kate murmured.

"A colonel who flew fighters in Korea and became a prisoner of war."

"Must be pretty old."

"Forty-two, but he doesn't look it. He had some deep stomach wounds from being shot down. He says he survived the prison camp because he kept his injuries a secret, even when infection set in. Now he has terminal cancer."

"God. Does he know?"

"Not yet. It doesn't seem fair, does it?"

"Life isn't fair."

"When the war was done, the Air Force tried to medically retire him because they couldn't get the infections under control. When he refused to go, they gave him a cushy job at the Pentagon."

"How'd he end up here?"

"His wounds finally healed and he petitioned for flying status. They gave him some transport time, but he says flying transports was like driving a bus, so he wrangled his way to Southeast Asia flying F-105s."

"Old airplanes flown by old men."

"Who told you that?"

"Some fighter jock."

"If it's true, why are so many guys waiting to get into the program here?"

Kate shrugged.

"So in Vietnam this guy gets shot down twice, and both times he bails out and is rescued."

"Proves it's better to be lucky than smart."

"Now he's got his own squadron. He's commander of the 385th."

"I'd hate to be the one to tell him he's half dead."

"Yeah. That's the rub. Survives all that stuff then gets brought to his knees by cancer."

When they walked into the lobby of the club, she was shocked to see Colonel Meyer Cobb talking on one of the public phones. He waved and held his hand up for her to wait.

"There he is," she whispered to Kate.

Kate studied him carefully. "Nice-looking guy," she said. "I bet he's good in bed."

"Kate! He's in no condition."

The colonel hurried over. "Hey, Sandy! This must be your roommate. She's prettier than I imagined." He took Kate's hand and lifted it to his lips.

"Kate Kiley," she said. "And you must be the infamous war hero Sandy's been telling me about."

"At your service." He bowed and grinned. "I finagled a six-hour pass and I want to celebrate. Can I introduce you two ladies to my squadron?"

Happy hour drinkers crowded the bar and thickened the air with cigarette smoke. As Colonel Cobb guided them along the polished bar, he reached up and rang a bell hanging above its center. Cheers exploded through the room. At one of the round tables a dozen flight suits stood in unison. "Put it on my tab," the colonel called to the bartender before he leaned over to explain. "The drinking bell is rung by anyone who catches someone in the place with his hat on. The unlucky sap then buys drinks for the bar. I rang it on myself, to celebrate.

"Meet our newest nurses, Sandy and Kate," he said to the still-standing men at the table. Then, to Sandy and Kate, "These guys are here to become real pilots."

The men, in their mid-thirties to early forties and all dressed in regulation green flight suits with a red one hundred–mission patch on one sleeve, proving they'd flown in Vietnam, protested loudly. Sandy caught only a few names as Meyer rattled them off.

"These lovely ladies have been on base for three weeks and not one of you gentlemen has discovered them," he said.

Kate looked to Sandy and winked.

"I'll have to report this to the couth officer." B.B., a slightly younger version of the rest, spoke with a Texas twang.

"Exactly my plan." Meyer raised one arm and waggled his fingers. "And as soon as I get a drink, I'll get to work on it."

"Where've you been, Colonel?" the waitress asked as she placed drinks around the table.

"Had a bit of an R and R," he answered.

As Sandy and Kate took the offered chairs, the men sat in unison. Sandy noticed Meyer holding his abdomen as he lowered himself into a chair.

"Better watch yourselves," he said. "These two are some mean women. They give you tubes in every orifice."

"But they got you on your feet again." B.B. raised a glass to him. "Thanks for the drink."

"Speaking of mean women," the one named Randy interrupted, "here comes another one."

The men again stood as one as a petite redhead slipped into Meyer's waiting arms. "I thought you were crazy when you said to be here," she said.

"Do I ever disappoint? Ladies," he said, "this is my girl, Sarah."

Sarah kissed his cheek and took the chair pulled out for her by Ralph, a man so tall he had to bend to push the chair into place. A glint of silver showed through the darker hair at his temples and deep laugh lines radiated from his eyes.

"You have to watch out for Ralph," Meyer warned. "Real lady killer."

Ralph laughed. "If my old lady would give me more kitchen passes, I could be."

"You've got too much to handle already," B.B. said.

"Five kids," Ralph admitted.

"And all conceived between remotes," Meyer added.

"Tell me, do you have a kitchen pass tonight?" Kate asked.

"Sooey!" Ralph threw an arm over her shoulder. "I think I do!"

"Where is your wife?" Sandy asked. The men laughed as she blushed at her transparency.

"She's staying with her mom in Louisiana until I get back," Ralph answered. "Not worth hauling the kids up here for a three-month rotation."

"They sent us Ralph from Langley," Meyer said. "Couldn't wait to get rid of his ugly face."

"Be nice, now," Ralph quipped. "Problem with you is, you don't like competition."

"With the ladies or in the air?"

"I'm talking about flying."

Meyer slapped his knee. "You're a gooney bird driver, Ralph. Be a long time before you can call yourself a fighter jock."

"Beat the tail off of you any day," Ralph shot back.

Meyer turned to the three women. "C-47 —better known as Puff the Magic Dragon. An old gunship used in Southeast Asia since the fifties. It's not a fighter."

"Oh, it's a fighter all right—just a little slower than most." Ralph waited for the men to stop laughing before he added, "Takes a Sierra Hotel guy to fly, shoot, navigate, reconnoiter, and still get his tail out in one piece."

"Who told you your tail was in one piece?" Meyer quipped.

"What's Sierra Hotel?" Sandy asked when the laughter faded.

"It's radio talk—for clarity. S and H—short for shit hot," B.B. explained.

"And don't let these guys fool you, Sandy. Anybody with a hundred-mission patch on their arm is Sierra Hotel." Sarah raised her glass to Ralph.

"But I got mine the hard way," he said, "not sitting in a Saigon bar like some hotshot fighter jocks I know."

"Yeah, right. Flying spookies and dreaming of being a real pilot," Meyer shot back.

"I can fly rings around you, Colonel. First chance I get. Boom. Out of the sky." He flew a spiraling loop with his hands and smacked the tabletop.

Meyer stared him down. "Can't touch me," he said.

"Give me one chance."

"Ralph has had too much to drink," Sarah said.

Meyer flashed a smile. "You'll get your chance, Ralph, soon as I get off medical."

"You're on."

"But he won't be flying this week," Sarah said. "He has better things to do."

"You bet your sweet ass I do." Now Meyer raised his glass. "To our newest lieutenants, Sandy and Kate. May the Air Force be everything you dreamed and more."

"Hear, hear."

The waitress began setting out another round.

∾

The next afternoon Sandy knocked on Meyer's open hospital room door. He was lying with his back to her, facing the window. "Come in," he said without turning.

"Meyer?"

He sat up and smiled. "What are you doing here?"

"The chief nurse is reassigning Kate and me. I'm on my way to meet with her about it. I came to say thank you. We had a tour of your squadron this morning. Ralph showed us everything: the airplanes, helicopters, base ops. He even let us sit in on a debriefing."

"What did you think?"

"I thought you guys are pretty darn brave. I didn't know the Thud has only one engine and one seat or that a small bird can take it down by flying into its turbine. And if you have to eject? Man, that's too much. I didn't know you get rocketed out and could get hit by the falling plane."

"No guts, no glory." His smile lacked its usual spark.

"You okay?"

"The doc gave me the scoop today."

She could think of nothing to say so she leaned forward and kissed his cheek. "I'm sorry, Meyer."

"Thank you, Sandy. Thank you."

"What did he say?"

"Said they want to ship me to Texas. Shoot my veins full of chemicals. Try to kill this damn thing."

"It could help."

"Just help?"

She wondered how much truth he wanted. She nodded slowly.

"How bad will it be?"

"Pretty bad. It will make you sick and tired."

"I guess I'd better get my personal affairs in order." He winked, pulled his legs up, and sat cross-legged on the white bed. "Then I'll buy me some party time."

Tears stung her eyes.

He reached out and took her hand. "First rule among fighter jocks and their women? No boo-hooing. When one of us runs out of luck and buys the store, the rest of us party until we drop. Absolutely no regrets. That's the way it's done." He brushed her tears away with a gentle touch. "No tears for a fighter pilot. It's important you understand, Sandy."

"Is there a second rule?"

He jumped from the bed and danced her across the vinyl floor. "Yes. Always have a quarter ready for the jukebox. You should never stop dancing."

"Have you told your squadron?" she asked.

"No, and I'm not going to."

"Sarah?"

"She knows I'm flying to Texas for more care. Nothing more. Nothing less. I may need you to fib for me."

"I'm not very good at lying, Meyer. If she asks, I won't be able to pull it off."

"She won't ask."

"How do you know?"

"She's a fighter jock's gal. She knows the rules."

She left him standing by the window but didn't realize he had given her the secret to surviving in a time of war. "No tears for a fighter pilot" would soon become her mantra.

∽

Major Pauline Roberts waited behind a polished metal desk, cigarette in one hand, lighter in the other, with both bloodshot eyes fixed on Kate, who sat in one of two chairs near the door.

"Come in, Lieutenant O'Connell," she said as she turned her attention to Sandy at the door. "Hot enough for you?"

"Yes, ma'am, it is."

"I hear they've been having some problems with the flying colonel on your ward."

Sandy didn't comment.

"Heard he had a run-in with the A.P.s at the gate."

Sandy remained silent.

"Drinking while on pass. They had to escort him to the hospital. He'll get no more passes."

"He's dying," Sandy said.

"We all are, Lieutenant."

"But he's dying soon and he knows it."

"Bending the rules for an officer doesn't look good for the hospital." The major tapped her cigarette on the desktop. "But we're not here to discuss the ills of Meyer Cobb. I've problems of my own. I'm short three nurses, and my two senior officers have received orders for Southeast Asia. I've been told I have to make do with what I have." She lit her cigarette. "So you're it."

"We're what?" Kate asked.

"You're my reinforcements."

Kate leaned forward and placed her folded hands on one knee. "Just what are you asking?"

The major's sudden laugh caused her to cough out smoke. "I'm not asking, Lieutenant. I'm telling."

"What are you telling us?"

"You'll be expected to perform well in some new assignments, and I won't warrant any complaints." She watched the smoke from her cigarette curl around her hand before she continued. "Especially not from your father, Lieutenant Kiley."

Kate placed both feet squarely on the floor.

"You'll be working O.R., evening shift."

"But—"

"Report Monday, 1300 hours."

Kate slumped and chewed her thumbnail.

"Lieutenant O'Connell. Obstetrics. 0700. Monday. You'll be in charge."

"I don't remember a thing about O.B. Isn't it considered a specialty?"

"You'd better remember fast. There're no specialties here."

"I don't think I'm capable of ..."

Major Roberts stopped her. "And, once a month, you'll each supervise the hospital for a weekend. You'll be compensated with two days off. Now, if you'll get out of here, I have more important things to do."

Kate stormed ten paces ahead. When they were out of earshot, she stopped. "What the hell am I going to do in an O.R.? It was my worst clinical. I almost flunked the damned thing. I don't know a forceps from a hemostat."

"Better bandages than babies. Want to trade?"

Kate scoffed. "No way. I'll take hemlock before I touch a baby."

They stopped by the post office on their way back to the BOQ. There was a letter waiting from Penny.

> *17 September 1967*
>
> *Hi guys!*
>
> *How's Meridian? Are you adjusting to the "real" Air Force? Not quite the picture painted, is it? I'm sure by now you're totally involved in the wild social life of a fighter base. Wish I could be there with you.*
>
> *Earning my wings isn't quite so easy as I thought it would be. The physical training is tough. The plane is noisy and gets pretty crowded when we move in all the equipment and litters. We had altitude chamber training last week. Remember what Kharkins warned us about not eating much before going into the chamber—that gases begin to expand at 18,000 feet? You don't? Well, neither did I. Let me tell you, I suffered big time. My poor tummy grew to twice its size and, when they lowered the oxygen levels, I got the giggles. I thought I had made a complete fool of myself, but my instructor said she hardly noticed a change from my normal state.*
>
> *Today we'll be learning ditching procedures. We have to jump from the plane into deep water in our combat boots and full gear. Scares the hell out of me, but I think the hardest part will be deciding which of the patients are worth saving.*

Our instructor says she won't consider us proficient until we can insert a tampon while flying through turbulence at 20,000 feet. I'd better make tracks to the simulator and practice—inserting IV lines not tampons!

Guess what? Bob has been transferred to Thailand. He says it won't be a problem for us since hopping flights to Bangkok will be easy and we can meet up there. Still, I'm disappointed. I could have requested a Thailand assignment but now it's too late. I've been assigned to PACAF doing long flights from Vietnam to Japan, the Philippines, and the USA.

Write soon and fill me in on all the wonderful men you gals have met.

As always,
Penny

ᘒ

Sandy had agreed to meet Meyer and Sarah at the club. As she accepted a seat at his squadron's table, Ralph and a flight instructor were flying an imaginary dogfight with their hands.

"The way I understand it," Ralph said, "if a MiG's coming in behind me, at three o'clock, I turn down and go inwards towards him."

"You got it. If he shoots it'll go wide. Then he's gotta come after you again, like this." The instructor did a quick downward spiral with his hand. "So you roll over on his inside, he shoots again. Misses. There you are. Six o'clock and on the money. Boom!"

"Seen it done?"

"There's one guy, Captain Zeke Spencer, who wiped out two MiGs on a single mission with it."

"Lot of flying for one guy," Ralph observed.

"Well, okay, Ralph. If you're not up to it, I can send you home to the little woman," the I.P. said.

"Hell, I'd rather take my chances with a MiG than face that." Ralph turned to Sandy. "Speaking of home, take a gander at these." He laid several photographs on the table.

Sandy studied the freckled faces for a long time without speaking. She had heard his voice in Kate's room during the night and now he was calmly showing her photos of his children and wife.

"They must really miss you," she finally managed to say.

"Sure. But they know this is my job. Grandpa here's got four college-age boys." He reached out and touched the shoulder of a man in his mid-forties. "And the old guy's volunteered for 'Nam again."

When the man grinned, his cheeks flushed and his brown eyes crinkled closed. "Real name's Ed." He stood and offered his hand.

Before Sandy was halfway out of her chair, all the men rose as one. She would have to remember to stay seated.

His hand was strong and warm in hers. "I volunteered so my boys won't have to go. If an old pro like me can't win this war, we're in deep doo-doo."

Meyer and Sarah arrived. "Gramps, you trying to steal my girl?"

"Looks like they're trying to drown her in booze." Sarah moved several full glasses aside to make room at the table. A gold wedding band glinted from her ring finger.

Meyer shook change in his pocket. "Come on, Sandy, help me feed the jukebox." He took her hand and led her away as all of the men stood.

As he fed quarters into the machine, Sandy noticed he chose only slow songs. He wasn't as strong as he let on.

"Meyer, how did you get another pass?"

"Didn't. I bribed a corpsman to give me my clothes. Shall we dance?"

She allowed him to take her loosely in his arms. Neither spoke until the song finished.

"Where did you learn to dance so well?" he asked.

"In the clubs back home."

"I bet you had every boy in town steering you around."

"Just one. There was always just one."

"And where is he now?"

"Still in Maine."

"Why did you leave him?"

"He went to Vietnam."

"You didn't wait for him?"

"I did. I saved every cent I earned for our wedding."

"What happened?"

"He changed."

He nodded as if he had heard her story before. "And he let you go?"

"I used my wedding savings for a car, and here I am."

The song "Moon River" began its soothing beat.

"Are you glad you came?"

"Yes. I wouldn't trade places with anyone."

"Good."

They danced comfortably together.

"Did you guys get married overnight?" she asked.

"What?"

"You and Sarah? She's wearing a ring."

"Boy, you don't miss a thing." He spun her around and pulled her closer.

"Well?"

"Sarah's husband is a POW at the Hanoi Hilton."

She didn't know what to say.

"Got shot down over the Red River in '65."

"But you and Sarah ..." She couldn't continue.

"She's living with her kids in the war widows' section of north base housing. It gets pretty lonely for her without any family near."

"Why doesn't she go home, like Ralph's wife?"

"Her husband is a confirmed capture. The government will allow her to remain in military housing as long as he's alive. This is where she was going to wait for him. Now, this is where she is stuck."

"Are you taking advantage of her?"

He laughed. "I don't think she'd say that. And I don't think he would either. War changes everything. Folks make concessions, agreements. We're all adults."

"I'm a small-town girl. I don't understand any of this."

"I suppose you'll have to go to war to understand."

"Explain it now."

"Okay. When I was in Korea I learned that taking care of my family was the strongest drive I had. Well, maybe right after the drive to survive and to keep the rats from stealing my rations in that hole of a prison. I had to go deep inside myself—to look at things differently, to see things more clearly. I realized that, without my family, I was absolutely nothing. My wife became my focus, my dreams, and my strength. The hope that I would touch her again got me through."

"You're married, too?"

"Was. My worst times were when I imagined how things might be for her. It drove me crazy."

"Didn't you trust her?"

"I was afraid she was having a hard time, or she might give up, or she would abandon me. When I got back, I realized we both would have had an easier time if we had agreed on some basic things."

She thought she understood. "Like sex?"

"Yes, sex, but other things too."

"What?"

"Legalities: a will, how the children should be raised, when to file for divorce if the wait is too long. I tell my guys that if they expect to survive they need to get all that stuff out in the open. I suggest they negotiate future plans with their wives."

"And do they?"

"Most do. Sarah's husband neglected some of the legal stuff."

"But they had other agreements?"

"Yes. Sarah would live normally, take care of herself, have no guilt, and be waiting when it's over."

"Do you think he'll make it?"

"His chances are good."

"I have so much to learn."

"You do, Sandy. But do you know what?"

"What?"

"When you learn all there is to learn, you're going to be one hell of a woman."

His words embarrassed her. She tucked her chin into his chest and allowed the rhythm of the music to lead her. He hummed to the tune.

"Meyer? Are you happy?"

"At peace. I can't think of anything I would do differently."

"And your wife?"

"We divorced two years ago." He moved to one side of the floor and stopped to rest.

"After all those years? Why?"

"She was afraid of my flying. She stayed when I got into transports, but when I switched to fighters she couldn't handle it."

"That is so sad."

"She'll be at the hospital in Texas when I get there."

"If I were her, I would be too."

"You're a lot like her, Lieutenant Angel."

"I wish I could have met her."

"When I've finished chemotherapy, I'll bring her up."

"I'd like that," she said, but her words were part of the elaborate charade. They both knew he'd never return.

☙

Monday morning she walked through the obstetrical ward with a civilian nurse.

"Could you call me Sandy instead of ma'am, Mrs. Sabin?" she asked.

"It's against regulations, ma'am. I'll just call you Lieutenant if it suits you better."

Sandy nodded. It was the best she could expect.

Screams from the closed labor room echoed through its double doors. "Is that patient typical?" she asked.

"I'm afraid so, Lieutenant. Most of the moms are first-timers and darn young. Some are louder than others." Mrs. Sabin's voice held the slow drawl of Kansas.

"Things must get a bit wild back there."

"Yes, Lieutenant, they do."

"When you say there's only one registered nurse on evenings and nights, do you mean she's responsible for patients in labor, delivery, and postpartum?"

"Yes, Lieutenant."

"If the nurse has a complicated delivery or several laboring patients at the same time, how does she manage?"

"The nursery nurse comes out to help."

"Who covers the nursery?"

"A corpsman."

"What if there's a sick baby and the nursery nurse can't leave?"

"We call the supervisor and see if she can help."

"And if she can't?"

"It's still up to the corpsman."

"So the corpsmen are trained in nursery and emergency care?"

"No."

Sandy placed her hands to her face. "Does it work, Mrs. Sabin?"

"No, Lieutenant, it doesn't, and it's one of the reasons you've heard our patient screaming."

∽

When her shift was done she found Meyer standing in the open door of his room. His blue pants and striped pajama top did nothing to diminish his officer stance.

"You look beat," he said.

"Oh, man, there's so much to do."

"But you can do it, right?"

She dropped her armful of papers on his chair and brushed several strands of hair from her face. "I can do it. But it's sure going to be work."

"Scared?"

"Are you?"

"No."

"Good for you. I'm scared out of my wits for both of us."

"I'm leaving Friday," he said.

"What time?"

"Ten o'clock medevac."

"I'll see you off."

He shook his head. "Too iffy. Plane could take off at ten or at midnight. Let's have a party at the club Thursday evening."

"Major Roberts says no more passes, Meyer."

"I've hidden my clothes."

She smiled for him. "I'm going to miss you."

"And me you."

"I hate good-byes."

"You'll get used to them."

"Even the hard ones?"

"That's where all the challenges are."

∽

On Thursday, when she stopped in to say good morning, Meyer's bed was empty. He had left at 0600 on the medevac. He had known the schedule all along.

With a heavy heart she pushed through the double doors for her first day in a labor room that barely accommodated three beds separated by curtains and only had enough space to allow one person standing sideways to squeeze through. The three beds were full.

In the farthest corner, Mrs. Sabin held an emesis basin for a young girl. "Could you help Mrs. Holern in Bed One, Lieutenant?" She pointed to the bed nearest the door. "She's been asking for the pan. You'll need to check her before you put her on. She's gravida four and was seven centimeters ten minutes ago."

Sandy smiled tentatively. At least she remembered enough of the language of obstetrics to know it was the woman's fourth pregnancy and she was almost fully dilated. She lowered the side rail and pulled sterile gloves over her hands. "Let's see how you're doing," she murmured.

The woman didn't speak, but let her knees bow outward on the mattress. Sandy pulled the cover back.

"No need for an exam," she called. "Baby's crowning!"

Mrs. Sabin stepped to the bedside. "I'll help get her into the delivery room, ma'am. Then you can take over."

Sandy leaned close and whispered. "I can't take over. It's been too long since I've been inside a delivery room."

The patient grunted and pushed a pale infant onto the bed.

"Grab the sterile pack," Mrs. Sabin coached. "Suction the baby first."

As Sandy began moving, everything she thought she had forgotten came back. She slid the baby carefully to a dry spot on the bed, wiped its face, and pulled a suction bulb from the pack. It made loud slurping noises as she cleaned the infant's nostrils and mouth. She pulled a blanket from the kit with one hand and rubbed the infant's feet with the other.

"How do we get a doc in here?" she asked.

"Pull this." Mrs. Sabin stretched over and yanked a cord on the wall.

A male voice came over the intercom. "Problem?"

"We need a doc in here," Mrs. Sabin answered.

The baby hadn't cried. His skin remained pale, his arms flaccid. Sandy flicked the soles of his feet. He shuddered, shook his tiny fists, and let out an earsplitting squeal. His entire body flushed pink. She wrapped him loosely in the blanket.

"A nice healthy boy," she said and lifted him onto his mother's abdomen.

His mother reached down to steady him. Between her and her child the umbilical cord pulsed and strained. Its persistent pumping seemed more miraculous than the crying baby. Its translucent whiteness against the bloody sheets reminded her of the spring birthing field back home.

"Should I clamp the cord?" she asked.

"We're allowed to clamp it but not cut it, Lieutenant." Mrs. Sabin reached in and handed her a plastic clamp.

She was surprised that it took both hands to place the first clamp over the pulsing cord. The second clamp secured more easily.

The older nurse took her hand and placed it on the woman's stomach. "You can tell when the placenta is ready. The uterus kind of rises up against your hand, then clamps down hard. The cord will move out an inch or two. Feel that? See?"

Sandy did feel and see.

The entire cord flattened into a lifeless string. Mrs. Sabin pulled it gently as she pressed the mother's belly. The afterbirth slid out like a fat, veined balloon.

"Shiny Shultz," she declared. "Always want to see them like this. All round and plump. Means the entire thing folded up neatly and slid out. If you get the rough side showing, it's a Dirty Duncan and spells trouble. Means you might have some left behind that could bleed or get infected. Always be wary of a Duncan." She pulled a pair of steel scissors from the delivery pack.

A doctor strode into the room and took the scissors. "You weren't really going to cut it, were you, Mrs. Sabin? You'll set a bad example for our new lieutenant. Make her think we docs aren't needed." He smiled at Sandy across the soiled bed.

"Our new lieutenant doesn't need any examples, far as I can see."

Mrs. Sabin patted Sandy's hand quickly and went back to her patient.

Meyer had been right; she would do fine.

CHAPTER THREE

It was Kate who suggested that Sandy visit the university library to research modern delivery protocols.

After four months of military surroundings, returning to a learning environment filled her with energy, but after a week of looking, she had found no answers.

She closed the last reference book with a sigh and slumped in her chair.

A man she had seen with other students every evening stopped at her table. "You look like you could use some coffee as much as I," he said.

She liked his smile and rugged Nordic looks. "Yes, I suppose I could."

"You're in luck. I was just about to buy."

"Are you a student here?" she asked as they filled their cups in the nearly deserted commons.

"Professor." He poured a generous portion of milk into his cup and stirred it with one finger. "History."

"You don't look old enough."

"Trust me, I am. What about you? I haven't seen you here before."

"Nurse. On Meridian. I'm doing some research." As they settled at a table with a view of the courtyard, the ubiquitous Kansas wind rattled the windows and sent a flutter of discarded papers across the brown lawn.

"What are you researching?" he asked.

"I work on the obstetrical unit of the base hospital. I'm trying to find a better way of doing things."

"Husband in the military?"

"No. I am."

"You? I never would have guessed that. What rank?"

"Second lieutenant."

He smiled. "We're on opposite sides."

"Opposite sides of what?"

"The war."

"I don't understand."

"I'm working against the war in Vietnam. I spend my weekends addressing student groups on protest methods."

"Oh." She really didn't know much about the protest groups, but she did know, from an Air Force perspective, that she shouldn't be spending time with him. She pushed away from the table. "Guess I'd better be going."

"Hey?"

"We are on opposite sides. I have friends who have been, or are about to go, there."

"I'll listen to your side of things, if you'll listen to mine."

"Why waste the time?"

"Because I'm a nice guy and you seem like a nice girl. I think we could be friends." His grin was lopsided and genuine.

"Are you a draft card burner?"

He pulled a wallet from his pocket. Handed her a dog-eared card. "I have no need to burn it. I've already served."

"Dave Peterson." She handed it back. "Where were you stationed?"

"Army. Served two years as an advisor in Vietnam."

"Well, that makes a difference. I'm Sandy."

He studied her face. "What's a girl like you doing in the library on a Saturday night? Don't you have a boyfriend?"

"I have an overabundance of boyfriends."

He raised his eyebrows.

"Sounds conceited, doesn't it?"

He nodded.

"What I mean is I live in a fishbowl of a BOQ surrounded by testosterone. It feels good to get away. Besides, I'm desperately in need of help with my job."

"What kind of help?"

"My patients are mostly young and scared to death. I need to find a way to let them know what to expect and how to manage the pain of labor. Right now we don't medicate them until the very final stages of delivery. Most of the time they're screaming and out of control by then."

"I think I could provide you with a contact person."

"Really?"

"Sister Anne. She teaches nursing a couple of times a week here and gives natural childbirth classes at St. Anthony's Hospital. My neighbors took her course and they haven't stopped talking about it. Sam went into the delivery room and you'd think he delivered the kid himself."

Sandy sat forward.

"I can give you her number."

"Would you?"

"Sure."

৬৯

Kate had left Sandy's mail on the kitchen counter: one envelope with no return address. Inside she found Meyer's only message of good-bye—a name card, white with silver lettering: MEYER HAROLD COBB, COLONEL, USAF. He had slit the card in two places. It cradled a shining new quarter.

She carried it to the couch, sat, and tried to control her feelings. She would not cry. She must not cry. For Meyer's sake.

An angry knocking caused her to look up. Sarah, white-faced and shaking, stood in the open doorway. She held an envelope at arm's length, as if it were at once too hot to hold and yet too dear to throw away. "Read this!" she demanded.

Sandy moved to her and took the envelope. It had no return address. With trembling hands, she pulled out a single sheet of white paper.

> *My dearest Sarah,*
>
> *Do you remember when we talked about temporary loves? You said, "It doesn't matter. Let's take what each other offers and let the future be what it will." Sweetheart, I'm afraid the future is here sooner than we expected and I am forced to say goodbye. I wish it were not true. Promise you will always remember me fondly. Know that when you rejoice at Jim's homecoming, I'll be rejoicing too.*
>
> *All my love,*
> *Meyer*

The letter blurred. Sandy raised her eyes as Sarah whispered, "He's dying, isn't he?"

She nodded and opened her arms. They stood in the center of the room and cried together for a very long time.

৩

Three weeks later, as a north wind swept the few remaining fallen leaves from the courtyard, Sandy cruised the library fiction shelves as she waited for Dave's meeting to end.

"Fiction?" He swung his load of books onto her table. "You mean you've found time for recreation at last?"

"Killing time waiting for you."

"I'm flattered."

"I've been to a meeting with Sister Anne."

He turned the chair, straddled it, and rested both arms on its back. "And?"

His left arm was shorter than the right and rested on the chair at an odd angle. She hadn't noticed that before. "She has exactly what I need. I came by to thank you."

"Can you thank me over some food? I haven't had dinner. I know a great place on the edge of town."

"I'm not used to getting into cars with strangers." She felt silly as she said the words.

He wasn't offended. "Follow me in your car. I'd rather not drive back anyway."

She followed him over a few miles of deserted roads until they came to a thorny hedge surrounding a clapboard building. Against the hedge lay piles of drifted leaves.

She laughed as she met him in the dirt lot. "You found them."

"What?"

"The leaves. The wind swept them all away. I wondered if they'd stop anywhere between here and Missouri."

"You missed them too?"

"I miss trees more. Maine is filled with big trees. Here most of them are drab and spindly."

"Maine? That's where you're from?"

She nodded. "And you?"

"Wisconsin."

They entered the dim interior of a roadhouse. Several men sitting at the bar looked up, then turned back to the television. A fire roared in a stone fireplace and candles glowed from globes on vinyl-covered tables. The fire crackled and sputtered as a gust of wind teased it from the chimney.

The waitress took their orders.

"Would you like a beer? They only serve three-two."

She nodded. "I'm still learning about this temperance stuff."

"Conservative state. Conservative politics."

"Suits me. The beer, I mean. I'm not much into politics."

The waitress brought two beers, some chips, and a small bowl of chopped tomatoes. "Tell me about Sister Anne," he said.

"She's amazing. Both parents attend her classes. She shows films that explain pregnancy from conception through birth and demonstrates breathing and relaxation methods. The fathers learn comfort techniques and how to recognize the stages of labor so they can do the coaching. I've never seen men so interested in having babies. And guess what?"

"What?"

"I get to coach a couple in this class. I'll help at the hospital when it's time."

She followed his lead and dipped a tortilla chip into the chopped tomatoes. Her first big bite caused her to choke. "Hot!" she cried. "So hot!"

He laughed as he handed her the beer. "It's salsa. Tomatoes and jalapeño peppers. I wanted to warn you, but I couldn't get a word in edgewise."

She drank deeply. "I do get carried away. Sorry."

"Don't apologize. I love it."

"Thanks," she said, "but I am talking too much. Tell me about you. Where did you come from? How'd you get here?" She sat back so expectantly they both began to laugh.

"Not much to tell," he said. "Graduated from the university in Madison. Dad teaches there. Runs in the family, I guess. I managed to squeak through my master's before the Army got me. Was aiming at becoming a combination history teacher and high school coach. That went by the wayside in 'Nam."

"Why?"

"Took some shrapnel. Can't physically do what I used to do." He sipped his beer, then rotated his left arm to show her its limited movement. "Besides, I couldn't see myself teaching high school kids a load of crap and then sending them to the slaughter. I used the G.I. bill to get my doctorate. And here I am. I love my job."

The waitress brought their food. Sandy leaned back until she could feel the fire warming her back. "I'm tired of living in my fishbowl. I've been apartment hunting," she said.

"What kind of place are you looking for?"

"One bedroom. Furnished. Close enough for me to be on call from the base. Far enough away for some privacy."

"I know something that might interest you."

"Where?"

"A couple of blocks off the main gate. Those friends who just had the kid? They've found a bigger place. They're in a duplex now. It's in a nice area, and quiet. Sounds like it might be for you."

"How can I see it?"

"I'll take you there after dinner."

"Isn't it a little late, especially when they have a new baby?"

"I'll call them." He was already on his feet. "If it's not all right, they'll say so."

An hour later they were walking along a path toward a low brick rambler. The door opened and spilled yellow light onto the wide planks of the covered porch. A young man with a baby in his arms welcomed them.

"Hope you don't mind," Dave said.

"Not at all. We're up late every night now, Dave."

They walked with her through the unit. It was much larger than the BOQ, and well furnished. The back door opened onto a communal lawn. A wide hall led to the bath and bedroom. The living room windows looked onto the porch.

"It's perfect," she said.

"You want it?"

"Do you think the landlord will rent it to me?"

Dave grinned. "I'm the landlord."

"You own this place?"

"Sure. I live on the other side. I'll have it painted before you move in."

"White," she said. "Do every wall plain white."

॰॰॰

At the end of the month Kate helped her cram her few boxes and portable television into the car and waved her off with a grin.

That night Sandy woke to hailstones rattling against her windows and, for the first time, sincerely wished she were more like Kate. The walls were too white and her bed was too big for one person. She had never felt so alone.

At dawn she carried a cup of freshly brewed coffee to the front windows and gazed out over the flat landscape. The wind carried a whirl of dust skyward as Dave stepped onto the porch. She watched as he collected his newspaper before she tapped on the window. "Coffee?" she asked.

He smiled and nodded. "If you provide the coffee, I'll provide the paper," he said as she opened the door.

"Deal." She wasn't so alone after all.

॰॰॰

Her first mail was a picture postcard of some temples in Bangkok.

Hi Sandy!

Hope I got the address right. Can't believe we're here. And we're engaged!! Wedding this time next year. Overwhelmed with happiness. Two more days before we go our separate ways again. More later. Luv, Penny

When she called Kate with the news, her friend seemed uninterested and distracted.

"Is something wrong?" Sandy asked.

"No. I'm glad you called. I was thinking of coming by."

"I have to leave for class in a few minutes," Sandy apologized.

"What class?"

"My childbirth class with Sister Anne."

"Can you get out of it?"

"My patient is due any day. I can't let her down."

"Darn."

"Kate. Are you sure everything is okay?"

"Yes. I just felt like visiting."

"How about tomorrow after work?"

"Sure."

But the next day Kate wasn't at work.

"Her mother passed away," Major Roberts told Sandy. "I took her to the airport this morning."

"I didn't know her mother was sick."

"I'm not sure she was."

"Kate didn't say a word when I talked to her last night. Are you sure she was okay?"

"She was fine. We all have to face these things, Lieutenant. There's no need to worry."

But she did worry, and she was greatly relieved three days later when a man who said he was Kate's family driver called with Kate's flight number and arrival time.

That evening Sandy paced the airport terminal and scanned the arriving passengers. When the area cleared and Kate hadn't appeared, she stepped onto the windblown tarmac. She found Kate huddled against the building.

"I'm so sorry," Sandy said as she moved toward her.

"Yeah, me too."

Sandy tried to hug her, but Kate pulled away. Unsure of what she should do, Sandy steered her friend into the terminal, collected her bag, and walked silently beside her to the car.

Once inside the car, Kate finally spoke. "She had a prescription. She took the whole bottle and went to sleep. She didn't say good-bye. Just went to sleep. She had no right to do that."

Sandy maneuvered the car out of the lot. A surge of anger welled up within her. "No, she didn't have the right."

"I can't believe she's gone." Kate's voice was flat and devoid of emotion.

Sandy turned onto the road to town.

Kate began to shake. "I need a cigarette. Do you have a cigarette?"

"You know I don't."

She laughed. "Of course you don't. I don't either—do I?" She rummaged through her purse, pulled out a crumpled cigarette, and used the car lighter.

They rode in silence for several miles.

At the first stoplight Kate rolled down her window and flicked the stub of the cigarette out. Sandy watched it brighten and spark as the wind carried it away.

"I hate him," Kate said.

"Who?"

"My father. He dumped Mom. He married a bitch." Dry sobs rocked her body as she began to bang her head against the dash.

Sandy reached out to restrain her. They were near the duplex. She turned into the drive and stopped.

"She's dead. Took all the pills and went to sleep. She's dead," Kate moaned.

"I think we both need a drink."

"Where are we?"

"My place. Come on." She pulled Kate from the car.

As they stepped toward the porch, Dave burst from his door. "Sandy. Sister Anne's looking for you." He stopped when he saw Kate's disheveled state. "Can I help?"

"No one can help," Kate murmured. "She's dead."

"We're going to have a drink." Sandy kept her voice even. "Come join us?"

He moved ahead, held the door. Once inside, Kate collapsed on the couch and threw one arm across her eyes.

Sandy sat beside her. "Have you eaten, Kate?"

"I can't. I left her alone with that bottle of pills. I wasn't there. She called me and I left her to handle it alone. Now's there's no turning back."

Human touch was the only thing Sandy knew to offer. Comforting nurse-words would be recognized at once. But when she touched Kate's arm, her friend slapped her hand away.

The phone began to ring. Sandy answered it.

"Your patient is in labor at St. Anthony's," Sister Anne said. "I've been trying to find you. Will you be coming?"

"Sister, something has come up. I'm not sure I can leave right now."

Dave signaled over Kate's bowed head. "Go," he whispered. "You have to."

She shook her head.

"I'll stay here," he said. He pointed to Kate.

"I'll try," she said into the phone. "I'll get there as soon as I can." She rang off and followed Dave to the kitchen.

"You have to go," he whispered.

"I could be gone all night. She can't be alone."

"I deal with kids like her every day."

"Her mother committed suicide. I'm scared for her, Dave."

He placed his hands on her shoulders. "I'll stay with her."

"I can't leave her."

"You've worked too hard for this. You don't want to let everybody else down, do you?"

"Oh, God. I don't know what to do."

He reached into the cupboard and began to pour whiskey into a glass.

"Beer," she said. "Kate only drinks beer."

"Then I'll have this one." He upended the glass, smiled, and turned to pull a beer from the refrigerator. "Are you going to stand around here all night," he asked, "or are you going to go meet Sister Anne?"

She looked toward Kate. She had let her friend down once; would this be a second time? She trusted Dave, and she did so want to have this opportunity. In the end she waited until Dave had settled onto the couch next to Kate and Kate had taken the offered beer, with a slightly dimpled grin, before she turned and hurried out the door.

∽

Nine hours later, she sipped the last coffee from her cup and flung the empty container in a hospital trash bin. She was exhausted, exhilarated, and envious. The couple and she had worked well together. For a few brief moments it seemed as if they had all produced the squalling baby girl, but then they had laughed, shuffled about, and regrouped. Now it was the parents' birth and their baby. She smiled. The method had worked. She could use it on her unit. She stopped at a phone booth and called Major Roberts.

"Did you pick up Lieutenant Kiley?" the major asked.

"Yes. She wasn't in very good shape."

"Is she at the BOQ?"

"No, she's at my place. I'd like to spend time with her today."

"You can't hold her up forever."

"Just one day."

"She'll come around. They always do. But, yes, take the day."

"Thank you."

"Call me if you need anything."

"Yes, ma'am."

At the apartment she tiptoed past Dave, who was asleep on the couch. Several empty beer bottles were on the kitchen table. Kate was asleep in her bed. Back in the living room, she whispered, "Dave."

He sat up. "How'd it go?"

"Great. What about here?"

"Okay." He pulled his shortened arm back and stretched carefully.

"Did she eat anything?"

"No, but she drank a lot of beer."

"That's normal."

"She's a bit mixed up."

"I know."

"She tried to get me into bed. When I told her I didn't think that was what she needed, she had a fit, cursed, kicked, and finally collapsed."

"She's exhausted. She didn't know what she was doing." Why couldn't she admit it? Why couldn't she tell him Kate handled everything with sex: Slam. Bam. Thank you, ma'am. All cares forgotten in a flash.

She leaned back in the big chair and changed the subject. "Do you have classes today?"

"Yes." He checked his watch. "And I'd better get going."

"Dave, thank you. I don't know what I would have done if you hadn't been here."

"Glad to help."

When the door closed behind him, she settled on the couch under the still-warm afghan. The scent of his aftershave was the last thing she noticed before she fell into a deep sleep.

တ

Kate, wrapped in a blanket, was looking down on her when she woke. "About time you get up," she dimpled. "I've been waiting for at least an hour."

"What time is it?"

"Fourteen hundred hours and I'm starving. Did you know there's not a donut or a beer left in this place? How do you survive?"

Sandy rubbed her eyes. It didn't seem possible that Kate could be back to normal after only a few hours of sleep.

"I think you should move back to the BOQ before you starve to death," Kate continued.

"We can go out and get something."

"I need my beer and donuts."

"Is that all?"

"And I'd like a walk."

They stopped at a grocery store, then drove to a park along the Arkansas River, where they found an empty bench under the limbs of an ancient white oak. Each ate a donut and opened a beer.

"That's one gorgeous hunk of a neighbor you have. I'm not surprised you keep him to yourself," Kate said.

"If you had visited before this, I would have introduced you."

"He's quite attractive."

"All men are attractive to you, Kate."

"Do you like him?"

"Yes, I do."

"How much?"

"What do you mean?"

"I mean, are you sleeping with him and, if you're not, do you intend to? And if you don't intend to, would you mind if I did?"

"You've never needed to ask my permission before."

"This is different. If he means something to you, I won't touch."

"You can't bargain for another person, Kate!" She tossed her empty beer can into a receptacle.

"Why not?"

She had no answer. She picked up the rest of the six-pack and walked toward the river. Kate caught up with her and took another beer.

"If he wants to go to bed with you, it's his business," Sandy finally said.

"Just tell me if you want him."

Trouble was, Sandy wasn't sure how she felt about Dave. They had been friends since they first met, but he'd shown no romantic interest in her. "It doesn't matter what I want, does it, Kate? In the end the decision is really his."

"Yes. But it takes two to tango. I won't even smile at him, if you want him."

"Your fidelity overwhelms me."

"Stop beating around the bush, girl. I'm waiting for an answer."

"Damn it, Kate. Why is everything so black and white with you? Can't you wait and see what happens?"

"Okay. I'll wait for a cue from you."

"You make him sound like a piece of meat."

"Well?"

"He isn't. He's a nice guy. I like him." She struggled to pull another beer from the box. "How can you expect someone to answer a question like that?"

"I could answer it."

"Sure. That's part of your personality. I'm not that ... spontaneous."

"Spontaneous!" Kate began to laugh. "You truly are a good friend, Sandy. Anyone else would have said 'loose' without batting an eyelash."

"I'm not very good at batting eyelashes."

"Ah, but you are. You're an expert and you don't even know it." She opened another can of beer. "But I do know something you're not very good at."

"What?"

"Decorating. You're going to have to do something about that virginal bedroom. When I first woke up, I thought I was in a morgue."

"There is something missing, isn't there?"

"Yes," Kate said. "A man."

They laughed together. Kate took her arm and they walked on. Finally, Kate said, "It happened so fast, it doesn't seem real."

Sandy waited.

"Mother was in California to see my brother before he boarded with his crew for Vietnam. He was halfway to Saigon when he got the news."

"So he was with you for the funeral?"

"No. He said there was no reason to return, since she was already gone."

"You never told me you have a brother."

"You never asked."

"That's the kind of thing most people volunteer."

She shrugged. "We Kileys are all selfish bastards." She tossed her can in the bushes and opened another. "She called. She wanted me to help her through the good-bye. I didn't go."

"You wouldn't have been able to get leave."

Kate didn't seem to have heard. "She'd done this kind of thing before—called me to help with some minor crisis. I always went. But this time I thought, 'Well, Mother, it's time you learned to handle things by yourself.' She'd never had to manage alone. She chose not to ever have to do it again."

"You can't blame yourself, Kate."

"I let her down."

"She let herself down."

"I let her down. So did my brother. We're really all alike, you know—like my father. We came from the same mold."

"Kate, you're probably going to get mad at me for saying this, but I'm going to say it anyway. This whole thing is too much for you. Would you consider talking to Dr. Gels?"

"The psychiatrist? My God! My personal proclivities would be all over the base in a week."

"You know that isn't true. You can trust Dr. Gels."

Kate began to laugh in the high, screeching way Sandy had first heard the evening before. "You are so damned naive." She poured the last of her beer onto the ground. It made a small red river in the gray Kansas dust. "Seeing shrinks was the in thing to do in my family. The first one I saw seduced my mother. The second one seduced me. Don't talk to me about trust. Do you want the last beer?"

"Yes, I do," Sandy said.

"I'm all talked out. Let's go." She turned and strode back the way they had come.

CHAPTER FOUR

The weekend supervisory office was a tiny room sandwiched between the main clinic and the E.R. It held a large metal desk, two chairs, and one telephone. Its only window looked toward the flight line. The crash bell hung high on the clinic side of the shared wall. The bell had a shrill tone that jarred her senses. On this, her first evening supervisory shift, it had gone off three times before dinner. Each time it rang she moved to the office window and watched several corpsmen hop into the boxy blue ambulance and speed toward the flight line. When it rang for the fourth time she was able to ignore its sudden jangling tone, thanks to a corpsman who explained it was simply a warning about a flying incident, from a light on in some fighter cockpit to a possible malfunction on the ground.

Now she calmly watched as the landing lights of three F-105s fluoresced against snow-laden clouds along the darkening horizon. Number four of the formation was late. Probably Gramps, who had become the butt of good-natured jokes because his bomber pilot skills caused him to land too slowly and too high and often forced him to go around and try again. She would be sure to tell him she'd watched him land. He'd like that.

Funny. He should be in sight by now. A chill raised the hair on the nape of her neck. She stood on tiptoe and searched the horizon for the returning ambulance. The prairie was empty. She stepped into the clinic.

Across the lobby, the E.R. staff hovered over their radio. As she neared the group she heard a calm voice announce, "Confirmed. Chute sighted."

Captain Smith, the 385th's flight surgeon, pulled up to the ambulance doors in an official car, ran into the clinic, and began to give orders. "I want everyone prepared. Get I.V. fluids hung and ready to start."

"Flier is on the ground," a voice crackled from the radio. "Chute intact."

The flight surgeon triggered the receiver. "This is Captain Smith. Report. Vital signs? Extent of injuries?"

"Negative on the signs, sir. I repeat. Negative on the signs."

"Absolutely sure?"

"Affirmative, Captain Smith. All negatives."

"Identification?"

Sandy held her breath. Please don't let it be Gramps.

"Identification as follows: Colonel Paul Hart. Commander, 385th Tactical Fighter Unit."

Sandy gasped. It wasn't Gramps but the one man she wouldn't have expected to crash—Meyer's replacement and the best of the best. Like Meyer, Colonel Hart had survived Korea and had flown two hundred combat missions in Vietnam. It couldn't be the colonel.

"Mobile Unit Three. Bring him in. Over."

"Proceeding as ordered. ETA 1735 hours."

She continued to stare as Captain Smith unzipped the top few inches of his flight suit and pulled in a ragged breath. "Cease and desist," he said to the room at large. "The guy didn't make it."

"Has to be a mistake," she whispered.

"They don't make mistakes, Sandy. We'll need some backup. Would you call Chaplain Terrence and have him report here ASAP?"

She went into her office and telephoned the chaplain. She had no time to catch her breath before the phone rang.

"Sandy!" B.B.'s voice sang into her ear. "They get the colonel over there? Tell the old son-of-a-gun that was a classic maneuver. Beautiful action. Tell him we'll all be over as soon as we debrief."

She couldn't speak.

"Sandy?"

She placed her hand over the mouthpiece and called out the open door to the flight surgeon. "It's B.B. from his flight. What should I tell him?"

"Let me take it."

Captain Smith sat on one edge of her desk and spoke calmly into the phone. "B.B., Len here. Listen, fella, he didn't make it. We don't have him in yet, so I can't say what went wrong. Spread the word quietly among the guys, would you? Don't let it leak out of the squadron until we tell Judy. You might have someone stand by for her. Okay?"

Sandy knew that each flight surgeon wasn't really a surgeon but a general practice physician who flew, attended briefings, and went to war with his men. He did their flight exams, counseled them, and cleared them for flying. He knew their wives and children much more intimately than any civilian family doctor could. She had never considered this painful aspect of the job.

The ambulance passed her window. She followed Captain Smith into the E.R. and watched as several corpsmen carried the body of Colonel Hart into the room. Coming in behind her, Father Terrence, the Catholic chaplain, whispered, "Sandy, we'll need you to come along when we tell his wife."

ᧁ

Twenty minutes later she shivered as the official car drove through the gates of base housing. She had not been warm since she had placed the colonel's orange scarf around his broken neck and helped two corpsmen lift his body into a morgue drawer. She wasn't here for this. She had set out on this adventure to heal her heart. She wasn't here for any dying.

As lowest-ranking officer, she exited the car first at the Hart home and then stood aside as the men stepped toward the door of the colonel's house. They waited and allowed her to knock. The door opened immediately. Judy smiled. Frowned. Her face became as pale as her husband's had been. Her head wobbled as his head had wobbled when they lifted him onto the slab. But she was not silent. She was screaming and trying to push the door closed against them. Father Terrence stepped forward. Judy swung at him with flailing fists. "No! No! No!" she screamed.

Someone should stop her. Someone should quiet her. Sandy looked to Captain Smith. He turned his face away. She moved forward, passed Father Terrence, and stepped into the stiff resistance of the woman's grief. She wrapped her arms around Judy Hart and held her swaying body up.

"Judy. No tears for a fighter pilot," she whispered to remind her. "No tears."

The commander's wife obeyed. She knew she must hide the pain inside and push down her fear. Perfect in his life, she now must be perfect in his death: a monument to hospitality, a greeter warm with hugs and downcast eyes.

Together the two women turned their backs on the men and entered the house.

∞

Hours later, when she returned to her apartment, Sandy was grateful she didn't have the same responsibility as the commander's wife. She kicked the couch, threw her handbag against the wall, and allowed the truth of her aloneness to fill the room. She wanted someone to hold her, to listen to the details of her pain, to understand the depth of her feelings. But the white rooms were empty and cold.

She had reminded Judy Hart who she was and how she should behave, but now wished she had allowed the woman to scream as long and as loud as she desired. Her husband was gone, not for a few months or a year, but gone forever, and now she too would have to sleep alone.

Sandy threw herself onto her unmade bed and stared at the ceiling until her reddened eyes grew tired and closed.

～

Three days later she again joined the charade as she drove to the Harts's hometown with Ralph, B.B., Gramps, and Randy. The day was cold, but the sun too inviting to ignore, so they put the top down on the convertible, rolled up the windows, and turned the heater on full blast. No one spoke of the purpose of the outing. It was another perfect day in another perfect year with a group of perfect friends.

At the cemetery, they walked proudly in dress blues beneath a leafless stand of persimmon trees along a white picket fence. Sandy silently offered a prayer for the colonel's fighter pilot soul as she hugged his two small sons. When three fighters flew their missing man formation, low and loud, chills ran through her. But when the F-105s rolled their wings in tribute and an honor guard fired a volley into the Kansas sky, she remained stone-faced and did not cry.

She watched with new understanding as two airmen folded the flag from Colonel Hart's coffin and carried it to Judy, who accepted it proudly. But the spell was broken suddenly by Judy, who, realizing the truth—that this flag was all she would have to replace her flesh-and-blood man—dropped to her knees in the dirt and sobbed into the white-starred triangle of cloth.

A soft hand touched Sandy's elbow. Sarah took her arm and smiled. "We wives wanted to thank you for helping Judy and her kids."

"It isn't nearly enough," Sandy said.

"It is for now."

They shuffled toward the line of cars. "How will she manage?"

"We'll look after her."

"She won't be alone?"

"No, we war widows stick together."

"How do you do this year after year?"

"The trick is not to let it make you hard, not to allow yourself to become cynical." She shrugged before smiling toward the men waiting by Sandy's car. "I pretend the person who died is either on a temporary duty assignment or has been transferred and we've lost contact. I imagine what they might be doing now, where they're living. It may not be the healthiest way to cope, but it gets me through."

They rejoined the men. Meyer's name remained unspoken. It was time to party.

෴

The next morning, Sandy groaned as she lifted the telephone to her ear.

"Good morning, Lieutenant," Major Roberts sang.

"God! What time is it?"

"0700."

"I'm not on the schedule, am I?"

Major Roberts laughed. "No, and it sounds like that might be a good thing."

"Send-off last night—for Colonel Hart," Sandy explained.

"I know." Sandy heard the click of her cigarette lighter. She waited for the intake of breath and exhalation. "I've put you back on for this afternoon and tomorrow."

"Why?"

"The president is coming."

"The president of what?"

"Of the United States."

"Why would he come here?"

"To give out some medals and make a speech. I need you to work."

"What time?"

"His advance party is here. There's a mandatory briefing at 1400. Tomorrow, all day."

"And there's no way out of this?"

"Be at the commander's office today at 1400 hours."

"Yes, ma'am."

She dropped the phone twice before she was able to dial Dave's university number. "Sorry, Dave, I have to cancel lunch today."

"Sister Anne will be disappointed."

"Would you apologize for me?"

"What should I say?"

"Tell her I have a mandatory meeting. The president is arriving tomorrow."

"LBJ?"

"Yes. He's going to hand out some medals."

"Wow! He sure didn't give much notice."

"His advance party is already here."

"What do you have to do with it?"

"I'm not sure. I'll know more tonight."

"I'll get busy and work up some protesters."

"You're kidding!"

"Would I kid you?"

༖

Later that evening, a sharp knock on the door interrupted her nap.

As Sandy poured drinks, Dave asked, "How was yesterday?"

"Fine. If a funeral can be fine."

"You feeling all right?"

"I don't know. How am I supposed to feel?"

"I guess it depends on how well you knew the guy."

"Not too well. Funny how the military can throw total strangers into the most intimate situations and get by with it."

"One of the oddities of war." He accepted a drink she offered. "How was your meeting?"

She sipped her scotch. "They've put in twenty-five thousand dollars' worth of communications equipment and confined all personnel with a history of protest or threat of protest to quarters. The Secret Service is everywhere. Still, the visit seems pretty thrown together. They intend the president to be just one hour on the ground."

"Will you take me with you tomorrow?"

"Onto the base?"

"You'll be near the action, won't you?"

"I'll be on the flight line, but I can drop you off near Kate. She's working the aid station. Why do you want to go with me?"

"I'm not welcome in some circles."

"You won't carry a gun or anything, will you?"

He laughed. "No, Sand. No weapons. Although I wouldn't be surprised if someone tried to do the guy in."

She stared at him. "How can you even think that, after Kennedy?"

"It's true. He's getting us so damned deep in this war we'll never get out."

"You can't blame him for all of it."

"Sure I can. He's playing politics. Why do you think he's coming to Meridian?"

"The guys say it's because the new wing commander is a buddy of LBJ."

"That may be true, but he also needs to draw out some votes. He's so damn scared to face his public, he's doing his campaigning on military bases where he's totally safe and the government can foot the bills."

"The war widows will be front and center. They're arriving in official cars and sitting in a special area next to the speakers' platform."

"God, he's a good old boy! He's saying, 'Looky here! See all these pretty little ladies who are sacrificing their best years for the good of the country.'"

"McNamara is coming with him."

"McNamara? I was sure he was on his way out."

"The pilots don't like him. They say he makes them sitting ducks because he won't let them hit a target until they get approval by the entire line of command. They blame him for their losses."

"We're all sitting ducks."

"If you go with me, will you promise to behave?"

"I'll be as silent as a spot on the wall."

∽

On the drive to the base the next morning, Dave tried to help her understand how a country as small as Vietnam could cause such big problems for America. She reminded him that communism was the problem. When he laughed, she decided it was best to change the subject.

At the gate, a contingent of A.P.s stopped all vehicles.

"See. If I tried to get in here on my own, they would turn me away. And they call this democracy?"

"They call this a military base, Dave. We have a right to protect it."

"Old LBJ must be scared shitless."

"Poor man."

"Poor man? He's a big fake."

An A.P. allowed them through.

She pulled over near the main hangar. "I'm going to drop you here. The speakers' platform is out on the flight line, but they won't allow onlookers past the chain-link fence. Kate is working the aid station around the corner. She'll bring you to the club later."

"Jesus, I wish I could have planted some hecklers."

She gave him a disapproving look as he climbed out of the car.

At the staging area an agent took her I.D. and checked her off his list. "Report to the commander's office, Lieutenant."

She pushed her way into the crowded headquarters building.

"About time you got here." Agent James, who had led the briefing the previous day, allowed his eyes to trail approvingly over her powder blue Chanel suit and navy heels. "We're riding with the wing commander. I'll brief you again as we go."

The flags up on the fenders of the general's car said he was already inside. Agent James held the door for her. "General Magnem, may I introduce Lieutenant O'Connell, our ladies' agent for today, sir."

"Nice dress," the general said. "Very nice." He patted the seat beside him.

She stepped into the car. "Thank you, sir."

The agent slipped in after. "I've got to pin you, Lieutenant." He folded a fluorescent metal tab onto the lapel of her jacket. "Check out everyone near you when you step out. Anyone else with a tab is Secret Service. If there's trouble, let them handle it." He handed her a crushable ammonia ampoule. "In case someone faints," he said. "Keep it in your pocket. Watch every woman seated in the chairs for unusual behaviors—groping in a purse, searching pockets, anything remotely suspicious that might be a problem. Use your womanly intuition."

"And if I see something?"

"Stand up. Walk toward the problem. Focus your eyes totally on the person you suspect. Our agents will be watching you. As you reach the target, step aside. They'll handle it from there. Do you understand, Lieutenant?"

"Yes," she said.

The limousine stopped. She stepped alone out onto the tarmac and walked before thousands of watchers to her seat. A flag-draped speakers' platform rose from the asphalt like an iced birthday cake. Steep airline stairs had been pushed to its narrowest end. Rows of folding chairs filled with women snuggled against its base. A man with a machine gun stood hidden from the crowd, behind it. The uniformed men who would receive medals waited at parade rest on the tarmac, facing the crowd.

In the chairs before her, a bevy of white gloves reached up to secure pillbox hats as a gust of wind threatened to carry them off. She scanned the men hovering about and had located three agents before Air Force One touched down. She watched as a DC-9 followed closely behind the president's plane but landed short and careened to a stop. A red-faced man signaled frantically from its open door. Flight crews rolled stairs across the tarmac. Before they could lock the stairs into place, a jostling flock of newsmen carrying cameras, lights, and microphones began to run down the stairs. They bent from the waist and raced toward still-taxiing Air Force One. As the bigger plane stopped, they formed an undulating ring below its main door.

The president stepped from the bowels of the plane and, with a gesture that conveyed dominance rather than respect, urged the defense secretary forward. The Air Force band labored to play "Hail to the Chief" loud enough to be heard above the wind and jet engines. General Magnem stepped from a line of suited dignitaries, saluted, and walked with the president to the stairs of the speakers' platform.

A man leading a small white dog brought up the rear. As the president climbed the steep stairs to the platform, the dog sniffed the bottom step, squatted, and relieved herself. The man led her behind the platform and stood near the agent with the gun.

As the speeches began, Sandy strained to hear what was being said, but the wind carried all but a few words away. "Continued determination to win … commitment of resources … use of the most modern technology available."

Several war widows laughed when the wind teased a long strand of pomaded hair over McNamara's face. The band played a march as the waiting airmen shuffled to the stairs. One by one they received their medals and shook the president's hand. Sometimes he reached out and hugged a man and sometimes he patted one on the back.

A sudden pause in the proceedings caused all heads to turn toward the empty stairs.

Sandy leaned forward to whisper to the woman in front of her. "Do you know what the problem is?"

"Colonel Hart was supposed to get a medal. They must not know he's dead."

Someone giggled nervously. A woman began to sob. Sandy reached into her pocket and felt for the ammonia ampoule.

Major Tim Schneider, the 385th's operations officer, ran through the crowd and bounded up the stairs. Dressed in a flight suit rather than his regulation A uniform, he nevertheless stood proudly in front of the dignitaries, accepted Colonel Hart's medal, and continued to the far side of the platform. The watching crowd shifted as the speakers turned and moved down the stairs.

The president strolled alone between the rows of waiting women. He said a few words to each. At times he offered a consoling hug. As he came closer, Sandy squeezed the glass ampoule between her nervous fingers. It shattered. Ammonia seeped into her skirt.

The president stood before her and offered his hand.

She surrendered her wet fingers.

His smile became playful. "You smell just like my dawg," he drawled.

She blushed. "She has better bathroom manners, Mr. President."

His smile broadened. "Yes, ma'am, she's got you there. She's never pissed in my hand."

She held his eyes and smiled. "I'm sorry, sir."

"What's your name, girl?"

"Lieutenant O'Connell, sir."

"No. No. I'd like to know your God-given name."

"Sandra O'Connell, sir."

"It's been very interesting meeting you, Sandra." He moved past to rejoin General Magnem.

"Find out who the hell forgot Colonel Hart has gone to his maker," he murmured. "I want that man's balls!"

Agent James hurried to her as she prepared to leave. "Lieutenant O'Connell, ma'am, your presence has been requested at lunch."

"I'm afraid I'll have to decline," she joked. "I have a date."

He took a firm hold on her elbow and smiled. "The president has requested your presence, ma'am. We haven't much time."

He drove her to the Officers' Club and placed her at a long table near the kitchen door. As men jostled for seats near LBJ and airmen waiters scrambled to place the hurried lunch, she realized she was the only woman in the room. A whiff of ammonia crossed her nostrils as she lifted her fork and pretended to eat. Movement at the main table caused her to raise her head. Chairs scraped against the floor, silverware jangled, everyone stood as one with the president. He moved through the throng, stopping to shake hands at intervals. As he reached her, he smiled. "Hello, Sandra," he said.

"Hello, Mr. President."

He cocked his head to one side and leaned closer. "You're an attractive young lady, Lieutenant."

"Thank you, sir."

He slicked back his hair with one large hand. "What's your job?"

"I'm a nurse, sir."

"What part of the country are you from?"

"Maine, sir."

"Ah. Logging. Fishing."

"Yes, sir."

"What does your daddy do?"

"He's a farmer, sir."

"Big farm?"

"No, sir." Thinking of her father caused her to relax and smile. "Very small."

"He make money at it?"

"No, he does some logging to make ends meet."

His expression softened. "I'm trying to help folks like yours. Trying to get all the help I can for them. But it's hard, Sandra. We've got this war. We've got these boys being killed. Hard times, Sandra. Hard times."

She didn't know how to respond.

He continued on. "Every day we sacrifice to win this thing."

One of the suited men tapped his shoulder and whispered in his ear. He listened intently, then with a laugh nudged the man aside. "Do you see how everyone wants my attention? Everyone has questions to ask, causes to push. Do you have any questions you'd like to ask?"

"No, sir."

"Come on. Ask me something. You have your president's undivided attention."

"What's your dog's name?" she blurted.

His laugh moved the crowd back. He slapped his thigh. "I just call her Dawg," he drawled, "but my girls call her Yuki." He was still chuckling as he pressed through the crowd and out the door.

Microphones pushed into her face. "What did he say? Do you have any comments on the president's speech? What's your name? What's your relationship to the president?"

She pushed through the hot throng of bodies and ducked into the ladies' room. The mirror reflected flushed cheeks, eyes that glistened in the light, and perspiration rings beginning to show on her dress. She went into a stall and placed her burning face against the cold metal of the door until she heard the jukebox blaring from the bar. She washed the ammonia from her hand and made her way through stacked crates of communication equipment.

Kate perched on a stool in her white nurse's uniform.

Dave lounged beside her. "You seemed quite at home out there in the limelight," he said.

"I need a drink." She waved back to Gramps at the 385th's table.

Dave handed her his scotch.

"What were you doing out there?" Kate asked.

"Working. How'd the aid station go?" Sandy waved again to Gramps.

"One guy with a headache."

"We should join the 385th before Gramps wears out his shooting arm," she said.

"Count me out," Kate said as she stood. "I've got to get out of here before Major Roberts catches me in my whites." She kissed Dave's cheek and sauntered away.

"Come on, Dave," Sandy said. "It's about time you meet the 385th." She led the way to Gramps.

"'Bout time you got here," Gramps chided. "It's been eating me up to know what you were doing out there with that bevy of beautiful gals."

"I was playing Secret Service agent." She sat so the men would. Dave moved a chair in beside her.

"Is that right? Were they going to let you shoot somebody?"

"Nah."

"Could you believe that thing with Colonel Hart?" Ralph asked.

"Some heads will roll for that one," Gramps said.

"Who's your friend, Sandy?" Randy asked.

"Oh, sorry. This is my neighbor, Dave."

Each man stood in turn and shook Dave's hand.

"I'm still curious, Sandy," Gramps persisted. "Why did they need you out there?"

"They wanted a female with the women in case any got out of hand."

"You have to be kidding me! Why in the hell would anyone worry about our gals?" Randy asked.

"They thought there might be some hard feelings."

"There are," Ralph added. "But if anybody was going to hurt anybody, it would be McNamara they would hit."

Gramps turned to Randy. "Didn't McNamara look like a snake though?"

Randy nodded. "You know what galls me? Those gals have too many problems to waste their time on world events, and those bastards put them right into the middle of politics."

Ralph smiled slowly. "Now, anybody in their right mind knows those gals don't know one goddamned thing about politics. And the truth is, they know they don't know a thing about it. That's why they leave the government to us men. It isn't the women LBJ should be worried about, it's us men."

Gramps leaned back in his chair. "Those little ladies aren't going to say anything, do anything, or sanction anything."

Dave smiled. "Those little ladies are going to surprise you one day."

"You think so?"

"I do. They've been saying quite a bit about the fate of their husbands. From what I understand, they're forming a nationwide organization, even going as far as hiring lobbyists."

"Now, who's going to be scared of them?" Ralph asked.

"Politicians. I heard a lot of placating in the speeches today."

"Hey, Dave, what are you? Some kind of infiltrator?" Gramps asked.

"I'm a low-paid history prof," Dave answered.

"You should stick to your history books, Teach," Ralph said. "I don't believe you've got your information straight. There isn't any organization among the gals. Why, they can't even tie their shoes without Uncle Sam taking them by the hand and showing them how."

"You might be surprised," Dave said mildly.

Ralph signaled the waitress for another round. "The only thing that would surprise me is if they stopped putting out on Saturday nights."

The men laughed.

"If you ask me—" Gramps started.

"Nobody did ask you," Ralph said.

"If you ask me," Gramps persisted, "I'd say old LBJ was here today because he knows we're all getting fed up with his pussyfooting around. Either we're going to fight this war or we're not. If he doesn't give us the manpower instead of all of McNamara's fancy equipment, and if he doesn't give us the right to make military decisions, then we're going to lose the darned thing."

Randy ran both hands through his crew cut. "The whole thing smacks of political maneuvering."

"You're right there, brother," Ralph said. "Old LBJ cut his teeth on the big deal."

"Poor little old country boy," Gramps crooned. "Why, he and Sam Rayburn were as thick as thieves down there in Texas."

Dave couldn't stay quiet. "If you're so against the man and his war, why are you training to go over?"

Ralph grinned. "It's a hell of a war, but it's the only one we've got."

Gramps turned to Dave. "How about you, Professor? How come you're not over there fighting?"

"Because it has a stink about it."

"Aha! I knew the truth would out," Ralph said. "It stinks so bad, you're not going to get your pretty little hands in it, eh?"

"That's right."

Ralph rocked back in his chair and whistled between his teeth. "And if we didn't get involved, who else would see to it that the communists don't take over Asia?"

"You're echoing the rhetoric of the Eisenhower administration, Ralph. Communism. Domino theory. General Ridgeway and others never agreed with that line of reasoning."

"So, Dave, what makes you an authority?" Ralph demanded.

"I'm writing a book."

"Well," Ralph scoffed. "Here we are. Write about us. We're the guys who'll win it for you."

"It's no nearer to being won now than it was three years ago," Dave persisted.

Sandy could sense Ralph's anger building.

"I can see you haven't been listening to Westmoreland," Ralph said. "He believes the end is in sight."

"He didn't say which end," Dave said.

"It's pretty easy to judge when you spend your days with hippie students thousands of miles from the action."

"True." Dave wasn't rattled.

"What'd you ever do for your country? Besides talk?" Ralph continued. "What gives you the authority to be an authority?"

"I've been over there," Dave said quietly.

"In what capacity?"

"Army."

"When?" Ralph challenged.

"Two consecutive tours. Sixty-four. Sixty-five."

"Where?"

"Central Highlands."

"See any action?"

"Some."

Meyer had told Sandy his belief about men and war: "The laggards come home with stories to tell," he had said. "The heroes are rendered speechless." Sandy believed Dave was one of the latter.

Ralph's tone was more respectful. "If you were there in '64, you must know something about the Tonkin Gulf incident."

Dave shook his head. "Didn't get there until October."

"But you must have an opinion about it."

"I don't believe it was real."

"Randy, you were flying then. What do you say? Was it the real thing?"

Randy's face reddened. He raised his hand, palm outward, to stop his buddy. "Don't ask me to stick my neck out. I could get canned for talking about the Tonkin incident."

"Politics, right?" Dave asked.

Randy smiled. "Now, I never said that."

"You were over the *Maddox* when it happened, weren't you?" Ralph was determined to top Dave.

"Yeah," Randy answered, "but I didn't see anything. We took a couple of shots at some MiGs that buzzed us. That was pretty normal at the time."

Ralph persisted. "We were attacked in the Tonkin Gulf. There were P.T. boats attacking the *Maddox* in international waters."

"Whatever you say, Ralph. Whatever you want to believe." Randy gulped his beer.

"The whole incident was debated and swept under the rug," Dave persisted. "Scuttlebutt said the *Maddox* was gathering intelligence on the North Vietnam coast and got caught in their waters."

Ralph conceded. "Hell," he said, "it doesn't matter. Got us a war."

"I don't understand any of it," Sandy said. "Why is it so important?"

"Because it gave LBJ the right to extend the conflict without saying it was war," Dave explained. "He used the Tonkin Gulf incident to jam a resolution through Congress and then jumped in with both feet."

"Past history, no matter how it went down," Gramps said. "Nobody's going to back out now. We're in it and we better gosh-darned win it. That's the crux of the whole deal. We have to get in there and bomb them out."

Dave emptied his glass. "Easy for you flyboys to say. For you it is all guts and glory. Fly in, drop your bombs, and go home to an air-conditioned club and a little poontang. For the grunts on the ground it's blood and guts and rats at night—both the human and the rodent type. The Vietcong are fighting for a cause. All the bombs in the world aren't going to stop them. And where does that leave us? It leaves us deeply in debt and with citizens who no longer believe in the goodness of the great white fathers. Give me a *for what*."

"For flag and mom and apple pie," Ralph quipped. "What the hell else is there?"

The waitress brought another round.

Gramps leaned over and tapped his glass to Sandy's. "Cheers," he said. "To LBJ." When no one else raised a glass, Gramps tried to lighten things up. "So. Tell us, young Sandy, what's he look like up close?"

"I was too scared to look," she joked.

Ralph shook her gently. "Bullshit. Tell us. What's he like?"

"He was kind of yellow and thin in the face, big in the belly. Like he'd been drinking a little too much gin."

"Kind of like Gramps." Ralph nudged the older man's paunch and grinned. "Did you see his landing this morning? Smoking along, foot on the brake, two sheets to the wind."

"Was that you, Gramps?" Sandy teased. "I thought you were flying the missing-man formation."

All talk of war and politics was finished.

ⁿ◦ⁿ

On the drive home, Dave offered to buy lunch.

"I've already had lunch, compliments of LBJ," she said.

He sat up straighter. "And you didn't tell me?"

"I made a fool of myself. I'll tell you about it another time."

"You're in your element when you're with those guys."

"How do you mean?"

"You're a perfect fit. You're so comfortable knocking things back and forth, pulling out one-liners. It seems to be the kind of life you were meant for."

"Compared to what?" she asked.

"Compared to the way you live at the duplex and the job you do. The two lifestyles seem to be complete opposites."

CHAPTER FIVE

The weather on Thanksgiving morning was unseasonably warm. Dave helped her move her couch and chairs to the front porch and set up tables in the living room for a long buffet. By early afternoon the new obstetrics chief, Jim Andersen, his wife and three young boys, four men of the 385th, several coeds from Dave's antiwar group, Major Roberts, Kate, and Sister Anne were all enjoying turkey dinner. Afterward the coeds showered the children with attention while the men gathered around the television in Dave's apartment to wager on the football games.

Sandy joined Connie Anderson on the porch couch.

"This is wonderful," Connie said. "The motel is so cramped. I haven't lived in such small quarters since I first met Jim."

"Were you in school then?"

"Heavens no! I was campus counselor and mother confessor at UCLA, where he was taking his residency."

"Did you like being a counselor?"

She nodded. "It was before draft anxiety changed everything. My friends tell me that when boys change majors or drop classes nowadays, their draft deferments are canceled and the military snaps them up."

"I suppose we should be thankful we were born female."

"Ha! Born female and look where we end up." Connie's laugh was a merry trill.

"Well, at least you're not barefoot."

"Being pregnant is enough. I sure don't look forward to the labor again."

"Do you have a hard time?"

"Horrible."

"What kind of anesthesia do you take?"

"I had a spinal with one, epidural with another, and with the first they knocked me clean out."

"Have you considered natural birth?"

"Are you kidding? I couldn't do it."

"You might want to talk to Sister Anne."

Jim came onto the porch and sat beside Connie. "Talk to Sister Anne about what?" he asked.

"Natural childbirth," Sandy volunteered.

He shook his head. "I've had a gutful of natural deliveries. They never work."

"This is a new method. I coached a first-time couple through a difficult labor and both say it was a fantastic experience," Sandy tried.

"I don't know about you women. We spend years developing anesthetics and then you girls want to go back to the Stone Age."

"It's not Stone Age; it's education."

"What more does a woman need to know?" Jim asked.

"How to control the pain."

"Women don't have much pain in a well-managed labor."

Sandy and Connie burst into laughter.

"Okay. Okay," Jim conceded. "There has to be some pain. But it's not horrendous."

"This method makes the pain bearable, doesn't sedate the infant, and uses no invasive techniques."

"Won't work. It always ends up with the patient screaming for a shot."

"A good coach can prevent that."

"Who coaches?"

"Usually the husband."

"During delivery? Not on my watch."

His resistance surprised Sandy. She had thought he would be open to anything to decrease the chaos on the ward.

"I'd like to try it on a limited basis," she said.

"In that tiny hole you call a labor room? Where in the world will you put the fathers? In bed with their wives?"

"My nurses are interested in training."

"You can do anything you'd like with your nurses, but don't mess around with my deliveries. And don't ask me to support you. I won't."

Dave had been standing in the open doorway, listening. He leaned into the conversation and tried to help. "Plains Indians didn't need anesthesia. Their women stopped beside the trails, delivered, and went on with their business."

"Sure they did. And after one delivery they had bottoms as open as railroad tunnels." Jim winked at Dave. "Now, that wouldn't be much fun for us, would it?"

Connie's voice tightened with anger. "Is that your first priority? Maybe we women should have some say in the matter."

"Now, Connie, if we didn't do a good repair, most women would develop bladder and other problems." He turned to Sandy. "Seeing one patient succeed with a technique doesn't mean it will work for everyone."

"I realize that, but Sister has been successful with it for more than a year, and she has three times more births than we do."

Connie looked to her husband. "We've done it your way three times. Maybe it's time we tried something new."

"Count me out," he said. "It won't work. If you want to try it, you're on your own."

"I could have one of my nurses be your coach," Sandy offered.

"It's a deal," Connie said.

Major Roberts joined them. "What's a deal?"

"Having a nurse be my childbirth coach," Connie answered.

"You're getting a little big for your britches, aren't you, Lieutenant?" Major Roberts warned. "I don't have funding to pay nurses for classes and I don't have enough nurses to staff the place while they go."

"The classes are free and I'll cover for their time," Sandy said.

"I'll hold you to that, and if things go wrong, it will be your ass in a sling."

                                  ᘓ

20 November 1967

Kadena AFB, Japan

Hi Sandy,

I finally got a crew rest and am trying to catch up with everyone. I got your letter and package. Thank you for all the stateside goodies.

It sounds like you can no longer be called an FNG or a feather merchant. I was sorry to hear about your friend Meyer. He sounded like a good guy and so tough.

As for me, I'm not as tough as I thought. I've gotten used to sights, smells, and danger, but not the long hours of flying. Still, I'm thankful not to be an army nurse. My patients have been cleaned up and treated by primary care teams. The army gals get them right out of the combat zones, and let me tell you, they're not pretty. Injured guys sometimes have to stay in the open for days before they get picked up. You can imagine the condition they're in. The grunts didn't ask to be here and I did, so the least I can do is offer them good care. I've had great training.

The battle zone at the moment is the Dak To Valley along the Ho Chi Minh Trail. The guys coming out say they routinely run short of food and ammunition because the firefights are wicked and supplies can't get in. And no matter what they say about the low number of deaths, I sure see a lot of body bags.

The scenery is absolutely incredible. When we fly under the clouds the colors are amazing. But there are also areas that have been napalmed or hit with vegetation killer and are a mess. I remind myself that the destruction is necessary to save this country and these people.

Bob Hope is coming for Christmas! Raquel Welch and other sexy broads are going to be in it. Seems a bit out of place, but the guys will love it and God knows they can use a boost.

As for your situation, getting off base was a good move. If you find your work too petty and political, consider putting in a volunteer statement. We can use all the good nurses we can get, and life is definitely not dull. Good wishes for Christmas. Remember me when you carve the turkey.

Always,

Penny

Near the end of Christmas week she stopped by the Officers' Club to join the men of the 385th for dinner and drinks. As they moved closer to deployment, every conversation revolved around the war. The club had taken on a louder tone as the newest pilot replacements trickled in. They were much younger than the seasoned professionals who had previously flown the Thud. Some were ROTC recent graduates.

The new operations officer, Tim Schneider, introduced her to flying ace Zeke Spencer, the squadron's newest I.P.

Zeke's piercing blue eyes commanded respect. A real lady-killer, Sandy decided as she pulled her hand away from his.

"I hear the V.C. are bringing in troops and supplies near Con Thien," Ralph said. "Something big coming down. Maybe a real battle."

"Never happen," Zeke countered. "The gooks don't know a pod of peas about a conventional battle."

"Mao's teachings of guerilla warfare give three phases: Hit and run. Larger action. And, when the time is right, big conventional battles," Tim said.

Zeke laughed. "We've got a cease-fire."

Tim shrugged. "Enemies have been known to ignore those."

"Over Tet?" Zeke said. "Shit. You sure as hell don't know much about gooks. They'd never offend their ancestors with a big fight."

"Unless they believe they're avenging those same ancestors," Tim shot back. "It's what they did with the French at Dien Bien Phu."

"If you're right, we could see some good action," Randy interjected.

Zeke disagreed. "It'll be the same old shit. The V.C. aren't that savvy."

Tim laughed. "We aren't any tougher than the French, or the Chinese."

"But we've got superior weapons," Ralph said.

"Ho Chi Minh is fighting for a cause. We aren't," Tim persisted.

"Let them come slithering down that goddamned trail. We'll take them hands down!" Ralph ended the discussion.

"So, Sandy, will we see you at our place for New Year's Eve?" Tim asked.

"You betcha you will, and I'll be by her side," Zeke said.

"Sandy?" Tim said.

"I don't know," she answered. "I may have to work." She wasn't sure she wanted to go anywhere with Zeke, even though she'd heard that most of the women on base were gaga over him.

"I'll pick you up at 2100 hours. Show you my new 'Vette. And you can show me the way to the Schneiders' place."

All eyes were on her as he waited for a response. "I'll have to let you know," she said.

❦

"Oh my God, Sandy. You have to go. He's the cutest guy yet and every gal on base would like to walk in your shoes. Maybe this is your chance to lose your virginity."

"I'm not sure about him, Kate. I don't think I like him. He's pretty opinionated and bold."

"Of course he is. He's a hero. He deserves a little swagger."

"I don't think he's for me."

"Sandy, look, you've got to get over this Sam guy. He's not worthy of you. Give this guy a chance, for heaven's sake. What do you have to lose?"

"My reputation. My respectability."

"Not worth the paper they're printed on."

"What?"

"Times are changing. Virginity is becoming passé. With the pill, we women are on equal terms with the guys."

"Ha! I'll know we're on equal terms when we can be something other than nurses or teachers. When I find a female bank president, then I'll agree with you."

"If I ever see a female bank president, I'll eat my bra."

They fell onto the couch in gales of laughter.

"Come on," Kate said. "I have a closet full of fancy dresses. Let's choose one for your New Year's date with the famous Zeke Spencer."

Sandy liked a modest black number, but again Kate chided her. "Why do you insist on hiding your assets? You should show off those long legs and shapely boobs."

In the end, she carried home a scarlet number that made her appear more sophisticated than she felt. Still, she convinced herself, Kate had been right—its velvet softness did highlight her tawny skin and silvery brown hair.

∞

When she opened the door to Zeke Spencer on New Year's Eve, his rakish whistle caused her to have second thoughts. He reeked of scotch. She pulled on a long coat and hurried him to his car, but his driving proved he'd had a snootful.

She was relieved when they arrived at the Schneiders' and he went in search of the bar.

General Magnem came to her aid. "You here alone, Lieutenant?"

"No, sir, but I seem to have lost my escort to the bar."

"He's a bit short of sense to leave a beautiful girl unattended."

"The girl can fend for herself." She smiled to soften her words.

"Good. I have yet to meet the Schneiders. Will you introduce me?"

They walked into a sunroom, where floor-to-ceiling windows revealed a distant view of city lights. The Schneiders were on the stairs to the upper floor, speaking to their two boys. When Tim caught sight of the general he scooted his children up the stairs and guided his wife into the room.

Ann Schneider's smile was dazzling. "Sandy." She offered her hand. "I'm so glad you came."

"Have you met General Magnem?" Sandy asked.

"Welcome, General. I'm sorry for the slight confusion. My children are a bit excited."

"I understand. I have three of my own. All grown," he said.

Tim was handsome in a tailored suit. He helped Sandy remove her coat.

"What a beautiful dress," Ann gushed. "Perfect for your coloring."

"Thank you."

"Nice house you've found," General Magnem said. "It's the only place I've seen in Kansas that's higher than the wind."

"But after Texas, Kansas seems positively mountainous," Ann said.

"Is that where you're from? I thought I heard an English accent."

"You're absolutely right. Suffolk. But I stayed with Tim's family while he was at Tan Son Nhut." She made a face.

"War widow," Tim said. The timbre in his voice sent small chills up Sandy's spine.

"And glad to have done with it," Ann added. "But, Sandy, I thought I saw you come in with our newest I.P.?"

"I did," she said.

"And his loss is my gain," the general said.

"With nurses as attractive as Sandy, we should visit the hospital and have our pulses checked or something, shouldn't we, General?" Tim teased.

"You will not!" His wife stretched up and kissed him lightly on one cheek. She turned back to Sandy. "Have you and Zeke been dating long?"

"It's actually our first and last date."

Ann patted her arm. "We all know how that goes."

There was a commotion in the next room. They turned to see Zeke struggling with a young woman.

"Apparently he's not doing very well anywhere tonight," Tim said.

"Who is he?" General Magnem asked.

"That's *the* Captain Zeke Spencer." Tim answered.

"Excuse me." The general walked toward Zeke. Tim followed.

Ann held Sandy's arm and watched them go. "I sure hope old Zeke flies better than he socializes," she said.

"He's going to feel pretty stupid about this in the morning." Sandy watched the two men escort Zeke into the kitchen. "I can see I should have come alone."

ⁿﾟ

Hours later, someone opened the front door so they could hear the city welcome in 1968. As explosions filled the air, the partygoers kissed freely. Sandy found herself in Tim's arms. His kiss sent shivers to her toes. A bit shaken, she turned away and was immediately caught by General Magnem. His kiss was more perfunctory. As more champagne was brought out, she sat on the couch with Ann and watched Zeke sip coffee—provided at the general's insistence.

"Are you sure we can't take you home?" Ann asked.

Sandy shook her head. "He's a bit more sober than when we drove up."

"And you promise you'll not see him again?"

Sandy laughed. "I definitely will not be seeing him again."

"I hear the new class coming in is jam-packed with young fellows. I will take it upon myself to find a good match for you, my dear."

Sandy laughed.

"I promise you I will."

The rooms began to empty. Zeke came to her. "Are you interested in some breakfast?" he asked.

"I have to work in a few hours. I'd rather go straight home."

"It's your call." He shrugged.

She accepted his arm as they walked across the icy drive, and murmured her thanks when he made her comfortable in the passenger seat of his Corvette. She snuggled into her coat and slipped off her shoes.

He lit a cigarette and watched the string of cars disappear over the hill.

When the drive was clear, she looked expectantly toward him. "Are we going?" she asked.

He snuffed his cigarette in the ashtray and slid one hand under her coat.

She brushed it away.

"Don't want any?" he asked.

"I just want to go home."

"Come on. Every girl likes to play a little."

She reached to open the door, but he slammed the car into gear and, with a rattling spray of gravel, sent them toward the hill. The car lost its hold on the ice. She placed both hands on the dash as they narrowly missed the edge of the drive. Near the bottom of the long hill he swung the wheel violently to the right. The car bumped and jolted across an uneven surface. Only her outstretched hands protected her from hitting the dash when he slammed on the brakes. Overhead, a mass of branches blocked out sections of stars. Her heart beat rapidly against her rib cage.

He switched off the ignition and lights and slid his hand behind her neck.

She stared straight ahead. "Zeke, I want to go home," she said in her best nurse voice.

"We're not going anywhere, sweetheart, until you put out."

She could make out a line of trees and what might be a house about a mile away. The blustery wind shook the car and rattled the frozen branches overhead. A windbreak, she thought, probably along one of the furrowed fields she had seen in the headlights on the way in. To her right a double string of barbed wire lined the lane. She had to remain calm.

He wrapped his hand in her long hair and pulled until her head tilted back.

She reached back with both hands and tried to free her hair. "I said no, Zeke."

He laughed and slid his free hand under her coat. "Every girl says that. At first."

His cold hand slid into the low neck of her dress and cupped one breast.

She released his hand that held her hair and tried to remove the one tearing at her dress.

He pushed her sideways against the door and covered her legs with one of his. With one swift pull on her hair, he forced her head back into an unnatural arc. His mouth came down on hers. His lips and tongue were sour with coffee and whiskey.

She turned her face aside. Door hardware bit into her ribs.

He bit her cheek.

The icy coldness of the window glass pressed against her face. His fingers twisted in her hair and forced her back to arch. "Stop fighting, bitch," he snarled. "You know what I want."

She blinked away tears.

His eyes glittered through the darkness.

She heard the dull tearing of velvet and felt cold air cross her bared breasts.

"Ah, there you are, my lovely beauties." He smeared spittle over her nipples with his tongue.

She tried to knee him.

"I'm lots bigger than you are, bitch, but if you want to fight, let's get to it. More fun for me."

She screamed as his teeth bit into her breast.

His responding growl was low and primordial.

Another searing pain flashed through her breast. Her piercing wail echoed through the small car's interior.

He pressed his knee into her stomach until her screams became empty gasps.

His free hand touched her face with unexpected gentleness. His fingertips crawled across her cheek, encircled her mouth. "Oh, girl. I've had my eye on you for days. You want me, don't you? You're just playing hard to get like your mommy taught you."

Fear glued her tongue to her teeth and rattled in every breath. She strained her head side to side in silent protest. Hair tore away from her temples.

"Don't tell me no," he hissed. His hand snapped her jaw against her neck cords, and cracked her head against the window. Something warm ran down her face.

A high-pitched whine escaped from her open mouth.

He threw back his head and laughed. "No one can hear you, hon. It's just you and me now."

He tore her dress to its hem, slid into the small space beneath the dash, and pulled her forward so he could bite the white skin of her belly. He pressed his hand between her legs.

Her knees knocked together rhythmically as she sobbed.

His mouth moved slowly, bit deeply. "Do you know what a belly button is for, bitch?"

Her eyes bulged painfully from their sockets. She wasn't going to escape. Zeke Spencer would have his way.

He lifted his face, rubbed his nose against hers, sniffed her nostrils, and whispered, "The belly button's the place where a guy stores his gum on the way down."

He slapped her again. "Laugh," he demanded. "Laugh at my joke."

His sharp fingers tore her panties. She pushed with hips and knees, felt a sudden painful jab, and gasped. He had won. He forced himself between her legs. His weight fell on her and crushed her twisted spine. He shifted for a better position, but the small space in the car wouldn't accommodate his size. He reached behind her and pushed the door handle.

Her upper body fell into the cold.

He lay on her, both hands beneath her buttocks.

Cold air filled her lungs. Her head cleared. His erection was too small. He couldn't penetrate.

"Help me, you bitch!" he shouted as he kicked at the driver's side door.

She bit her lips so she wouldn't scream. "Zeke." The cotton in her mouth made the sound inaudible. She tried again. "Zeke."

His fetid breath hovered over her. "What?"

"Zeke." She stretched her head up to find his lips, almost gagged, and fell back. "Zeke, there's no room. Let's get out on the ground. Oh, hurry."

"You sweet bitch. I knew you wanted it."

He released her slowly, without shifting his weight. "No tricks, now," he said. "Just slide nice and easy with me. If you try anything, I'll have to hurt you." He wrapped his hand in her hair again and slid clumsily with her toward the frozen ground.

Her head hit with a thud. She opened her eyes. The barbed wire fence was strung tight. As his legs cleared the car, she twisted hard on the frozen ground and pressed all her strength into one push against his chest. He fell against the fence. His bare buttocks and upper back caught on the barbs. He screeched with pain. For one second he lost his hold.

She tore her hair away and scrambled on all fours for the cover of the trees.

He grabbed for her trailing coat.

She half-stood, began to move along the fence line. Briars and brush tore flesh and hose from her legs. Her coat caught on something. She pulled free and lifted it to her thighs. She was upright now, could feel her legs under her.

He thrashed through brush not far behind. She cleared a small rise, came out into open sky. She couldn't see how far the land fell off. She wouldn't think about it.

She cleared the fence, as she had cleared many fences in her youth, in one clean leap. As she hit bare earth, she pulled her knees up. She rolled, pulling the coat with her. Furrows. She was in a plowed field of wide ridges and deep trenches. Her lungs screamed for oxygen. Her legs wanted to run. Instead, she rolled into the next furrow, brought her knees up, and covered the whiteness of her face and limbs with the dark coat.

He came out of the trees. She could hear him adjusting his clothing as he walked along the fence line.

"Sandy? Ah, Sandy, come on. I was only kidding. I had a little too much to drink. Come on. You'll freeze to death out here. Come on and I'll take you straight home."

She shivered on the frozen ground. Her breath came in short rattling gasps that echoed loudly in her ears. He could hear her. He must hear her. She wanted to run, but if she did he would know exactly where she was. She tensed, felt something beneath her hand. A cold Kansas rock. She would kill him. She would smash his face. She silently willed him to come ahead. She wanted to see him dead.

He paced outside the fence, back and forth, grunting his dissatisfaction like a bull in rut. After what seemed an hour, he clapped his hands together, and began to move away.

Underbrush cracked and snapped.

Silence.

She did not move.

The engine of a car turned over. Bright headlights swung over the field.

Cold slowed her brain. She peeked from her coat as the lights moved away.

She lifted her head and watched the car descend the hill, stop once near the bottom, then speed up and disappear toward the city.

She pulled herself up, then fell backward as her numbed feet found no purchase in the ridged contours of the field. She squatted and pulled her coat closer. She was not thinking right. If she stayed here frostbite would take her exposed toes and the cold wind would erase all reason. She straightened, placed one bare hand on the frozen wire to steady herself, and stared across the open field. It was impossible to judge the distance to the row of trees where the farmhouse might be.

She would have to climb the hill to the Schneiders' house.

It took two tries to get over the wire. Its barbs pierced her legs but she felt no pain. She hoped her shoes had fallen from the car, but she could find only one. She tossed it into the field, buttoned her coat with numb fingers, and forced herself to move forward. The pavement brought the sensation of scalding heat to the soles of her feet. She moved to the dirt shoulder, pulled her face into her upraised collar, jammed her hands into the narrow pockets, and began to climb.

She reached the house an eternity later but could not pull her hands from her pockets. She leaned against the door and tapped it with her head. It opened in a golden glow of light. She fell at the feet of Ann Schneider.

"My God!" Ann cried. "Tim, come here. Oh, my God!"

Sandy felt arms reach under her, lift her into the warm interior, and settle her on the long couch. The soft plush of velvet caused her legs to shiver with a painful heat. She opened her eyes, turned her face away from Tim. She couldn't bear his touch.

"What happened? Where's Zeke? Did you have an accident?"

"You're nearly frozen," Ann soothed. "I'm going to take your coat and put you in a warm blanket."

Sandy cringed with shame, clutched her coat, and shook her head.

"Tim, call a doctor," Ann said and wouldn't be pushed away.

Sandy was too weak to fight. She allowed Ann to remove her coat. "My God, Sandy! What happened?"

She pulled at the torn edges of her dress and felt a blanket fall over her. When she tried to thank the woman, only a sob broke free.

It was then she heard heavy footsteps and recognized General Magnem's voice. "Sandy," he said. "Where's Zeke?"

"For God's sake, somebody call a doctor!" Ann said.

"Sandy," the general tried again.

"Can't you see what's happened?" Ann shrieked.

Sandy felt panic rise. Her limbs trembled uncontrollably. She pushed herself up, took a deep breath, and shook her head. "No," she begged. "Don't. Please."

"Don't try to talk," Ann crooned. She tucked the blanket around Sandy's face and gently stroked her hair. "There's ice in your hair. I'll get a towel."

Sandy reached out and held Ann's arm in a viselike grip. The general came back into view. "Did Zeke do this?" he demanded.

He was too close. He needed to back away.

"Sandy. I have to know. Tell me. Where's Zeke? Did you have an accident?"

"For God's sake," Ann said.

Sandy shook her head. "No," she said in a voice that wasn't hers. "No accident."

"There, Sandy," Ann said. "You're safe now. We'll take care of you. Close your eyes. Rest."

"Ann."

"Shh. Don't talk. I'm going to make some warm tea."

She closed her eyes at the thought. Tea. Tea mixed with milk, swirled in a golden well, and served in a thin white cup. She longed to sip from the lacy edges of that cup, feel the tart cleansing liquid on her tongue, and taste its smooth sweetness. But all she tasted was the rusty bitterness of her own blood and the thick cottony felt of fear.

She could hear voices muffled in argument from another room. She shouldn't have come here. She should have stayed in the dirt with her shame. She should have allowed the Kansas cold to seep deeply into her bones until she was no more. She could never live with this.

She heard someone moaning and realized the voice was her own. She struggled to sit up.

Ann's voice: "Shh." She felt Ann's arms come around her. "Shh, Sandy. Shh."

She was too tired to go on. She felt herself sinking into a warm place and gave herself over to it. She sank slowly away and slept.

∾

A bell jarred her awake. Something was wrong. She jerked with fear until she heard Ann's voice.

"It's okay," she said. "It's just the door."

Her body tensed. Zeke. Zeke at the door. She forced her eyes open. Three men stood together, murmured, and glanced toward her. They were discussing her, she was sure of it. One man moved toward her.

"Sandy," Jim Andersen said.

A rush of emotion overwhelmed her. She reached out to him.

He wrapped her in his arms. "You all right?"

She nodded. Thank God, she thought. Thank God it was Jim. No one else should see her like this.

He turned away and spoke to the general. "I'll have to examine her. Can we use another room?"

Ann answered. "Yes, this way." She helped Sandy into a small bedroom.

Jim pulled a surgical kit from his flight emergency bag and arranged bottles and instruments on the dresser top while Ann gently removed Sandy's torn clothing and covered her with a smooth bed sheet.

Sandy breathed in the familiar scents of iodine, alcohol, and dry gauze and watched as Jim expertly assessed each wound.

"I'll have to suture a few of these," he murmured. "Sandy, are these bite marks?"

She nodded as he gently injected Lidocaine into a tear on her arm. She turned her head away as he began to stitch the open edges of the wound.

"I'll have to check you in a few days," he said as he worked. "The chance of infection with human bites is pretty high. I'll clean those up but have to leave them open. They may scar. You know what to watch for."

She nodded.

"I'll have to do a pelvic now, Sand," he said.

She sat up straight, pulled the sheet to her chin, and shook her head.

"Has to be done. In cases like this my testimony in court will be crucial."

"He didn't do that," she said. "He couldn't. I fought. I got away."

"You're in shock, Sandy. I'm sure you're hypothermic. You're not thinking straight. After what you have gone through, I understand, and I can see you fought, but still ..." His words trailed off as she began to climb off the bed.

"No," she said. "There's no reason. No."

"Sandy, this has to be done."

She was standing now with the sheet wrapped closely around her. "No. The car was too small. He couldn't do it. When he let me get out of the car to make it easier," she shuddered at the memory, "I pushed him into the barbed wire and he let go."

"It's best to have records, just in case."

"I can't," she said. "I just can't."

"It's against my better judgment," he said, "but I can't force you." He patted her shoulder paternally. "Okay, kid. It's your show and I'll have to take your word for it." He moved closer and touched her hair. She pulled away. "I need to check your scalp, Sandy. I'm not going to hurt you. What happened to your hair?"

She turned her head to one side and allowed him to study behind her ears and the nape of her neck. "He pulled it hard so I couldn't move."

"Looks like he yanked quite a bit of it out. You're going to have some bald spots."

"I need to shower," she said. "I'm supposed to be at work."

"You won't be going to work anytime soon, kid. You look like you've been hit by a truck."

"There's nobody else."

"I'll call the major."

"You can shower here, Sandy," Ann offered. "I'm sure we're the same size. I'll find you something to wear. If you'd like I'll cut your hair too. I was a hairdresser in a previous life. How about it?"

"A bath will warm her faster," Jim said. "I'll go speak to the general."

An hour later Sandy reluctantly reentered the living room wearing a pair of too-tight jeans and one of Tim's oversized sweaters, with her hair cut into a short bob.

The men stopped speaking. She raised her eyes and looked for the source of tension that held each in an angry stance.

Tim studied the floor and fluffed up the thick strands of carpet with one foot.

General Magnem, his lips thin, his jaw tight, paced between the sofa and the front door.

And Jim—ah, there was the angry center. He paced, mouthed silent words, and eyed the general with unabashed indignation.

"Okay! Okay!" he blurted suddenly. "I can understand the point, but I can't accept it. Sandy has been brutally attacked by a member of the very forces meant to protect her. You can't let him get away with this. It's not right!"

The general faced him. His eyes were cold and sure. A bulldog of a man, Sandy thought. Someone who knew his own mind and demanded that others bend to it. "We're talking about a military problem, an altercation between two officers in my wing. An altercation that, if misunderstood, can seriously damage our mission here."

"An altercation? An altercation? Look at her. Does she look like she's been part of an altercation? That man is guilty of assault and attempted rape. And where is he, General? Are the police out looking for him? Or is he out about town forcing himself on another helpless female?"

"He's at home, Captain Andersen. And he's been ordered to stay there."

"Oh, sure. And he's really going to sit there like a good boy and wait for you to decide his fate?"

"He's an officer and a combat-proven fighter pilot. He's had two tours in Southeast Asia, where he conducted himself honorably. He'll follow the orders of his commander."

Jim pumped one closed fist. "I don't give a damn what he is to you, General. I only care about what he's done to Sandy. If you aren't going to report this, I certainly will!" He picked up the telephone.

"You'll do no such thing, Captain. Unless you're looking for a general court martial." He stepped over, took the phone, and looked to Tim. "Do you have you some brandy?" he asked. "I think we could all use something to relax us."

Ann went behind the bar and began sorting through half-filled bottles. Sandy watched as she poured the golden liquid.

The general accepted a snifter, sat on the couch, and crossed his legs. He looked to Jim. "Sit, Captain, and we'll talk about this like reasonable men."

Jim walked to Sandy and sat on the arm of her chair. It's us against them, she thought, but what were they fighting for?

She accepted a brandy with both hands, wrapped her shaking fingers around its warmth, and leaned over to breathe in its earthy aroma. She wanted to flee, to run home to Maine. She couldn't remember why she had left in the first place.

The general studied the contents of his glass.

He's buying time, Sandy thought, just as Meyer had advised her to stall when faced with a difficult event. She took a deep breath as he began to speak.

"I intend to handle this internally. If you disagree I'll be happy to entertain comments." He studied each person again before his gaze fell on Sandy. "Can I ask you some questions, Lieutenant O'Connell?"

She nodded as she, too, bided her time.

"Have you known Zeke Spencer long?"

"No. He's only been on base a few weeks."

"And where were you introduced to him?"

"At the club."

"And have you two been dating these past few weeks?"

"No, sir. This was our first date."

"So you drove to the party tonight and you both had a little too much to drink and, on the way back to the base, when he suggested you might stop and enjoy the view, you said, 'Well, why not'?"

Sandy felt indignation rise. She sat forward on her chair. "No," she said as calmly as she could. "That's not what happened."

She felt Jim's hand on her shoulder, followed by a small affirming pat.

"Really, Lieutenant? Tell me what did happen." His tone seemed to mock her.

Slowly, her face burning with shame and her voice trembling with remembered fear, she told him what she could remember, beginning with Zeke's loud knock on her door, until she jumped the fence and heard him drive away. Somewhere in the middle of her telling, she realized she was becoming less afraid. When she was done she placed her empty brandy snifter on the coffee table and said, "That's what happened, General, and if you don't believe me you can go to hell."

She heard Ann cheer involuntarily, and Jim mutter, "Oh ho!"

From across the room, Tim sent her a quick approving smile.

"And if it did happen the way you say it did, Lieutenant," the general persisted, "then surely Captain Spencer will have some marks, some bruises from your fending him off, some scratches where you clawed him?"

"No, sir," she said and again followed Meyer's advice to include a bit of humor in every encounter with brass. "He didn't give me a chance to bite or scratch, but the fence most definitely put a few deep marks on his rear."

Everyone chuckled quietly. Jim muttered, "Good girl."

"Well then," the general placed his empty glass on the table and reached for his coat, "that's that. I have your story and I have your assertion that you're completely innocent in this episode." He turned to Tim. "Major?"

"Sir?"

"Did you observe Captain Spencer and Lieutenant O'Connell over the course of the evening?"

"Yes, sir. Often."

"Would you say Lieutenant O'Connell was provocative?"

"Beautiful, but not provocative, sir."

"Not with Captain Spencer?"

"No, sir, just the opposite. She was avoiding him. He'd had a lot to drink."

"If he's only been at Meridian a few weeks, Major, how can you make that judgment?"

"You saw how he was acting, sir."

The general turned back to Sandy. "Lieutenant O'Connell, shouldn't you have felt you were taking a chance by coming here tonight with a man you hardly knew? And once you were here and witnessed his behavior, shouldn't you have been more prudent and found another way home?"

"He's an officer, General Magnem. I trusted him the way I trust all the men under your command."

"Despite his behavior?"

"Yes." She studied her feet. Her toes were changing from white to pink. She raised her eyes and fastened them on the general. "You've had a lot to drink and I wouldn't be afraid to drive home with you." She looked each man in the eye. "Or with you, Tim. Or you, Jim."

"And were you behaving like an officer, Lieutenant?"

He seemed determined to discount her story. "Yes, sir, I was."

He strode across the floor and stood before her. "I believe you, Sandy. I want you to understand that. I'll deal harshly with Captain Spencer. But at the same time my duty lies with the organization. I have to protect my wing. To that end I do not intend to report this incident to civilian authorities. It's a military matter. And I intend for it to remain a military matter." His eyes went to Jim. "Do you understand, Captain Andersen?"

"Yes, sir, but I don't like it."

"I'm not asking you to like it." He turned back to Sandy. "I know this will be difficult, Lieutenant. You've been terribly mistreated. But I believe you have the strength to pull it off."

His sudden gentleness disarmed her.

"Can you trust me to take care of this without the newspapers and gossips sticking their noses into our business?"

The word *gossip* clinched it. "Yes, sir," she said.

She heard Jim's disapproving grumble.

"Good girl," General Magnem said. "And for every person in this room, I never want to hear a word or insinuating reference about the events of this night. Do you understand?"

She couldn't see Jim's reaction.

He turned to Ann. "As you're a civilian, Ann, I have no authority over your actions, but I have to tell you, if you value Tim's military career, it is in his best interest that you maintain silence."

"I will, General, but only because it's what Sandy wants."

"This matter is settled. I'll take you home, Lieutenant O'Connell."

She didn't move. She didn't want to drive with him.

Jim understood at once. "Not to worry, General. I'll get Sandy home."

She remained seated as everyone else stood. At the door, General Magnem turned. "Happy New Year," he said. "I'm sure it will be a wonderful one for all of us."

 measuring ∽

She was relieved of duty until her bruises faded. She told everyone who phoned she'd been in a fender bender on the ice. She allowed only Dave to visit. She lied to him too.

When a package arrived in the middle of the week, she was grateful to Penny for breaking into her sadness. Dave helped her cut the tapes and laughed when yards of multicolored silk spilled into her lap.

"It's a quilt," she marveled.

Dave picked up an edge of the material. "Some peasant girl spent hours on her knees tying all those knots."

"It's handmade?"

"Yep. Made on a small handloom."

She ran her hand over peacock blue, crimson, red, and pale lavender. "I've never seen anything like it."

"One of a kind," he said.

"I've got to try it on my bed!"

He helped her replace her bedspread with the rainbow of silk.

"Much better," he said and raised his glass. "To many hours under an Asian quilt," he said.

And definitely not alone, Sandy thought.

CHAPTER SEVEN

27 December 1967

Dear Sandy,

I've been sitting here, staring at the ring on my finger and wishing you were here so we could talk. I have bad news. A week ago Bob was in a midair collision near the Cambodian border. He and three of his crew survived but he has been burned over sixty percent of his body. He is too unstable to be medevaced home, so is at Kadena with a trach, in much pain, unable to speak, and completely withdrawn. He does not appear to want to live. I'm still flying constantly and have only seen him twice. Both times he turned his head away and refused to acknowledge my presence. I had to speak to the back of his head. I told him how important he is in my life and how important his survival is to me. He did not respond. I tried to spark some will to live in him, to give him my strength, but he refused it. I clutch at straws. I know it's not possible for one person to will another to live. If it were, I would have no dead bodies at the end of my flights.

I am torn between Bob and the many who depend on my care. At the moment I am on an eighteen-hour crew rest and should sleep, but I can't.

Bob Hope has arrived and the crowds are huge. I want to go over and tell Raquel that she is a stupid piece of shit. I've seen such a slice of life in the past few months and so much pain that I know I am the one who is stupid. I need to save Bob. I don't want him to die. I desperately need a friend. I wish you were here. Pray for us, will you?

Always,

Penny

$\backsim\!\!\!\!\!\!\backsim$

When Gramps and Randy insisted, Sandy accepted their invitation to graduation. She had returned to work in time to say goodbye to her favorites from the 385th. They were all living in future tense now—looking forward to the war and the beginning of another great adventure.

Bile rose in her throat when she saw Captain Zeke Spencer at the speakers' table. He had not contacted her since the incident. She trusted that his egoistic need to continue flying and his obedience to General Magnem would keep him away. The general had been called to the Pentagon earlier in the week and he had taken Tim with him.

Ralph took her hand. "Come on, Sandy. Smile. It's not like this is the end of the world."

She laughed on cue. "What are you, a mind reader? I was thinking that my friends are all leaving me at once."

At the main table, Zeke moved the program along with ribald humor. At the end he turned up the microphone. "Hey! Listen up here! Listen up."

The room hushed.

"There's one more event on the agenda tonight. We've added something extra. A bit of a door prize, you might say."

Applause drowned him out. He raised both arms for silence. "We're going to have an auction. All proceeds go to the bar, so you know it's a good cause." He grinned as he waited again. "I've got a shoe here." He held it aloft. "Some little lady lost it at one of our parties. She wants to have it back, along with the man who buys it."

He held up the shoe Sandy had lost in his car on New Year's Eve.

"That's Sandy's shoe," Kate shrieked from across the room.

"Too bad I'm married," Gramps said.

"And way too slow," Randy retorted.

"And too old," Ralph added.

"And too late," another man said as he stood and shouted, "I'll give you ten bucks."

Gramps held Sandy's shaking hand. "I haven't agreed," she shouted.

Her words were lost as Zeke bid, "Twenty!"

Oh, God, please, no. She clutched at Ralph's arm. "Tell him no," she begged.

"Twenty-two," Ralph shouted.

"Thirty!" Zeke's eyes met hers. He smiled.

No one knew the danger. She looked across the table to Randy. "Please stop this," she begged.

"Thirty-five," a new voice said.

"Forty." Zeke slammed the shoe onto the tabletop.

A long silence closed over the room.

Sandy leaned to Ralph. "Please, Ralph, tell him fifty."

"Fifty," Gramps hollered.

"Hey, Gramps, this war thing's got your blood up!" someone yelled.

"Sixty," Zeke said.

Ralph leaned toward her. "What do you have against old Zeke? You can't do better than him."

"I hate him." She turned to Randy again. "Please," she begged.

"Come on, Sand. Lighten up. It's all in fun."

"Damn you all to hell," she said.

Gramps leaned anxiously toward her. "Sandy?" He raised one hand. "Sixty-five."

"Go, Sand!" Kate shouted.

"Seventy," Zeke said.

A new voice shouted, "Seventy-five." B.B. caught her eye.

"Eighty." Zeke again.

"Ninety."

"Ah, hell, B.B., she's not worth a sawbuck. Take her," Zeke conceded. "Going. Going. Gone." He banged the shoe on the table.

Sandy slumped in her chair.

"Nice job, Sandy. Nice job. Paid for the bar. Thank B.B. for us, okay, kid?" Ralph said.

B.B. moved to her. "You look terrified."

"I am so grateful," she said.

"It's Zeke, isn't it?"

The room emptied into the bar. "I feel so stupid," she said.

"Not me," he smiled. "I feel lucky. Damned lucky. Want to get out of here?"

She nodded.

He steered her toward the main door. A crowd from the bar saw them and began to shout. Zeke stepped out. "Hey, B.B., pay the barman." He raised a glass to him. "Have fun, pal. I hope you get as lucky as I did."

"Bound to," B.B. said, and pulled her through the door.

He drove her home. At her front door she took his hand. "I don't know how I'll ever be able to thank you. I wish I could explain. If I invite you in for coffee, will you understand it's all that I'm offering?"

"I won't see many round-eyed girls for almost a year. I'll take you up on coffee."

"Come in," she said. "I just bought some new L.P.s."

৶

The next morning Dave adjusted the newspaper to catch the lamp's light as she poured coffee into cups. "General Wheeler is saying there may be a big offensive. And they don't even give it front page coverage."

Sandy sipped her coffee. She had sent B.B. off to war with a quick kiss on the cheek. Why couldn't she have, just once, been more like Kate? What was wrong with her?

"So let's see what we get on the front page," Dave continued. "Famous actress comments on the need for prostitutes, not actresses, as USO entertainment because the boys need relief, not more frustration." He tossed the paper aside. "No mention of the Pueblo incident or the fact that they're calling up the National Guard."

"Sex makes better reading," Sandy said.

"Those boys can get sex on any street corner of Saigon." He stood suddenly and strode through the door without saying goodbye. Minutes later she heard the tapping of his typewriter.

She turned on the TV. A note of urgency in the newscaster's voice caught her attention. Khe Sanh. Something about Khe Sanh. Dave's typing stopped. He was pounding on her door.

"Did you hear?" he shouted. "The offensive has started. The V.C. have attacked Khe Sanh with an army of troops."

"Kate's brother is there," she said, but he didn't seem to hear.

"I hope the shit-hot jocks of the 385th are well trained. Looks like they'll be arriving just in time for their dirty little war."

 ❦

After work the next day she stopped by the club to cash her check. Zeke stood near the cashier's booth, surrounded by new students. He spotted her at once. "Sandy. Come over here and meet some FNGs."

She pretended not to hear as she handed her check to the clerk.

Zeke grabbed her shoulder. "Come on, Miss Prissy Pants, I've got some new jocks I want you to meet."

"Don't touch me, Zeke," she warned.

He turned toward the men behind him. "Whooie! This one is a real fighter."

She took her cash and turned. A tall captain stood in her way. He had the greenest eyes she had ever seen. She smiled uncertainly and pushed past.

He followed her into the parking lot. "Could you give me a lift?"

"Sorry, I'm in a bit of a rush."

"It will only take a minute."

She climbed into her car. "Where are you going?"

He pointed across the street. "VOQ."

"I think you can walk that far."

He grinned. "I'll buy you dinner."

"I have plans for dinner, thanks."

She drove away. Typical fighter jock, she thought. Cocksure that he has the world by the tail.

At the duplex she found another letter from Penny. It had been written ten days earlier.

> *10 January 1968*
>
> *Dear Sandy,*
>
> *Bob shipped out stateside while I was on a flight. He didn't say goodbye. When I came back and saw his empty bed, I felt like someone had hit me in the stomach. At first I thought he had bought it, but one of the nurses told me he had been medevaced. His leaving makes me feel so small. He took my heart with him.*
>
> *The holiday cease-fire is holding. My flights are routine. The weather is terrible. But the mighty B-52s are still flying. When I hear their takeoffs they remind me of Bob, as he was, healthy and happy and returning to me in one of those birds.*
>
> *If you happen to get down to Texas Burn Center or have friends who do, could you see if you can get some info about him? I believe he owes me that much.*
>
> *Penny*

◌◌

Sandy slept fitfully until instinct drove her from her bed and over icy roads for an early start. Overflowing laundry hampers and the scent of ether—clear signs the unit was busy—did not cause her anxiety. Her extra hours worked had resulted in her mastery of obstetrical skills.

"Mrs. Andersen is in unit three," the night nurse said. "And Kathy has the flu."

"And Kathy is Mrs. Andersen's coach?"

"Yes, ma'am."

"Who do we have to replace her?"

The nurse's eyes cleared the top rim of her glasses. "You're sitting in the hot seat, Lieutenant. You'll get no help today."

Sandy fell back in her chair and covered both eyes with her hands. "My luck can't be this bad, can it?"

"You've got one delivering now and two in the hopper. I can stay awhile to get you started, but I have little ones at home and their daddy's already left for work."

"If you can finish up the first delivery, I'll be okay."

When she finished her round, she peered into the window of the delivery room. The night nurse gave her a high sign: one down and two to go. Jim had done the delivery. She pushed open the door to the labor room.

Connie appeared to be sleeping as a younger patient cried with nerve-jangling persistence. Sandy spoke to the girl. "I'm going to be the nurse who helps you have this baby."

"I'm not having any baby." She screamed.

Sandy smiled. "There doesn't seem to be any other way out of this, Judy."

"It hurts."

Sandy pulled the curtains closed between the beds.

"Let's see how long your contractions are lasting." She laid her hand on the girl's stomach.

"It's not a contraction. It's a god-awful pain." The girl closed her eyes, threw her head back into the sweat-dampened pillow, and broadcast her anguish to all four walls.

"I want to help you, Judy. Open your eyes and look at me," Sandy commanded.

"Tell me quick," she said, "because I think I'm about to die."

"Has the pain gone?"

"Yes."

"Good. I want you to lay back and let your whole body go limp. Let your breath out. Let every part of you go."

"I can't."

"Start with your hands. Open them and lay them on the bed."

She soothed the girl's open palms as she explained how she could relax her entire body.

Another contraction began. Judy's eyes flew open, her hands clenched into fists.

"We're ready for this one. Let your tummy relax. Take a nice deep breath and let your bottom relax. Think about the breathing. Relax and think about getting a nice big breath of air."

"I can't!" She wrapped her fingers around Sandy's outstretched hand and squeezed.

"Let me hear you breathe, nice and loud. Like this." Sandy breathed with her, led her away from the pain. "Good girl. That's better, isn't it?"

The girl nodded.

"Now hold your breath gently and relax," she whispered. From behind the closed curtain she heard Connie moan, and below the curtain she saw Jim's scrub pants move to his wife's bedside. She placed one hand over the girl's contraction.

"That's the worst for now. Let the air out nice and slow. Let it come out and sink back into the bed. Relax. Fall back. Rest."

The girl sank into the bed and closed her eyes.

She pretended not to know Jim was present. "Connie. Hi. You're awfully quiet over there. Is your breathing working?"

"I don't know if I'm doing this right or not. I wish Kathy was here."

"Me too. Have you been listening?"

"Yes, but I can't concentrate. I'm so tired."

"When you get your next contraction, breathe with it. Are you relaxing between them?"

"Yes. Oh, God. Here it comes." Her voice rose.

Judy was beginning a contraction too. Sandy looked into the teenager's eyes. "Now, deep breath," she whispered, "nice deep breath."

The girl reached out and grabbed her hand. Sandy guided it back onto the bed. "Relax this hand," she coached. "Now breathe. A deep slow one. That's the way. Slowly. Slowly."

Connie moaned. Sandy could hear the sheets rustling.

"Connie?" she called over her shoulder.

"What?"

"I want you to take control of the next contraction. Remember your exercises. Deep breath. Hold it. Hiss it out. Do you remember?"

"I remember but I just can't do it."

"Try it with the next one. Okay?"

Jim grunted his disgust.

"Jim? Have you finished your delivery?"

He didn't answer.

Sandy felt her face grow hot. She had to do this. She had to prove the nurses could conduct controlled labors despite inadequate staffing. Beneath her hand she felt Judy's contraction ebbing.

"Good work," she said. "Now, relax. Flop like an old pillow. Take all those wrinkles out of your forehead. Good girl."

"Sandy!" Connie cried.

She heard Jim murmur. "I'm here."

"Sandy! Help me. I can't do it."

It was time to jump in with both feet. "Connie," she called, "breathe in. You know how."

Connie's response was a ragged scream.

Sandy's shoulders tightened until she heard Connie begin to hiss through the pain. She turned Judy's pillow to the cooler side. "I'm going to take three steps over to Connie," she said. "I'll be listening."

She pulled the curtain back, stood between the beds, and coached Connie through a contraction.

"I'm getting it," Connie said.

"You ladies have a nice little rhythm going here," Jim said in a voice edged with sarcasm. "Maybe we should put some money on who gives in first."

Sandy ignored his pessimism. "There are other techniques to this besides breathing, Jim," she tried. "I could show you a few before Connie gets too far along."

"I've told you. I'm not into mumbo jumbo. You just tell me when to call in the anesthetist and we'll be square."

She moved to Connie and began to demonstrate effleurage. Jim walked out of the room.

An hour later she called him to examine Judy.

"Eight centimeters dilated and completely effaced. The head is beginning to descend the birth canal." He looked across the girl's belly and added. "It's your show, Sandy. Prove me wrong."

"You're on, Doc." She leaned close to Judy and said, "The hardest part is coming up. You're going to have a lot of work to do."

"No!"

Jim smiled and sat beside Connie.

"Judy, you need to listen to me. Can you hear me?"

"I'm going to throw up."

She held a basin ready. "Take little breaths. In and out, in and out. Now take a deep, deep breath and blow it out hard. We're going to clean out all that dirty old air and clear your brain. Come on, one good deep breath. That's it. You are so good at this."

The uterine muscles remained rock hard. She watched the second hand of her watch. Sixty seconds. Seventy. She looked toward the ceiling and silently begged. Come on. Let it relax a little. Give the kid some room. Slowly the muscle softened, but there was no time for cheering. Another contraction began immediately.

"I have to pee!" the girl screamed.

"It's the baby moving down." Sandy scolded herself for not having checked her bladder sooner. Too late now. "Let your bottom relax and if you pee, you pee. I have plenty of padding under you." As she was speaking she heard the girl give the unmistakable grunts of the final stage of labor. "Do you need to push, Judy?"

"Yes." A deep grunt followed a piercing scream.

Sandy helped her breathe through the contraction and turned to Jim. "Are you taking this one or is Arnold?" she asked.

"Arnold."

Sandy pulled the call button. Within seconds a corpsman was at the door. "Call Dr. Arnold, would you? Tell him primip, ready in about ten."

"Yes, ma'am."

The girl started bearing down as Sandy unlocked the brakes on the bed and pushed it into the delivery room.

The girl looked up. "Is it almost over?"

"Almost."

"You'll stay with me?"

She wet a cloth and wiped the girl's face. "I'll tell you what to do every step of the way," she promised.

The baby delivered less than a minute after Dr. Arnold arrived. "Eight pounds of boy," she whispered to Judy. "What a great little mother you are."

"I was so scared."

"You did it all. No reason to be scared now, is there?"

She cleared the baby for the nursery, left Judy to her sergeant and Dr. Arnold, and moved back to Connie.

"If you don't take something now, it will be too late," Jim was saying. "You'll be delivering and taking a spinal at the same time. That's not what you want. Remember the last time?"

Connie pulled off her gown and threw it. "Leave me alone," she shouted. "Just leave me alone."

"Jim," Sandy offered. "Want a little break?"

"Not now!" he said.

She stepped closer, picked up the discarded gown, and placed it over Connie's chest.

"You got her into this, Sandy. Now you tell her it's time for me to take over."

She couldn't give up. "You're tired and worried," she began.

"I am not worried! I know what she needs. Just who is the doctor here?"

"At the moment you're a husband. I promise, if I can't help Connie over this last hump, I'll give her the shot and I'll never say natural childbirth again."

"No. She can't do this. We'll need to use forceps in the end, and then where will she be? I'll tell you where. We'll be facing general anesthesia and we'll really have our hands full."

Sandy was about to give in when Connie spoke. "I've lost it, Sandy. I can't remember what to do. And my back is killing me."

"Want me to help?"

"Yes."

"Turn over on your side. I'll rub your back." She helped her into position and pressed her spine. "Is that where it hurts?"

"Yes. Right there."

Sandy looked to Jim. "Posterior presentation?"

He nodded.

"Let's relieve the pressure, Connie. Remember what you learned in class. Knee up and pillow to support your tummy?"

"Yes."

"Let's try it." She placed the pillows and began to rub the small of Connie's back. She turned to Jim. "What was she at last check?"

"About five, but high."

Connie began to moan.

"Breathe, Con. Listen to my breathing and concentrate. Her hands worked in rhythm with her breathing. She could feel Connie's spine relaxing.

"For Christ's sake. I've had enough of this garbage," Jim's voice startled both women. He swung his arms and strode to the door. "I'm not going to sit here and listen to someone who's had one-fiftieth of the experience delivering babies as I have tell my wife to relax when it's damned obvious it won't help. I know what to do for her. Sandy, I'm ordering 75 milligrams of Demerol and 50 milligrams of Sparine. Stat!"

Sandy stood away from the bed, defeated. She couldn't defy him. By law she had to follow his orders. She was starting for the door when Connie spoke.

"Okay, Jim. I've had enough of you. Get out of here."

"You don't know what you're saying. Do you think I would do anything that is wrong for you?"

"I'm not in a position to argue, Jim. I'm the one having this baby. We've done it your way three times. I think it's my turn."

Sandy saw her hands clutch the sheet as another contraction started.

He folded his arms across his chest. "I'm not going anywhere. Get that shot, Sandy."

Connie's face contorted with pain. "Fuck off!" she whispered through clenched teeth. "Get the fuck out of here, Jim!"

His anger was evident as he retreated.

He'll be back, Sandy thought. And he'll bring the shot and Major Roberts. It was his right. He was in charge of the unit. But — she smiled as the thought came to her — he wasn't in charge of his wife. She turned to Connie. "Okay, girl, let's really get this show on the road."

Connie's answer was a deep transitional groan.

He didn't come back until she pulled the call button, and by then he was too late. With one good push, Baby Girl Andersen was born in the labor bed, with no fanfare, no sweet smell of ether, no needles, and no forceps.

Connie put her arms out to him and he kissed her before he took Sandy's neck in a pincer grasp. "Nice job, nurse," he said with a grin. "I take back all those nasty things I said."

"Apology accepted." She stood to one side as Doc Arnold cut the cord.

"It does worry me a bit," Jim added. "We give you girls an inch and maybe you'll want to take over the whole show."

"Not the whole thing," Sandy said. "Just the parts that are naturally ours."

"Look, Jim," Connie squealed. "She has your eyes."

He hurried over to hold his daughter.

ᥫᩢ

At the end of the day, Sandy nearly burst with excitement when Connie volunteered to organize natural childbirth classes for the entire base.

Dave wasn't home and she had no one to tell about her day. She dressed, drove to the club, sat in a dark corner of the bar, and watched for Kate.

The barmaid placed a drink on her table and stopped to chat. "The place isn't the same without Gramps, Ralph, and Randy, is it?" she asked.

"No, and I hadn't realized how lonely I would be without them."

"Oh, you. You'll meet some nice young fellow soon. Pretty girl like you has her choice. Some of the women who come in here look real good but they're not so nice when you get to know them. You? You never change, except to get happier and prettier."

"Thank you." She sipped her drink in embarrassed silence.

"Well, if it isn't the girl who doesn't give rides."

She felt her heart race in a way it hadn't since the day her first love had come home from the Army. She looked into the tall captain's eyes. No man should have eyes that green.

"Mike Hopkins." He bowed. "Let me buy you a drink." He sat beside her.

"Thanks. I already have one."

He lifted her glass and drank it down. "Now you don't."

She blushed.

"Hey." He took her chin in one hand and turned her face toward the lights over the bar. His touch sent a rush of emotion through her. "Is that a blush I see? My God, it is. I haven't seen a woman blush in years."

She didn't pull away.

"My car came in yesterday. Let me take you to dinner."

His eyes hypnotized her. She looked deeply into them and for one breathless, vulnerable moment—one fatal moment that she would never be able to take back—she could not move.

"Okay," she said.

～

As they climbed the stairs to his club in the city, she admired the way his leather jacket clung to his broad shoulders and the way his lips curved when he smiled. She wanted suddenly to feel the softness of those lips on hers.

As an Asian woman poured from the bottle of champagne he had purchased at the Officers' Club, he conversed in French. When the woman departed, he raised his glass to Sandy's. "To us. May this be the first of many hours together."

She became tongue-tied. She sipped her champagne and tried to think of anything to say. "You speak French well," she blurted.

"Honed my skills in Vietnam."

"You just got back?"

"Yes. Let's drink to that." He raised his glass again.

"To what?"

"To finding you on my first day back."

She changed the subject. "Are you one of the new students?"

"Do I look young enough to be a student?"

"Not many of the 105 students are young."

"They will be soon. I hear the old Thud is being phased out. Not many career guys will want to get stuck in a dying program."

"And you?"

"A step up for me. I'm a new I.P. in the 385th."

The waiter brought a plate of rolls and served their salads as Mike placed a complicated order.

"I'm impressed," she said.

"What? With my French or my improved status?" He chose a roll and tore it into pieces.

"Your French."

"All of the romance languages are easy after Latin."

"Now I know you're pulling my leg. No one speaks Latin anymore."

"Catholic priests still do."

"If you're a priest, I'm a nun."

His eyes fell on her in a caressing way that made her want to lean toward him. "You'd make a good nun. You have a quietness about you."

She concentrated on her salad.

"Seriously," he said. "I was going to be a priest at one time. I flunked out."

"Couldn't pass Latin?" she teased.

He shrugged. "I didn't have what it takes. Disappointed the hell out of my mother. She wanted me to pay off her debts to the Great Master."

"What kind of debt?"

"Sins of my father." He leaned forward and rolled his eyes before he whispered, "His sins were so bad, I can't mention them in a place like this."

"Mention them anyway." They were close enough to kiss.

"He made a fortune selling rotting cars to little old ladies. He took their savings, and when the cars stopped running within months, refused to deal. Not a nice man."

"My father warned me about used car salesmen."

"You would do well to heed his advice."

"He wouldn't like you."

"Why not?"

"He's very Catholic. Failed priests are not on the top of his good list."

"My mother shares his sentiments."

"You haven't told me how you flunked out."

A smile played at the corners of his mouth. "I had a problem with the celibacy part. I prayed. I studied. I worked hard. Nothing worked."

"No wonder your mother was upset."

"She sent me to my grandfather for discipline. The old bird congratulated me and gave me this." He pulled a chain from his jacket and dangled a gold watch between them. He flipped open its filigreed top to reveal a porcelain face and golden hands. He turned it over and showed her its inner workings.

"It's beautiful," she said.

"My lucky piece," he said. "Never leaves my pocket." He polished it with his napkin and slid it back into his pocket.

"You've never been sorry?"

"About the priest part? Heck no. Being cast out was the best thing that ever happened to me."

"It's a big leap."

"What is?"

"Going from priest to fighter pilot."

"Not much else I could do with a major in philosophy and religion."

"You must be awfully smart."

"Foolish, some might say. But at least I'm smart about one thing."

"What?"

"Women. I picked you, didn't I?"

Another rush of emotion filled her. "That doesn't place you above average." She tasted the artichokes on her plate.

"You don't like artichokes?" he asked.

"I love them. I always save the best for last."

"Will I be the last?"

"Maybe," she said. She was drowning in his eyes. "But then again, maybe you'll actually be the first."

When they had eaten and finished the bottle of champagne, he took the back roads to the base at one hundred miles an hour.

"Do you like tempting fate?" he asked.

"Not really."

He pulled in next to her car. "Are you afraid of me?" he asked.

"Yes," she said.

"Why?"

Because you're as smooth as spider's silk, she thought, but aloud she said, "Because you seem like the kind of guy who likes to do everything fast."

"And you don't?"

She smiled a Kate smile. "I like going slow," she said.

He placed both hands on the steering wheel and stared off to the spot where runway lights disappeared into the black sky. He leaned over and pushed open the door for her.

I won't see him again, she thought. I'm definitely not his type.

‿

The next morning she awoke early and stepped into the winter cold with a full basket of laundry. A thick ice fog covered the land. She had forgotten her gloves. She went back inside. As she came back toward the door, a man materialized in the open frame. "Dave!" she cried and stepped to him.

"Dave? Just who is Dave?"

"Mike? What are you doing here?"

"Taking Dave's place, apparently."

She laughed. "Dave lives here. I mean he lives there." She pointed toward his door. "How did you get here?"

"I talked the club clerk into giving me your address. I'm on my way upstate to see the salt mines. Thought you might like to ride along."

"I was on my way out."

He lifted the basket back into her living room. "You can do your laundry anytime. How often will you see a salt mine?"

"You're absolutely right," she said.

As she settled into his car he studied her closely.

"You've had your hair done."

She laughed. "No, this is just how it looks in the morning."

"I'd like to see more of you some morning."

"I bet you would."

They rode in silence for several minutes.

"You ever been to a mine?" he asked.

"No. I stopped in a cave on the way to Texas. It was cold and dark."

"Kind of like Kansas."

"I like Kansas."

"You do? All I see is Bible Belt and a bunch of wagon train dropouts."

"I like the people. They're as flat and smooth as the land. What you see is what you get. Steady and honest."

"And you find that attractive?"

"Yes, I do."

"God, you're more of a goody-two-shoes than I thought."

"Who called me that? Zeke?"

He laughed. "Zeke has a lot of pet names for you. I think he likes you."

"I don't like him."

"That bad, eh? What happened, he get fresh with you?"

The general's warning never to speak of her encounter with Zeke echoed in her mind. "Oh, look," she said as she pointed to a pond. "Wild geese."

"Must have come through during winter migration and decided to stay awhile. I'll have to remember this spot. I wouldn't want to run into a flock of them when I'm flying."

"Wouldn't be much fun."

"No. What do you do for fun?"

"Just about everything," she said.

"Everything?"

"I said 'just about.'"

He smiled, turned up the radio, and began whistling along to "Moon River."

She was foolish to have come, she thought. He was too fast for her.

❧

When they finished their tour through the white-walled caverns and were speeding back toward the city, he checked his watch and asked, "It's nearly three. Want to take in a movie?"

"I should get home."

"For what? To do your laundry?"

"And other things."

"Like what?"

"I have a date."

"We can catch the matinee if we hurry," he persisted. "Then I'll throw in dinner and maybe a dance or two. What do you think?"

I think I've never stood up a date before, she thought. But what the heck. There was a first time for everything. "Okay," she said. "You're on."

"Great. Let Dave wait."

They were late for the movie. He took her hand and pulled her along the sidewalk, held it while he bought a bag of popcorn, and led her into the theater. They found seats in the darkness.

"What is this?" she whispered as a young woman ran across the screen, nearly naked.

"Adult entertainment," he said. "The guys in the squadron say it's great."

A few minutes later she closed her eyes as a girl got herself laid on a pool table. She didn't know where to look. Was he hoping she would be turned on? Should she pretend to be sophisticated and cool? She couldn't pretend. She was mortified. She leaned away from him.

He leaned with her. "You don't like this, do you?"

"No."

"Want to leave?"

"Yes."

He stood up. "Let's go."

Her cheeks burned as they threaded their way out of the row.

In the lobby, he stopped. "Sorry," he said. "I miscalculated."

"Do you always run your life on calculations?"

"No."

"Then why start now?"

"Look, I said I'm sorry."

She strode to his car.

He sat behind the wheel. "Hey. You shouldn't be mad."

"I'm not. I'm embarrassed," she admitted. "Let's go."

"How about a walk?"

She shook her head.

"There's a great park along the river," he persisted. "Just a walk."

She remembered the big trees she and Kate had found and gave in.

He tossed handfuls of popcorn as they strolled past empty picnic tables and closed swimming spots. A raucous crowd of crows and pigeons tailed them.

"Look at this old guy," he said as he patted the trunk of a cottonwood. "Let's climb him." He tossed the remainder of the popcorn to the ground, swung onto the lowest branch, and reached down to her.

She took his hand and climbed.

"I dare you to slide out and tempt fate," he said.

She surveyed the limb. It was long and thick, with splayed branches spread out low over the water.

It looked easy. She straddled the limb and moved to its end. "Come on," she called.

He scooted out and settled behind her with his long legs dangling toward the water.

The sun disappeared and the wind began to rise. A chill penetrated her coat. She shivered.

He placed his arms around her and pulled her back against his chest as they leaned and swayed on the rocking bough. He nuzzled the back of her neck and kissed her hair. The rising wind shook the branch.

She felt a sickening lurch as the smallest tendrils dragged over the muddy water.

He tucked one hand under her breast and trailed soft kisses across her cheek.

She wanted more. She tilted her head back until she found his lips. They were soft on hers and tantalizingly slow to open. That slowness caused her to abandon her reserve and touch her tongue to his. She liked the popcorn taste of him.

He wrapped his arms more tightly and kissed her more deeply until she was weak with wanting him. The wind shook the tree and caused them to tilt.

"Come on," he said. "We're going to end up in the drink if we stay here."

She followed him blindly, overcome more from his kisses than the cold. Her legs wouldn't hold her when they touched the ground.

He pulled her to him, pressed her close, spread warmth to her loins. She strained against him.

He buried his face in her hair. "Let's get out of here." He draped one long arm across her shoulder as they walked back toward the car.

She clung to him, buried her face in the warm lapel of his coat, and breathed in his cologne.

"Shall we go to my place?" he asked.

She shook her head against his chest.

"Is that a flat-out no?"

"I don't know."

"Do you want to sleep with me?"

She nodded without looking up.

He stopped walking and pulled her face from his coat with one finger under her chin.

She looked into his eyes.

"You want to, but it's too soon?"

"Yes."

He brushed the blowing hair from her face and kissed her nose. "Okay," he said. "I can wait."

They walked entwined to his car. At her door he kissed her with tantalizing slowness. "How long will I have to wait?" he asked.

"Not very long," she answered.

⁓

She slept poorly. Erotic dreams stirred her as a howling wind sang and spatters of ice pelted her windows. Each time she awoke she chided herself for being a fool for his arrogant manliness. She wondered if she could sleep with him and not wake in the morning with pangs of guilt—or worse, wake with the knowledge that he didn't like her, that he thought her too much of a child and too old-fashioned. He was interesting, complex, and experienced. He knew exactly how to arouse her. He would be a good lover. But what if he kissed and told? What if she became another Kate on the base?

Throughout the night, one stubborn fact kept growing. She wanted him. And by morning light, she had decided. She stepped out of bed more sure than she had ever been. Mike Hopkins would be her first. She smiled into the mirror as she dressed.

The sound of Dave's typewriter cut through her thoughts. She scampered across the porch, avoiding small piles of drifting snow, and tapped on his door.

He opened it at once. His shirt was as travel-worn as his face. "Did I wake you?" he asked.

"No. I'm happy you're back."

"I'm on my way to early Mass and to get some breakfast. Want to come?"

"Sure," she said. "It's snowing."

He stepped onto the porch and peered into the driveway. "Hell, there must be six inches out there."

"It's a blizzard. It's wonderful."

"Shall we walk?"

"Fine with me."

They walked arm in arm into the wind. When her scarf blew off, he rewound it around her head and neck. "You're practically bursting with excitement," he said. "Tell me what's happened."

She launched into a review of Connie's birth and the progress they had made. "We're actually going to have a full program," she concluded.

"I knew you would do it. You sure put in a lot of hours."

"But no more," she said. "I'm able to take all my days off now."

"There's more, isn't there?"

She hesitated. "Nothing else. Same old stuff."

"Hey, this is Dave, remember? You're higher than a kite. I've never seen you like this."

He pushed open the doors to St. Nick's. The lights were dim and the chapel cold.

∽

When communion was offered, they made their way to the front with a row of worshippers. She hadn't been to confession, but she knelt anyway. It was then she was struck by the enormity of her future sins. She hoped the priest couldn't see her lips quiver as she accepted the sacraments with a heart black with plans for birth control and sex.

When Dave guided her back out into the wind, her heart felt as light as the blowing snow. She would have freedom.

"Where have you been all week?" she asked, a half hour later, as they ate their fast-food breakfast.

"Meeting in Berkeley."

"The way you travel is crazy."

He cradled his coffee cup in both hands and allowed the steam to warm his face.

"Why'd you go there?" she asked.

"I met Derringer and Spock. I can hardly believe the scope of this project."

"What project?"

"Organizing the protesters. Getting all the different factions to come together for common goals. We need to stop the violence at marches."

"I thought violence got more attention."

He shook his head. "We've had bottles, eggs, and rocks thrown into the crowds. The kids get hot and start throwing stuff back. We've got to stop it before it gets too far out of hand."

"How?"

"That's what we're working on. Conservatives believe we can naturally keep things cool, but there are factions deliberately lathering up the kids."

"Why?'

"They want a revolution."

"In America? That's crazy."

He shrugged. "Human nature. Lots of good intentions end in bloodshed."

"Could it happen?"

"Might. The draft is taking boys from poorer areas and sending them over while kids with connections get deferments and into the National Guard. The dichotomy is becoming obvious. Soon there won't be a family in the lower classes that hasn't had someone come home from the war wounded, hooked on drugs, or in a box. Once they realize they're being sacrificed, there could be a backlash."

"Dave, do you really believe they're sacrificed?"

"You should come to a march. If you could see the vets who show up in wheelchairs or blind, you might believe it too. Most of them say, 'I went to fight for something I believed in, but it was a lie. Now here I am. Look at me. This is how they sent me home.'"

∽

Back at the duplex, he went to his typewriter and Sandy, desperate to tell someone about Mike, called her friend in Maine. "I'm going to sleep with him, Rita," she said.

There was a long pause and then, "Isn't this awfully soon?"

"No, it's way late. I'm twenty-two years old. You've had a bed partner for four years!"

"Yes, but we dated all through high school and we knew each other pretty darn good."

"It's a new time. Out here everybody is having sex."

"What if you get pregnant?"

"I made an appointment to get birth control pills."

Rita couldn't keep the shock from her voice. "Sandy, that's a major sin. Using birth control says you're not having sex for the pure purpose of having children, and you're planning it, like you would plan a dinner party."

"Exactly."

"Sandy!"

"I'm tired of being a good girl. I'm tired of sleeping alone in a big bed. I want this guy."

"What do you really know about him?"

"He's tall and handsome and very sexy."

"He sounds like a rogue to me."

"I'm not planning to marry him."

"Why can't you find a nice Catholic guy? What about your neighbor, Dave? Didn't you say he's handsome?"

"Sure, but he treats me like his sister and best friend. There's no chemistry. Rita, I can't count the number of guys I've dated since I've been here. Not one of them made me feel the way this guy does. Besides, he is Catholic."

"Don't you want to wear white on your wedding day?"

"I wanted that once and look where it got me. It's time for me to get some experience. And Mike can provide it."

"Didn't you tell me he's a friend of that guy Zeke? Don't you think birds of a feather flock together?"

"I shouldn't have told you about Zeke. I'm not supposed to talk about him."

"Hey, kid, this is Rita, remember. Your general can't tell me what I can and can't talk about. He shouldn't be telling you either."

"It's part of the job. Protect the organization or leave it. I love this job. Besides, with Zeke I could have lost my virginity in the worst way. I might as well give it away and enjoy it."

"Sandy!"

She giggled then, and made Rita giggle too.

"You're crazy, Sandy. You know that, don't you?"

"I hope it's crazy in a good way."

"It is, old friend. It's in the very best way. I just hope you know what you're doing."

෴

Sandy visited a civilian doctor and received the pills on Monday. That evening Mike picked her up for dinner.

"Do I get to meet Dave now?" he asked as he took her in his arms.

She smiled at his curiosity. "He's back," she said, "and I'd introduce you, but he's working on his book."

"Now that's intimidating." He nuzzled her neck until she relaxed, then began to move his hands down her back.

She liked being teased out of her puritanical shell. When he pulled her closer and rested his hands behind her waist, she raised her lips to his and lost herself in his warmth.

His hands moved slowly over her until they cradled her face. His elbows rested against her breasts. His tongue sent shivers through her. He moved his lips to her ear, caressed the soft part of her neck with his chin.

She felt his erection against her belly and moved shamelessly against him.

"Jesus, Sandy," he whispered. His voice was husky and low. "Say yes. Say it now."

She pulled slowly away. "Not yet," she said.

He reached for her again, slid his opened fingers around her waist.

She relaxed against him, put more energy into her voice. "It won't be long. I promise."

He laughed, lifted her feet off the ground, and swung her in a small circle. "Oh, girl. If you knew what you do to me."

They drove to the base and had dinner at the club. Kate came in, sat down, and flirted openly. When she flitted away, he turned to Sandy and said, "Too bad you're not a little more like your friend."

She was stung by his words. "Why?"

"I didn't mean it literally." He leaned across the table and took her hand. "I mean she does her thing and doesn't give a damn what anyone else thinks. She's a free spirit."

"I don't think she's as carefree as she seems. Sometimes she's just the opposite."

"She doesn't look any the worse for the wear," he said.

But she is worn, Sandy thought.

He placed his napkin beside his plate. "Shall we go into the bar and say hello?"

Because she didn't trust herself to be alone with him again, she agreed.

Zeke, Tim, and a group of new students were gathered at one end of the bar.

"Well, my my and lookie lookie. My friend Mike has caught the cookie!" Zeke sang out. "How'd you do it, man?" He clapped Mike on the back and threw one arm across Sandy's shoulders.

She pulled away.

Mike moved into the crowd of men.

Zeke persisted. "I've heard this guy is really good." He turned to the bartender. "Hey, give these lovebirds a drink."

When Zeke moved toward her again, Tim stepped between them and guided her to a barstool.

"Zeke likes to give you a hard time," he murmured, "but I don't think you have to worry about him."

"I hate him!" she whispered.

"Ignore him."

When she turned back, Mike and Zeke were having a dogfight with their hands at the other end of the bar. The new students surrounded them.

Fighter pilots, she thought, know their aircraft better than their women. She excused herself and went into the ladies' room.

Kate scooted through the door after her. "Where in the world did you find that one, Sandy?" she asked. "He's the most gorgeous piece of maleness I've ever seen."

"He's off-limits, Kate."

Kate's eyebrows shot up. "Aha!" she gushed. "Sandy's finally been bit. Is he good?"

"Don't go there."

"Ah, Sand. I do get carried away." She rolled her eyes and laughed. "Is he?"

"Cool it," Sandy said.

"Okay. Okay. Don't take it personally. I just want everyone else to sink to my level." She flashed a smile in the mirror as she drew a perfect line of red over her lips.

Sandy smoothed blusher on her cheeks.

Kate leaned against the mirror. "So how's old Dave these days?"

"Fine. He's been working his buns off."

"Ha, and you'll have to admit, those are some fine buns."

Sandy didn't comment.

"So, if you've got the hots for this Mike fellow, does it mean Dave is free game?" She studied Sandy's face as she spoke each word.

She could be so irritating at times, Sandy thought. "Dave's always been free game."

"If you want him, say so now."

"I have no dibs on him."

"Good. Best of luck with Mike."

As she followed Kate out she heard Zeke laugh and felt his eyes on her. Mike had either completely dismissed the fact they were on a date or he expected her to hang around until he was ready for her. She walked to the lobby booth and asked the clerk to call a cab.

"Going somewhere?" Tim stopped on his way toward the exit.

"Home," she said.

"Can I give you a lift?"

"You wouldn't mind?"

"Mike's loss, my gain."

As he drove across the base, she turned to him. "What makes you guys think you're so god-almighty great?"

"Because we *are* great," he said with a grin. "Why are you mad at me? I'm not the one who dropped you."

She giggled because he was right. "The truth is, I'm not sure who dropped who."

"Don't tell Mike it was me who delivered you to your doorstep."

"You don't have to worry. I'm never going to speak to him again."

"This is serious." He passed through the back gate. "Which way?"

"Take a left."

When he pulled into the driveway, she jumped from the car. "Thanks," she called with a wave. "I owe you one."

Dave met her on the lighted porch. "Hey, what is this? You leave with one guy and come home with another?"

"The first one was a jerk and the second one is married. Frankly, I think you're all a bunch of idiots."

He raised both hands in surrender. "Don't take it out on me, girl. I'm completely innocent."

"Sorry," she said. "Bad night."

"Want to make it worse and come out to the university with me? I left my exams to be copied and I need to proof them before tomorrow."

"Sure." This way, if Mike called she wouldn't be tempted to forgive him.

Dave tucked her into his car. "Must be the story of my life. I'm always third on a match."

He drove in silence for a few minutes before he stopped for a light and looked at her. "The general came by earlier."

"The general? What in the world did he want?"

"He had bad news."

She sat up straighter.

"Gramps bought it yesterday. Augered in. No chute sighted."

Sandy slumped. "Not Gramps."

"They were near Hanoi and couldn't go back for him. They're sure he didn't survive."

"Oh, God, his poor family." Tears stung her eyes.

"I wanted to be the one to tell you. I didn't think a note from the brass was right."

She reached out and touched his sleeve. "Thank you."

The war had changed her boyfriend back home and she hadn't understood, but now, the stark reality of someone like Gramps giving up his life brought it into clear focus. Gramps's sons and thousands of others could follow. It wasn't worth the cost.

CHAPTER EIGHT

January 28, 1968.

On Tuesday, a sweet bouquet of winter holly created a flurry of speculation among her staff. She tucked the card into her pocket and didn't explain. The next morning gardenias arrived, and the next, a dozen roses.

"Come on, Sandy, tell us who your suitor is," Jim begged.

"I haven't read the cards."

"For Pete's sake, why not?"

"I like the mystery." She left the flowers on the unit and stayed away from the club. She would not trade Mike's bad behavior for a few flowers.

❧

On Friday evening she attended Dave's protest meeting and listened to a debate on what might happen when Secretary McNamara retired. Most believed it would be the beginning of the end of the war and that, without the hawk in control, moderate voices would be heard.

As the meeting wound down, a student ran into the library and announced, "The U.S. Embassy in Saigon is under attack!"

They moved to a TV in a dorm lounge and watched news footage as a camera followed a Vietnamese officer down a street littered with wreckage. Suddenly the officer raised a pistol to a man's head and pulled the trigger. Everyone screamed.

It has nothing to do with me, she thought. It's far away in a foreign place. But even as she thought it, she knew it wasn't true. It had everything to do with her. She was part of a killing machine.

The screen changed. General Westmoreland assured Americans their territory had not been violated and the military remained in charge.

Dave tried to calm the students. "Networks shouldn't have shown that," he said. But in the car he told her, "It's time everyone sees what war is really like."

They drove home in silence.

∞

That weekend, fighting in Hue, Saigon, and towns in between filled the TV news. She watched marines win back hamlets, burn villages, and call in bombs and napalm. As she cringed at the human voices screaming their painful responses to the carnage, she prayed for Penny, the 385th pilots, and Kate's brother.

∞

"What the hell's going on?" one of the pediatricians asked on Monday morning. "This place looks like a funeral home."

"Lieutenant O'Connell has a new admirer," Jim answered. "He beat on the side door all weekend."

Sandy turned to him. "He came here?"

"He seems damned determined."

"Any guy who spends this much on flowers must either have a lot of money or a big, big crush," the pediatrician said.

She shrugged. "Or else he's in the doghouse."

"His doghouse is getting pretty expensive," Jim said.

"Isn't that military policy? An officer messes up, you hit him in his wallet?" She shuffled her stack of unopened cards. "Anyway, he's almost paid up."

Jim patted her hand. "Be careful, Sandy. Some guys fall pretty hard."

"I doubt this one will need a safety net."

That afternoon she didn't look up when a pot of fragrant lilies was set on the ledge above her desk. But when a deep voice said, "I am sorry," her heart leaped. Her legs trembled as she stood.

"Say again," she whispered.

He leaned across the ledge. "I really am sorry."

She held his eyes. "Apology accepted, but you shouldn't be in here. This is a restricted area."

"I won't leave unless you agree to have coffee with me."

"In the cafeteria," she said. "Go out and come back through the front door. I'll meet you in the hall."

"When?"

"Ten minutes. I have to change from my scrubs."

"Good. That outfit is crummy."

She laughed. "Go."

∾

Outside the cafeteria he tried to take her hand. She pulled away. "Not professional," she warned.

He turned and peered into the crowded room. "Isn't there somewhere we could be alone?" He backed her down the hall without touching her. "What's this?" He pushed against a closed door.

"The morgue," she said.

He pulled her inside.

"Mike! We can't be in here."

"God!" he said. "You're full of rules."

Before she could speak his lips were on hers. He nudged her deeper into the darkness. It was not the coldness of the room that sent a shiver through her.

"Not a place for making love," he said.

She melted against him.

"But what the heck." The nylon of his flight suit made a rustling noise against her starched whites. "Why'd you run out on me?"

"I wasn't getting enough attention."

"Is this better?"

"Yes."

"And why didn't you answer my calls?"

"I wasn't home."

"Where were you? With that damn Dave?"

"Yes."

"Do you love him?"

"I told you, he's my friend."

"Why don't you like my friends?"

"I do."

"Even Zeke?"

She stiffened and pulled away.

"He's a problem?"

"Yes."

"He's one of the best pilots we've got."

"Is that all it takes to be a winner with you guys?"

"Should we care about anything else?"

"The world isn't full of fighter planes. It's full of living, breathing people who deserve to be treated with respect."

"I respect you."

Her senses were full of him. His warm closeness clouded her thoughts. His tantalizing touch silenced her. Electric tension pulled them closer. She raised her face and kissed him without restraint. His hands moved more boldly.

"So, you'll go to dinner with me tonight?" he said as she pulled away.

"Can't," she said.

"Why not?"

"I promised Dave I'd go to a faculty party with him."

"He's still more important than me."

"At the moment."

"Tomorrow?"

"What time?"

"Early. I'll pick you up for breakfast. You can help me move into my new place."

"Tomorrow," she promised. "Now, I've got to get back to my ward before I'm missed."

"I've missed you all week. Doesn't that count for anything?"

"No," she said as she pulled away and pushed open the door. "You deserved to be alone."

She hurried away.

᎑

The next morning, fresh from the shower, in her heavy terry robe, her hair wrapped in a towel and fuzzy slippers warming her feet, she opened the door for Dave and his newspaper. He too was wearing his robe. She heard a voice and looked behind him. Mike strode up the walk.

"Morning," he called.

"Mike! You're early."

"And I caught you two lovebirds in the act, didn't I?"

He moved past Dave, kissed Sandy lightly on the cheek, and turned back. "Well, come in. You must be Dave."

They all laughed.

"Nice pajamas," he said.

"Saturday morning ritual. Will you join us for coffee?"

"Don't mind if I do." He unbuttoned his coat and tossed it on the couch.

The two men shook hands and followed her into the kitchen. She set cups and the full pot of coffee on the table, excused herself, and hurried into her bedroom, where she pulled on jeans and a sweater, fluffed up her short hair, and dabbed on some lipstick.

As she entered the kitchen, Mike reached out and pulled her into his lap. "Are you ready? The moving van is at my place."

Dave walked to the door. Mike helped Sandy with her coat and the three stepped out into the winter wind.

Dave's good-bye wave was tentative.

Mike drove two blocks up the street and pulled behind a block of new townhouses.

"Is this it?" Sandy could not keep a note of surprise from her voice.

"Yep. I bought it between trips to the flower shop. I can't see renting, since I'll be here a couple of years."

They stepped through the door. The stairs to the main living area were carpeted in gold shag. Stacked boxes lined one side of the honey-toned living room. Floor-to-ceiling windows looked over a small park.

"Come see my favorite room." He placed his hand on the small of her back and steered her into his bedroom. The walls were a series of mirrors broken by louvered doors. The floor was polished hardwood softened with white flokati rugs.

"Look at this." He threw open a closet door. The space was as large as her bedroom. The shelves were already well organized, with sweaters stacked by color. Racks held pants and jackets. Pressed dress shirts of every possible color filled an entire wall.

"It's like a men's department store," she said.

"Feel this." He pulled a black jacket from the rack and held it out to her.

She ran a hand over it. It was the softest material she had ever touched.

"Cashmere," he said. "Someday I'll wear it dancing so you can feel how it moves. I guarantee it's quite seductive."

She needed to change the subject. "How did you carry this around with you through all those assignments?"

"I didn't. I buy new wherever I go."

"On a captain's pay?"

"My grandfather was a generous man. He left me an annuity that allows me to enjoy life." He opened another door and stepped onto a small balcony. "For midnight meetings and other things," he whispered in her ear. "I've ordered one of those Napoleonic lounging chairs and an extended stereo system. Would you like to spend a night with me out here?"

"Yes," she said. "I would."

"I knew it."

"Captain Hopkins," a man called. "I have your furniture order here."

As Mike showed him where to place large pieces of teak and black leather furniture, Sandy wandered through the kitchen, running her hands over the new counters and appliances.

"Like it?" he asked as he returned to her side.

"I was wondering if you know how to cook."

"Cook? Oh, lady, I will prepare meals you've never dreamed of." He pushed the door closed behind him, gathered her in his arms, and began to rock her gently.

She gazed into his face. Everybody should be afraid at first, she thought. Everybody should be careful with such overwhelming feelings. The door crashed into them. Sandy pulled away.

"Captain Hopkins," the mover said. "We have a problem with the bar. It won't fit against that wall."

"Then take it back," he said. "I'll pick out a smaller one tomorrow."

෨

When the movers were done, Mike and Sandy had a late lunch accompanied by a bottle of wine before settling into a corner of the couch with his photo album held between them.

"It's my flying days," he said. "From graduation on. I'll have to take some pictures of you for the Meridian part."

"I hope it's not full of women," she teased.

"How could there be no girls when it starts in Del Rio, sin capitol of the world?"

"That's where you trained?"

"As a pilot or 'other?'"

"Other," she said.

"Great postgraduate course."

"After the theology part?"

"Well, you have to admit, I had some catching up to do."

The wine allowed her to laugh.

"Here's my first tour in 'Nam."

She studied the picture. He was much younger, with a short haircut and spare frame.

"Is that your C-130?"

Amusement filled his eyes. "Don't I look like a weenie?"

"Yes," she agreed.

"See the patches on her bottom?"

"Those shinier squares?"

"Hits from ground fire. She was a damned good girl."

Sandy turned the page.

"Saigon," he said. "Streets full of noisy mopeds and traffic that would kill you. Sidewalks full of whores."

He felt her stiffen and quickly kissed her. "Sorry, but it's true. You can get anything you want in Saigon. Those little gink bastards will sell you their mother if you ask."

She didn't comment. It was that seedy side of Saigon that had destroyed Sam.

"Look, that's the monastery. Beautiful Catholic piece of architecture."

Sandy studied the picture. "I thought most Asian countries were Buddhist or Hindu. When did we Catholics get there?"

"Centuries ago. It was the French priests who organized the first trade out of Vietnam. I'm surprised they didn't teach that in parochial school."

"Until a few years ago, I'd never heard of Vietnam."

"President Diem was Catholic. His oldest brother was an archbishop in the church."

"Really?"

"I learned that in the seminary." His laugh was sardonic. "I wanted to be assigned there. The most ironic thing is, when I finally did get over there, it was to bomb the people rather than to serve them."

She studied his face. Religion and philosophy turned into mayhem and bombs. What kind of concessions does a man make to accomplish such a transition? Before she could ask, he turned the page and changed the subject.

"Look! Do you know what this is?"

The picture was confusing. Cars lined two sides of a city street. A small group of people watched something burning in the center of the narrow way. "What is it?"

"That's a Buddhist monk committing suicide. I was in Saigon with a friend and we came across him. I snapped pictures while the guy burned up. No one tried to intervene. Asians have more respect for the spirit and less for the flesh. It was quite a year. The whole of the south was in chaos."

"Do you think it will settle down soon?"

"Not for years."

"And we got involved because of one guy. Diem?"

"We should have butted out."

"And not save them from communism?"

He laughed. "It has nothing to do with communism."

She was bored with history. She wanted to feel his lips on hers and his hands touching her body, but he continued on.

"Diem and his brother used some pretty ruthless tactics to keep their government in power. When Lodge went over he expected them to do everything his way. They didn't and we all became murderers."

"I'm not a murderer."

"Maybe not directly, but still guilty as part of a group." He closed the book. "I'll get us some more wine," he said.

The set of his shoulders and his heavy stride told her something had touched a nerve. She would have to stay away from talk of the war. She wondered what made men fear yet become obsessed by war.

He placed a full glass into her hand. "You can get anything you want on the black market over there—stereo sets, cameras, women, drugs. The pot isn't such great quality though." He smiled. "I get better stuff here in Kansas."

She didn't respond. She had never smoked a joint and was stunned that he would.

"Uh-oh. You don't approve."

She shook her head.

"You ever try it?"

She shook her head again.

"Why not?"

"Because I can get high enough on real life. I don't need a smoke to make me happy."

"You like booze. What's the difference?"

"I don't know. Maybe it's the 'Mary-will-wanna' my parents drummed into my head."

When he laughed again she thought he was laughing at her and she felt anger rise.

"I think we need some music," he said and began to sort through his records.

She reopened the album to a series of pictures of him with an Asian girl.

"Aha. You've found my secret." He sat beside her again.

"She's very pretty," she said.

"Le Chi. A bar girl from Saigon. Her entire family was killed when the French were ousted. She fled from Hanoi to Saigon and got a job working at a club."

"I know what a bar girl does."

"You do?"

"My old boyfriend explained that to me."

"What did he say?"

"That they entertain customers, tell funny stories, play games, and provide sex for a price."

"Did your boyfriend indulge?"

"In everything. It ruined him."

"Did he teach you any of the games?"

"No. I'm a good Catholic girl. I was waiting for marriage."

"Are you still waiting?"

"I was, but I've decided not to wait any longer."

"You remind me of Le Chi."

"How so?"

"A bit of a kitten. Naive. Young. Trying to appear sophisticated in a world you don't understand."

"Is that how you see me?"

"Yes, it is." His reached out and stroked her face. "But I also know that isn't all there is to you. Just as I knew there was more to Le Chi."

"What happened to her?"

"Last I heard, some do-gooder had brought her back to the States and had married her. She was only seventeen."

"You took advantage of her."

"Like I'm going to take advantage of you." He folded the book closed and placed it on the floor. He slid an arm around her waist and pulled her to him.

She softened with his kiss, allowed him to sweep her away. They stretched out on the long couch, touching, straining to be closer.

"Will you sleep with me?" he asked.

"No," she said. "Two more weeks."

"Why?"

"Because that's when my birth control pills take effect."

He laughed. "Now that makes us a nice church couple—the failed priest and the nice girl using contraception. What would your mother say?"

"This is not my mother's world," she said as she watched his agile fingers unbutton her blouse.

෮

The next morning, over coffee, Dave worried about the war's escalation and the continuing protest marches. "We've got to cast out the hippie image and show America our real face."

"What face is that?" she asked.

"Yours. Mine. Middle-class Americans who go to work every day. We need to get the blue-collar workers on our side and get the churches involved. Look."

She read the headlines he held up: Protest Marchers Blockade New York, Boston, and Madison.

"Together we can bring this administration to its knees," he said.

"How?"

"We're dividing the ranks into hawks and doves, protesters and hardhats, peaceniks and warmongers, in the press, on the campuses, in the churches, and on the streets. We're showing them who we are."

"Who are we, Dave?" she asked.

"People. We're the people who made this country great. And all we want is to live in peace."

∽

Two weeks later Mike took her hand and helped her into a red Cessna parked at the city airport.

"Tired?" he asked.

"Exhausted. The midnight shift never does agree with me."

"But it got you extra time off."

"True." She smiled.

He looked toward the tower. "I have to file my flight plan," he said. "You won't run away, will you?"

"Only with you," she answered.

When he disappeared into the airport tower, she took Penny's letter from her pocket and began to read.

> *11 Feb 68*
>
> *Dear Sandy,*
>
> *I'm having my first break in three weeks, and I find myself unable to relax, unable to eat, unable to rest. I have been flying nonstop since the offensive began. We sleep where we can, eat when food is put in front of us, and often can't take a potty break for hours.*
>
> *We could see the offensive coming. Villagers were sandbagging hooches and buildings. When the cloud cover forced us to fly low and slow we could see steady streams of Vietnamese leaving the cities.*

Everybody said it was normal; they visit their ancestral homes to honor their dead during the Tet holiday. I thought they were taking an awful lot of their belongings with them for such a short holiday.

I was in Saigon, at Tan Son Nhut Air Base, when the fighting broke out. Luckily my crew was loading the plane as the first mortars came in. We were airborne fast, but found nowhere to go. Almost every airstrip was under attack. In the end, we were forced to return to Saigon. They assured us the base had been secured, but there were still plenty of incoming rounds and gunfire. The city was in chaos. Entire neighborhoods were in ruin. People crowded into the streets and hospitals near the American facilities looking for protection. We refueled and went to work. I have been flying in country since the first day, moving wounded to connecting flights to Japan, the Philippines, Guam, and Thailand.

Saigon is a mess. The streets are littered with debris and bodies. We never know when a firefight will break out. Ambulance crews get caught in the crossfire and cut off from hospitals. The hospitals are putting two in a bed. There is no blood available, little food and few medicines. The only shops open are the coffin makers. Their business is booming.

Our planes are packed with seriously injured and we're bombarded with extras trying to hitch rides whenever we land. Just keeping in a straight line is a test of nerves for the pilots. The air corridors are jammed with fighters, cargo planes, helicopters, and us medical guys. You can imagine the jam-ups when clouds hover to ground level and rain is as thick as jelly and everyone needs to be somewhere else.

I was so tired one night I slept on the floor of hooch and didn't know sappers attacked us. When I woke up several buildings had been destroyed and one of the hangars didn't exist anymore.

From what I hear, there are six thousand Vietcong fighting in Hue and things are really bad at Khe Sanh. I'm supposed to fly *that way tomorrow.*

I've heard of atrocities committed by both sides but it's hearsay so I won't pass that on.

I'm going to have a cold shower and see if I can find something to eat. I hear they have clean water and a mess hall here. Therein lies the difference between this war and those that have come before. Thanks to our airpower, we are only hours away from a more civilized life.

As always,

Penny

She put the letter aside as a rush of cold air followed Mike into the plane. "Whew," he smiled. "I hope I can get this baby off the ground. The wind will be against us all the way to Stapleton. We might be in for a rough ride. Still up for it?"

"Definitely," she said.

He leaned across and pulled her to him. "You won't be sorry."

Sandy tugged her seatbelt tighter.

The man in the tower gave them thumbs-up. The small engine roared against the wind.

Her stomach fluttered. She closed her eyes and tried to concentrate on what was ahead—Colorado, skiing, and sleeping with this sexy man. When she forced her eyes open, they were swooping above the brown prairies.

"We'll follow the railroad west and north and then cut across the state along Route 70. Be there in no time." He didn't take his eyes off the controls as the plane dipped and shook in the gusty winds. "There's a blanket there in the back, if you want to wrap up and get some sleep."

"Sleep? You expect me to sleep?" She laughed and leaned toward him. "I'm so excited I can hardly sit still."

His eyes told her things no man should say while flying in a small plane in a windstorm.

◦◦

At Stapleton a new Land Rover waited for them. When he saw the question in her eyes he said, "It's a shared family thing. It goes with the condo." He tipped the parking attendant as they drove out.

When she glanced into the rearview mirror she saw eyes that glittered with a piercing light. I'm exhausted, she thought, and I look it. She rested her head on his shoulder and closed her eyes. It was the last she remembered until his deep voice awakened her.

"We're almost there," he murmured. "I don't want you to miss this view." He had pulled off the road.

She sat up and rubbed her eyes. The snow lay in drifts as high as the windows. Ahead of them, the road dipped into a valley where wood smoke drifted lazily from hidden chimneys. There was no graceful way to turn back now. Somewhere down there she was going to lose her virginity. "It's like a Christmas card," she said.

"It's my Christmas card to you. Better late than never."

She met his eyes. "Thank you, sir."

He touched her face. "Life doesn't get any better than this."

"You're sure?"

"I'm sure."

"Me too." She kissed him then in a way she had never kissed a man before, with clear promise and unfettered desire.

He pulled back onto the road. It fell away steeply to the floor of the valley. "There it is," he said, pointing to a large chalet. "The Hopkins haven."

When they arrived, he unlocked the door and stepped aside so she could go first. Windows soared three stories to the peaked roof, flooding the room with light and providing an unbroken view of mountains and village. A log fire crackled in a stone fireplace. She was way out of her element. This was a playground for the rich.

He dumped their suitcases in the marble entry and came to her. "Like it?" he asked.

"It's not what I expected," she answered.

"What did you expect?"

"A log cabin in the woods, with an outhouse out back and plumbing problems in the kitchen."

"No such luck," he said. "I go first class all the way." He took her hand and pulled her into the room. The carpeting was as soft and thick as snow.

She struggled to take it all in.

"You look frazzled," he said. "My flying and driving too much for you?"

"Never."

"Tell you what. It's perfect powder on the slopes. I'm dying to get up there. You go upstairs and have a good sleep. I'll come back in time for dinner. That way we'll both be at our best later."

She relaxed against him.

"Sound good?"

She nodded, rubbing her cheek against the soft wool of his coat.

"I'll find my skis and get out of here." He broke away and began to sort through racks of skis in the marble foyer. She climbed the stairs.

The second floor had two bedrooms. Colorful toys and children's beds filled the first. The other appeared to be a dormitory, with an open closet and six beds stacked up in twos along the outer walls. She continued up to the third floor, where she found the master bedroom. Below, a door slammed. She watched through the window wall as Mike, skis over one shoulder and racked boots swinging from the other hand, strode off toward the lodge. She stripped to her underwear, climbed under the down comforter, and fell into a deep asleep.

When she woke it was dark. She stared through the windows until her eyes focused on the lights of a distant ski run. Dark figures moved sinuously down the slope. She rose from the bed and, without turning on a light, peered over the rail to the living room below. The fire had burned low. The room was empty. Her stomach told her it was past dinner hour.

She shivered in the cold air cascading off the windows as she crept down the stairs. Folding her arms against the chill, she hurried to the fireplace and placed two logs on the glowing coals.

I'll have some milk, she decided, but when the light from the open refrigerator door exposed her near nudity, she grabbed her suitcase and bolted up the stairs like a small creature caught in a flashlight beam.

Breathless, she pulled the curtains over the loft entrance and turned on the lights. She would shower, dress, and demand dinner before all else.

She was blotting her lipstick when she heard the door open below. She stepped through the curtains and sprang down the steps into Mike's cold arms.

His cheeks cooled her flushed and feverish lips. He swooped her into his arms. "The snow is fantastic," he said. "I couldn't get enough of it. You must be starving."

"Are you?"

"Famished. We'll have a huge dinner at my favorite place. Can you wait while I shower and change?"

"Do I have to wait?"

"No," he said, pulling her closer. "You can join me if you want."

She wasn't sure if it was his cold lips brushing across her earlobe or his words that excited her so. She laughed and pulled away. "No. You go. But, hurry, please. I'm starving."

"You'll be sorry."

She smiled. "No, I won't. Good things come to those who wait."

He grinned then. "They do, don't they? I'll just be a few minutes." He bounded up the stairs.

∽

Ski racks lined the wall of a restaurant nearly buried under snow. A band played in a room to one side.

"Nice to see you again, Mike," the waiter said as he led them to a table. "Up with the family?"

"Nah. Just me and my friend this time," Mike answered.

"How'd you manage that?"

"Planning, man. Very good planning."

"Usual to drink?"

He nodded. As the man retreated, Mike moved closer. "Glad you came?"

She couldn't take her eyes from him. "Yes. I never dreamed life could be this easy."

"You do know how to ski, don't you?"

"Would it matter if I didn't?"

"Depends on how good you are at other things."

She surprised herself. "I can do anything I put my mind to."

"Anything?"

"Definitely."

He leaned over and kissed her until the waiter brought their drinks.

When they had eaten, they moved into the side room and onto the dance floor. As he pulled her into his arms she recognized the luxurious softness of cashmere. "You've worn your seduction jacket," she laughed.

"Just for you and with the very worst of intentions." He kept his eyes and hands on her until she was flushed with anticipation and desire.

She could sense others watching them but didn't care.

"Let's go," he whispered into her hair. He took her hand and ran with her up the hill.

Once inside he pulled her to him, melded his body against hers, and covered her face and throat with kisses. She was beyond doubting, beyond waiting, beyond anticipation. He slammed the door shut with one foot. "Come on," he said. "Hurry."

They shed their coats and moved to the stairs.

She stumbled on the first flight.

He caught her by the waist and pulled her sweater over her head.

She looped her arms over his neck and trailed kisses over his eyes and forehead as he removed her bra. She ran her hands through his hair as he used his tongue and lips to warm each breast. She pulled the cashmere jacket away and pulled his sweater over his head, then moved her bare skin against his smooth chest.

"If we don't move up these stairs, I'm going to take you right here," he groaned.

She tried to slide out of his arms but he caught the waist of her slacks, kissed the soft flesh of her belly, and pulled her zipper free. His cold hand slid over the warmth of her lower stomach, smoothed the tangle of hair there.

She pushed onto the landing. He caught her shoes, pulled them off, and tossed them down the stairs behind them. He did the same with her slacks.

She scampered up the remaining stairs, pushed into the curtained room and, breathless with desire, waited for him.

He was naked when he pulled the curtains wide and flooded the bed with moonlight.

She could see his erection silhouetted against the windows.

He came to her and covered her mouth with his. His cool hands moved with tantalizing slowness over her hot skin until she was frantic for him. He lowered her to the bed and removed her panties. His body covered hers as she begged, "Please. Please."

"When?" he breathed into her ear. "When?"

"Now," she answered, opening to him. "Now. Now. Now."

He rose up and pressed against her. He was moving too slowly.

She had to have him. She raised her hips and slid her hands over his buttocks and pulled him into her. The sensation sent her into a frenzy of desire.

As waves of carnal sensuality overtook her, he grasped her hips and moved with her, stoking her desire and bringing her close to something she could feel but not touch.

She needed to taste him, to feel his tongue against hers.

He responded with an open mouth. His hands moved to her waist. His movement heightened her excitement and caused her body to quiver violently. He thrust into her hard and fast until she was wanton and uncaring except for the pleasure he was bringing. And then he was touching that something and causing such ecstasy she couldn't think, couldn't speak, could only reach for more.

As his buttocks began rhythmic spasms she pressed him deeply into her, pulled on him with her hips, made him cry out as he collapsed on her. Bathed in sweat, they continued to slide against one other as they slowly cooled.

He fell asleep with his head against her chest.

She lay fully awake. She wanted to press closer to him, to wake him, and ask him to do it again. Her mother's warning came to her: "Once you say yes, you'll never again be able to say no." She pushed the words away. She had been a good girl far too long. If her body felt this aching need from this day forward, so be it. She could handle that. It was small pay for such pleasure.

❧

As morning light fell over their tousled bed, he turned to her, trailed a slow parade of kisses over her nakedness, and silenced the remorseless voices of the night. "You're beautiful," he whispered. "I can't believe you've kept this body to yourself."

"I'm sorry I did. I had no idea sin would feel so good."

"Should we ask for absolution?" His hands stirred her.

She pulled herself up on one elbow and ran her fingers over his bare chest. "I don't intend to ask forgiveness from anyone," she said.

"Then I won't either."

The chill in the room caused gooseflesh to rise on her exposed skin. He pulled the comforter over them and pulled her onto him. "You know, when I first met you, I didn't believe you could be so innocent. I thought you were a tease."

"Why?"

"Zeke said."

She recoiled and rolled away. "What did Zeke say?"

He tried to pull her back.

"Tell me what he said."

"He said the squadron auctioned you off to the highest bidder."

She kept her back to him. "Did he tell you how high he sent the bidding? That the whole sick thing was his idea?"

"Sandy. It isn't important."

"It is to me. What else did he say?"

"He hinted he'd made it with you."

"So you decided to get in line?" She pushed her legs over the side of the bed.

"Oh, Christ, Sandy." He wrapped his arms around her waist and trailed his lips over the soft skin of her back. "It wasn't like that. Call me a schmuck, but don't pull away from me."

"You are a schmuck. A total jerk."

"I am," he agreed. "But you've got to admit I'm a damned good schmuck. There's no turning back now."

"The hell you say."

"You've proved he's a liar. I know I'm your first. You can't fake that. Let me make it up to you." He pulled her back and caressed her belly.

She didn't move as he rose up and ran his lips over the fleshy edges of her breast. "How?"

"Like this." His fingers slipped intimately over her.

She lay against him and smiled. "Love me like you did last night."

"I'll do it better than last night." He turned her to him and began to pleasure her with kisses and bites and fingers until she forgot about Zeke and gave herself up to the hunger of their bodies.

∞

After breakfast he helped her select boots and skis from the dozens on the racks. They carried their gear toward the lifts. "You do know how to use these once you put them on, don't you?"

"Are you still worried about that?" she teased.

"Are you?"

"No, but you'll have to show me how to get on and off the lift."

He stopped walking and turned fully toward her. "How can you ski if you've never been on a lift?"

"I did okay with making love, didn't I?"

He laughed. "But this time you could break your pretty neck."

"You show me how to navigate the lifts and I promise I will ski."

He insisted on the bunny slope. She stood on the small hill and grinned at him. "Okay, here goes. Wish me luck." She pushed off, quickly found her balance, and glided to the lodge.

He skied down to her. "You minx," he said. "You're an expert."

"I'm from Maine, remember? We skied to school most mornings."

∽

At dinnertime she retreated to the lodge and watched as he took one last run. When he came into view he was not alone. A tall girl moved beside him on the crowded lower hill. She left him at the entrance to the lodge.

His clenched jaw drew his mouth into a tight line as he came into the room. "Ready to call it a day?" he asked.

"Yes," she said.

"Let's go."

The girl was waiting by the racks when they stopped for their skis. "Don't go away mad, Mike," she said.

He raised one pole and pointed it. "Sandy, this is my cousin Alicia. We ran into each other on that last run."

"Literally," Alicia said. She stared at Sandy. "You up for the weekend, Sandy?"

"Until Monday."

"How about you, Mike?"

"Yes."

"Oh, that's so convenient," she said. "Where are you staying, Sandy?"

Sandy looked to Mike.

"She's staying at the cabin with me," he said.

"Gee, Mike, how does the family feel about that?"

"I didn't think to ask." He pressed Sandy toward the path.

"A lot has changed since your tour, hasn't it?" Alicia persisted.

"Yes," he answered. "It has. Good night, Alicia."

"Well, don't run off. I'd like to talk to you for a minute if Sandy wouldn't mind."

"You go ahead, Sand." He handed her his keys. "I think I need to have a few words with my cousin."

"How long will you be?"

"Not very." He turned and walked back into the lodge with Alicia.

She moved up the hill, turning now and then to look back and study the lodge. She had hoped to be anonymous, but he was well known here. She wondered what his cousin wanted. Whatever it was had made him edgy.

At the chalet, she found a roaring fire and several dishes of cold cuts, vegetables, and rolls waiting on the sideboard. "Hello. Anybody here?" she called.

No one answered.

Their bed had been made and the clothing they had discarded on the stairs was neatly folded. Sandy pulled the curtains, showered, perfumed her skin and hair, and pulled on the sleep set she hadn't needed the night before. In the living room, she lit every candle and turned out the lights. She poured scotch over ice in a crystal glass, turned on the television, and settled onto the sofa to catch the evening news.

A series of clips showed Marines racing wildly for cover, airplanes flying low, and tanks tumbling over crumbled walls. Now she understood how people became obsessed with war; having friends involved made all the difference.

The door opened. Mike dropped his boots and skis on the marble floor. "I'm sorry, Sandy. Alicia's a bitch. I had to talk to her."

"What did she want?" She patted the seat next to her.

"She wanted to know more about you. You know how families can be." He turned away. "Let me get out of these clothes." He bounded up the stairs.

She heard the shower start. When he came down, he was wearing a robe. He turned off the TV and pulled her to her feet. "You look damned inviting, and smell good too." He nuzzled her neck. "But I'm starving and I think I'm going to need my strength."

She laughed and followed him to the buffet. "Who did all this?" she asked.

"The housekeeper."

"Do you always request candles and champagne?"

"Why? Are you worried you might not be the only girl I've brought here?"

"The thought crossed my mind."

"Well, uncross it. I've been away. Remember?"

When they finished eating, he opened the champagne and blew out all but one of the candles. The fire crackled and hissed excitedly. Sandy's heart beat in harmony. They settled on floor pillows, looked out at the blowing pines, and watched the full moon rise.

"Let's bay like wolves." Mike growled.

"And act like wild animals?" she whispered as she felt his hands slide under her gown.

"Let's not act."

She opened his robe, kissed his bare chest, ran her fingernails along his ribs, moved her lips lower and nipped his belly.

He blew out the last candle and pulled her to him.

❧

They skied early the next morning, swam in the lodge pool, skied again, and then as the sun was about to set, changed into snowmobile gear.

The housekeeper had packed a lunch and thermos in a small backpack.

Mike pulled a snowcat from the garage behind the chalet. She held tight as they moved into the darkness of the big woods. Clouds covered the moon. He navigated expertly between trees until they came to a large clearing with a covered fire pit. Within minutes he had a fire started. They snacked and drank hot toddies on a heavy throw in the snow. The wind whistled fiercely through the evergreens.

"I want to give you something," he said.

"I don't need anything more than this."

"You earned your wings." He took off his gloves and pulled a silver chain from his pocket. A tiny winged charm, an exact replica of his uniform wings, sparkled in the fire's glow. "This is just the beginning," he promised.

"I have nothing to give you." She couldn't get close enough in the heavy suit.

"You've already given your gift to me."

༄

On the ride back, their light cut small beacons through an increasingly heavy snowfall. The machine slid on a curve, went over a small embankment, and tossed them into a drift. She fell on him and covered his face with kisses as the snowmobile came to a precipitous stop nearby. He laughed and brushed snow from her face with a cold glove before helping her to her feet. Together they righted the machine and set it back on the right course.

Back at the condo, they hung their snow-covered suits on hooks, and, too aroused to wait, made love on the throw on the marble floor as snowmelt dripped, cold and refreshing, on their overheated bodies.

The next morning as a strong tailwind propelled them home, she remembered Meyer's credo: Here and now, give freely, take happily, and share enthusiastically. For her this was the right time, the right place, and most definitely the right man.

༄

When they pulled into her drive, Kate's car was parked behind Sandy's. The lights were dim in Dave's place. Mike carried her suitcase to her door and kissed her. "Meet me at the club after work tomorrow?"

She shook her head. This was all too new and too private for the club. "No."

"Later then? I'll come here."

"About seven?"

"Will you wear the black thing I saw in your bag?"

"If you don't think it will get in the way." She stepped into the house and watched as his car drove off.

Dave came to her door. His face was troubled. "It's Kate again," he said. "Her brother was killed."

She followed him across the porch. Kate was curled in fetal position on his couch. Sandy touched her arm. "Kate?"

"What?"

"I'm sorry. I'm so sorry."

"For what?"

"I'm sorry you've lost your brother."

"He's not lost. He's dead. They took him away."

Sandy waited.

Kate stood up, angry and confrontational. "He was the only person who ever cared about me and he's dead."

"That's not true. I care about you."

"Friends can't care the way families do."

"Friends don't hate the same way either."

"How dare you say that?" Kate raised a hand toward Sandy's face.

Dave moved between them and grabbed Kate's hands as he forced her back onto the couch. "Sorry, Sandy. She's tried to take a few pieces out of me too."

Sandy stepped aside. "We do care about you, Kate."

"I called you. I couldn't find you."

"I was skiing."

"Where?"

"Aspen."

Kate's eyes opened wide. "Did you like it?"

"Yes, I'm a good skier."

"I'm sure you are. It's about time."

"She's been like this all day," Dave said.

"Says you," Kate muttered.

He moved into the kitchen. "Sandy, would you like a drink? I'd say yes, if I were you. I think you're going to need it."

Sandy sat beside Kate.

"I'd like one," Kate shouted. "If it isn't too much trouble for you."

"It's too much for you," he called. "You've had more than your share already."

He came back and handed a glass of scotch to Sandy.

Kate snatched it and drank it down.

He shook his head. "She needs to fly to Arizona for her brother's services. Major Roberts made flight reservations for both of you for tomorrow. You're to pick up the tickets at the airport. The funeral is at three."

"I told *you* to come with me," Kate said.

"And I told *you,* I'm on a flight to San Francisco in the morning," Dave said. He turned back to Sandy. "The major said you should wear your Class A's. You can ride with me to the airport if you want."

Sandy repacked a bag and spent the night in the BOQ with Kate. While her friend slept, she retrieved Kate's uniform parts from the closet floor, sponged and pressed them, and packed Kate's bag.

∾

Dave showed up at seven.

Sandy didn't tell either friend this was her first flight on a big jet. She followed Kate and watched as the girl upgraded to first class, settled into a seat, and ordered a drink. When the stewardess told her she would have to wait until they were airborne, she laughed and said, "That's okay. Just stack up my orders and bring them all at once."

Kate was very drunk when they deplaned. She lounged on a chair at the baggage claim as Sandy retrieved their bags.

A black-suited man stepped in and lifted both bags. "It's about time you arrived," he said without introduction. "I expected you yesterday." He strode to Kate. "We have only enough time to make it to the chapel," he said. "You won't have time to change."

"Hello, Father." Kate stood and followed him.

A limousine waited at the curb. Sandy settled stiffly into one corner. Kate moved close and reached out for Sandy's hand.

"I want to get some things straight before we get there, Kathryn," her father said. "I'll have none of your hysterical outbursts or sarcastic remarks to your stepmother. Nor will I have any ostentatious emotionalism. We are adults and we shall perform as adults. Is that understood?"

"Yes, Father."

The silence in the car grew thick.

A robed minister held the church doors. They filed in, father first, Kate second, and Sandy, feeling awkward and out of place in her uniform, third. An overflow crowd spilled to the sides and back of the aisles. The floor was carpeted in red. At the altar, a flag-draped casket reclined on a silver bed guarded by uniformed marines. A blond young woman stood to allow the three into the front pew. Sandy assumed she was Kate's stepmother, although she appeared far too young for that role.

As the ceremony droned on, as cold and formal as the man who had ordered it, Kate's head lolled to one side. Her feet stretched toward the altar and she began to slide from her seat.

Sandy prodded her.

Kate struck out with one hand.

Sandy pressed her into a formidable woman in the next space. The woman recognized the problem and pushed back. Together they propped Kate into an upright position.

Sandy helped her stand when Marines lifted the casket from its bed and hefted it onto their shoulders. She steered Kate down the aisle behind her father and his wife and into the waiting limousine.

Stunted desert trees passed silently by in a landscape without color, life, or hope. "They're returning him to Mother," Kate muttered as the drive sloped upward.

They sat in a semicircle of folding chairs on an artificially green knoll where a marble mausoleum waited in windless solitude.

The Marines carried the casket through iron doors, folded the flag, brought it out, and held the blood-red thing toward the blond. Kate lurched forward and snatched it from the woman's hands. Holding it against her chest, Kate faced her father. He reached out, hesitated, and dropped his arm.

"We're going now," Kate said. Sandy followed her down the hill to their driver. "To the airport," Kate demanded.

❧

It was morning again when they arrived in Wichita. Only one day had passed, but one more life was gone and many more were changed forever. Kate carried her flag as Sandy paid the cabbie and unlocked her door.

"I'd rather go to the BOQ," Kate said.

"I'll drive you over after we've both had some sleep," Sandy said.

"I won't sleep."

"I have some Valium the flight surgeon gave me for Colonel Hart's wife. You can have my bed." She found the bottle in her bedside drawer and handed it to Kate.

Kate popped open the cap and tossed all three tablets into her mouth. "Okay," she sang. "That should do it."

Sandy waited until she heard even breathing from the room before she settled under the afghan on the couch.

Soft tapping on her door awakened her. The room was dark. Thoughts of Mike sent her flying to open the door. She hoped he would understand why she'd stood him up.

It was Dave. "What are you doing back so soon?" he asked.

"I should ask you the same."

"Short meeting and school deadlines," he said.

"Short funeral. And her father's an ass. He was sorry to see us arrive and happy to see us go."

"How is she?"

"A mess. She's sleeping under the influence of Valium."

"Here?"

"Yes."

"I haven't had dinner, have you?"

"No dinner, no lunch, and no breakfast."

"Whoa. I'll take the two of you for Mexican. Think she'll go?"

Of course she'll go with you, Sandy thought, but aloud she said, "Yes, she needs to eat."

"Good. Come get me when you're ready."

When Sandy told her their dinner plans, Kate smiled, broke open her suitcase, showered, and reappeared in a skirt and heels. She's like a finely formed steel spring, Sandy thought. Pushed to the limit, she always manages to spring back. Yet how much of that resilience was real strength and how much was improperly forged was impossible to tell.

Throughout the evening, Sandy's friends managed a running dialogue of history, war, and the upcoming presidential campaign. By the time dinner was over Kate had charmed and snared Dave.

The next morning Jim Andersen waited to begin his rounds. "Where have you been?" he asked. "We missed you. You look different. Did you redo your makeup or something?"

"What are you talking about?"

"Your face is different. It looks even nicer than usual."

She knew exactly what had changed. She had seen the same softening of her corpsmen's faces when they released pent-up sexual tensions on their wild forays on the town. "Must be the tan," she said.

"Where'd you get a tan in the middle of winter?"

"Colorado. I went skiing with a friend. Any more questions?"

"Nope. None of my business." He picked up his charts. "So, where'd you go? Who did you go with? Does your father know?" He walked down the hall laughing.

When she turned around, she realized why he was so tickled. Mike stood at the desk.

"Here I am, slipping in the side door again."

"Mike! I'm so glad to see you." If the desk hadn't been between them she would have fallen into his arms.

"Sure. Like, so much you stood me up."

"I'm sorry. I had a good reason."

He leaned over the desk and whispered. "Meet me in the morgue. I've been thinking about that table all weekend."

"That's gross!"

He laughed. "I had a fantastic time."

"Skiing?" she asked.

"No," he whispered, leaning so far over the desk he could almost kiss her, "making love."

She blushed, hot and crimson.

He laughed and stood up straight. "I love to make you blush."

"Why?"

"It makes you different from every girl I've ever known. I like that you're so transparent."

"I don't."

He propped one elbow on the counter top. "Promise you won't ever change."

"Mike, stop."

"Stop what?"

"Stop talking like that. Here. You're not supposed to be in here."

"There's that nurse again. Turn her off and tell me you liked making love."

"If I do will you leave?"

He nodded.

She smiled.

"You won't stand me up again?"

"I flew to Arizona with Kate. For her brother's funeral."

He stood upright as a flash of pain crossed his face. "And here I am playing pretty boy. I apologize."

"You didn't know."

"I'm flying in an hour and then I'm free. Come to my place as soon as you get off?"

"Yes," she said as she glanced around to be sure no one could see. She stood, leaned across the desk, and promised him with a kiss.

Somewhere behind her she heard Jim laugh.

CHAPTER NINE

Spring came gently to the prairie, a slight warming of the wind, pastel tints hazing over the stark lines of the horizon, browns turning to pale greens, grays becoming rich browns and the sky, as if restrained too long by the shale clouds, rejoicing in brilliant shades of blue. The persimmon trees that grew in symmetrical lines around farmers' fields unfolded quietly, and so did Kate.

As she and Dave spent time together, Kate became more subdued and less edgy. Their shared interests led them into the McCarthy presidential campaign.

On a sunny Sunday the two couples drove to Dodge City to drop off some campaign information and tour the town. For a short time Sandy was able to put the death of another friend in Vietnam out of her mind. But when they passed a child standing by the road she recalled the five freckle-faced children hotshot Ralph had made fatherless when he crashed into the China Sea the previous week. Now his affair with Kate had become unimportant and that part of Meyer's creed became more acceptable.

Mike pulled her to him. "I saw that look. No more of it. We're here to have fun."

Fighter pilot's girl. Fighter pilot's credo. She struggled to replace the pain with a smile. "I still say they could do more with Boot Hill than sell ice cream cones," she called to Dave, who was driving.

"Not much to see, I'll admit. But the natives were friendly."

"I thought it was boring," Kate said.

"Too small for a big city gal," Dave said.

"No town is too small for me," Mike quipped. "Nor any gal too slow."

Sandy smeared his face with ice cream as he bent to take another taste.

"Show him who's boss, Sandy," Dave said into the rearview mirror.

"He's always like this after a night in the war widows' camp with the boys," she laughed. "Too big for his britches."

"And exactly the right size for yours," Mike shot back.

"Mike!"

He hugged her. "Speaking of big britches, Dave, how does the McCarthy crowd feel about Bobby Kennedy entering the race?"

"Aargh! Just when I was beginning to relax, you have to bring that up."

"You still think McCarthy has a chance?"

"Hard to tell. He had pretty good odds when he was the only antiwar candidate, but with a Kennedy in, who knows which way it will go."

"Does that rule out LBJ?" Mike asked.

"Hell no! With the votes split, he could slip through like a greased pig on the Fourth of July. Old politicians like him have a sixth sense about such things."

"He's the incumbent and he's doing an awful lot of maneuvering," Kate said. "He kicked Westmoreland to the curb."

"And last week he sent thirty thousand more troops over," Dave added.

Thirty thousand more to die, Sandy thought.

"Speaking of war," Mike said. "I've got to change our plans for next weekend."

"Oh no." Sandy waited for an explanation.

"My sister's coming up for an unexpected visit."

"Well, that's neat," Kate said. "Now we'll get to meet some of your family."

"No, it isn't neat. She's got a two-year-old who'll pull my whole place apart. And she's not exactly in stable mental condition."

"What does that mean?" Sandy asked.

"It means she's in the middle of a divorce and looking for moral support."

"What a good brother you are," Kate said.

"Right. Tell me what a fighter pilot knows about two-year-olds or a woman in crisis. I'm a good old boy, remember?"

They laughed with him.

"Okay," he said. "Tell me, Nurse Sandy, where do two-year-olds sleep? What do they eat? Can they talk? Do they still crap in their britches?"

"Can't answer," she said. "Newborns are as far as I go." She couldn't imagine his place with baby things.

"She'll only be here for a couple of days."

"Personal Affairs Office rents equipment. I can handle it," Sandy offered.

"You wouldn't mind?"

"I'm at your service," she said.

She spent the next few days helping him set up and expected he would introduce her to his sister, but on Friday, when he was supposed to call, he didn't. She called his squadron. Tim said he had taken leave. His sister was probably in worse shape than he had expected, she rationalized. Facing a weekend alone, she traded supervisory shifts with Kate.

On Monday morning she stopped by the club to have breakfast and spotted Mike in the dining room with a stunning woman and a small child. She turned and walked out. If he didn't want her around, she certainly wasn't going to force the issue.

Dave was on the porch when she got home. "Something wrong, Sand? You look down."

"Fighting with myself," she said. "I know it's early but I sure could use a drink. Join me?"

"Sorry," he said. "I have a meeting."

"Where's Kate?"

"Took off for Kansas City. Said she had some shopping to do. Where's Mike?"

"At the club having breakfast with his sister."

"How is she?"

"I don't know. He hasn't called since she arrived, and I ran away when I saw them."

"Why?"

"Because she looks like a porcelain doll and is way out of my league. I don't have the courage of a flea."

"That's not like you."

She turned away. "It's so weird. Mike not wanting me to meet his sister is a big thing. He's shutting me out of his other life."

"You don't know that, Sandy."

"I feel it."

"He knows what he's found. Without you his life would be pretty dull."

"Will he get bored with me eventually?"

Dave shrugged. "That's a chance you have to take, isn't it?"

"I couldn't turn back now if I wanted to."

"Then throw in your chips like everyone else has to. What have you got to lose?"

Myself, she thought. I'm afraid I'll lose myself. But he wouldn't understand. She slid Penny's letter from her pocket. "Here's the latest bulletin from the war. I think you'll find it interesting."

5 March 1968
Dear Sandy,
The good old U.S. of A. seems farther away than ever. I read

your letters and realize things are pretty much unchanged in your lives, while over here things keep getting worse. Now we've been asked to carry the dead as well as the injured. To make matters worse, every time we stop, someone desperate to get to a battle zone jumps on. Today we were filled to the max with critical patients and waiting in line to take off, when this hot-shot-bastard-of-a-reporter pushed his way through the door. I told him we had no room but he climbed in. "Sure you do, honey," he said. "I'll sit right here." He climbed onto the full body bags! He acted like the whole thing was a big joke, but no one was laughing. The men threw him off the plane. I swear if I'd gotten my hands on him I might have killed him.

The fighting is winding down at Khe Sanh. I can't see that one hill is going to make one damned bit of difference in this war, but it has become as symbolic as the Alamo. My God, Sandy, you should see the kids we bring out of there. They are caked in mud and exhausted. We can't fly into camp, so we pick up them up wherever the dust offs put them down. Some of them have had treatment from Army hospitals, but most have had only a minimum of first aid. The injuries are awful.

We aren't getting crew rest. The fighters and bombers are flying three hundred air strikes a day, and the cargo planes try to keep supplies going in and wounded troops coming out. One guy on the radio said, "It's beans, bullets, and bandages in and body bags out." And that sums it up.

I don't mean to get all mushy on you, Sand, but I do want to say thank you for your letters with your glimpses of life back home, and for your care packages. They help me to keep some perspective. For a short time I can remember what this is all about, and when you tell me about your friend Dave's protest groups, I am strengthened because it makes me know I'm not the only one with doubts about this mess. I feel like I've been

caught in some terrible nightmare that goes on and on and on.
Home seems far away. Thanks for being the kind of friend I can
be totally honest with.

　　As always,
　　Penny

∽

Three days later Mike showed up at her door. He offered no explanation for his behavior and she didn't ask for one. His sister had returned to California.

April arrived with bullets in Memphis that stilled Martin Luther King's voice, and race riots in the streets of Detroit and New York. The war in Vietnam seemed to be giving way to a bloodier one at home. Sandy preferred not to think about it.

When Mike wasn't TDY to California for bombing practice or cross-country training flights, they carried their favorite books to the riverbank and spent afternoons reading to one another.

She didn't tell him when B.B. was listed as missing in action near the Cambodian border or that she finally understood "MIA without a chute sighted" really meant "killed in action." With him holding her close under the sun she temporarily forgot blood and guts and Vietnam. Life was easier without reality.

Summer came early. They spent hot, dry afternoons around the club pool and drank French 75s until few men were left standing. Mike gave her a heart-shaped charm for her birthday and Dave gave her a party at the duplex.

For the first time, someone passed a few joints through the crowd. Mike inhaled deeply. Sandy declined. Kate disappeared for a long time and came back giggling hysterically.

"Make a wish," Mike said when Dave brought out the cake. She closed her eyes and wished for love. Mike pulled her into his arms and kissed her. She didn't like the taste of pot.

As graduation loomed for his first class of pilots, Mike became distracted and short-tempered. Another squadron lost a plane and even though the student successfully punched out, the loss of a Thud put a crimp on flying hours.

The general ordered all I.P.s to ground any man seen drinking within twelve hours of a scheduled flight. Tattling was not in a fighter pilot's bag of tricks. While most accepted the order, Mike felt it had been directed toward him. He railed against senior brass, inept commanders, and stupid regulations. He began to spend more time with Zeke.

"I'd take you with me," he said one afternoon in their hidden spot on the river, "if only you'd be friends with Zeke. I'll never understand why you don't like him."

"Shh," she said. "Let's not talk." The attack had happened a lifetime ago, but she still felt dirty when Zeke was near.

He pulled her closer on the blanket. "I haven't been much fun lately, have I?"

"I could use a little more."

"Fun, or this?" He slid his hands under her waistband and pushed her shorts over her hips.

"Both," she said.

He laughed but lay back again and stared at the darkening sky.

She took his hand. "Mike, what is it? Something's bothering you."

"I don't know." He placed both hands behind his head and closed his eyes. "I think I'm actually having qualms about sending my guys off to war. Maybe Dave and Kate are rubbing off on me."

It was her turn to laugh. "Fat chance. You haven't given an inch since you guys began debating the darned war. Besides, the men you train are volunteers. Could anyone have stopped you?"

"A lot has changed since then."

"Like what?"

"Like the planes have gotten older and the pilots have gotten younger and the war has heated up and the protesters are saying we're a bunch of pawns."

"That didn't stop you from going a second time."

"I didn't know you then."

"What difference does it make?"

He rolled onto her, pushed her hair back from her face, and kissed her forehead, her temples, her nose, and finally her mouth. She wrapped her arms around his neck and pulled him closer. As he lifted her hips and helped her remove her shorts he whispered, "The difference now is that I love you."

Most days through midsummer he was on a more even keel. They lounged near the river, partied with friends at the club, and boated on a nearby lake. She had hoped for many things in her life but had never dreamed of a man like him.

Events in the war and at home didn't touch her. Bobby Kennedy's assassination, although tragic, was another marker of history and nothing to do with her. There were always a few weirdoes waiting to do bad, she rationalized, but for the most part, people were good and kind and wanted happiness as much as she. Penny's letters were from another world, a world far away and uncontrollable. Even the growing violence at antiwar marches failed to shake her unwavering belief in the goodness of the American way.

At the beginning of June she had another letter from Penny.

28 May 1968

Dear Sandy,

Loved your letter. Mike sounds wonderful. How lucky you are to have found him. I'm envious, but living life large in Australia at the moment. The fighting started again just before I escaped. I hear they are calling it "mini-Tet." That's funny because I hadn't realized the first Tet had ended. I can only hope the peace talks in

Paris will make a difference.

A week ago, I was bringing a bunch of injured grunts out of Saigon, and today I'm on R and R in the lap of luxury in the hotel Bob and I had planned to visit. Two other nurses came over with me, but they have gone on to meet their boyfriends.

The Aussies have welcomed me into their hearts and have plied me with great drinks and good food. They are wonderful, warm-hearted, heavy drinkers, and slightly mad. It's been fun, but I'm not able to completely shake the anxiety that sometimes overwhelms me.

Tell Kate I am taking her advice. She wrote in her last letter I should "go out and find a good screw." I am doing that and can report it does relieve a bit of my pent-up emotions. Tonight I'll try again.

Must go,
Penny

When Mike and Dave discussed the differences between McCarthy's believers in the political process, Dellinger's pacifist ideals, and the call by Rubin for all-out revolution, Sandy tuned out.

When Kate told her Dave was walking a tightrope, with the threat of mob violence, she decided Kate was exaggerating the danger and shouldn't be involved anyway. Politics were for men, who were expected to debate the issues, but women should be soft and yielding.

As scorching heat settled over the plains, a series of fierce electrical storms birthed tornadoes. One missed the base but hit a nearby turkey farm. She and Mike drove past it on their way to his townhouse with supplies for a squadron party to welcome a new class of pilots.

"Man, would you look at that!" He pulled the car under a stand of persimmon trees stuck with turkey feathers. "They're like a line of Indian chiefs' headdresses," he said. "Can you imagine a power that can do that?"

Your love, she thought, and then out loud for the first time said, "I love you, Mike."

He sat still and unspeaking for a few seconds before he whispered, "I'm glad." He put the car in gear and started off again. The words she had held in so long had been expected and were accepted.

At the townhouse they threw open the balcony doors to accommodate a crowd of graduating pilots and new students. She took over the kitchen.

Dave was in Detroit. Kate was on the balcony entertaining a laughing group of new men.

An FNG who seemed younger than any previous student sat on a kitchen stool and chatted nervously as she worked. Behind his head, through the open balcony doors, another line of black storm clouds gathered along the horizon. She glanced at them occasionally as she listened to him tell the story of a T-38 accident he had seen at flight school.

"And this guy pulls back, but the bird looks like it doesn't have enough power. He's just off the end of the runway and the 38 goes belly up across the field like it's standing on its tail. The jock must have decided he couldn't pull it out, because he fires his canopy and punches out. Ka-pow! Flattened like a pancake. That's why I'll never punch out of one of those babies. I'd rather go down with my craft."

Each time he made his hand dive, Sandy caught a glimpse of rounded black clouds moving toward them.

"Do you know how they identify a pilot's body after a crash?"

She feigned ignorance. "How?"

"From footprints. Boots protect the soles of our feet. Only thing left if we auger in."

A blast of wind came in through the open doors and sent a stack of paper napkins onto the floor.

The boy turned. "Looks like another doozy of a storm. Do they scare you?"

Sandy nodded.

"It's the geographical location," he said and sipped his drink. "We're in a unique place where air masses coming down from Canada are predominately cold Arctic air. But the stuff coming up from the southwest is warm and dense with water. The two completely different masses collide right here and loosen huge amounts of energy."

"Is that what makes the thunder so loud?" She tried to remember his name. Scott, that was it.

"No, the land is so flat the noise has nowhere to go but out. It explodes along the ground, causes things in its path to shake."

"How do you know all this, Scott?" she asked.

"I got my degree in meteorology. Actually asked the Air Force for training as a navigator. I was more surprised than anyone when I got tapped for pilot training."

Outside the sky had begun to take on a strange greenish cast.

He turned again. "See that green? That's hail. Maybe we'd better ask Mike if he has a basement."

"Do you think there'll be tornadoes?"

"Could be. They usually come at the end of the storm."

Sandy looked for Mike and spotted him standing with Zeke by the living room windows. They appeared to be arguing. "Where are you from, Scott?" she asked.

"Iowa. I've got a girl back there. Soon as I get back from 'Nam we'll get married."

Don't bet on it, she thought, and turned to see large hailstones pelting the pots of flowers on the balcony. Kate and her men hurried to get under cover. "I'd better get those plants in," she said.

"I'll help."

Together they threaded through the retreating crowd and slid the pots to the shelter of the roof overhang. Lightning streaked across the sky. The thunder was instantaneous and earsplitting. Inside, laughter increased.

She pulled the balcony doors closed and walked toward Mike. As she approached she heard Zeke say, "Boys' night out is boys' night out. Everybody does it. Shit, man, what's happening to you?"

Golf ball–sized hail began cracking against the windows. The sound of shattering glass rose from the parking lot below.

"Jesus!" Zeke shouted. "My car!" He and Mike ran toward the stairs.

Out the window, she saw a dark mass barreling toward them.

"Tornado!" Scott yelled.

Mike shouted, "This way!"

Sandy stood frozen at the windows as the funnel cloud touched the ground two streets over. The crowd jammed up at the top of the stairs. Bolts of lightning split the air as the twister skipped along like a stone on water.

She became aware of Scott pushing her down the stairs. The interior garage door blew open as the wind tore at the metal outer door.

Just as her feet touched the cooler concrete floor of the basement, the lights went out, causing her to trip and fall against another body. She recognized Kate's expensive perfume and laughed.

"Sandy," her friend said. "Guess what I've done?"

"What?"

"I've put in my volunteer statement. I'm going over there."

A sound like a freight train barreling down on them cut off further conversation. It was followed by complete silence until someone laughed and everyone began to talk at once. She could feel the crowd pushing back toward the stairs.

Someone opened the front door and allowed light to flow in. They filed into the street, tilted their faces into a blue sky. Ice melted rapidly on the summer sidewalk, but on the far side of the park, where a row of small buildings had stood, there was not a tree, shrub, or structure.

Behind her she heard Scott say, "We'd better see if we can help."

She was unable to move. It had happened too fast, was too final to be real. She needed to find Kate and ask her exactly what she had done, but Scott began to run toward the destruction and she followed.

Miraculously, many of the homes had been emptied in preparation for more townhouses to be built, and those few occupants who remained had found shelter and suffered only minor injuries.

When Sandy looked for Kate, she was nowhere to be found.

The storm had jolted her sensibilities. She no longer felt untouchable and safe. Although nursing had taught her to respect the fragility of life, now the fragility of life circumstances was brought clearly into focus. She understood why Dave worried so about the chaotic forces being unleashed in response to the war, and she had new empathy for Penny, who had lost the future she and Bob had planned.

Her respect increased for women like Sarah, left adrift by her husband's poor planning and the military's rigid policies. And she regretted that she hadn't understood when her high school sweetheart returned from war and wasn't able to fit back into her small dreams.

That night she and Mike made fierce love. In the morning she saw him off for another deployment.

When she couldn't locate Kate, she took her pager, book, and transistor radio to the river park. There, with her back against their ancient tree, she heard a broadcaster report that the military had decided to abandon Khe Sanh. Gramps, Ralph, B.B., and Kate's brother were gone forever, and for nothing.

Shocked at the pain that developed in the pit of her stomach, she cried out. An old man sitting on a bench nearby looked up from his newspaper. "Are you okay, young lady?" He put his newspaper down and started to stand.

She rubbed her eyes with the palms of both hands. "I'm fine," she said.

"You don't look fine."

"I'm sorry." She tilted her head toward her radio. "Just the news."

He nodded. "Yes," he said. "I understand. The news has been terrible of late." He sat back down.

She gathered her things and left the park. At home another letter from Penny waited.

> *24 June 1968*
>
> *Dear Sandy,*
>
> *I'm back to reality, ferrying bodies between war and civilization and feeling less like a heroine every day. There are more injuries than ever, but we have been told to keep a running count only of the dead. Body counts, theirs and ours, have taken on great importance as measurements of winning and losing. No one wants to count the mutilated because they reveal the foolish face of war. Since the "peace" talks have started I sometimes feel the two sides are like little boys who have been caught fighting on the school ground and are separated by the teacher. Now as they stand with her, waiting to be judged, they both take furtive, ugly swipes at one another, because each wants to get in the last punch.*
>
> *With every planeload of broken bodies, I ask myself:Why are we still fighting?Why are we bringing these broken, nearly lifeless bodies home?Will it be okay with their mothers and wives if they spend the remainder of their days in a veterans' hospital? But questions are not allowed for we "angels of mercy" so I push the shock and fear to the back of my brain and deal with the here and*

now. I sometimes feel like I'm working with only half of my brain and one eye and the other part of me has shut down, a kind of half-life or emotional death. I have no time to deal with questions. Reality is racks filled with "heads"—brain injured men—all seizuring at once. Some of them have shrapnel imbedded in their brains and leak gray fluid through their bandages. They stretch out their hands like claws and roll their eyes and I can't help them, because we have used up all but a few cc's of our anti-seizure medicines.We, two nurses and three corpsmen, huddle together and make decisions, like, which of these men have a chance of making it and so deserve the last of the medication? And we hug each other as some of the men die and we realize we have squandered precious medication on the wrong one.We hurry between shaking litters and move oxygen supplies from the dead to the living.When the oxygen gets low we negotiate with the aircrew until they agree to descend to conserve what oxygen we have. They, of course, stay in the front of the plane, and rarely venture back. I want to move up front with them.

I have asked to go back to the shorter in-country runs. My nerves are beginning to tell on me: my hands tremor and shake. My survivor instinct is telling me I need a break, but I just had one.

A reporter stopped me the other day, asked my opinion of the upcoming presidential candidates, and how I would be voting in November. I told him I would vote for anyone who promised they would stop this mindless massacre. He wrote that down and then searched my chest for my nametag.Thank goodness I hadn't pinned it on. All I need is for someone in power to read my views and end my career. Thanks for letting me cry in my beer.

As always,

Penny

The next Saturday night Sandy was hospital supervisor.

"You've got your work cut out for you," Kate warned as they met. "Had a medevac diverted from Oklahoma because of weather. The patients are staying overnight. One of them is a nurse from Vietnam. She's in early labor."

"How early?" Sandy asked.

"She's not sure. I paged Jim Andersen. He's on his way."

"Good."

"She's not married. Her boyfriend's MIA. The Air Force is booting her out."

"Kate?"

"What?"

"Have you really volunteered for Vietnam?"

"Yes."

"I had no idea you planned that."

"I didn't plan it."

"Why are you going?"

"I want to see what everyone gets out of the experience."

"Does Dave know?"

"I wrote. He hasn't answered."

"Do you think he'll be upset?"

"He shouldn't be. We've had fun and a lot of good sex but neither of us is committed to a relationship."

"I hope you know what you're getting into. I sure don't want anything to happen to you."

"Fat chance. My father has used his influence. I'm going to Cam Ranh Bay, the safest place in the country."

Jim Andersen was at the desk reading the pregnant girl's medical record. He pulled a chair in so Sandy could read with him.

"She's a sad case," he said. "Lost her boyfriend before she could tell him about the baby. Can't go home because her parents are the religious sort and have refused to see her. She's between four and six months along and having contractions. Medevac nurse wrote she appeared depressed and withdrawn."

"I would be, if I were her."

"Is pregnancy considered a service-connected disability?" he asked.

"The military makes it clear to us gals, Jim. Get pregnant and we're out. No questions. No compensation."

"So she has good reason to be depressed."

"As if losing her guy wasn't enough."

"Well, let's go take a look. We sure don't want her to lose the baby too."

The girl was the only patient in the labor unit. Her face was gaunt. Her hospital gown fell loosely from her shoulders. Sandy could see how she had hidden her pregnancy.

She glared at them. "What do you want?"

"I'm Dr. Andersen. You must be Cindy." Jim took her hand. "I need to ask you some questions and examine you."

Relief showed on her face. "I was afraid you were another administrative type," she said.

Jim laughed. "No, just a doc. And this is Sandy, my charge nurse. Lucky for us, she's supervising tonight."

The girl's smile changed her face into that of an impish child. "Lucky you, Saturday rotation, eh?'

Sandy nodded.

"Been there, done that," she said.

Jim opened her chart. "You've been having some contractions?"

"A few. Too much flying, I think."

"How far along are you?"

Cindy shrugged. "It took me a while to believe I was knocked up. I'd guess about five months."

"Baby moving?"

"Hell, yes. The little shit's been kicking like a mule."

"And there's no father?"

"There was a father. He was shot down. No chute sighted." She shrugged again. "I thought I could fake it until I was due and then get the Air Force to deliver it, but my supervisor guessed and here I am."

Jim laid his hand on her abdomen.

"I think I was a little dehydrated from the long flight. I'm feeling okay now."

"I don't feel any contractions," Jim said.

"They've slowed."

"Have you had any bleeding?"

"No. Like I said, I was fine until they forced me onto the plane."

"Physically forced you?" Jim asked.

"Ordered me. I told them I had nowhere to go and no money to go with, but they wouldn't listen."

"What will you do?" Sandy asked as she prepared the girl for the exam.

"I don't know."

Jim completed his exam. "I don't see any changes in the cervix. I agree it's probably been too long a flight with too much anxiety. We'll let you rest here tonight."

"Thank you," she said. "I was scared to death you were going to put me out on the street."

Jim patted her foot.

"I'm a fallen soul." The face she made caused them to laugh.

"When did you last eat?" Sandy asked.

"I haven't had much of an appetite."

"I'm going to move you to a postpartum bed for the night, so you won't be woken up if someone starts labor. I'll go to the kitchen and get you a sandwich." She turned to Jim. "What do you think?"

"I think food is in order. This baby is hungry."

"Good point," the girl said.

Sandy moved her to a private room and returned to the desk. "Jim, if she's pregnant and not married, the Air Force will take care of her medical expenses, won't they?"

"I called the hospital commander. He says as long as she's near a medical facility she can receive care until she delivers, but they won't give her a leave of absence and they won't continue her pay."

"She can't work much longer."

"According to the regulations, it's not our problem."

"Bet me," Sandy said.

"I'd never bet against you, Sand. I lose my shirt every time. But this time you won't win. The regulations won't change for one pregnant woman."

"Then I'll have to find a way around them." She didn't tell him she felt compelled to help the girl because she could so easily be in the same mess.

The kitchen was locked up tight. Sandy called Kate, who delivered a hamburger and milkshake to the side door. The three were on a first-name basis before Cindy finished the burger and giggling friends by the time the milkshake was gone.

"Where will you go?" Kate asked.

"I have no idea. Once my commanding officer discovered I was pregnant, I had no time to think," Cindy answered.

"What about your boyfriend's family? Wouldn't they want to know about the baby after losing their son?" Sandy asked.

"By the time I thought of them, all of B.B.'s things had been sent out. I have no address. Once the baby's born I'll look for them."

"B.B.? What's his last name?" Sandy asked.

"Gunz. Isn't that hilarious? When I first heard his name I nearly died laughing."

"I knew B.B. You couldn't have picked a nicer guy. I was so sad when I heard he was MIA," Sandy said.

Cindy began to cry.

"How did you end up here?" Kate asked.

"I said my home of record was Oklahoma, because I knew it was near Kansas. B.B. loved it here." She laughed. "But when I looked out the window of the plane I couldn't imagine why. I mean, man, it's flat."

"You get used to it," Sandy said.

"Doesn't matter anyway. I only have enough money for a YWCA and who's going to hire me in this condition?"

"I'll try to help," Sandy said.

"Why?" Cindy said.

"I owe B.B.," Sandy answered.

"Oh, my God." Cindy began to sob into her hands.

Sandy touched her shoulder.

"I am so scared. This baby is so important to me. Oh, God."

Sandy's pager sounded. "I've got to go," she said. "I probably won't get back tonight. Will you be okay?"

"Yes."

As they walked to the side door, Kate surprised her by saying, "We're all in this together, aren't we?"

"In what?" Sandy asked.

"This woman thing. It's why I volunteered. The men go off to war and we women wait. If the worst happens, it's us who spend the rest of our lives picking up the pieces. I've decided to become part of the big adventure and not sit on the sidelines."

"I wonder if it will be worth it." Sandy held the door for her.

"None of us will know until it's done, will we?"

⁓

Early the next morning, Cindy was up and dressed.

"Going somewhere?" Sandy asked.

"I can't lay around in my pajamas all day, even if they are flattering as all get out."

"No contractions?"

"Not a one. And baby is kicking away. I think he liked the milkshake."

"Do you want to stay?"

"Yes."

"Then you'd better get back into bed. The medevac crew will be here soon. I'll call Jim Andersen and tell him you're having a few contractions. Then we'll have another week to get your orders changed and figure out a plan."

"Will it work?"

"Can't see why not."

Cindy climbed into bed.

"Can we talk business?" Sandy asked.

"Sure."

"How much money do you have?"

"Severance pay. Three hundred and eight dollars."

"Have you talked to family services or personal affairs?"

"No, they shipped me out too fast. They did say I would have commissary privileges until the baby is born."

"That will help."

"Sandy?"

"What?"

"Did you and B.B. have a thing?"

Sandy laughed. "No. He helped me out of a terrible jam once. Honest."

"Will you tell me about that?"

"I can't, Cindy. You'll have to trust me."

"Fair enough."

∽

Sandy spent the next week lobbying General Magnem, Major Roberts, and the Personal Affairs officer while Kate placed multiple calls to her father. By the time the next medevac flight arrived, Cindy had permission to receive care at Meridian Base Hospital. By then her sense of humor and irony had already bonded her to the staff.

Cindy was cleaning the break room when Sandy brought the news. "Your discharge is approved, a social worker has been assigned, and there's a tiny apartment on the bus line, waiting."

"God, Sandy, thank you. What a relief."

"The place is a one-room efficiency, but the price is right and there's no lease. Major Roberts created a temporary position so you can work here as an aide until the last month."

"How will I ever repay you?"

"I'm the one with the debt, remember?"

∽

The next evening, Mike and Sandy wandered to the riverbank to enjoy the city's Fourth of July fireworks. He carried a book and a blanket. She carried a small lunch.

As they lay in their hidden spot, Sandy watched the contrails of a jet split the sky into even halves. "My mother liked to say the trail left by a plane was the spirit of a pilot on his way to heaven," she murmured.

Mike laughed. "Certainly not a fighter pilot."

"Why not?"

"A fighter pilot wouldn't be caught dead in heaven—too boring."

"Where do they go?" She turned toward him and traced the silky contour of his eyebrows with one finger.

"They stay right here and follow pretty girls home every night. What about nurses? Where do they go?"

"You're the theologian. You tell me."

"They can't get into heaven after taking the pill."

"Maybe they stay and follow studly guys around." She laughed, pulled his hand away from her breast, and kissed his fingers. "If you could come back from the dead, what would you want to be?"

"A rat." He pointed to the river's edge. "Like that one."

Sandy caught a movement in the grass and sat up. "God! I didn't know there were rats here!"

He laughed. "Been here every time we have. I didn't tell you because I knew it would freak you out."

She watched the grasses shake.

"We think the park is ours, but he knows it's his." Mike lay back and began to page through his book.

A chill ran through her. "Why would you want to be a rat?"

He shrugged. "What more could I ask for? I'd live in this park, have lots to eat, and watch couples make love all night."

"I didn't know you were a voyeur."

"Maybe not so much voyeur as realist. Everyone has the secret desire to watch someone else making out."

"Really? It must be a guy thing."

"Come on, admit it. Don't say it doesn't interest you."

"It doesn't." She needed to change the subject. "What are you reading?"

"Ginsberg. The beat poet." He handed her the open book. "Here, read this one. It's pretty interesting stuff."

She read the poem on the open page. "This isn't poetry," she said. "What do Walt Whitman, supermarkets, and death have to do with America? What's he talking about?"

"He's talking about the death of America as we know it. It's over, don't you see? Walt Whitman's America is dead!"

She rolled onto her back and pushed the book toward him.

He laid the book by her head and smiled. "*You* could use a little more Ginsberg instead of that fluffy stuff that clogs your mind."

She closed her eyes to hold back sudden tears. "*I* like what *I* read."

"But Ginsberg is what life is really about. He tells the truth about sleaze, degradation, and life's little deceits. He doesn't harp on about trees and snow and leaves floating in springs." When he realized she was crying, his voice softened. "Do you know what I mean?"

"No."

He laughed as he tried to pull her into his arms.

She resisted and sat up. She couldn't find anything funny about what was happening in America and she didn't understand his cynical view of death. "I don't want to understand."

"Why?" He sighed and sat up next to her.

"Because I'm a nurse and I already know enough about dying. How can that man call what he writes poetry? I might like it if he said things in a nicer way."

He leaned toward her, nudged her hair back from her face and touched his lips to her cheek. "But, Sandy, my love," he whispered, "if he said it in a nicer way, no one would understand."

She relaxed against him, responded to his kiss, but when she thought she saw the rat's eyes peering from the tall grass, she stiffened and said, "Now you've done it, Mike. I won't ever be able to love you here again."

"Bet me," he said, pressing her back onto the blanket.

"Well, if you're going to be a rat," she said, yielding to her body's needs, "at least you'll be a very sexy one."

CHAPTER TEN

August brought rainless, head-splitting heat that baked the land night and day. Sandy cranked up the air conditioner and invited Cindy to visit often. Mike was away most weekends. Dave was away until after Labor Day and Kate went back to one-night stands.

One late evening, when Mike was to return from a cross-country flight, Sandy drove by his townhouse. Her spirits flagged when she saw no lights. As she passed the small park, her headlights caught a feminine shape in pink and white, ducking between the trees. Sandy slowed and watched as the wind caught and lifted the girl's blond hair before a man, who so resembled Mike, pulled her playfully into the darkness. Sandy felt her breath catch painfully. She was jealous of a tiny stranger because she herself would go home to another sleepless night in her empty bed. She drove on.

In the middle of the night, thunderstorms blew out the electricity. Without the air conditioner and with the thunder shaking the small house, it was impossible to sleep. She dressed in total darkness, drove to the hospital, and slept on the couch in the nurses' lounge until her shift began.

After work she went by Mike's again. He hadn't returned, but her spirit was renewed when she found three letters in her mailbox. She opened Penny's first.

> *2 August 1968*
> *Dear Sandy,*
> *I have been grounded and assigned to the Kadena hospital. My body reneged. My heart gave out before my brain. (Maybe there is more to the idea of "heartsick" and "broken-hearted" than we modern day medics care to admit). I have been diagnosed with an anxiety disorder that caused my heart to go out of control.*

I'm on medication but still have episodes of anxiety and fear. My psychiatrist (yes, they make me see a shrink!) says it will take time to recuperate from the traumatic events of the past nine months. He says I will have to go through a grieving process. When I asked what I am grieving for, he said, for Bob, of course. He says I have been forced to put the good of many before the good of one, namely me. He says by shouldering the responsibilities of my job at a time when I should have been resolving my own problems, I have traumatized my psyche. He assures me I will get well. Sometimes he seems a bit over the rainbow to me.

I have terrible nightmares. I see bodies on stretchers, bloody but able to speak clearly enough to beg for death. I see body bags floating in air and water. I see bloody rivers and raging maniacal people wandering in search of water until they come to the barrels full of bodies. Almost biblical, don't you think? A few nights ago I saw Bobby Kennedy marching in the New York City Saint Patrick's Day parade, but he had no legs and a horribly elongated face. (And no, I haven't tried LSD, although it's been offered.) Sometimes I think the whole world has gone mad.

So tell me, why is Kate leaving a guy like Dave to come over here? So many of the things you tell me about Dave, what he says and what he thinks about politics and stuff, are very interesting. Did you tell me he had been over here? I seem to remember that. How can Kate go from working for Eugene McCarthy to volunteering for a war she doesn't believe in?

Some of the boys are angry with people back home. There's talk of castrating draft dodgers who go to Canada and resentment for the little rich boys who stay in college, or worse, manipulate their way into the National Guard. They're right of course, about the rich boys, I mean. When I meet officers who are in cushy desk jobs, inevitably they're upper crust. The boys who are fighting, being injured, and getting killed are country and inner city kids. They haven't had the benefit of a higher education and have little worldly experience. They realize soon enough they've been selected to do the dirty work. When the reality of their situation hits home some of them turn to drugs that are available everywhere. I say, whatever gets you through, especially when the outcome of this war seems so dark.

Oh, the power of the written word. If there's one thing I'll take away from my experiences over here, that's it. And the TV camera. They provoke a more powerful image of an event than the actual reality of the situation. Now that I have the time to read up on the things I've witnessed, I wonder if some of the newsmen have actually been in the same place as me. A few correspondents have been over here too long and are a little wacko. (It happens to the best of us.) That's a catch-22, isn't it? I mean: Have they been here so long they can see the overall picture more clearly than a short-timer, or have they been here so long their very experiences have distorted their reality? (Now I'm starting to sound like my psychiatrist.)

I've had some news of Bob. A nurse, who came over from the burn center in Texas, says he is still in the unit. When she left in June he was undergoing skin grafting. She said he is an angry and difficult patient. He faces years of grafting and hospital time. At least he is alive. But it makes me wonder how many of the boys we sent home curse us for helping them survive. I doubt we have done some of them a favor. I'm full of laughs, aren't I? Can you take one more? I've put in for Meridian for my next assignment. You and Kate being there were two good reasons, but there's another. Bob will eventually be discharged to his home of record. That's Kansas City. I have to see him, Sandy. Just once more. He owes me a good-bye. I can't hope to be normal again until I am done with him. Hope to see you in a few months.

As always,

Penny

The second letter was from Dave.

Chicago
August 9, 1968
Hi Sandy,

I hope things are okay at the duplex. I miss all of you guys and am looking forward to coming home soon. It will be a relief to have this part of the campaign finished. As the convention looms, our ranks remain split. Now McCarthy refuses to allow demonstrations. He wants to keep his platform clean and go into the convention with the message we can change the war if we can change the President. (For me, his belief in the power of one is a bunch of horse manure. One person, alone, cannot budge the establishment.) But, he makes my first foray into national politics interesting.

I feel we anti-war folks have been back-pedaling since LBJ copped out and we lost our best target. The war itself is far too nebulous to provide a good antagonist. That means we have no strong candidate to pit McCarthy against.

Rubin is dying to have a great confrontation and has surrounded himself with a motley group of druggies that frighten even me. I can't imagine middle-class Americans falling in line behind them but it does worry me. I can almost touch the violence that lies beneath the surface of the crowds. Dellinger wants passive protests outside the convention hall—a quiet stand of non-acceptance. I'm not sure we can pull it off. I have permits to take my students into the convention hall. I hope I'm wrong about the violence.

I stopped by to see my parents for a few days and thoroughly enjoyed the visit. I miss having Kate's help, but she writes she is busy getting ready for her big adventure.

Well, Sandy, it's down to the wire. I'll be driving home when the convention is over. Watch for me in the crowds on television. I'll wear a white hat, just for you. Wish me luck.

Dave

The third letter was an invitation and a short note from the 385th squadron.

Langley, Virginia

9 August 1968

Hey kid! Do we have great news for you! The fellows of the 385th are coming to Meridian on Labor Day weekend for the annual Hundred Mission Convention. Here are formal invitations for you and Kate. Hope you'll be there to help us celebrate.

385th, WGFP

∽

She was in the shower when Mike called. She hurried to the townhouse and nearly knocked a beer from his hand as she fell onto him. He kissed her until she was weak with her need for him.

"I'm wearing nothing under this shift," she whispered. He laughed, pulled the madras dress over her head, stood, and quickly removed his own clothing. "We should close the curtains," she said.

"Can't stop me now," he murmured as his touch sent shivers of desire through her.

Something hard bit into her back. She lifted her hips so he could remove a catalog and drop it onto the floor.

"You drive me nuts," he said.

"That's what you get for leaving me alone too long."

"You're going about this all wrong. If this is what I get on return, I'll go more often."

"Shh," she said. "Or you'll get way more than you bargained for."

"Try me," he said. "Let's see who's first to cry 'uncle.'"

Later, as they lay spent, he fished about on the floor with one hand until he was able to heft the discarded catalog onto his chest. "I have something for you," he said.

"What?"

"You'll see. Sit up."

He moved with her until the arm of the couch supported their backs and allowed them to read the catalog together. "I've been thinking about this for weeks," he said.

She watched as he opened the catalog to a marked page and pointed to pictures of glass stones. "What is it?" she asked.

"They're loose diamonds. I want you to pick one."

"Why?"

"Because I want to buy you one. I need you to choose a setting."

She gasped and sat up.

"We should choose a set of gold bands while we're at it."

"Mike! You don't mean it."

He smoothed her shoulder with one hand and kissed her. "I mean it."

"Oh, Mike!" She knocked the catalog from his chest and threw her arms around him. "Is this your idea of a proposal?"

"Will you pick one?"

"I say again, is this a proposal?"

He grinned and pulled her onto him. "Isn't it obvious?"

"No. Who in the world proposes with a catalog?"

"Surprised you, didn't I?"

"Yes."

"Will you marry me?"

"You idiot, of course I will."

He pulled her closer, kissed her face and hair. "Good," he said. "Life isn't worth living without you."

In the middle of the night, he turned on the light in the bedroom and insisted they get serious about the rings. Together they chose a setting and a diamond and he chose two intricately carved gold bands. In the morning she showered quickly and woke him with a kiss.

He opened his eyes. "You aren't going to change your mind, are you? I'm sending this order in today."

"I'll never change my mind," she said. "I'm going to open the door and shout it to the world."

But when she arrived on the ward and Jim Andersen looked up from his desk and said, "You look awfully happy this morning. Mike must be home," she didn't tell him she'd become engaged, and when Major Roberts said, "You look so refreshed. That man must treat you awfully good," she didn't take the opportunity to say, "And he wants to marry me, too." She hugged her secret to her the entire day because she wanted Dave and Kate to be the first to know.

Sanity returned, and with it the decision that she wouldn't tell anyone on base until Mike placed the ring on her finger. At home she called Rita, because Sandy wanted her to know she wasn't a fallen woman after all.

That evening, Zeke joined them at their table at the club. "Hey Mike, have you signed up for the convention?"

"That's affirmative," Mike answered. "How about you?"

"Did it today," Zeke said.

Sandy waited until Zeke was out of earshot before she said, "I'm going to the convention too."

"Not so fast," he laughed. "It's invitation only, and a man's thing."

"I have an invitation," she said. "Kate and I were both invited."

He stopped smiling. "But you're not going."

"Of course we are."

"No, you're not."

She was sure he was teasing. "Who are you to say whether I go or not, Mr. Smarty Pants?" she quipped.

"You don't belong there."

"You can't be serious."

"I am. It's not a place for women."

"My friends must think it is, or they wouldn't have invited us."

He was shaking his head.

"Mike? I don't understand."

"Why would you want to be with a bunch of drunk pilots? And with Kate, no less. What's she going to do, go for a record?"

"I can't believe you're saying this. It's not like you're the only person in my life. I've been invited and I'll go."

He threw his napkin onto the table. "Fine. Hang out with Kate. Cheapen yourself. But don't tell anyone you're my girl." He stood and grabbed her shoulder. "Let's go," he said. "I've lost my appetite."

He drove her home and dropped her at the door without a word or a kiss. The next morning he left for Nevada.

She called Sarah to ask for advice.

"Some of the women from my neighborhood are going," Sarah said. "I'd love to go too, but I have a meeting in D.C."

"Washington, D.C.?" Sandy asked. "Why are you going there?"

"We're organizing, Sandy. The POW wives are going national. No one seems to care about our husbands, so we're going to put pressure on the administration until they sit up, take notice, and bring our men home."

"Wow. You girls are brave."

"Somebody has to fight. I'm sure learning a lot. And, Sandy?"

"What?"

"Not standing up for what you believe in, and not taking action on what your intuition tells you, is self-defeating. If I were you, I

wouldn't worry about what your boyfriend thinks. Go to the convention, have a good time, and don't look back."

Sandy felt better after their conversation. When Mike learned
other women would be at the reunion, he would have to admit she
should go.

He showed up at her door Saturday morning, still wearing his
flight suit. She fell into his arms.

"You missed me," he said.

"Yes."

"Good."

He pulled away and held her at arm's length. "And you've forgotten all about the convention?"

"I talked to Sarah—" she began, but he interrupted.

"What? Sarah who?" He had the strangest look on his face.

"Sarah Robins. My war widow friend from north base housing. "

"I didn't know you know Sarah."

"I didn't think you knew her, either. She hasn't been down this
way for months."

"What about her?"

"I called her and she said that women from north base housing
have been invited and are going. Kate and I won't be the only girls
there."

"I don't want you to go."

"Why?"

"I just don't."

"That's not a good reason."

He dropped his hands. "You go and I'll stay home."

"Mike?"

He turned to leave.

"You're not going to make me choose between you and my old
friends, are you?" she asked.

"Are you going to do the same to me?"

"I don't understand."

"And I won't explain." He strode down the walk.

She waited until he had driven away before she called Kate and asked what she thought about his actions.

Kate answered with a laugh and then said, "He's a guy. What do you expect?"

"I expect him to get over it," she said. "Do you think he will?"

Kate didn't hesitate. "If he treated me like that, I'd say to hell with him, go to the convention, and dance the night away. But, then, you know me. I wouldn't spend the entire night dancing, but I'd sure let him know he couldn't boss me around."

∽

Sandy thought about her decision through another week of silence before she began shopping for a dress.

On the evening of the convention, her mascara brush quivered as she did her makeup. When her face was done, she said aloud, "That's good," and then laughed because her own voice startled her. She had been alone before Mike came into her life, and she had grown used to it, but now two weeks without him was impossibly long. She didn't want to ever be alone like this again.

∽

At the hotel, she and Kate were greeted by excited voices and wrapped in hugs.

"Jesus! You look great! One in a million!" Randy shouted above the din.

"Sure, Randy," Sandy said. "I heard you say exactly the same thing to Kate."

"Oh, well, Kate." He worried one hand over the back of his neck and raised his eyes toward the ceiling. "If Kate were an angel, I'd change my mind and request heaven when I leave this world."

"You'd be out of place up there, my friend," Tim said from behind Sandy. The two men shook hands.

Someone shouted across the room, "Sandy! Kate! Over here!" The men pressed her forward. A tremor of fear, the kind she felt the night Zeke had auctioned her off, ran through her. Maybe it was a mistake to come, she thought. Maybe there were too few women and too many men. She forced herself to smile. As she took an offered seat at the table, she pulled her dress over her knees and crossed her ankles. Randy caught the gesture and laughed. "Same old Sandy, I see."

Sandy returned his smile. "And same old Randy."

"Not really," he said. "I've been relegated to a desk job. I'm teaching at the academy. Who would've thought?"

"You're not flying?"

He shook his head. "Not married either." He waved his hand to show his wedding band was missing.

"Oh, no!"

"I don't take it personally, kid. One of the ravages of war."

She studied his face as he turned to greet another pilot. There was sadness in his eyes, and he had deep grooves on the sides of his mouth. His brash swagger had been replaced by a false cheeriness.

He turned back to her. "She hardly waited until I'd stepped off the plane before presenting me with papers. Great homecoming."

"At least she waited until it was over," another man said. "Mine sent the news by cable before I'd flown my fiftieth mission. Made for one hell of a wild R and R though."

"I wish she'd told me earlier," Randy said. "I could have enjoyed Hawaii too. Having her there was like taking a box lunch to a presidential dinner." He raised his glass for a toast.

Someone shouted, "Hear, hear."

"That's sad," Sandy said.

"But so true," Randy added. "Hawaii in the middle of a war was a big mistake—trivial, after all the uppers of flying combat and dodging missiles. Hell, it wasn't possible to have anything in common with my wife."

At the table behind her she heard a woman's voice. She started to turn to smile, until she caught the woman's words. "What's up with Mike and Shirley? Wasn't he bringing her?"

She couldn't hear the answer. It couldn't be her Mike, she decided, but when the double doors from the kitchen opened and shed light on a table at the farthest wall, she clearly saw Mike standing with Zeke and a bevy of women. Sandy turned her ear toward the table behind her again and caught a few more words.

"… mad about him. And I thought he was about her too."

The second woman's voice said, "She's serious, but I think he's just fooling around. I hear he has a girlfriend at Meridian."

"He must be quite a stud. He's been staying over at Shirley's for days at a time."

"Have you seen him there?"

"Sure. When I was having that fling with Zeke, they drove up together. He's much smoother than Zeke. Shirley's head over heels for him."

"I can understand. He's got it all: money, looks, charm. What more could a girl want?"

Across the table, Tim was staring at her with a look of concern. She felt her stomach churn. She was going to be sick.

She tried to concentrate on what Randy was saying. "We couldn't hook up. She was full of problems and funny little stories about the kids. I couldn't wait to get back to the war. But I didn't realize what she meant to my sanity. World's greatest fighter pilot, world's greatest father, world's greatest flop."

A waitress placed a dinner plate in front of her. She felt her stomach churn again.

"Now I can ask you out, Sandy," Randy tried.

"Won't get you anywhere," Tim said. "Already hooked up."

"Is that right, Sandy?" Randy asked.

She nodded numbly as forks began to rattle against glasses. A drink. Her mouth was dry. She needed a drink. She lifted her wine glass and emptied it. She shouldn't have come. She became aware of a deep silence settling over the crowded room. "Angel passing by," she said softly.

"Where?" Randy stood, put his hand on his forehead, and scanned the room. Everyone at the table laughed.

"Down, boy," someone said.

"I was sure you meant Kate," someone said. "Ah, yes, you did. Here she comes."

Kate was heading their way. Before she had moved a few yards, Mike pulled her to one side. Behind her Sandy heard the woman say, "I wonder if that's his girlfriend?"

"Not her," the other voice said. "That one is a nurse, but a real sleep-around."

"Seems like they'd make a pair," the first woman said with a laugh. "Mike's done just about every girl in our circle."

"Including you?"

Sandy didn't hear the answer. She stood and searched for a way out of the room. Randy put up a restraining hand. "Where you going, Sandy?"

"To the ladies' room. Do you know where it is?"

He pointed toward a lighted hallway.

The room reeked of deodorizer. Bitter wine rose into her throat. She went into a stall and struggled to stay on her feet.

"Sandy?" Kate's voice echoed against tile.

She didn't answer.

"Hey, I know you're in here. I can see your shoes. You all right?"

She wanted to run. She wanted to go back to Maine, but there was nothing there for her either. There was nowhere to hide.

"When I saw Mike with all those women I went over and asked him what he was doing. Do you know what he said? He said he was fucking with your brain. You need to go out there and scratch his eyes out," Kate called through the door. "You shouldn't hide in here and cry."

"I'm not crying," she called back.

"Then what are you doing?"

"I'm throwing up."

"That's even worse. Are you done?"

"Yes. With all of it."

"Then get out there and tell him off."

"I don't want to make a scene."

"You have every right to make a scene."

"I want to go home."

"Okay," she said. "Come out and let's go before I can't control myself and I tell the jerk where to get off."

Kate drove her home and offered to stay, but Sandy turned her away.

She splashed cold water on her face and grabbed a towel. Mike's aftershave filled her nostrils and caused a pain-filled moan to escape from the center of her soul. She wrapped the towel in her arms and, still fully dressed, curled up under her Asian quilt. Everything she had thought real was a mirage. How could she have been so naïve? How could he have been so deceptive? She tossed and turned, but couldn't cry. Her heart raced, her breathing stuttered. She wanted to feel pure anger, to be like Kate, to demand answers. By the time she realized there were no answers, only more questions, she had fallen into a restless sleep.

The doorbell jarred her fully awake. The bedside clock read four-thirty a.m. She knew it was Mike, as clearly as she knew that he had to be faced. She moved slowly to the door, opened it, stepped aside, and allowed him to enter.

He stumbled and steadied himself on one arm of the sofa before he threw himself heavily onto the cushions. "Did you have a good time?" he asked.

She sat on the arm of the chair opposite. "Did you?"

"I asked first."

"I had a lousy time."

"I warned you."

"About what? About all the times you were supposed to be TDY but were actually out partying with Zeke and sleeping with every willing woman in the war widows' annex?"

He shook his head. "None of that means anything."

"Oh, Mike. Maybe not to you."

"There is only one girl for me."

"And I thought that was me."

"It was. It is."

"What about Shirley?"

"Fuck Shirley."

"I heard you did."

"Ah, for Christ's sake, Sandy. What are we talking about here?"

"I don't know. I don't think there's anything that can be said. Go home, Mike. Please, just go home."

"I'm not going anywhere." He crossed his legs and settled one hand on his knee. "I'm staying right here. We're going to clear this thing up. We're going to set some rules. We're going to decide on our future."

"We have no future." She stood and opened the door. "Go home."

He stood, slammed the door, and held her paralyzed with his eyes. "We're engaged, remember?" he said softly. "Me and you. We're going to be married."

As she watched his finger wag between them like a worm dangling on the end of a fishing line, hatred filled her. "Over my dead body," she hissed. He pulled her to him and tried to kiss her. His breath reeked of alcohol. She pushed away.

"Get out of here," she said. "Just go."

"You don't mean that. Not even for a minute. You won't give up on me because of a few recreational fucks."

"Is that what you call it?"

"Don't give me any high-and-mighty moral shit. You're getting what you want."

"Who do you think you're talking to?"

"I'm talking to you, Lieutenant O'Connell, ma'am." As he bowed drunkenly toward her, his face contorted with pain and his voice faltered. "I'm talking to you, Sandy." He said her name so softly and with so much love she felt herself soften and begin to yield. He opened his arms and held them out toward her. "Please. Come here."

A deep sorrow filled her, made her want to fall into his arms, to be comforted by him, and to go back to the way it was. But her intellect said he had held other women in those arms and begged other women to come to him. An intense intuition of deception overpowered her softer side.

"Go home, Mike." The strength of her voice surprised them both. "Go home. We'll talk about this tomorrow."

"Tomorrow will be too late. We have to sort this out tonight."

"There's nothing to sort out."

"We need rules."

She shook her head.

"Yes," he said. "We need some rules of you and me."

"There is no you and me."

"Of course there is. We're great together. How do you think our marriage should work, Sandy? Could we allow for an occasional outside fuck? For variety? To keep the home fires hot?"

"Stop! Please! We're not having a marriage, Mike. We're not having anything."

"What? Just like that? Forget the whole thing? Come on, Sandy. You're a bigger girl than that."

She reached past him and opened the door again.

"I see. One little slip from Mike and it's all over. One little step over the line and we're through. I don't play the game like that, Sandy. That's not my style."

"I heard about your style tonight. I heard the women talking about you, Mike. About how many nights you spent at Shirley's and how you slept with as many of the war widows as were willing. It made me vomit. I loved you." Pain overwhelmed her. "I don't understand." She needed him to go so she could breathe.

"Don't be stupid, Sandy. Throw me away and you'll be throwing away more than you'll ever know. I love you. Those women meant absolutely nothing to me."

He jerked her closer until their eyes were locked together. "Tell me that doesn't matter to you."

He caught her hand before the slap could reach his face.

"Get out," she said. "Just get out." His lips were so close she could breathe in his essence.

He released her. "If that's how you want it. Fine. I'll forget I ever knew you. I'll forget all about you. But let me tell you this, girl. You'll never forget me. I'll make sure of it. You'll never forget me. Never."

He turned and staggered onto the porch.

She closed the door with both hands and held it closed. It was over. The big warm love of her life was done. She should cry hysterically. She should scream until the pain subsided. She should run after him and shout obscenities. Instead, she turned, leaned her back against the door, and stared, thoughtless and without hope, at her snow-white walls.

CHAPTER ELEVEN

The Kansas sun forced its way through the low front window. Sandy stumbled to her bedroom, pulled off her dancing dress and pulled on her white stockings, threaded shining white buttons into the holes on her starched white uniform, and drove, white-faced and white-lipped, through the white-hot pain of lost love, to her place of duty.

There were only two patients and both were waiting for discharge. Her staff gathered in the ward kitchen, sipped coffee, and laughed often as they planned a surprise baby shower for Cindy. Sandy stood at the side door and watched the flashing blue lights of the crash crew disappear behind the flight line. One of the corpsmen came in with a cartload of supplies and said, "I heard on the radio a Thud is down in some farmer's field west of the city."

Sandy walked with him to the utility room and began restocking the supplies. She wouldn't think about a crash. She wouldn't think it could be Mike. Methodically she placed linen covered trays onto shelves, hefted jugs of antiseptic liquids into low cabinets. As she worked she tried to hold back the feeling that is *was* Mike. The realization came to her clearly. Her intuition knew it was so.

Kate came to the door. "One of the 385th has bought it," she said. "They say it's official."

"I know," Sandy said. "It's Mike."

Kate's eyes widened. "Don't be silly, O'Connell. I went back to the reunion. By the time it was over, Mike was too drunk to drive, let alone fly. You know the rules."

"He doesn't believe in rules."

"He wouldn't mess with his flying status," Kate said.

Sandy continued putting white sterile packs into drawers until Kate gave up and walked away. Restocking done, she moved to the center of the room and stared until the green walls became white and the tiled floor turned to ice. She heard someone answer the telephone at her desk. A murmur of voices filtered in from the break room before an unearthly silence settled over the unit.

She waited until she heard the double doors at the far end of the unit open and close before she forced her legs to take her to the middle of the hall. She turned and faced the four people moving toward her—Kate, Chaplain Terrence, Major Roberts, and Jim Andersen. Kate broke from the group and ran to her. Sandy felt her legs become rubber as whiteness enveloped her. When Kate's words came to her it was through a haze of white noise.

"Sandy, I'm sorry. I'm so sorry."

Something painful stung her arm. Someone told her to sit. Another voice told her to walk. She allowed herself to be guided into a bright light. "It's hitting her now," she heard Major Roberts say. "Take her home."

She wanted to go home, to start over in Maine, to have another chance, but she knew it was fruitless to expect redemption. She hadn't been to confession in months and had swallowed a birth control pill yesterday.

Someone asked her what was funny when she laughed. She didn't know. She was floating, light and weightless, into a sea of white. She was in a lovely dream, being swept along by gentle currents, bumping into soft pillows as light and weightless as she. She was nothing. She was nothing at all.

ை

"How is she?" a voice whispered. Billowing whiteness became pink, red, and finally startling black. The wild beating of her heart caused her to stir. She opened her eyes and looked about. She was in her bed, under her bright quilt, and it was night.

Something was wrong. Everything was wrong.

If only she could stop right here.

She stared at dim walls, a blank canvas, and her last fling at purity.

Stop, she silently begged. Give me back this space. Please give me another chance.

A glimmer of light showed from her living room. Voices murmured. Mike. Mike was here. No. Dave. Dave and Kate. She reached behind her, felt the empty space on the bed. Mike wasn't sleeping with her. Because Mike was sleeping with everyone else.

She sat up, propelled by the sound of someone screaming. A light came on. She closed her eyes against it.

"It's okay, kid. It's okay," Dave's voice said.

She tried to push him away, but her arms were weak. She lay back. "No more," she said.

"No more what?" he asked.

"Just no more. Nothing. No more."

"What, Sandy?" Kate asked.

"The shots. I felt the shots. No more."

"But—" Kate started.

"She's right," Dave said. "No use putting it off. She has to face it eventually."

She felt his cheek close to hers. "I'm sorry, Sandy," he said. "I am so sorry."

Her body was rigid in his arms. She opened her eyes.

Kate stood behind him. "Feeling better?" she asked.

"I feel terrible."

"I'll help you stand. Come on." Dave pulled the quilt away. Sandy was still wearing her scrubs.

"You look tired," she said as he helped her to her feet.

"Chicago was the pits," he said.

"Life is the pits."

"Are you hungry?"

She shook her head.

"Dumb question," Kate said.

"What time is it?" Sandy asked.

"Eight-thirty."

"What day?"

"Same day, Sandy." Kate stopped as they entered the hallway. "There are people waiting," she whispered. "They want to ask you some questions."

"Who?"

"The general, Major Roberts, and Mike's flight surgeon."

"I can't talk to them."

"You have to."

"No," she said.

Dave moved her into the bathroom. "Kate, tell them she just got sick and they will have to wait until tomorrow." He closed the bathroom door.

"I'll go with you tomorrow," he said as he settled her on the closed commode.

"I won't go tomorrow either."

His voice became hollow and distant. "Sandy? Sandy?" She could hear worry in his tone but it didn't matter. Nothing mattered. She gave herself up to the whiteness.

෴

Morning. The sun shone through her open window blinds. Her bladder called for relief. She pushed the quilt aside and staggered toward the bathroom. Kate stood in the way.

"Have to piddle," Sandy said.

"Good," Kate said. "When you're finished I have some coffee on."

Sandy held a cold washcloth to her face and leaned against the sink. In the mirror her face appeared shrunken under flat strands of tangled hair. She brushed out the tangles, took several deep breaths, and walked to the kitchen.

Kate sat at the table holding a mug of coffee in both hands. "You all right?"

A full cup sat before an empty chair.

Sandy sat in the chair. "Will I ever be?"

"In time."

She sipped the bitter liquid.

"There's a meeting at 1300 hours."

"Why?"

"They have questions about the accident. They're convening a board to investigate."

"Mike's flying has nothing to do with me."

"They want to know about the twenty-four hours before. What he did. Where he went."

"Everyone knows where he was. I don't know what he did."

"You'll never get away with that."

"Shut up, Kate! Just shut up!" She stood and stumbled to the living room.

"Come back here!" Kate shouted.

Sandy sank into the living room chair and stared at her magic white walls.

Kate followed. "You have to do it. There's no way out."

"I didn't mean to yell at you."

"Yell all you want. I'll scream too. What else can we do?"

"Cry."

"Can you?"

"No."

"Me either." Kate flopped onto the couch.

"Will you go with me?"

"Yes, and Dave too. He's coming back at noon."

"Did the major give you the day to babysit?"

"Yes."

"Then we'd better get on with the job. I'll get dressed."

∾

She felt very small in the chair, surrounded by men in uniform. The general hadn't allowed Kate or Dave in. A secretary recorded questions and answers.

"You called Mike's moodiness 'graduation syndrome.' What did you mean by that?" the general asked.

"That he was uptight before his squadron's graduation."

"Only at that particular time?"

"No. Particularly at that time."

"Did you often see him upset?"

She shook her head and studied the ribbons on his uniform.

"How long did his 'graduation syndrome' last?" he asked.

"A couple of weeks."

"And what prompted its ending?"

"I don't know."

"Why do you think he acted moody and angry?"

"I'm not a psychiatrist. Ask someone else."

Everyone shifted restlessly.

"I'm only interested in what you think," the general persisted.

"I can't think."

"You said Mike became sullen and distant around the time of his squadron's graduations. How many times did this happen?"

"How many graduations was he here for?"

The flight surgeon interrupted. "Did Mike ever experience weak spells? Dizziness? Heart palpitations?"

"He was never sick."

The flight surgeon tossed a heavy file on the table between them. "He took a lot of time off for sick call," he said.

That surprised her. "Did he?"

The general leaned back in his chair and tugged on his jacket to pull the buttons into line. "No one ever found a basis for his symptoms."

"Did you see Mike in the twenty-four hours before his accident?" the flight surgeon asked.

"Yes."

"Where?"

"At the Hundred Mission Convention."

"You were there together?"

She glanced quickly about the room. "No. I went with Kate. Mike drove himself."

"Alone?" the general asked.

"I don't know."

"Did he appear stressed?" the flight surgeon interrupted.

"I don't know."

"What did you talk about?" he asked.

"At the convention?"

"Yes."

"We didn't talk. He was at another table."

"And you didn't speak to him all evening?" he persisted.

She shook her head.

The general stood and paced to the window and back. "Sandy," he asked, "did you see him after the convention?"

"Yes."

"Where was that?"

"At my place."

"What time?" he asked.

"I lost track of time."

"Was it morning?"

"No. It was dark."

"What kind of mood was he in?" the flight surgeon asked.

"He was angry."

"Did you argue?"

"Yes."

"But you made up?" General Magnem interjected.

"No."

"Had he been drinking?" the flight surgeon persisted.

"We all had."

"After you argued, did he leave?"

"Yes."

"What time was that?" the general asked.

"I don't know."

"Was the sun up?"

She shook her head.

The flight surgeon retrieved Mike's medical record, neatened it so all the sheets lined up, and placed it on the table. "And he went home?" he asked.

She nodded. "I think so."

A tall man she hadn't noticed stepped forward from the corner. "Did it occur to you that he'd had too much to drink to drive?"

"To drive?" She was astounded by the question. "Of course he had too much to drive."

"And did you think to stop him?"

"He lives up the street from me. I didn't care how he got home."

"So you didn't just have an argument. It was more serious than that?"

"We broke up," she said.

"Can I ask you why?"

"No."

She saw the general smile, heard the flight surgeon mumble, "So we have a slight time lapse. A few hours unaccounted for."

The tall man answered, "Yes. Let me see that statement from his friend again."

The tall man's eyes bored into hers. "You're absolutely sure he didn't spend the night?"

"I would tell you if he had."

"Ah, here. 'I met him at base ops at 0800 hours. He was still in his suit from the convention. He asked to fly.' That's from Captain Zeke Spencer."

"There's more, isn't there?" the general asked.

"Yes." The tall man turned a page and continued. 'I asked him if he had slept and he laughed and said, *Of course I did. Didn't you? I* asked him where he'd slept and he said, *With my girl.*'" He looked at Sandy again. "And you say he left at five. Are you sure about that?"

"I didn't say a time," she said. The wall behind him was neither gray nor green nor white but rather a wide transparent glow of nothing. It didn't matter. Nothing mattered. She rested her eyes on the wall and began to blot out the pain, pass above the voices, and go beyond the anger rising in her chest. She heard the general's voice coming from inside a deep tunnel.

"Sandy? Sandy?"

She thought she heard Kate and Dave, or maybe it was the flight surgeon. She couldn't tell. She closed her eyes and floated away.

ᥬ

Dave insisted she attend the memorial service. Kate helped her dress. Black sweater. Black wool skirt. A comb run through her tangled hair. Black shoes clicking across the parking lot of the base chapel. They helped her to a seat.

"How many times have you done this, Dave?" Kate asked.

"One too many," he answered.

Zeke came into her field of vision, with a tiny blond girl wearing a wrinkled dress and no makeup clinging to his arm. Her eyes were red-rimmed. Her face was gray. A jolt of recognition made

Sandy look again. It was the blond girl she had seen in the park the night she had looked for Mike—the one who had made her jealous as she laughed at her tall companion. That was Mike, she realized. And the girl must be Shirley. Sandy had expected her to appear matronly, wife like.

As he helped the girl to a seat, Zeke turned and flashed a know-ing smile. She held his gaze until he turned away. When the service was done, she waited as Zeke allowed the girl to exit first.

"Why, Zeke? Can you tell me why?" she whispered.

He shrugged his shoulders. "Because he could." She heard his low laughter long after he was gone.

∽

Kate's orders had been cut and she had to go. Dave insisted Sandy go to the airport with them. Sandy hugged her friend and moved to the back of the terminal so the couple could say their good-byes.

Dave was quiet as they returned to the duplex, where they found Cindy waiting on the porch. "Mailman was here. I hope you don't mind, I signed for a package." She followed Sandy into her apartment.

"I'm going to run into my place for a minute," Dave said.

Sandy showed no interest in the package.

Cindy placed it on the television. "How are you doing?"

"They shot me full of Valium. It's taking a long time to wear off."

"I know how hard this is. When B.B. bought it, I didn't want to go on, but at least I had this baby to look forward to. I want to help. If you get really sad will you call me?"

Sandy nodded.

"And you're okay? Truly?"

"I think so."

They stood looking at one another until Sandy turned away and settled into a chair. She wanted to be alone.

Dave came to the door. "You ladies okay?"

"Yes," Cindy said. "I was just leaving."

"I'll drive you home. Sandy, will you ride along?"

"No. You go ahead."

"Why don't you come with me?"

"No." She met his eyes to reassure him.

He stepped forward as if he would insist, but she stopped him with an upraised hand. "I'm fine. Honest. I need to be alone for a while."

She stood, locked the door after them, and began to pace the room. How had it come to this? What had she done that was so wrong? She hadn't loved Mike when she decided to sleep with him. But she had been a virgin far too long and he was a good choice, the perfect choice. They had fallen in love.

How could that have been so bad? She went into the hallway and began to alternately shout and thump the walls. "Why didn't I do something to stop him? Why didn't I see his pain?" Her pace increased, became more frantic. "How could he have lied to me all those times? Why did he ask me to marry him?" She screamed at the white walls, demanded they answer her.

The walls echoed her words. She couldn't breathe. She had to get away. She ran to her car and drove to the river.

Clouds hung along the horizon, holding tight to the last piercing rays of sun that bled gold onto the brown landscape. The wind blew from the north, cold and full of moisture. A few leaves swirled in mini tornadoes on the pavement. She hadn't worn a coat.

She folded her arms across her chest and hurried to their spot along the curve of the Arkansas. She threw herself onto the grass and stared at the silted, slow-moving stream. "You should be here, Mike," she said aloud. "I am so sorry. So sorry."

A movement in the dry rushes caught her eye. A sleek black river rat crept along the water's edge. It raised its head and peered at her. "Eye to eye," she said, "but never soul to soul."

The rat scampered toward the river. She stood and moved forward until she could see its tail slithering lightly on the water's surface. Its movement in the stream cut the water into rippled lines. Three feet out, it turned and looked back. She moved to the river's edge. The rat paddled slowly in a circle and watched her.

The musty smell of rot filled her nostrils. She was guilty—guilty of letting Mike down, of not listening, of judging harshly. No, he had let her down. He was the one who had destroyed them. It was all his doing.

She buried her face in her hands. The tall man at the inquiry had known she was the guilty one. A dry sob escaped her. She'd made one mistake and now Mike was dead. She opened her eyes and looked to the river again. The rat waited. Flies buzzed about her head. She stepped into the water.

"Hey, lady!" The voice came from behind her, high up on the bank.

She moved into the water, felt the heels of her shoes sink into the slime. The water was surprisingly tepid. It splashed soothingly about her ankles and then her calves. The rat moved into the deepest part of the river.

"Hey, lady!" the voice called again.

She lifted her head and turned. A boy stood on the bank. He had clear blue eyes and brand-new front teeth that were slightly crooked. His brow was fixed in a worried frown. "I wouldn't do that if I were you, lady. My mom says that water is polluted from the summer runoff. You're gonna get sick."

"It's not polluted," she said.

"Yes, it is. Can't you see that rat?"

"It doesn't scare me."

"It will bite you."

She was suddenly confused. Why had she come here?

The boy backed up, as if afraid.

The water had become colder. Its chill penetrated her feet, but when she tried to move, her shoes stuck fast in the mud. "Oh, hell!" she shouted as she lost her footing and her shoes.

"You shouldn't say bad words either." The boy backed into the grove of cottonwood trees. "God won't like you if you curse."

She stepped from the water in her bare feet. "God doesn't like me anyway." She crested the hill and stood a few feet from him.

"Yes, he does."

"Oh? How do you know?" She was suddenly too exhausted to go farther. She sat on the grass.

"Because," he said so softly she could barely hear him, "he made you pretty. He wouldn't have done that if he didn't like you."

"Does that mean God doesn't like ugly people?"

"No. He gives them other gifts. Ones you can't see so good."

"Who told you that?"

"My mom."

She stood again and looked upward through the ancient trees. "Your mom must be pretty smart," she said.

"Yep. But my dad is smarter."

"Why is that?"

"He knows lots of things. He sells cars and makes lots of money."

"Is that what you're going to do when you grow up?"

"No!" he shouted. "I'm going to be a priest."

He turned and bolted into the park.

She followed.

He disappeared across the parking lot and into the street. She stood at her car and caught her breath. Inside, she laid her head on the steering wheel and closed her eyes.

She wouldn't recall driving home. She had a vague recollection of Dave waiting by her door, scolding and upset. She remembered him rinsing the filth from her feet and helping her into her scrubs. And she remembered climbing under the quilt of many colors to find the deep peace that waited in the depths of her white walls.

                            ᥫᩬ

Voices came and went: Dave, Cindy, Major Roberts. Darkness turned to light and back to dark again. Jim Andersen held her hand. His voice was kind. "Come on, Sandy. Come back to us," he begged.

Someone brought tea; the smell made her stomach churn and she turned away. Tim and Ann stood beside her bed.

"Zeke is gone," Tim said. "Reassigned to Point Barrow, Alaska. You'll never have to deal with him again." That put some color onto the wall.

She drifted in a silent world until the odor of turpentine burned her nostrils. She opened her eyes and saw a man painting on the wall. Hallucination, she thought, and drifted away.

When she awoke next, there were trees with orange and yellow foliage and sturdy earth-bound trunks growing on the wall. The man was still there, a paintbrush in his hand, whistling mindlessly as he grew another tree. She watched him without speaking.

Sometime later she heard water running. Cindy came in, pulled her from the bed, and insisted she bathe. She obeyed, allowed the girl to shampoo her hair and wrap her in a robe. "What day is it?" Sandy asked.

"Saturday. The seventeenth," Cindy answered.

She nodded and turned away.

"Dave's taking you for a ride, so you'll have to get dressed," Cindy said. "Here are your clothes."

She started to refuse, but Cindy's eyes said she was not being given a choice.

She pulled on the jeans and shirt. "Where did you get these?" she asked. "They're not mine. They're too big."

"They are yours. I pulled them from your drawer. You haven't been eating."

"Yes, I have," she countered.

"Ha! Tea and toast is not food."

Cindy walked her to Dave's waiting car. The sun was warm. The wind was cold.

She slipped into the car and allowed Dave to place a blanket over her knees as if she were an invalid. "I'm not sick," she said.

"Bet me," he countered.

He turned west into the sun. "Aren't you going to ask where we're going?"

"No."

"Not interested?"

She looked fully on him. "I trust you."

"Did you like the wall of trees?"

"Yes. Who was that man?"

"One of the art students. Sandy?"

"What?"

"Maybe you should go home for a while. Recharge your batteries. Spend some time with that good friend of yours."

"Rita?"

"Have you considered that?"

"The last time I talked to Rita, she said my lifestyle was against her Christian beliefs. She said I'd made my bed, now she hoped I'd enjoy lying in it. That's pretty much what most of my family would say." She looked out at a dust cloud blowing over the open plain. "Not a good day," she said.

"No, there don't seem to be many good days lately."

His words caught her attention. She watched him for a few minutes before she asked, "Are you okay?"

"Feeling a bit more cynical and no wiser," he said.

"Me too."

He patted her knee and caused the car to swerve. The movement made her light-headed.

"I think I'm hungry," she said.

"It's about time."

She'd been in hibernation, suspended in a painful sphere that required no sustenance. She raised her face to the sun, leaned back on the seat, and closed her eyes.

After what seemed like a very long time she felt the car slow, turn, and stop. She opened her eyes and watched Dave push open a pasture gate. They drove under a thin canopy of maple and cottonwood trees above a small ravine where a stream of water ran into a natural rock pool.

"It looks like home," she said.

"I thought it might. It belongs to a friend from the university. He plans to build a house here someday."

He pulled a cooler from the trunk and carried it to a grassy spot above the pool. "Cindy packed us lunch."

They sat on a blanket, ate sandwiches, and drank an entire bottle of wine. "If I'd brought my suit I would swim," she said.

"I won't look if you don't."

They stripped to their underclothes and climbed down to the water. Her body trembled as the icy water covered her. She ducked her head and allowed herself to sink. Dave pulled her up. She floundered near the middle of the pool. "Float for a bit," he said. "You're still weak."

She floated on her back, opened her eyes to the sky, inhaled the scent of water mixed with the dust of the land, and began breathing normally again. He swam by her side.

They lay together on the blanket. He pulled the tablecloth from the picnic hamper to cover her chilled skin.

When she was warm, she sat up and wriggled her toes in the Kansas dust. He turned on his side and rose up on one elbow.

"Do you want to talk about what happened?" he asked.

She shook her head.

"You'll have to someday."

"Not if I don't want to. Let's talk about something else. What did you do? You went to the convention. How was that?'

He laughed. "You always have been good at changing the subject."

"That's the nurse in me," she said. "Always best to steer away from painful things."

"Then we definitely shouldn't talk about Chicago."

"Was it bad?"

"Worse."

"Who got the nomination?"

"Humphrey."

"You worked so hard."

He lay on his back and closed his eyes. "Too many strong personalities, wild ideas, free drugs, and rumors."

"What kind of rumors?"

"That we were going to put LSD in Chicago's water supply. Mayor Daley wouldn't have us messing with his city. He activated the National Guard. It was us against the Army."

Sandy turned on her side and stared at him.

"We wanted to march quietly but he said they would shoot to kill."

"Kill protesters?"

"I should have known better. I knew about the Madison riot last year and how the cops went wild with clubs. I didn't believe they would actually use violence against a bunch of kids at a public convention."

"That happened?"

He nodded. "Daley sent in bulls. They beat the hell out of us. I had a group of twenty-two clean-cut kids. We made it to some park just as some guy took down the flag and hung his bloodied shirt from the pole. That really pissed off the cops. They came marching in, swinging their clubs and chanting 'Kill! Kill! Kill!' It was unbelievable."

"Why?"

He shrugged. "I don't know."

"Was that the end?"

"No. The next night we went to the convention hall to hear the acceptance speeches. It was supposed to be an educational look at our political process. They wouldn't honor our passes to the hall. We were trying to decide what to do when another busload of cops arrived. They made a bloody mess of my kids. We made a run for it, but a big cop stepped in my way and said, 'Come on you fucking commie, come and get it.' Something snapped. I knew I couldn't let them hit another kid. I beat the living crap out of a uniformed cop."

He took a deep breath and shielded his eyes with one arm. "I won't ever be that naive again. I learned we have no rights when the enemy is the government." He moved his arm and squinted up at her. "The rich and powerful have taken over. It's us against an elitist few. If it takes my entire life, I am going to fight for what we've lost."

She was tired and cold again. She lay down and pulled the tablecloth over them both. They dozed.

⚭

She dreamed Mike was sleeping with her, snuggled against her back with one arm lying loosely across her breasts. She pushed gently against him and felt him respond, but when she awoke slowly from the dream, she realized it was Dave who was aroused and that it was his attempt to gently disentangle himself that had stirred her.

In that dreamlike state, she pulled up her knees and removed her panties, turned, wrapped her arms around his neck, and pressed her invitation close to him.

"Please," she whispered. "I want to feel alive again."

"This is wrong," she heard him say, but their bodies were too close and too warm. Neither of them hesitated again.

Afterward, she lay with her eyes closed, her body sated, but her soul remorseful. She had used Dave's kindness, and it meant nothing.

"I'm sorry," she said.

"Why?" he murmured in her ear.

"I have no self-control."

"We take comfort where we find it," he said. "It's not a big deal."

"I've prided myself on fidelity."

"And you're being faithful to whom?"

"Another illusion shattered." The lightness of her laugh surprised them both.

"At least you haven't lost your sense of irony," he said.

"You know what's ironic? All that time I was so in love and so faithful, Mike was fooling around. Did you know that?"

"Kate had heard rumors, but I didn't think they were true."

"They were. He was doing the war widows."

"It's a new world. Everybody is doing everybody."

"Is that why you and Kate are so casual?"

He laughed. "Kate is Kate. She's a free spirit and no one will ever change her."

"You are too."

"Me? Yes, I suppose you're right. I'm like everybody else on campus. The tenured staff trade partners on a weekly basis."

"Even married ones?"

"Especially married ones."

"Where have I been? I always believed love meant monogamy. I'm all mixed up."

"Sex with anyone can help us over bad times, but when it's part of love it's more like a prayer."

"I thought that's what I had with Mike, but it was an illusion."

"He loved you, Sandy. You have to believe that or his death will drive you nuts."

"I think it's already begun to do that."

They swam once more, dressed, and drove in silence back to the city.

"I can stay if you want," Dave offered.

"You've already spent weeks on me," she said. "I'm beginning to feel better. Honest. Go on. Get your work done."

She stood in her living room and wondered what to do next. She could not allow herself to sink into the whiteness again. She turned on a lamp and noticed the package on the television. She carried it into the kitchen and slit the taped seams with a steak knife.

The spicy scent of the Orient wafted into her nostrils. Something from Penny. She lifted the lid. Three velvet boxes. Her hands shook as she opened the first. A diamond glittered brightly from its silken bed. She snapped it closed, fell onto a chair, and dropped the package onto the table. The boxes scattered across the tabletop. A small card fluttered after them. She picked it up and read its message: "I love you. Marry me. The sooner the better. Mike."

The card fell from her hands and fluttered slowly to the floor. "Oh, God," she cried. "Why, Mike? Why?"

She wouldn't remember how long she sat, opening the cases that contained matching wedding bands and allowing their spring-loaded tops to close with a click, before she carried them to her bedroom and tucked them under the mattress. When they were safely out of sight, she undressed, climbed beneath her bright quilt, and fell into a deep sleep.

◌

When she awoke Cindy was in the room. Watching the girl move about, smiling, chattering, and collecting soiled clothes, made Sandy feel ashamed. She climbed from the bed and stripped the linens.

They carried her laundry to the small Laundromat behind Cindy's apartment and stood together to fold towels and sheets. This is right, Sandy thought. She and Mike began with a basket of laundry and they were ending the same way.

When Sandy's things were done, they washed and sorted the baby clothes Cindy had collected. Heat trapped in the shack caused perspiration to drop from their foreheads.

Cindy stopped folding and placed one hand against the small of her back.

"Contractions?" Sandy asked.

"No. Just some soreness from standing with this lummox kicking at my diaphragm."

"Go inside and lie down. I'll finish up."

"I think I will." She stepped through the open door but quickly turned back and whispered, "Look. There goes Mr. Sipher. See him? In the carport."

Sandy peered into the twilight and saw an old man hurrying down a path between backyards.

"He spends his days drinking beer and watching TV, but when the sun gets low, he toddles over to the widow's for the night. Convenient, eh?"

"Isn't convenience a prerequisite for love?"

Cindy laughed.

"Well," Sandy said as she placed a tiny gown into the basket, "babies sure aren't very convenient."

"True. And this one is becoming a real hassle. But, just think, in a few weeks I'll be holding him in my arms." As she patted the round ball of her tummy, her eyes became soft and glowing.

"And then what?"

"And then I'm off to California."

"California?"

She pulled a letter from her pocket. "One of the gals I knew in Thailand is head nurse in the emergency room at UCLA. She'll hire me. She sent the forms for my license and says I can stay with her until I get settled."

"Wow. That's great."

"I want me and baby Broward to start fresh somewhere away from the noise of fighter planes."

"Broward? Isn't that a boy's name?"

"Yep. That's B.B.'s real name."

"No wonder he shortened it." Sandy smiled. "But what if he's a girl?"

She shook her head. "Boy. Definitely boy."

Sandy folded the last tiny shirt. "I wish I could go away," she said.

"It won't help." Cindy held the door. "You'll take Mike with you wherever you go. I can still feel B.B. hanging around."

"Do you want him to go away?"

"Never. What about you?"

"I don't think I have a choice."

They crossed the yard to Cindy's room.

Sandy turned to leave. "I have a meeting with Tim Schneider. He's been appointed Mike's summary court officer. I'll call you when I'm done and treat you to dinner."

Cindy laughed. "No phone, remember? But I'm too tired, anyway. I'm going to have a long nap."

၏

Tim was waiting on her porch. He spread his papers on the kitchen table. "So," he said, "the biggest question is about Mike's grandfather's watch."

"What about it?" she asked.

"His mother believes he gave it to you."

She shook her head.

"She wants to talk to you."

She glared at him. Cindy had told her that angry flare-ups were part of grieving, but she blamed them on pure guilt. "Why?"

"She's a mother who lost her son."

"And I'm a girl who lost her boyfriend."

"I'm sorry. We're all sorry. But I do have to clear this up. If you talk to her, I'm sure she'll see what a nice girl you are and she'll recognize your honesty."

"I can't. I just can't."

He reached across the table and touched her hand. "Sandy?"

"I wish Dave were here. He'd tell her."

"What would he tell her?"

"He'd tell her how Mike used to take the watch out of the pocket of his flight suit and polish it on his neck scarf. Dave saw him do that as often as I did. He never flew without it."

"Where is Dave?"

"He's on a sabbatical to work on the Humphrey presidential campaign."

"Do you have a number for him?"

"No. He moves around."

"You miss him."

"I don't feel safe when I can't hear his typewriter beyond the wall."

"How are other things going for you? I heard you were sick."

Her laugh sounded edgy even to her. "I wasn't sick. I was nuts. I belong in a loony bin."

"That's pretty normal after a shock like this."

"This long?"

"Jesus, Sandy. It's only been a few weeks."

"So, you're telling me I'm normal?"

He smiled. "Completely."

"Well." She smiled back. "That's a relief."

They sat in silence.

"The general wants to see you in his office at 1500 hours tomorrow," Tim said.

"Why?"

"He didn't say. Better wear your uniform."

❦

The next afternoon she stood before General Magnem's desk.

"Sandy, relax," he said, as he held a chair for her. "This meeting is off the record."

"Sir?"

"I want to help."

She studied the flight line out the window. "I'm doing fine."

He leaned across the desk. "No, you're not."

"How do you know?"

"You'd be surprised at how much I know about you."

"Like what?"

"Let's see. You're from a small town in Maine where you excelled in school. Your hospital coworkers thought highly of you. I have a snapshot of you with the high school sweetheart everyone expected you to marry. Your neighbors say he was nuts to let you get away. Your college psychological profile says you're highly motivated. And this organization provided you a high security clearance."

"I don't understand."

He stood and moved to the window. "When I accepted this assignment I was given the files of several officers I should watch, those thought to have the potential to excel—the achievers and the thinkers. Do you know who gave me your file?"

She stared at him.

"The president of the United States. He provided three names and yours was one."

She thought that was a very curious thing.

"You had lunch with him, didn't you?" he asked.

"I had lunch with him in the same room you did," she corrected.

"See? That's why I'm impressed with you. In all these months, you've never spoken about the privilege."

"It wasn't exactly a privilege."

He laughed. "If I were to venture a guess, I'd say that's exactly why he chose you, Sandy. Because, in this whole country, there is not one other person who would go to a luncheon with the president and come away believing it was no big deal."

She wished he'd get to the point.

"I watched you after the episode with Captain Spencer. You kept your promise to me despite his jibes and insults." He pulled on his collar. "The president put you on my list, Sandy, but I moved you to the very top of it."

She wanted to go home, but he would not be stopped.

"You've taken everything thrown at you and you've tossed it back—with spirit and honesty. And never once have I seen you fail."

"I failed Mike."

"This has been too much for you, hasn't it?"

"Yes." She closed her eyes against the pain.

"You're going to make it through this, and when you come out the other side, you'll be a little stronger, a little wiser, and your name will still be at the top of my list."

She didn't care about his list.

"I know this doesn't mean much to you now, but it will, I promise you. You have a great career ahead of you if you want it. I've never said this to a woman officer before, but I'm saying it with all honesty to you. You have everything it takes to make it to the very top, and I'd like to help you. If my friendship can't help you emotionally now, it can help you professionally in the future. If you decide to stay with us and make that commitment, I want you to call on me and I'll help you get to where you belong."

She shook her head.

"I won't listen to any negatives. Think about what I've said. Get back into the thick of things. Get back to work. You have too much to offer to allow Mike's death to pull you down. Will you promise me, Sandy?"

She had made many promises and they had all turned out badly.

"Say you'll try?"

"What's the use?" she said. "Nothing is what it seems. No one is who they say they are—even you."

But he had touched a chord, the one thing they had in common—the belief that work could conquer all. She could see herself back at the hospital, and she knew that if she filled her time entirely with work, she would survive.

৵৹

Two days later she climbed into a government station wagon with Tim and drove to Mike's townhouse. She held her breath as they walked through the door.

"Are you sure you're up to this?" he asked.

"Do I have a choice?"

"No."

He held her arm as they climbed the stairs to the second floor. The space was filled with the cold odor of an unoccupied home.

She went into the bedroom, opened the sliding doors, and stepped onto the balcony. The bright flowers had died in their pots.

She stepped into a closet and collected some clothing and her sleep sets. In the bathroom she found her perfume and a comb. Her umbrella lay by the kitchen window.

"That's all," she said.

"You're sure?"

"Yes."

He shrugged. "That's that, then. The movers will be here tomorrow."

A snapshot of her and Mike was tucked into a corner of the hall mirror. She remembered that night, how they had danced and how the flash of the camera had blinded her just as she had thrown back her head to laugh. "Can I take this?" she asked.

Tim peeled it from the glass.

Her legs shook as she walked to his car. By the time they had driven the short distance to her place, she was nauseous. She stumbled on the porch stairs.

He took her gently in his arms. "I know that was hard."

She held the snapshot in her hands. "I wonder sometimes if any of it was real."

He laid his cheek against her hair.

"Do you think Mike and I could have made a go of it, if he hadn't crashed? Do you think I could have made him happy?"

He thought for a long time before he answered. "I don't know that any person makes another happy. It has to come from within."

"But Ann and you are so perfect together. Doesn't she keep you mellow?"

"Sure. And being in the kind of job I am, that means a lot. But she isn't the only reason I'm content."

"Then what does it for you?"

"I don't think you're really interested in what makes me happy, Sandy. I think you're really asking, Why wasn't Mike happy?"

"Yes, I guess that is what I need to know." She pulled away and moved into her apartment.

He followed closely behind. "Mike lived the way he flew: reckless, edgy, always pushing the envelope. You made his life more interesting."

"But in the end I couldn't make him happy."

"He was careless. It wasn't your fault."

"I'm trying to believe that, but I know I had a part in it. Other people think so too."

"Like who?"

"Your flight surgeon and the tall guy who interviewed me."

"The attorney?"

"Yes. They both acted like I should have known Mike was going to fly drunk and I should have told someone."

"Oh, sure," he said. "And what gal in her right mind would squeal on a fighter jock? Do you think I would stay married to Ann for one minute if she interfered with my flying? There was nothing you could have done."

"I wish I could believe that. I think he'll haunt me until I die."

CHAPTER TWELVE

Halloween evening she handed candy to hobgoblins as she watched the news.

LBJ halted all bombing of North Vietnam while Humphrey's opponent, Nixon, made promises to strengthen South Vietnamese regulars so U.S. troops could come home.

Earlier in the day Sandy had faced the final inquiry board and signed her statement. Afterward, Tim had driven her to his house, where Ann had dinner and strong martinis waiting. Sandy liked the giddy numbness the martinis provided.

Now, alone again, she felt at odds with the world. When she opened the door for the last group of kids, she noticed the air had cooled considerably and the wind had picked up. As she stepped back into the living room, heavy rain began to clatter against the windows.

She slammed the door against the wind and hurried to answer her ringing telephone.

"Sandy?" Cindy's voice was high and shrill.

"Yes."

"You've got to come get me. Please. I'm bleeding bad."

She could hear wind howling in the background and rain pounding on metal.

"Where are you?"

"In the phone booth down from the apartment."

"Have you called the ambulance?"

"Yes. But they won't come. They said it's not authorized because I'm not military."

"Oh, Jesus. Have you had any contractions?"

"No. I thought my water broke, but it's blood, lots of blood. Come get me, please. I'm losing my baby."

"I'll be right there. Don't move. I'm on my way."

She dialed the supervisor's number at the base hospital.

Kate's replacement, whom Sandy had not yet met, answered.

"This is Lieutenant O'Connell, the O.B. charge nurse," she said. "I'm bringing in Cindy Howell. She's at term with sudden hemorrhage. I want you to call in Jim Andersen and the O.R. team."

"Who are you?" the girlish voice asked.

"Don't ask questions, Lieutenant," Sandy said. "Just do as I say and do it now." As she hung up the phone, she realized she had spoken in the same harsh tones as Major Roberts.

She drove to Cindy's through a wall of rain, pulled in near the lighted phone booth, and left the door of the car ajar with the engine running. Rivulets of blood mixed with the rain in the dim light of the partially open booth door. Cindy lay in a crumpled heap with her face pressed against the glass.

"Cindy?"

Her eyes flew open. Her hands reached up. "The baby, Sandy. We've got to save the baby."

There wasn't enough room in the booth for both of them. "Roll out toward me." Sandy tried to keep the panic from her voice. "If you roll out I can lift you."

Cindy squeezed her shoulders from the booth and kicked with her feet to push her swollen belly out.

Sandy leveraged her body between the girl and the booth and hefted her to her feet.

They were both soaked to the skin by the time they stumbled into the car.

"He wouldn't let me use the phone," Cindy mumbled.

"Who?"

"Mr. Sipher. He was drunk. He called me a whore. I begged him. 'Please,' I said. 'I'm bleeding. I need to call the base.' He pushed me out."

"It's okay," Sandy said. She sped along the base perimeter road. "We'll be there in minutes."

Cindy didn't answer.

The A.P. saluted her through the gate. She took the straightest route to the hospital.

Two corpsmen met them at the E.R. doors and lifted Cindy onto a wheeled gurney. "My baby, Sandy. Please save my baby."

There was too much blood. "We've made it. We're here."

"Get your fetoscope and listen for the baby," Cindy insisted.

"No time," Sandy said. "We're taking you right to the O.R."

"Pray for me, Sandy. I can't think anymore. Pray for me."

"Hail Mary, full of grace, the Lord is with thee," she started as she cut off her friend's wet clothing.

The E.R. doc shoved a needle into a pale arm. "We need blood," he shouted to a corpsman.

"Blessed art thou among women," Sandy continued. "Blessed is the fruit of thy womb, Jesus." She placed a hand on Cindy's abdomen. It was as soft as a balloon losing air. "Holy Mary, Mother of God, pray for us sinners, now and at the hour of our death. Amen."

"Let's roll." The doc pushed the gurney toward her. She took hold of a front corner and began to run. They maneuvered the cart around hallway corners as fast as possible. Her wet shoes squeaked on the vinyl floor. Her heart raced.

A warm blast of air, saturated with antiseptic and formaldehyde, brushed her face as they plowed through the double doors of the operating room suite.

Jim Andersen, gowned and gloved, stood by the far wall. Sandy saw a blur of bright lights, green walls, and sterile gowned figures.

They lifted Cindy onto the operating table. "Don't leave me, Sandy, please." Her voice was a whisper. "Say the 'Hail Mary' again."

"Hail Mary ..." She heard the click of the anesthesia machine, sensed rather than saw the tube jammed down Cindy's throat, heard the dull rush of oxygen being forced into lungs. "... pray for us sinners."

Jim shouted orders. "Sandy, out. You're wet and dirty. Out." She looked up and saw the blade in his gloved hand. She kept her eyes on it as she backed out of the room. She allowed the doors to close, then leaned into the window.

Jim's scalpel drew a red line from Cindy's belly button to her pubic bone. The green figures shifted and moved around the table. Blood was hung from a pole already heavy with bottles of fluid. An infant incubator was wheeled forward. Another doc pushed past Sandy. She recognized the newest pediatrician on the staff. "Too late. Not much chance," she heard Jim say. The door closed against her again.

And then she saw him, a tiny baby lying face up in the gaping wound, surrounded by graying, purplish tissue. His eyes were open, but as the pediatrician took him from Jim, the baby's limbs hung flaccidly toward the floor.

The doc placed him on a sterile pad, beneath warm lights, inserted a plastic tube into his lungs, and breathed for him. Someone connected a bag to the tube. A nurse pressed her fingers into the tiny chest, forcing his heart to contract. The doctor pushed a needle into the umbilical vein. Life-giving fluid ran into tiny vessels. The nurse's fingers continued to push against the tiny chest. The black bag breathed. The baby did not.

Sandy watched as another team went through the same procedures with Cindy, except someone began pumping blood into her veins and someone else pushed hard on her chest and counted loudly. The monitor showed flat lines. Jim drew another red line with his scalpel, called for retractors, opened Cindy's chest, wrapped his hands around her heart, and tried to force lifeblood to her brain.

The placenta lay in a basin on the table's edge. A Duncan—dirty, rough, and gray. She saw Jim throw up his bloodied hands as he stared at the monitor. All sound seemed to fade away.

She stepped back slowly until her shoulders felt the coolness of the wall. "Holy Mary, Mother of God, pray for us sinners, now and at the hour of our death."

She slid down the wall until she felt the solid floor beneath her, pulled up her knees, pressed her face into her wet jeans, and closed her eyes. There was nothing more anyone could do.

∽

She made a statement to another inquiry board, but this time she had as many questions as the attorney.

She asked the board why a female officer had been treated as Cindy had. Why were male officers allowed to take leave and make arrangements when they had personal problems, but a female was automatically rifted without so much as a thank-you for her service?

When male officers became single parents because of death or divorce, they were allowed to remain in the military. Why not females?

The hospital had agreed to provide care for Cindy. Shouldn't that have included emergency care such as an ambulance when she was hemorrhaging?

She received no answers.

Major Roberts, who had been appointed Cindy's summary court officer, didn't like the tone of Sandy's questions. After the inquiry, when Sandy asked for the address of Cindy's parents, the major refused. "You're angry and it won't help anyone to point fingers."

"It will help me," she answered.

"You'll have to toughen up, Lieutenant."

She accompanied Major Roberts to empty Cindy's place. There was little to pack. She carried the basket of baby clothes to her car.

"Planning on some little changes in your own life, Lieutenant?" the major asked.

"Don't you wish," Sandy answered. "Cindy bought these when she didn't have enough money for a phone. I'm going to take them to the Salvation Army so they get used."

"Did I tell you her parents are having the bodies shipped home?"

"Nice gesture," Sandy said. "A little too late, don't you think?"

"It's never too late. And speaking of that, there's some unfinished business with Mike's mother."

Sandy placed the basket in her trunk and slammed the lid hard. "What now?"

"The lawyers say you have to talk to her. I'm having Major Schneider set it up. He'll be contacting you in the next few days. You will talk to her, Lieutenant. That's an order."

༄

The lady at the Salvation Army wished her the Lord's blessings.

Paid for with blood, Sandy thought, but she smiled for the woman, whose flat Kansas accent made the words seem like an afterthought.

༄

Two letters from Penny waited in her mailbox.

> *12 October 1968*
> *Dear Sandy,*
> *I'm pretty sure they are going to give me the Meridian assignment. I should arrive just after Thanksgiving. I'm going to*

spend the holiday with my family in Sacramento and then drive my new sports car up. I bought the car through the BX system. It's my reward for having served and saved. To tell the truth, I'm kind of scared about coming home. I don't know what to expect and am afraid I will no longer fit in. I've been given responsibilities over here that stretch the limit of nursing practice. With all the rules in normal nursing, I may not be able to restrain myself from using the advanced skills I've mastered. And that means I may not fit into a normal nursing job in a normal hospital. Is it possible to go backwards and like it? The antiwar sentiment has reached us. I am beginning to see some of those peace signs on necklaces and bracelets. Will I be booed when I deplane?

Your last letter seems long ago. Are you okay? I had a quick note from Kate and she said she expects to be sent to Camranh Bay, but she didn't say when. I was sure looking forward to seeing both of you again. She will be coming here at a really troubled time. The morale of the troops is sinking and the spirit of camaraderie that has seen most of us through the bad times is sadly lacking now. We are seeing more and more lifers, you know, the guys with a dog-eared copy of policy and procedures on their clipboards? There is more talk than action and a serious mistrust has developed between those who would speak their true feelings about the war and those who stubbornly want to continue it. The rift between officers and enlisted seems to be widening. Small incidents are blown out of proportion and repercussions are instantaneous. Do you feel this kind of change stateside?

I am not as proud to be part of this organization as I once was, and that is something, coming from a military brat. My father would disown me if he heard me say this, but I will anyway—sometimes civilian life looks pretty good. Well, I have three more *years until I have to decide, hopefully this damn war will be over by then. Hope to see you soon.*

    As always,

    Penny

The second letter was much shorter.

    22 October 1968

    Dear Sandy,

    I am so sorry. I just learned of Mike's death from Kate. I thought your long silence meant something important was happening, but I expected happy news. By now you've probably heard enough expressions of sympathy to last you a lifetime and I would tell you, "be happy Mike died doing what he loved most," but I don't believe there is any happiness to be found in such a loss. My sadness for you can't be expressed in words.

    I did get the assignment to Meridian and will definitely be arriving after Thanksgiving. I wish I were already there so I could do something to help. I'll write more in a few days.

    Hope to see you soon, hang in there.

    Love,

    Penny

Tim arranged a telephone conference with Mike's mother. He came to Sandy's door carrying a bottle of wine, his briefcase, and a plate of cheese and crackers.

They sat in the living room—he on the couch, with legs crossed and his eyes moving to the telephone every few minutes; she on the big chair, watching him.

"You look like someone about to experience the Great Inquisition," he joked.

"That's exactly how I feel," she admitted.

He twisted the cork from the wine and filled two glasses. "We'll make the call as soon as you're ready," he said.

She tapped her glass on his. "To proper endings." Her hand shook when she raised the glass to her lips.

After the second refill, she relaxed. "Okay, let's do this."

He dialed the number.

She waited while he said a few words to Mrs. Hopkins, then she took a deep draught of wine and took the phone. "Hello." Her voice broke.

"Miss O'Connell?"

"Yes."

"It's about time I spoke to you. I suppose we should get right down to business." Her voice was crisp, but with a girl-like quality. "We have some important subjects to cover."

"Yes," Sandy mumbled. The telephone was slippery in her hand.

"The general has approached you about Michael's watch?"

"Yes."

"And?"

"And I've told him Mike carried it whenever he flew."

"I do not believe you."

"But it's true, Mrs. Hopkins. I'm not the kind of person who—"

"I'll make my own decisions about what kind of person you are," she snapped. "I'm well aware of the type of girls Michael preferred. He certainly wouldn't have chosen you for your virtue."

"You're insulting me, Mrs. Hopkins."

"*You* are the insult. I am sick to death of your lies."

Sandy looked toward Tim.

"Hang in there," he whispered and refilled her glass.

She turned her attention back to the phone.

The woman continued. "If it's money you want, I can more than compensate you for the watch."

"I don't want your money." She tried to keep her voice from rising.

"If you desire a memento I can send you any number of his things. I want the watch. Do you understand?"

"No." She upended her glass. "I don't understand."

"I think we've all made it quite clear to you I will not rest until you give back what you've stolen from me."

"I'm telling you the truth, Mrs. Hopkins."

The woman laughed. "Oh, heavens, I would never expect a girl like you to lie, would I?"

Sandy's brain failed her. She could think of no retort.

"He had a lot to offer a girl like you, didn't he?"

"What do you mean?"

"I mean the kind of girl who has no conscience. The kind who will do anything to get what she wants. The kind who will lure a man away from his wife and baby. They didn't matter at all to you, did they?"

"What are you talking about?"

"I'm talking about you, Miss O'Connell."

"I don't understand."

"Oh, I think you do."

She couldn't bear one more word. She placed the receiver firmly into its cradle.

"My God. What did she say? You look like you've seen a ghost." Tim pulled her to him.

Her hands clenched and unclenched as she pushed him away.

"Sit," he said.

She obeyed.

"What did she say?"

"She said Mike was married."

He turned away.

"He was, wasn't he?" Sandy asked.

"He was divorced earlier this year."

"And he had children?"

"One."

"A toddler," she murmured as she remembered the visit from Mike's 'sister' nearly a year ago. No wonder he had not allowed them to meet.

"So you knew?" Tim asked.

"Maybe you should go now."

"I can't leave you like this."

"It was his choice," she said.

"What was?"

"When and how he left. It was always his choice."

"Sandy?"

"There's nothing to say, Tim. Nothing anyone can say. You really need to go."

He stepped toward her again. She backed away, met his eyes, and attempted to appear confident. "I need to think about all this. I need to think."

"It's a lot to take in. I'll go. I'll have Ann call you when I get home. Maybe by then you'll feel like talking."

She panicked. "No. Please, Tim, don't tell Ann. Please don't tell anyone. I can't face that. I just need to think. I need to figure this out."

He raised his arms to comfort her again, but she pushed past him and opened the door. "Please, Tim, go. I promise I'll be fine."

She shut the door behind him, collapsed into the chair, and poured the last of the wine into her glass.

Married. He had lied from the beginning. He had gone after what he wanted and, when he got it, had realized he didn't want to give it up. She would have hated him had she found out. He knew that. She hated him now, but it was too late. Nothing could be changed.

"Oh God," she prayed, "I have been so arrogant. I believed I could keep him faithful when even you had failed at that."

His accident had been so painful it had almost destroyed her, and for what?

She ran into her bedroom, pulled the velvet boxes from beneath her mattress, carried them to the car, and drove like a madwoman to the river park.

Bold and unafraid, she ran down the gravel path to the tight bend of the river.

There was no movement on the green sheen of sluggish water. Reflections of a golden moon drew yellow edges along the icy shore. Gray reeds hung their heads listlessly from frozen stalks like hooded mourners in a darkened church.

She hurried to the water's edge, looked for movement from the rushes, watched for her rat.

A dog barked. Another answered him. A third began to howl.

Downriver, someone slammed a car door and called out in a loud voice. Another door slammed and the engine faded away.

She could hear her harsh breathing in the sudden silence. He's here, she thought. He's hiding in a bed of bones and discarded papers.

She folded her arms against the cold and waited. When he didn't come, she opened the first box and drew out a small gold band; opened the second and drew out a larger band. She opened the third. Diamonds sparkled with a fire that had no warmth.

"No truth," she said aloud. "No love. No meaning." She dropped the boxes and held the brilliant rings up to the moonlight. They gleamed richly, gave off a dozen points of light before she wrapped her hand tightly around them and threw them over the water.

"My offering to Charon," she shouted to the night. "Mike's fare to cross the River Styx." She laughed as she watched the water ripple. When she turned to run back up the bank her laughter neared hysteria.

∽

The next morning she waited for Major Roberts at her office. She'd had enough. She was ready to move on.

"Are we talking about a change of assignments, Lieutenant, or a change of orders?" the major asked.

"Assignments. I'm done with babies."

"You could ask for a change of duty. You've been in a year. I could get started on that."

"Ha!" she laughed. "You think I'm staying longer than the two years I signed up for? No way. In eight months I'm done with this man's world. I've had enough."

"Excuse me, Lieutenant." The major left the room.

Sandy paced. She needed challenging work. She needed to put all her energy into her job so the time would pass quickly and she could be on her way.

She scanned the papers on Major Roberts's desk with disinterest until one caught her attention. Highlighted letters announced Eyes Only, immediately below the letterhead for Air Force headquarters.

She knew she shouldn't, but she was in a mutinous mood. She slid the other papers aside. The directive requested head-to-toe snapshots of every female officer under the hospital administrator's command and had been forwarded with a paper-clipped note from General Magnem. The note read, "They aren't interested in male nurses or medical officers, only the gals."

She moved away from the desk as the major returned with Jim Andersen.

"What's this, Sandy? You want a new job?" he asked.

"Yes."

"I don't understand. We get along so well. I love the job you're doing. Why now? Don't you think you should give this some thought? You've come through a terrible time."

"That's why I have to move on." She raised her hands in a gesture of surrender. "I can't do it anymore."

"I need a better reason. You can't run away from life."

She laughed then. "I am running away. I'm an emotional wreck and everything I do in the unit seems to make it worse: footprints, blood, babies born with their eyes wide open. Even the flight suits going up the walk outside my window give me a start."

"Still not good reasons."

"How about this, then. I need a challenge. I need something new in view every morning. The ward is running at top efficiency. There's little challenge for me in my job. It's time for a change."

"I can accept that."

She smiled for him.

"But I won't like it," he said.

"Thanks, Jim."

"We're a good team, Sandy. I'll admit I'm totally selfish in wanting to keep you."

"And I'm totally selfish in wanting to go."

He looked to Major Roberts. "Where will you put her?"

"Medical unit. I need a new charge over there."

Jim excused himself and left. Major Roberts turned to Sandy again. "So, Lieutenant, let's talk about the other half of this."

"What other half?"

"Your plan not to re-up. You have a free ticket, you know. The sky's the limit for you."

"What are you talking about?"

"The general told me about the president's referral."

Sandy felt genuine laughter well up. "Haven't you heard, Major? LBJ didn't run. Mr. Nixon is going to the oval office. That free ticket is as worthless as a Confederate dollar."

"You still have the general. He has a lot of clout."

She shook her head. "Not interested."

"Why not?"

She walked around the desk. "Because of things like this." She tapped the letter from headquarters. "Why do you think they need full-length snapshots of us? Are we going to be promoted on the length of our legs? Will we get assignments because we're a size five? I want to be measured by my merit, not my looks."

The major shrugged. "Then stay. Use your energy to change things. Make this a woman's world too."

"It would be a long, hard fight."

"Think about it," Major Roberts said. "Don't make any decisions now."

❦

When she returned to the ward, she was surprised to see a stranger sitting at her desk. The woman stood as she approached. "Sandy! Surprise!"

"Penny!" She hurried forward. "I didn't recognize you. What have you done to your hair?"

"Natural," she said. "Bleached out from the sun."

"And shorter. I like it."

"Had to keep it short, no time for styling."

"You look so different."

Penny pirouetted and laughed. "Gained a few pounds. Never knew when we would get the chance to eat, so I ate at every stop." Her oversized sweatshirt flapped against faded jeans as she danced.

"But the same old Penny."

"I hope so. Boy, have we got stories to swap!" Her eyes had not lost their warmth, and her smile was as generous as ever.

"Come into the break room and grab some coffee," Sandy said.

She squeezed Sandy's arm as they stepped across the hall. "It sure is good to see you. I've been worried about you."

"Me? You're the one who's been living on the edge." Sandy took two cups from the shelf and poured coffee. She handed one to Penny and peered over her own cup to study her friend more closely. "I thought you were taking leave."

"I'd planned to stay home for a while, but I began to get on people's nerves, so I decided to go while the going was good. Drove up. Nice weather. Relaxing time."

Penny had changed, Sandy decided. Her voice lacked the happy lilting quality that had been her trademark at Officers' Training the previous year. Had it only been one year? To Sandy it seemed a lifetime had passed. "Does everything look different to you?"

"Yeah. I'm trying to figure out where I fit in. Everyone warned me the hardest part of war is coming home, but I guess I didn't think it possible my own family would act like I'm a stranger."

"Did you stop to see Bob?"

She shook her head. "He's in rehab at the Kansas City V.A., but I haven't decided how to accomplish a reunion."

A corpsman came to the door. "Another labor patient coming in, Lieutenant. They could use a hand."

"Sure. Be right there." She turned to Penny. "I have to go, but my friend Dave should be back today and I'd sure like you to meet him. His campaign for Humphrey failed and he may not be in the best of shape, but you'll like him."

Penny laughed. "I found your place and already met Dave. He invited me for dinner too. You guys are like two peas in a pod. Meant for each other."

"Friends," Sandy said. "I'm glad to know he's home."

"He said six; that okay?"

"Come at four. We'll have some drinks and catch up."

∽

When Dave arrived at six, Sandy and Penny had already finished a bottle of wine. He popped the cork on a magnum of champagne. "I thought we should have a celebration," he said.

Sandy pulled three champagne glasses from the cupboard and passed them around.

Dave quickly did the honors and raised his glass.

Penny and Sandy raised theirs. "To friendship," Penny said.

"And to Kate," Sandy added, "who should be here too."

"And to Kate," they said together.

Sandy brought out the snapshot she had received in Kate's last letter. Dressed in full combat gear, including a canteen on her belt and a rifle in her hands, she smiled from the ramp of a C-130.

"Yes, that's our Kate," Penny said. "God broke the mold after he made her."

After dinner, Sandy began having difficulty following the conversation. "I hope you guys don't mind," she said. "I haven't had much sleep and the champagne has dulled my brain. I'm going to bed. Dave, would you be sure the door is locked when you leave?"

He nodded, but didn't take his eyes from Penny.

∽

In the privacy of her bedroom she read Kate's letter again.

3 November 1968

Hey Sandy!

If it weren't for the military planes in their jungle camouflage, the rows of Quonset huts, and the high fashion jungle fatigues, I'd think I was still stateside. This place is almost exotic. It has a beautiful sandy beach and bright, blue ocean. I've already managed to deepen my tan.

Our hospital is huge and well equipped, but not the sea of suffering I had imagined. Our patients are mostly support staff and the OR schedules routine circumcisions. They tell me that's because most of the action is to the north, west and south of us and we are not on medevac routes. Trenches, barricades, and the ocean separate us from the real war. The social life is fantastic, an endless supply of horny men and a shortage of round-eyed women. They had a wild welcoming party for me and another nurse, Dee, who was on the same flight. We share hooch in a compound with no men allowed. That's probably a good thing. The testosterone levels are so elevated, sometimes even I am overwhelmed.

We've been invited to an embassy party in Saigon and our superiors are bending over backwards for us to go. We'll be relieved of duty for five days. I believe Dad may have arranged the invitation and I tried to renege, but they told me no one turns down an ambassador's call. A local seamstress is sewing Dee and me hand-embroidered dresses and matching silk sandals for the grand sum of two dollars. Doesn't war sound like hell?

The weather is hot as an Arizona spring, but with more rain and oppressive humidity. Do you like my picture? I make a good grunt, don't you think?

As ever,

Kate

CHAPTER THIRTEEN

On Thanksgiving Sandy double-shifted all weekend and on Christmas she avoided socializing by taking an extra shift.

Snow was her excuse to avoid every invitation for New Year's. When the whistles and fireworks began to sound at midnight, she opened a bottle of champagne and drank it alone. Sometime later she heard Dave and a giggling female go into his place.

A pang of jealousy for the fun they would have marked her body's reawakening. But Dave wasn't her type. Fighter pilots were, and although she might welcome one into her bed again, she knew she would never again allow one into her heart. The girl who had so easily fallen for their charms was dead. She had gone to the grave with Mike and Cindy and the tiny son of B.B.

Tim and Ann Schneider, Jim and Connie Andersen, and their families became her touchstones, her hold on normalcy, but the void in her life was quickly becoming an aching need that couldn't be filled by friends.

෮

Another letter arrived from Kate.

> *27 December 1968*
>
> *Hey girl!*
>
> *I can get Coors and I can get stereos and I can get laid, but until your package arrived, I couldn't lay my hands on one powdered sugar donut. Thank you and Sara Lee for the case. I may survive here after all. I've settled in. I spend my free time on the beach drinking beer and giving the troops something good to*

look at. There sure are lots of rich and attractive folks lolling on this beach.

They say this complex was originally set up as an R and R base, but was filled with so many lonely soldiers the military began sending in round-eyed women to take care of their needs. They say it wasn't long before senators and businessmen began having their sons sent here so they could pretend to have kids in the war. Looking around I sometimes wonder if those stories aren't true.

We have our own fishing village with locals who go out in little sloops and use hand nets to fish. They continue on with their lives in the old way, weaving between huge tankers and carriers as if they don't see them. They must think we Americans are crazy for our love of beaches. They use beaches as honey pot dumps and garbage pits and allow the tides to flush out the mess. They seem so happy that I wonder what it is they have that we Americans do not. I understand why Dave talked about them with so much affection. When I shop in the village the atmosphere is so foreign I can forget I'm on a military base. But, and this is a big but, one whiff of the ubiquitous fish sauce odor and my dream is over. Whew! Bad stuff!

As for me, here's how it goes. I have regularly scheduled duty hours, regularly scheduled meals and so much free time I can indulge in pleasure after pleasure. (And right now, my friend, I can hear you saying, "Boy did they send Kate to the right place!") If I compare myself to the Army nurses who come through, I don't measure up. They have something I lack. Maybe it's a sense of the mission or the satisfaction of knowing they help guys who didn't ask to be here and definitely don't want to die here. They have reached a level of maturity I will probably never see.

At the moment we are being fed dire warnings about the impending monsoon season and my high-maintenance self

says, "but how will I live without sunbathing?" Give Dave a
kiss for me.

Love,
Kate

Another note arrived in late February.

12 February 1969
Hey Sandy,

New Year's meant a week of parties but shortly thereafter I
was introduced to the reality of war. I hopped a flight on a C-130
to hook up with a guy at U-tapao. The plane had some kind of
hydraulic failure and full fuel tanks. We were flying in a tight, low
circle to dump fuel when the damned VC started taking pot shots
at us. At first it scared the hell out of me. But then I was rather
taken with the idea of looking death in the eyes. When the pilot
put down at Da Nang we hit the runway with a God-awful thud.
The planeload of Marines started screaming and jumping for joy.
It sent chills up my spine. Now I know why the guys sometimes say
coming close to death is very much like an orgasm.

Good thoughts and wishes.
Love,
Kate

In March, General Magnem earned a second star and sent
out invitations to his promotion party. Sandy planned to send her
regrets, but Ann convinced her to go with them.

Sandy bought a pair of panty hose, the newest fashion acces-
sory. They allowed her lavender dress to be very short. She pinned
her hair up before she slipped into the strapless dress, silk pumps,
and a gauzy wrap that covered her bare shoulders. When she saw

her image in her full-length mirror, she gasped with surprise. After months of drab scrubs, starched whites, and shapeless uniforms, she had forgotten how soft and feminine she could feel.

When Dave brought over a bottle of wine and whistled his approval, she felt fresh and renewed. But then Ann called.

"My kids have some kind of flu," she said. "I waited until now to decide, but I just can't go."

"Oh, no," Sandy said.

"Well, it's all right. I mean, I really don't mind. Tim has no choice. He has to go."

"I'll come over and watch the kids. You and Tim should go."

"He's already on his way to collect you. I wouldn't enjoy it anyway. Take notes so you can tell me all about it."

Sandy saw lights on the drive. "Oh, Ann, he's here already. I guess I'll have to go. Will you wish me luck on my social reemergence?"

"Have a wonderful time," Ann said, and rang off.

"You are stunning," Tim said as he held the car door for her.

Later, as they made their way toward the reception line, he warned, "We're going to cause a stir, showing up together without Ann."

"I'll give my name separately, and as a lieutenant."

"You'll take their breath away," he said.

She patted his lapel and teased. "You too, you handsome devil."

When she offered her hand, General Magnem pulled her in and kissed her cheek. "I'm glad you came, Sandy," he whispered. "I'll have to thank Major Schneider. You are lovely."

"Thank you and congratulations," she said.

As he greeted Tim, she heard him say, "Where's Ann?"

"Kids are sick, but she sends her congratulations."

General Magnem leaned forward and whispered something Sandy couldn't hear. Both men laughed.

She excused herself as they cleared the line. There was no use fueling gossip.

She moved through the crowd, greeting friends and looking for a safe ground-hugger to spend the evening with. A young legal officer stood up from one of the round tables. "Sandy," he called. "Come join us."

He introduced her to the new judge advocate, the judge's son, and the son's friend, John, who had flown in for the party.

John's warm hand touched her shoulder as she accepted the chair he held. He was tall, with a wide smile and the large-boned features she found especially attractive. He turned his back to the rest of the table. "Please excuse us, gentlemen. Sandy and I have important things to discuss."

"Here he goes again," the judge's son said with a laugh. "Didn't I tell you, Dad? This guy always picks the best-looking woman in the room and doesn't give anyone else a chance."

"You've got that right," John said without taking his eyes from her.

She liked his brazenness and enjoyed his good-humored conversation through dinner and far too many drinks. When the music started, he guided her to the dance floor and took her in his arms.

"Where are you stationed?" she asked.

"Laredo, Texas."

"I've heard it's a tough town."

"You wouldn't like it." He pulled her close and spun her rapidly around the floor. "Not much of interest there."

"There's not much of interest here either," she said.

"Oh, I dunno. I find *you* interesting." He held her away for a few seconds as he glanced about the room. "And many others seem to, also."

She laughed. "That's only because I arrived with a happily married man, and his wife isn't with us. I'm sure tongues are wagging."

"Trust me. It isn't the man they're watching."

The music stopped. He held her hand as they walked from the dance floor.

"Uh-oh," he said. "Here comes the judge."

General Magnem grinned as he cut between them. "You have good taste, Captain," he said. "Picked the best of the best. But now it's my turn to dance with Sandy."

"Yes, sir." John stood aside.

The general held her more tightly than John had, and danced with less grace and ease. She had difficulty following his steps.

"John comes from an old Air Force family," he told her. "Dad was an ace in Korea. Granddad was a general in World War Two. He's a good catch."

"If you're trying to catch something," she said. "I'm just here for the beer."

He laughed and swung her wide as the music picked up and turned to rock. "Can't dance a step to this." He led her back to their table.

She leaned toward John and asked, "So what do you do in Laredo?"

"Pilot training," he answered. "I hope to get into fighters. Man, I love to fly."

Sudden tightness in her chest made it difficult to breathe. She wanted to run but forced herself to stay calm. She glanced about the room.

Tim caught her eye and smiled.

She waved. "Will you excuse me, John?" she said. "I think my escort is ready to leave. His kids are sick and he's probably anxious to get home."

"I can drive you," he offered.

"Maybe that would work. Let me go check."

She moved across the room on shaking legs. "Are you ready to go?" she asked Tim.

"Yes. But it looks like you're having a good time. I can wait."

"No, I'm ready."

He raised his eyebrows and pulled her aside. "What's wrong? Did that guy do something?"

"He's a fighter pilot."

"Are you going to boil us all in the same pot?"

"I want to go, please. I need to get out of this gracefully."

They stopped by the table and the two men shook hands. "I've got to go," she said.

"My wife called and my son's fever is up," Tim lied. "Sandy has volunteered to check him out for us."

"Wow! That's too bad. The party is just getting started," John said. "I'll walk you to the door."

Sandy and Tim said good night to their host. Icy rain was falling.

"I'll bring the car around," Tim offered.

"No," Sandy said. "We've got to hurry."

Before either of the men could speak, she stepped off the curb and into the driving rain. Tim ran after her. John was left standing in the doorway.

They were thoroughly soaked when they settled into the car. She caught Tim's quick glance and realized her dress had become transparent. She pulled her wrap closer.

"Are you okay?" he asked.

"Cold," she answered.

"I'll let the car warm up while the windshield clears."

"Thanks for helping me out."

"My pleasure."

"What did the general say in the reception line that was so funny?"

"Just a guy joke."

"But about me?"

"Well, kind of."

"Tell me."

"He said, 'Could be your lucky night. You might be in for a lot of TLC and maybe a deep protein injection on the side.'"

"And you laughed at that?"

"You know how it goes, Sandy. If the general tells a joke, we mortals laugh."

He turned on the heater and defroster and they sat in silence as the car warmed. By the time they passed the hotel entrance, John had disappeared.

The driving rain forced Tim to go slowly. The road dipped and rose again. They both strained to see ahead. At the bottom of another dip, a wave of water thundered against the floor of the car. The engine sputtered and quit.

Sandy looked through her window and saw black water.

"Now, I should know better than this," Tim muttered. "Damn. I bet the coil's wet." He turned to her. "Ann will kill me. These are new shoes. But I'll have to have a look."

"The water's deep on this side," she said.

"Gully washer. It will pass. I've got a flashlight in the glove compartment."

He moved across the seat as she leaned forward to open the glove box. His body pressed warmly against hers.

Startled, she turned to meet his eyes. For a long second they stopped all movement and stared wide-eyed at one another.

He reached out and touched her face before his lips met hers, hot and searching.

Her hands moved to his neck, his face, and his hair. Something denied, something forbidden, became something too sweet to ignore. She wanted him. Not later, not tomorrow, not next week, but now, firmly and insistently now.

His caresses spread warmth as he slid her wet dress above her thighs. His hands moved smoothly over the tight silk of her hose. She stretched out on the seat and lay beneath him. As he struggled with her hose she whispered, "Tear them. Just tear them off."

Something bright cut through her closed eyelids and forced her to look up. A bright light glared through the window on his side. She gasped and froze.

He pulled away.

She was afraid to move, afraid to speak.

He sat up and sheltered her from the light.

She could see a badge and a hand tapping against the glass as she pulled herself up and cowered behind Tim.

Tim lowered his window.

"You need some help?" the sheriff asked.

"Yes," Tim said. "I mean, I know it doesn't look like we need help but …" He shrugged and lifted both palms up.

"Let me try that again," the sheriff said with a laugh. "Do you want some help?"

"Yes, we do. The car stalled and I can't get it started."

"That's plain to see. Damned dangerous place to park," he said. "Some car coming fast down the hill would total you."

Tim nodded. "Yeah." His voice quavered.

"I'll push you up a ways. There's a station ahead where you can sit and let her dry out."

"That would be great." He slouched against his door and held the wheel with one hand.

Sandy didn't move. Her dress had wrapped around her waist from top and bottom. She found her wrap on the floor, covered her breasts, and pulled her clothing back into place.

The sheriff's car bumped them from behind and began to grind up the hill. They stared ahead at the road. Neither spoke. At the station, Tim stepped out and opened the hood. As she watched his movements, she craved his touch.

He climbed back in and turned the key. The engine purred to life. They finished the drive without speaking. In her driveway he turned off the ignition and lights. "I won't apologize," he said.

"I don't expect you to."

"I know I have no right to say this, but I will. We're not some strangers going at it in the night."

"I know," she said. She was afraid to move or look at him. She was afraid of what she would do.

"What should I say?" he asked.

"I don't know. It's you who has everything to lose."

"And everything to gain."

"Tim," she said in a reasonable tone. "We've both had too much to drink." She turned and looked fully on him. "It's been a long night. Neither of us is really in our right mind."

"I'm totally sober." He placed one hand on the seat between them. "My brain is totally intact. I want you."

She touched his hand. "I want you too."

"Oh, God." His fingers curled around hers.

"We need to think about this. Maybe it will all seem different tomorrow," she whispered.

"Yes."

She reached for the door handle.

"Sandy?"

She paused.

"I'll stop by tomorrow and we can talk."

"Okay." She ran through the rain to the safety of her porch.

◐

Her sleep was troubled. Each time she awoke she hoped what had happened with Tim was simply an erotic dream, but she knew it was real and they had crossed a dangerous line.

In the morning, when Penny called, she agreed to a day of shopping. She wouldn't be home if Tim came by. They were both too sensible to fall into an affair. It was best to chalk up what had happened to too much alcohol and her pent-up needs. But when the telephone rang again, her hand and voice shook as she answered it.

Ann was on the line. "Did I wake you?"

"No. I'm on my second cup of coffee," Sandy answered evenly. "How are the kids?"

"You won't believe it. Both are fine today. No fevers and already fighting over the TV."

"I'm glad. But you missed a nice party."

"That's what Tim said. He didn't go into details. I think social affairs exhaust him. He tossed and turned all night."

"We all had a bit too much to drink," she said.

"I'm sure, but he seemed pretty sober when he came in. Hey, Sandy, the reason I called is this: A bunch of us are going to Hutchinson to an estate auction today and I hoped you could come along. We're leaving our husbands home."

"Oh, gosh, Ann. I'm spending the day with Penny."

"Well, maybe next time."

"Sure."

"Tim tells me you met a handsome guy last night."

"Yeah. A pilot type up from Laredo."

"Was he nice?"

"You mean was I interested?"

"Yes."

"I think so. Time will tell."

"That's good news. Gotta run."

She hung up, dressed, and was ready when Penny knocked. They shopped all day and had an early dinner at a drive-thru.

She had done the right thing, she decided. She and Tim had not gone so far that they couldn't opt out now. She would avoid the Schneiders for a time, find herself a nice safe man to sleep with, and go on as if it hadn't happened. That had worked just fine with Dave.

But when Penny pulled into the drive, Tim was standing on the porch. "Oh, my God."

"What?" Penny asked.

"Tim."

"So?"

"It must have something to do with Mike," she lied. "God, I hate this. Come in with me, Penny."

"Can't. I have a meeting at the university with my advisor for the master's program."

"Please?"

"Sorry, kid, gotta go."

Her heart began to beat out of control as she passed him on the porch and unlocked her door. He followed her in.

As he shut the door, she turned and faced him.

"I thought I'd lost you," he said softly. "I've been back and forth a dozen times since this morning."

Her voice was a whisper. "I hoped you wouldn't come."

"You didn't want me to?"

"I hoped you wouldn't."

"But now?"

"Touch me," she whispered, "and I'll tell you."

He moved to her and took her in his arms. His lips found her neck; his hands pressed her against the full length of his body. As his mouth opened on hers, she knew there was no turning back. Sobriety hadn't changed a thing.

She broke away, led him down the hall, and fell with him onto her bed. Mike had always taken control, orchestrated moves, and stirred her with his touches. This was different. This was a dangerous fire that could consume souls and hold bodies in bondage with heat and unbridled emotion—and one she didn't have the strength or desire to stop.

She helped him remove her blouse, her bra, and her skirt. He kissed her in places only Mike had touched. When all that remained were her panties, he gave a little laugh and said, "Do you want me to tear them off?"

She laughed then too. "Yes, do it," she said and partially rose to watch as he tore the seams, pulled the silk away, and kissed her there too.

She was frantic to feel his bare skin against hers. No longer shy, she slid from the bed, knelt, and removed his shoes. He pulled his shirt over his head and lifted so she could pull off his jeans. She reached out then and pulled him to her, kissed him as he had kissed her, and slid up over him. They rolled, smooth and hot, onto the colored silk of the Orient, with full knowledge that their needs were carnal and forbidden, yet both eager to share the sin.

Hours later their desire still burned. They had led one another to fiery heights—one needing, sated, the other sated then needing. Sometimes both needing and sated at once, but moving again, never quiet, never still, never done. She was shameless. He was adventurous. When she became playful, he became brazen. Both were unrestrained and reckless.

The sound of Dave's car pulling up on the drive brought them back to earth. They lay still and waited to hear the car door slam before they crept into the darkened living room and lay together on the couch. She could hear Dave's typewriter clicking away as the springs of the couch began their own throaty rhythm. Dave couldn't hear them, yet she found herself listening and worried he would know. Tim's car was on the street.

"No one can know," she said then.

"No one needs to."

"Ann."

"I never imagined a woman could be like this."

"Like a tramp?" she asked.

"You're not a tramp."

"I would be in Ann's eyes."

"Ann and I were never like this. For months I've wanted to kiss you, to touch you, but I pushed the thought away. I'll never get enough of you."

She looked into his eyes. "I'm totally out of control. It scares me."

"You have no reason to be afraid."

"Have you done this before?"

"Before what?"

"Have you done this with anyone else since you've been married?"

"We married young."

"So you have?"

"Yes."

"A lot?"

"No. We had an agreement when I went to 'Nam. I've been there twice. Does that tell you enough?"

"Do you still have an agreement?"

"No."

"She's my friend. She trusts me. I don't think I could live if she knew I'd betrayed her."

"I don't consider this betrayal."

"What is it then?"

"I don't know."

"Neither do I." She pulled herself up, sat in the curve of his belly, and stroked his face. "Have you ever had a lover?"

"No," he said. He grasped her hands and kissed her fingertips. "Do I have one now?"

"If Ann were to know, I couldn't love you like this."

"She doesn't need to know."

"Promise me she never will."

He promised, dressed, and slipped out into the darkness.

She hurried to her bed, pulled the cool quilt over her feverish skin, breathed in the scent of him, and fell into a deep and dreamless sleep.

∽

The next day another letter arrived from Kate.

2 March 1969

Dear Sandy,

Okay, so there really is a war going on. We were attacked last week and I have to say I was scared as hell. Some sappers with explosives got into the compound and did some real damage. For the first time I heard the sound of incoming rockets and grenade explosions. It was totally unexpected and in the middle of the night, so we could do nothing but climb under our beds and hope for the best. Dee and I were afraid to even whisper because men were running beneath our windows and bullets were hitting the walls of our hooch. It only lasted about an hour, but that was enough for me to decide there are some parts of this war that are not for me—like all of it. It was a miracle none of us were hurt. Our hooch was damaged and the front wall of the officers' mess was blown off. It's probably a good thing we'd had a wild party and most of us were three sheets to the wind and too relaxed to do anything foolish.

The next night we had dust offs come in with some pretty grim injuries and had to work through until morning. My Vietnamese seamstress has not shown up for a couple of weeks, which says she either knew about the attack coming or has been injured in one of the battles that are becoming more frequent around the base. I don't know whether I should be angry with her for leaving us like sitting ducks after all the business and freebies we have given her, or if I should be worried about her. There have been reprisals for some Vietnamese who serve Americans.

I am hoping there are no more attacks for a while because I had my buttocks imprinted on the ceiling of the O club one night and I can't get the blue dye off my butt. Can you imagine if I were sent home in a body bag with a royal blue butt?

We are all a bit wild. There was a rumor going around one of the female majors had set up a sex-for-pay operation. We nurses had some good laughs about that. Some of us agreed it was about time officers pay for sex like the enlisted do. Why shouldn't some round-eyed female reap the benefits of this war? The major was relieved of duty and sent stateside. When we went to see her off, she had a big grin on her face. She brought out a wad of cash and laughed. We couldn't decide if she was being sarcastic because of the rumors or if she was simply saying, "gotcha!" When one of the new gals said she thought it was terrible someone would prostitute herself in the middle of a war, we had another good laugh because lots of us are already doing that, but not getting paid.

Luckily there's a lot of weed around to help us see the humor in all of this. I can see you frowning. Don't worry; I'm a big girl.

Love,

Kate

∞

Sandy and Tim began to meet at motels every Sunday. She told herself he was a loan, a love to see her through. He told her he wanted all of her and soon began to beg for more.

One evening they ran into each other at the club and went to her place. Dave was away. They lost track of time and made love far into the night. He called Ann and said he'd had too much to drink but would be home soon.

They weren't so bad, Sandy rationalized; they weren't really taking anything away from Ann. Yet they were never free of her.

After that night Sandy gave him a key to her back door. He began parking his car two blocks away and creeping across dark lawns for an hour of lovemaking. He told Ann that Sandy had found a new love and was too busy to visit. Ann was happy for their young friend.

In truth, Sandy spent evenings watching TV and sipping scotch while she waited for her lover. Sometimes she met Penny at Dave's or Dave at Penny's. The two were seeing each other regularly. Penny was happier than she'd been since O.T., but she insisted it was because her visit to Kansas City to see Bob was inching ever closer. Dave rarely spoke of Kate.

One night as Tim and Sandy lay intertwined on her bed, he brought up Ann.

"She's beginning to ask questions," he said. "She says I'm spending too much time at the club."

"We should go back to Sundays."

"It's never enough, Sandy. I can't stay away. I keep thinking maybe we'll get tired of each other and slow things down, but I only love you more."

"Do you want to be tired of me?"

He kissed her hair. "No. But I catch myself wanting to tell Ann everything, spilling my guts and going on from there."

She pulled away. "Never! She doesn't deserve that."

He pulled her back and quieted her with kisses. "Sometimes I hate myself," he said.

"Stay away awhile."

"I can't. I need you more than I've ever needed Ann."

⚮

Three weeks later Major Roberts summoned her. "How about a little vacation?" she asked.

Sandy had expected another plea to re-up. "A what?"

"I've been directed to send a charge nurse TDY to San Antonio. The general recommended you. Want to go?"

"Yes," she said.

"Report on Monday. Fly or drive. I can give you two days' travel time, leave Saturday morning or Sunday night."

"I'll drive."

"Good. I'll have them cut your orders." She paused momentarily before she added, "Lieutenant, I'd be careful if I were you. The general seems to have a thing for you."

That night, as soon as Tim arrived, she broke the news. "I'm going TDY to Texas for six weeks," she said.

His smile faded.

"They're short-staffed and need help in San Antonio. The general recommended me."

"He knows about us," he said with a slowness that frightened her.

"How could he? We've been so careful."

"I have orders for San Antonio too, for more training in the flight simulator. I leave in two weeks and stay for four. It's too much of a coincidence."

"Major Roberts said I should be careful. Do you think that's what she meant?"

"I doubt he would have told her, but I was told the general personally signed my orders."

"Why?"

"He doesn't miss a trick. He's good at reading people. He's probably thinking if we have enough time together we'll get this out of our systems. Maybe he's right."

"He won't tell Ann?"

"He's doing this so *no one* tells Ann. He's doing this for his command and for our own good."

"He may be right, you know," she said.

"About us cooling off?"

"Yes."

"Shall we find out?"

"What if Ann realizes we're both in the same place?"

"That's why you leave first and I go two weeks later. He's a wise old bird." He sat up on the side of the bed. "You'll have to call Ann."

"Why?"

"To tell her about your trip and how excited you will be to see your pilot friend in Laredo. I'll tell her about my orders after you're gone."

"I can't lie to her."

"Why not? I live our lie every day."

CHAPTER FOURTEEN

San Antonio, Texas. May 1969.

Top-down weather, Texas at its best, the grass greened from rivers swollen with winter runoff. Sandy checked into the Visiting Officers' Quarters and kept her whites and duty shoes there. Tim took a room at a motel on a country road between the two bases. It had a pool and very few guests.

They both did their day jobs well, but in their free time they avoided the bases, danced to fiddle music at country taverns, and drank local beer. They saw a rodeo with real bulls and bucking cowboys, spent weekends in Galveston and on San Pedro Island, and made more leisurely but no less passionate love.

At times, when she thought about General Magnem and his interference in their lives, a deep resentment festered, but other times, when she could kiss Tim in public or not worry when their bedsprings squeaked, she was grateful for his understanding. But if the general thought the fire of their relationship would burn out, he had miscalculated.

They found they were compatible in other ways. They laughed constantly, played jokes on each other, and were equally grateful for a simple walk, a good show, or a sweet song. They slept wrapped in each other's arms and every morning woke with their desire rekindled and burning hot. Sandy foolishly began to believe life could be clean, unblemished, and uncomplicated.

On their final day she drove him to the airport for his flight. They stayed in the car kissing and talking until the last possible moment.

"Why do I want to cry?" he asked.

"I don't know, but it's contagious."

"I don't think I can go back and not make some changes," he said.

She leaned comfortably against him. "Sometimes I think, to hell with it. Why not be selfish? Why not take what's good and not worry about anyone else? But the reality is we can't build our happiness on someone else's grief. Neither of us is made that way."

"Would you hate me?" he asked.

"I'd hate myself."

"We can't go on leading half lives."

"We have no other choice," she said with a firmness she didn't feel.

"We're going to be found out. You know how things go on a base. If the general suspects, others can guess."

"I think Dave has suspicions. He says I watch too much TV."

"You're putting your life on hold. I don't want that for you, but I can't stay away. When I was flying in the simulator and crashed and burned, I thought how easy it would be if I had the courage to crash. Then there would be two women free."

She felt as if he'd physically hit her. The world closed in. She began to shake with intense fear.

He realized instantly and tried to pull her closer, but she pushed him away, scrambled to open her door, lurched to the pavement, and was sick.

"Oh, Jesus, Sandy. I didn't mean that. I'm sorry."

She should fall down on her knees. She should prostrate herself on the hot asphalt and beg forgiveness. She would do anything if only she could go back and not hurt anyone else.

He stood beside her, tried to hold her. She clawed her way free, leaned against the hot metal of the car, and faced him.

"I'm so sorry," he said.

"Oh, Tim. I'm sorry too. I never meant to hurt anyone. I have no right to love you. I've done all of us a terrible wrong."

"You're right," he said. "We've gone too far."

After he had flown off, she began her own drive back, but in Oklahoma City she stopped and called the major. "I'm having car trouble," she lied. "They say it will take until tomorrow to get the parts. I won't make it back until Tuesday."

"It will be unauthorized leave," Major Roberts warned.

"What does that mean?"

"You'll have to work next weekend."

"That's fine with me. There's nothing I can do about it."

"So get the car fixed and take care of anything else that needs taking care of. How was San Antonio?"

Sandy wondered if there was some innuendo in her phrasing. She answered quickly, "Exciting. Busy. The time went too fast."

"I heard good things about you. I had a call from your commander. They were impressed."

"I guess I did some things right."

"You certainly did. I'll see you Tuesday, Lieutenant."

She checked into a motel with tequila and margarita mix. Three drinks later and well after midnight she placed a call to Dave.

"I'm having trouble sleeping," she said.

"So you called me? Am I so boring?"

She laughed. "No, but you are dependable."

"Where are you?"

"I'm in Oklahoma City. I'm on my way back. I thought you might still be up working."

"I am. I'm trying to write a speech for a rally next week, but I'm having trouble thinking."

"You work too hard and think too much."

There was a long silence during which she thought she was interrupting his work. "I'll hang up and let you get back to it," she said.

"No. I've missed you. It's nice to hear from you."

"So tell me how the war is going. I haven't watched the news in weeks."

"Did you hear Nixon started up the bombing again?"

"Why?"

"It gives him some wiggle room, so he can begin withdrawing troops."

"That's a good thing, isn't it?"

"Not if the cost is the morale of the military. Pulling forces out a little at a time means the troops will only have to keep their heads down and serve their time. No purpose; no mission. It's the equivalent of a jail sentence."

"Boring?"

"And stressful as hell. So how will they get by?"

"I haven't a clue."

"They'll sit tight, keep their heads low, and start looking for some way to make the time go faster."

"And?"

"With cheap drugs available and a lot of time to kill, what do you think they'll do?"

"Party?"

"You got it."

"Is that what your speech is about?"

"That, and how history repeats itself."

"You mean all of this is predictable?"

"No. Only the men involved are predictable."

"I don't understand."

"All the basic survival and predatory instincts are still in us. We have better technology, more efficient machines, and proven methods, but the beast himself hasn't changed."

"Or the beast herself," she said.

"Do you have something on your mind?"

"Ask me something else."

"Was Texas okay?"

"Yeah. Texas was great."

"What then?"

"I think I've lost my equilibrium."

"I've been a little worried about your drinking."

"That's part of it."

"You've changed a lot since Mike died."

"For good or bad?"

"I'm not sure. It depends on who he is."

Her stomach did a flip. "Am I that transparent?"

"No. It's that I'm good old Dave. And old Dave keeps a close eye on the people he loves."

"And what advice would old Dave give a friend who's in love with a married man?"

"He'd say, 'I hope he's a damned nice married man because the girl deserves the best.'"

"And what if his friend knows the married man has a great marriage that is part of his very psyche and leaving it would cause tremendous hurt to everyone, and yet he wants to?"

"Old Dave would say it depends."

"On what?"

"On how much his friend truly loves the married guy."

"What does that mean?"

"It begs the question, Does the woman love the man enough to give him up?"

"That's what I thought."

"So when are you coming home?"

"I'm starting out in the morning. I should be there by nightfall."

"I'll leave the lights on."

She had never been married, but she had been in Ann's position twice and she knew the shadow of pain it left in a heart. She could not, would not, cause that kind of pain to another, especially some-one as kind and generous as Ann.

But she had already caused pain for Tim, and that in turn would transfer to Ann. There was no way out, unless she could convince him to be reasonable, unless she could make the break as cleanly and honestly as possible.

But all bets were off her first night home when she heard his key in the door and was in his arms before he'd crossed the kitchen floor.

He held her fiercely. "I'm going crazy," he said. "I can't be with-out you. I can't live like this."

"Tim."

He wouldn't be stopped. "Listen. Listen for just a minute. I've been frantic with worry."

"I needed time to think. We both needed time to think."

"Well, I've thought and thought and I keep coming back to the same place. I love you, Sandy. I love you and I don't want to live another day without you."

She wished she could cry. She hadn't cried since the early deaths of her friends, and now every emotion and every hurt she'd expe-rienced was buried so deep inside it was only when they made love that she had release.

"I only meant to borrow you," she said. "I never meant for it to come to this."

"I kept waiting for you to ask, for you to say, 'Tim, I can't live like this. Leave Ann and marry me.' But this weekend, when you didn't come back, I realized you're never going to say it.

"I was mad at you. I wanted to shake some sense into you. And then I got mad at myself for wanting you so much. And finally I took it all out on Ann and I made the kids cry. I love my kids and I don't know if I could live away from them, and so I vowed to myself I would never touch you again. But when I saw your car in the drive I forgot every vow I'd made."

She shouldn't have raised her lips to his, or touched his face, or allowed him to push her robe away. She should have stopped him before his hands spread fire and desire blotted out all the resolutions she too had made on the lonely trip up Highway 44. She should have, but she didn't. And in the end she had to ask the only question she was sure could finish them. She looked fully on him as she asked, "Tim?"

"What?"

"Would you give up flying if I asked?"

He laughed at the absurdity of the question. "You don't mean that."

"Yes, I do. Would you do it?"

"Jesus, Sandy. I've never even considered that."

"Has Ann ever asked that of you?"

"No."

"You see? That's the difference between us two women. And do you know what I think?"

He attempted to hide his discomfort with a smile. "No, and I'm afraid to ask."

"I think if I honestly asked it of you, and you had to choose, flying would win."

He didn't comment but he did flinch, and she knew in an instant she had hit her mark. If he needed a reason to leave her, this was it. And because she knew in her heart she could not trust a fighter pilot with both their lives, she was sure this was the one thing that would break their love.

"If you asked me that question seriously, would you give me time to think it over?"

"I am asking seriously," she said.

❧

The next morning Ann called her at work. She'd had a fight with Tim, she said, and he hadn't come home all night. He was deeply troubled but he told her not to question him. He never touched her anymore and she was sure he was sleeping with another woman.

Sandy could have won him at that moment. She could have said, if she was a cruel and selfish woman, "He was with me, Ann, but don't worry—we only made love twice," but she didn't. She listened and murmured and comforted and when she hung up the phone she walked up to Major Roberts's office and signed the papers that committed her for two more years and gave her the right to reassignment. Then she called Tim at his squadron and told him she needed to see him after work.

"I have to drive up to the firing range," he said. "I have duty in the pit tomorrow. Put on your uniform and go with me."

"Pick me up," she said.

Early the next morning they headed north in an official Air Force car, belted in and sitting rigidly apart.

As they drove through the Flint Hills he turned his head and said, "I talked to General Magnem yesterday. I requested reassignment."

She smiled. "I met with Major Roberts yesterday. I requested reassignment. How's that for mental telepathy?"

"I had a terrible scene with Ann."

"She called me."

"What did she say?"

"She said you stayed out all night and she's sure you're sleeping with someone else. She said you never touch her anymore."

"I don't."

"I had a horrible thought when I was talking to her, and it made me realize how hard I've become."

"Why?"

She told him what she had thought to say.

"You would never do that."

"No, and I can't do this any longer."

He reached out and took her hand on the seat. "I can't either."

They drove in silence for a few miles. "What assignment did you ask for?" she finally asked.

"F-4s. The National Guard will get the 105s soon. I'll train in Texas and California before I take an accompanied tour overseas."

"Not in Southeast Asia?" she asked.

"No. Europe somewhere. It will be four years if I take the family."

"Did he say when?"

"Within weeks."

"So, he does know."

"I didn't ask, but he said he thought my decision was a wise one. We left everything else unsaid."

"I don't want to leave anything unsaid between us. We have to say and do everything and then make the break, clean and permanent."

"What about when we grow old? What if things change anyway? What if I find I can't live without you?"

She wanted to crawl over to him, but she stayed belted in. "I don't have that much willpower. We have to make it like a death." Her voice broke. "Oh, God, Tim, I'm not sure I can do it."

He pulled the car onto a dirt road, moved slowly into some scrub trees, and met her in the middle of the wide blue seat. They kissed in that passionate and deep way that only lovers saying good-bye kiss, and for once, it was enough.

They ate dinner as any military officers on assignment would, and she waited at the restaurant while he checked into the motel. He returned for her and pulled to the back so they could go into the room without being seen.

They had never been together in uniform before, so they pretended he was a general and she was a private and he seduced her, one kiss, one touch, one item of clothing carefully removed at a time. And it was like their first time, but sweeter, and they were both sated when it was done.

When the first light of morning showed through a crack in the drapes, she rose up on one elbow and gazed at him. He was half covered by the sheet, his hair dark against the white pillow, his breathing even and deep, and his chest flaring seductively under his Texas tan. She was filled with love for him. As she breathed in his scent and held back her desire to touch and taste the saltiness of his skin, he opened his eyes and pulled her to him.

"Good morning, Private," he said. "Are you scheduled for on-the-job-training again?"

"Oh, General," she exclaimed. "Do you think we could?"

"Yes, Private. There's a learning curve we've got to hump over."

"Are you sure you're up for it?"

He pulled the covers off and said, "Does it look like I am?"

For the first time since Texas, they laughed as they made love.

She wore her uniform, went with him into the pit on the firing range, and watched as the latest class of fighter jocks took target practice on fences, concrete bunkers, and battered tanks. It frightened her to see the 105s dive from the sky, fire, and immediately pull up. Tim told her that if the pilots looked at the target after firing their missiles, they would crash and burn. Several of them were slow to pull up, and she felt her heart pound against her ribs until the plane was high in the sky again.

She wrote the scores on a pad as he called them out. At the end of the day, they drove slowly back toward Meridian.

∽

Major Roberts's car was behind hers on the drive.

She jumped out with her overnight bag. "Go," she said. "Don't let the major see you." She carried her overnight bag to the porch as Tim backed out and drove up the street.

The major was standing in Dave's living room, her back to the open door. Sandy opened her own door, put the overnight bag inside, and calmed herself before walking back across the porch.

The major met her halfway. "What the hell are you trying to pull off, Lieutenant?" she demanded. "Where the hell have you been?"

"I had to go somewhere."

The major followed her back to her living room, talking the entire way. "You were scheduled to be at work. I've had the hospital commander on my ass all day."

"Penny covered my shift."

"You know the rules. You notify me of any changes. Are you sick? Why didn't you report in?"

"I didn't have time."

"But you had plenty of time to spend with Major Schneider, didn't you?"

Sandy couldn't speak. Her pulse roared against her temples. She stood mute and defiant in the middle of the room.

"Did you think you could keep such a secret on a base?"

"Who else knows?" Sandy asked.

"Does it matter?"

"Yes. It matters a lot."

"Sit down and tell me."

"There's nothing more I want you to know."

"Oh, kid, there's a lot you've got to learn. You're a tender young thing. We were all like you at one time."

Sandy didn't speak.

"How long has it been going on?"

"Since January."

"Five months? Does anybody in his squadron know?"

"I don't think so." It was all an accident, she wanted to say. None of it was planned.

"I had an idea something was going on when the general sent you off to Texas. Did you request that?"

She shook her head.

"Major Schneider's wife came to the hospital looking for you this morning."

"Why?"

"She needed a friend."

"Did she know I was with him?"

"Honey, I don't think she has a clue. She said he had gone up to the firing range and she was going to ask you to stay with the kids so she could join him. Isn't that a hoot?"

"It's not funny at all."

"No, I'll agree with you on that. She arrived just as the Personal Affairs officer came to my office looking for you. I decided to drop in on my way home and I ran into Dave, who told me you went up to the range yesterday. Now you tell me, Does two plus two equal three?"

Sandy studied her hands. They were unusually cold.

"Do you love him, or is this just a kick?"

She nodded.

"You love him. Dumb question for someone as straight as you." She sat heavily in the chair. "You have an ashtray?"

Sandy handed her a candy bowl from the side table and watched as the major lit a cigarette.

"He's leaving soon," she said.

"And then what?"

"Then nothing. We're going separate ways."

"For how long?"

"Forever."

"Who are you trying to kid?"

"It is forever. It has to be, because of Ann."

"I have to say this and you won't like it, kid. You have a poor way of being a friend."

She stood rigidly with fists clenched. "I said we've decided, and we have."

The major's eyebrows arched with surprise. "Well, wonder of wonders, I've made the kid mad."

"Stop calling me kid. I've made mistakes and I'll fix them. It's nobody's business but mine."

"You're wrong there, Lieutenant. When you're a military officer, your business is everybody's business."

"You mean if you're a female officer."

"Not true. I'm sure General Magnem is as concerned about Major Schneider and his domestic situation as I am about yours."

"Why were you looking for me?"

"I have a dispatch the Personal Affairs officer was trying to deliver. It's about Lieutenant Kiley." She held out a folded piece of white paper.

"Kate?" Sandy unfolded the dispatch and began to read.

26 June 1969 (stop) As per request of First Lieutenant Kathryn Kiley (stop) It is with regret that I inform you of her death, Bangkok, Thailand, 06 June 1969 (stop) Death from natural causes (stop) Signed Ron Larson, Captain, USAF, SEA Command

Her hands shook as she stared at the message. "It can't be," she began, but her voice trailed off as dizziness nearly overcame her. She reached out one hand and steadied herself on the wall. "Not Kate. Oh, God. When will this end?"

"I'm sorry, kid. I'm trying to find out more, but I haven't had any answers yet."

"Have you told Dave?"

"Yes."

"Did you know he and Kate had a thing?"

"I didn't know."

"I need to go over there."

"We're not finished."

"Yes, ma'am, we are. I'll say good night."

She walked out and hurried to Dave.

CHAPTER FIFTEEN

July 3, 1969.

Her mother had told her that life was all about learning; that problems arose to teach a life lesson, and if an individual learned the correct lesson, she would never have to face that same problem again. Either her mother had been wrong or Sandy still wasn't getting it right. She had loved three times and all had turned sour.

She hadn't been able to sleep well all week, and now, as she rode toward Kansas City with Penny, her voice gave away the deep fatigue she felt. "Every time I fall in love, it turns out badly. What am I doing wrong?"

"Don't ask me," Penny scoffed. "I obviously haven't solved anything in that department."

"You're definitely braver. I could never do what you're about to do."

"Even if it were Tim who was injured?"

Sandy kept her voice steady. "What do you know about that?"

"I've seen him go in your back door with a key."

"We didn't plan it. It just happened."

"You don't need to explain."

"I've never needed anyone the way I need him. Now that he's safely away, I fight every day to not beg him to come back."

"Do you think he would?"

"No, I made sure he'd be afraid to want me that much."

"How?"

"I asked him to give up flying for me," she said. "His answer was to put in for reassignment." She laughed at the irony. "Isn't it weird? He wanted to tell his wife, and leave his family, but when it came to the flying part, he couldn't do it."

"Would you really want him to stop?"

"I don't see you dating pilots since Bob's accident."

"No. And I never will. They're too short-lived."

"But so damned exciting. I wish I could find a fighter jock's soul in a ground-hugger." Sandy's sigh filled the car. "I think Kate had the right idea. Take what they have to offer and get on with it. She sure had spunk."

"You haven't learned anything more about her death?"

"No. But I did write to her roommate."

"She was such fun."

"Does Dave talk about her?"

She nodded. "With lots of emotion and some regret."

"I'm glad he talks to you." Sandy said. "He was stunned when we got the news."

"I think they were like those proverbial two ships passing in the night. They enjoyed what they found and moved on. None of us can afford to look back."

"Then why are you making this trip?"

"Why do you still want Tim?"

"We'll always have a connection."

"And so will Bob and I."

"I'm going to meet Tim one last time in St. Louis."

"Sandy! That is so dangerous. Can't you leave it where it is?"

She laughed. "So, how's your sex life?"

"What?"

"It's been four weeks. I need a fix. How do you manage that?"

"I tried Kate's way. It wasn't very satisfying. Truth is, I've been sleeping with Dave."

It was Sandy's turn to be surprised. "How did that get under my radar?"

Penny smiled, shrugged, and kept her eyes on the road. "We're pretty much seeing each other exclusively."

"You've been busy while I've been distracted. I'm happy for you."

"I was afraid you'd feel I'd betrayed Kate."

"They were both screwing around while they dated."

Penny took her eyes from the road. "Do you think he's doing that now?"

"If he says he isn't, he isn't. What does he think about you and Bob?"

"He says I have to resolve the past before I can look to the future."

"Typical Dave. See? That's the problem with ground-huggers. They're always so practical."

༆

They stopped on the outskirts of Kansas City and had a drink to buoy their courage. The hospital was easy to find. On the elevator, Sandy said, "As soon as you both get over the initial speeches, I'm going to the cafeteria. Okay?"

Penny nodded. The color had drained from her cheeks and perspiration beaded on her forehead. A nurse provided them with masks and gowns and pointed out lockers for their purses. "Room 502," she instructed as she opened the double doors of the burn unit.

Penny knocked.

"Come in." Bob's head appeared unusually large above the back of a wheelchair.

"Bob?"

When his body jerked, wisps of straw-colored hair stood up from his nearly bald scalp. He didn't turn. "Hello, Penny. I watched you get out of the car down below."

"You've had an unfair advantage then," she said. Her tone was too light and practiced.

He backed the chair in an arc. A patchwork of colors covered his face and neck. A twist of thick red replaced his nose. One ear was missing and the other was just large enough to bolster a thick bandage. His cutoff hospital trousers revealed stockings made of white gauze and tape.

Only his eyes were normal: pools of bright blue, shining from sunken orbs. "Come to see the freak?"

Penny's voice was strong. "I came to see the man I loved."

"Have a good look at what's left."

"Thank you, I will." She walked closer and studied him with clinical detachment. "They were right," she said. "The gloves saved your hands." She reached out, took his hand, and ran a finger across his palm.

He pulled away.

She moved behind him and held his shirt away from his back. "Healing nicely here. They've accomplished a lot."

His eyes focused on Sandy. "They use the skin on my butt for grafts."

"Can you walk?" Penny asked.

"I take physical therapy a couple of hours every day. What the hell for, I don't know."

"How much longer do they say?"

"Years."

"Then what?"

"I don't know."

"Do you have to stay here?"

He shrugged.

"You should make some kind of goal," Penny said.

"Goal? Shit! My only goal is to die or get out of this goddamned wrap of pretend skin. Why the hell did you come here?"

"I came to hear you say good-bye."

"Good-bye."

"Look me in the eyes and say it!"

"Go to hell!"

"I've already been to hell, Bob. I want a final good-bye. You owe me that much."

"I owe you nothing!"

"I want you to say it to my face." She stood waiting.

Sandy moved toward the door.

His head wobbled on his thin neck. His hands grasped the padded arm of his chair so tightly his knuckles were as white as the patches on his hairless arms. "I can't."

"And why not?" she demanded.

Tears spilled over his ravaged cheeks and made dark blue spots on his shirt. "Because I love you," he whispered.

As her anger fell away, Penny moved to him and dropped to her knees.

Sandy walked down the hall, tearing off the mask and gown as she went. At the desk, the nurse looked up and said, "Leaving already?"

"They don't need me here."

She found the cafeteria and carried a salad and pop to the only free table. A tall man balancing a loaded lunch tray, a briefcase, and a newspaper walked past. He scanned the room and turned back. "Can I join you?" he asked. "There doesn't seem to be another empty chair."

"Please," she answered. "I never have liked eating alone."

He spilled coffee as he tried to settle his tray on the table. She reached over and took the cup from him.

"Thanks," he said. A scattering of faded freckles ran across his cheeks to a bristled mat of russet sideburns. "Name's Pete Kennedy."

She smiled. "Sandy O'Connell."

"Are you new on staff?"

"No," she answered. "I'm visiting with a friend."

"Did I take his seat?"

"No, she's in the burn unit visiting *her* friend. They needed some time alone."

"Oh? Who's she seeing?"

"Bob Gale."

He nodded. "Tough nut to crack."

"Are you in the nut-cracking business?"

He laughed. "Social services. Try to set the vets up with lives."

She sipped her pop and nodded.

"Are you from K.C.?" he asked.

"No. I'm in the Air Force. Stationed at Meridian."

"Really? What do you do?"

"I'm a nurse."

"You like the military?"

"Yes."

"I bet the social life is great."

"Yes. It can be."

"Not much social life for me," he said, and checked his watch. "I've got ten minutes for lunch. You won't mind if I scarf this down?"

"Go right ahead."

He swallowed his chili without chewing and didn't speak until he was done. "Young guys keep me busy. Battered bodies. Drugs. Alcohol." He checked his watch again, gulped down his coffee. "I've got a guy upstairs. Fried his brain. Family wants him home. I don't think it's advisable." He began stacking up his things. "We're up to our eyeballs in basket cases. No place to put them. If the folks want to take them home, so be it. I do what I can."

"And I thought my job was tough," she said. "Leave your tray. I'll take it back."

"Thanks. Is your friend a relative of Bob's?"

"Why? Do you want us to take him home?" she teased.

He laughed easily. "It's a thought."

"Old girlfriend."

"Not Penny?!"

"Do you know her?"

He shook his head. "He talks about her. She may be exactly the medicine he needs."

"But the question now is, *is he* the medicine she needs?"

"On that note, I'll say good afternoon, Sandy O'Connell."

"Nice meeting you, Pete," she replied.

Penny decided to stay another day. They checked into a motel, had a light dinner, and bought a bottle of wine to share in the room. Sandy tried to sleep. Penny wanted to talk. "I need to get him out," she said. "He has to realize there's more than pain to look forward to." She scribbled notes on a legal pad as if she were angry at the paper itself.

"Penny," Sandy finally tried. "Go to sleep. Finish in the morning."

"I've got to get this down."

"What?"

"This experience. I want to remember it all clearly."

"Why?"

"It will be a great master's thesis—the adjustments after war, coming home, new realities."

"I'd think you'd want to forget."

"I brought a whole mess of guys like Bob back. Their lives must be a living hell. I can help."

"Haven't you done enough?"

"I've got to fix it."

"If you don't go to sleep, you'll have to fix me too."

"I'm sorry. I didn't think. What will you do tomorrow? You can take my car."

"I've got it covered," she answered. "Some social worker guy left a note with the clerk. I'm going to tour Kansas City with him."

"You little devil," Penny laughed.

෨

Pete Kennedy picked her up in the lobby of the hospital after his rounds. "I met Penny," he said as he settled her in his car. "She'll be good for Bob."

He drove through the city and pointed out grain elevators, stockyards, and slaughterhouses.

They bored her.

"I'm not much of an upper, am I?" he asked.

She tried to make him comfortable. "It's okay."

"I'm out of practice."

"Me too."

He smiled. "We could take in a movie."

"Yes." She was relieved she wouldn't have to converse.

They laughed through a spaghetti western.

෨

It was nearly dark when the two women began their trip back to Meridian.

"How was your date?" Penny asked.

"Not like a date with a fighter jock. He's very serious."

"More so than Dave?"

She nodded. "I couldn't make him laugh, and I tried darn hard. How did it go with Bob?"

"Good. He needs me."

"What about Dave?"

"I don't think Dave needs anyone."

"You're wrong about that."

Penny took her eyes from the road. "Honest, Sandy, my intentions are good." She turned back. "Anyway, I have other things to consider besides men."

"Like what?"

"Getting my degree, plotting out a plan for my life." She laughed. "And finding myself."

"I didn't know you were lost."

"We all are. Some of us just don't know it."

"Meaning me?"

"We both have a way to go," she said softly.

∾

Three weeks later they again drove toward Kansas City, where Sandy would catch her flight to St. Louis.

She pressed her temple against the cool window. If only it could be different. If only she and Tim had met years before. Foolish thought. If she had never known Mike she would not have been as freely giving with Tim. If he had never known Ann he would not be the kind of man he now was. If. If only there were no ifs.

She turned to Penny. "You still think this is a mistake, don't you?"

"I don't think anything."

"You have to have some opinion."

"Right now, Sandy, I'm thinking this rain had better stop or none of us will get anywhere."

Sandy peered at the road ahead. If only she had some insight into what was to come. If only she could see how it all turned out. "God, Penny, I'm so mixed up."

"You aren't alone."

"My mother would say it's because I'm impetuous and willful. Yet I've never thought so long and hard about anything in my life."

"Our mothers would see our entire lives as sinful if they knew," Penny said.

Sandy sighed.

"Pete Kennedy asked about you."

Sandy didn't comment.

"He wants to call," Penny said.

"Did you discourage him?"

"He asked if you have a steady guy."

"And?"

"I told him you were still looking."

"I plan to be completely single and unattached."

"Maybe you shouldn't be so fast to turn him off."

"You like him, *you* turn him on."

Penny laughed. "Don't you think I have enough man problems at the moment?"

"Don't you think I do?"

The sky cleared slightly; the rain slowed. Sandy cracked her window and breathed in the freshly washed air. Tim had rescued her from the worst time of her life. Now she would have to stand on her own again. That thought made her want to fade away. She sat up straighter and turned on the radio. She needed to matter, to have a purpose, to feel important to someone but not be expected to change. Tim had made her feel good about herself, completed. One day she might allow herself to be as open with another man, but he wouldn't be married and he wouldn't be boring and he definitely wouldn't be a fighter pilot. She rolled up the window and turned to Penny.

"This year has been hell," she confessed, "yet the part that is the worst is that I betrayed Ann. You must think I'm pretty rotten for that."

"No, Sandy, I don't. We do whatever is necessary to get through."

"Deceit feels terrible."

"You wouldn't be on your way for a final good-bye if you were truly deceitful."

"I'm afraid. I don't know if I can pull it off gracefully."

"Then don't be graceful. Just be yourself and get it done. No one ever said love had to be dignified."

They had reached the airport. Sandy hugged her friend and ran through the rain to the terminal. I could still turn back, she thought. I could say I didn't make my flight.

But she had plenty of time before her flight. She browsed through the newsstands that headlined dire predictions about the mission to the moon. She bought a paper and attempted to comprehend the mechanics of the Apollo flight. She couldn't concentrate. She bought a blank card with an envelope and wrote a final note to Tim.

> *Dearest Love,*
>
> *There is no need to describe how deeply I love you, but I desperately want you to understand why I have to say goodbye. You have been on loan to me and now I must give you back. The fire we started will never burn itself out and, if allowed to grow, would consume everything and everyone within its reach. We can't build a lifetime of happiness on that kind of pain.*
>
> *I am sad, but not unsure because I know many lives depend on what we do.*
>
> *I don't have to speak to you or see you to know you exist. I have a feeling of you all the time. Our souls have melded together and cannot be torn apart. There is a part of my heart that will be forever yours. I have to say good-bye for now, but I will visit you in your deepest sleep. Watch for me in your dreams.*
>
> *All my love,*
> *Sandy*

She tucked the letter in her bag and boarded the plane.

Tim was waiting at the gate with an armful of roses. She fell headlong into him, crushing some blooms underfoot and lofting sweet scents of summer into the air. They clung together as they were overcome with the intensity of their feelings.

"I thought you'd never get here," he said. "It was like the first day when I thought I'd lost you. My God, it feels good to hold you."

She didn't speak but pressed closer. His arms wrapped tighter, his lips brushed her temple again and again. As the gate began to refill, they were forced to move apart. They retrieved as many roses as they could and moved down the corridor.

"I found a perfect room. Top floor, windows, balcony, and privacy," he said.

"And I have an extra day off to watch the moon walk." She released his hand, took his arm, and pressed closer. This is what he gave her, she thought, this peaceful outlook on the world and this sense of belonging.

As if he read her thoughts, he stopped and pulled her to him. "I love you," he said. "I don't know what else to say except that. I love you, Sandy O'Connell."

"And I love you, Tim Schneider, more than you'll ever know."

"I've felt empty and lost. Now I feel whole again."

"I know."

At the hotel they made love hungrily, then carried a bottle of champagne into the Jacuzzi bath to pleasure one another in a more leisurely way.

In the morning they walked up the street for breakfast, bought another bottle of champagne, and went back to the hotel, where they turned on the TV, lay together on the bed, and listened to broadcasts as the astronauts orbited the moon, again and again. When one of the astronauts spoke of earthshine, Tim lifted his glass to hers. "To earthshine," he said. "Can you even begin to imagine that? Man, what I wouldn't give to be in their shoes right now."

She clicked her glass to his. "To Tim Schneider, future astronaut."

"If I weren't so tall I'd consider it," he said. "But then, I'm a real chicken when it comes to medical stuff." He turned her face to his and kissed her deeply. "What about you?" he asked.

"Me?"

"Sure. They're training women now."

"You're teasing me."

He stretched out beside her and trailed his lips over her temple and earlobe. "Me? Would I tease you?"

She laughed softly as her body responded to his touch. "You're a monster."

"I'm serious."

"I'd never pass the physical."

"Oh, you'd pass the physical part just fine." He moved his lips to her neck and carefully nibbled along the edges of her shoulder until he reached the soft fleshy part of her underarm.

She shuddered with her need for him. "I wouldn't like being poked and prodded by the docs."

"How about by me?"

"I can't get enough of you."

∾

That evening they walked through the largest shopping mall in the world. "Someday they'll have hotels right in the middle of these things," he said. "Then we'll be able to park the car, shop all day, and walk to a room for the night. They'll have a captive audience."

"Not for me," she said.

"What? No designer clothes and mink coats?"

She shook her head. "I've seen all I'll ever need of that kind of life. Money gives a person too much free time and too many choices. I'd rather be poor and happy."

"With me?"

"Tim."

"Sorry. I just can't see an end to us."

"This has to be the end."

"I'll have time at Christmas, before we transfer overseas. I'll come to Kansas."

She pulled him into a darkened corner between two stores. "Stop," she said. "We have to do this."

"I don't want to."

"We have no choice."

"I'm still waiting for you to say, 'Leave her, leave all of it and come to me.'"

She had to be brutally honest. "I'm never going to. We're going to say good-bye and we're going to go on with our lives with good memories. It's all we can ask for."

She felt him stiffen before he broke away and moved into the crowded walkway. She knew he was angry, but she didn't follow. She stepped to a window and pretended to study briefcases and Pullman bags. When her rapidly beating heart slowed, she turned and walked his way. He was waiting for her three stores down. They didn't speak as they drove back to the hotel.

∽

That night fierce storms blew in from the plains and tornado warnings sounded as howling winds shook the windows. Tim opened the curtains wide. Bolts of lightning split the sky and thunder rattled the balcony doors.

"Maybe we should go to a shelter," Sandy murmured when he settled back into the bed and pulled her against his chest.

"That's a negative," he said. "If we're ever going to be struck by lightning or blown away by a tornado, I couldn't choose a better time. I'm willing to die right here, right now."

She curled against him. If only it could be so, she thought. If only I didn't have to give this man up.

∾

They stayed in bed until noon, ordered room service, and watched the astronauts begin their descent to the lunar surface. When Neil Armstrong pronounced the *Eagle* had landed, they burst into applause.

"Never, never, never will I forget this day or us," he said. "When I telephone you thirty years from now, I want you to promise you won't hang up on me. If a man answers, I'll ask for Sandy Schneider."

"I won't hang up," she said.

They read the newspaper to one another. The drowning death of a girl at Chappaquiddick brought cold reality. Ted Kennedy had been driving the car but didn't save the girl.

"I would never leave you drowning in a car," he said. "I would die trying to rescue you."

"Good intentions can't soften the sin. Deep down, our souls are all as black as Teddy Kennedy's."

He pulled her to him. "I'll never agree with that. And don't think I don't know what you're doing. I'm not going to get mad at you on our last day."

She collapsed in his arms. Her heart was dying but no tears would flow. She couldn't bear to let him go. She couldn't walk away. "We're too much alike," she said.

"No," he said. "We just love too much."

"Can you say good-bye for me? Can you be the one to do it?"

"I can't. I just can't."

But they had to. They dressed and drove to the airport where they stood together, holding tightly to one another, speechless and unmoving. The flight was called, passengers boarded, and still they stood, locked together in a time warp of their own making.

"Last call," the flight attendant said in an official tone, and then more softly, "You'll have to go if you want to board this flight, ma'am."

Sandy nodded, pressed her letter into Tim's hand, and broke away.

"Good-bye," she whispered before she turned and ran through the open door.

ᕦᕤ

Penny had promised to meet her at the Wichita airport, but Sandy found Dave waiting.

"Where's Penny?" she asked as he hugged her.

"Got tied up in Kansas City. She asked me to pick you up, said you'd need a friend."

"She was right."

"Bad trip?"

"It was like you said. I had to let him go."

"I don't think you'll be sorry."

"Then why do I feel so bad?"

He pulled her under his arm in a brotherly hug but didn't answer. They walked in silence to his car. She hadn't needed an answer or, worse, patronizing words. He knew her well, too.

"I just got back from Kate's alma mater," he said as they drove home. "I tried to find someone who knew her, but had no success. Things are a bit of a mess at Berkeley."

"No one remembered her?"

"Not a soul. She must have breezed in and out of there like she breezed in and out of here."

"I miss her."

"This world could use more Kates."

"And fewer sad sacks like us," she said.

"We have grown awfully serious, haven't we?"

"How could we not? Two years ago I would never have imagined there could be so many changes in my life."

"Comes with age," he said with a grin.

She punched his arm gently. "Don't put that one on me, Dave. I'm only twenty-four. You're the one who's ancient."

He laughed but didn't say more.

"So what called you to Berkeley?"

"A couple of months ago, a group of hippies took over a parking lot, dug out the asphalt, planted a few trees, and made it a gathering spot. The administration called the police to take it back and somebody started shooting. A bunch of kids were hurt and one guy died."

"Why?"

"Why did they start shooting or why did they want the park turned back into a parking lot?"

"All of it."

"Who knows? Governor Reagan called out the National Guard. Who in the hell needs the Guard to take back a damned parking lot? I'm part of the inquiry."

"Everybody's afraid."

"We have good reason to be, when there's a mini war in the middle of the university over a parking lot," he said with a chuckle.

His laughter gave her hope that everything would become normal and they could return to their original selves. "So what's next?"

"I'm not sure. Nixon is a foxy man. He says the war is winding down."

"If it's winding down, where are all the injured guys at the V.A. coming from?" she asked.

"Casualties are up, deaths are down. That means both sides are avoiding big confrontations. The V.C. can sit back on their haunches until the victims kill themselves."

"Our guys?"

"Yes. The stories coming from the war make my hairs stand on end."

"Like what?"

"Fragging."

"What does that mean?"

"It's short for fragmentation grenades. If the troops feel a commanding officer is putting them in danger, he has a sudden accident."

"That can't be true!"

"I believe it."

"They'd be court martialed."

"They don't get caught. Someone puts money and the target's name in a tree. Whoever chooses to do the deed takes the money and does the job. That way no one ever knows who ordered the job or who carried it out."

"That seems pretty far-fetched."

"It's not the only story I've heard. There are whispers of rapes, executions of civilians, and massacres of whole villages."

"Americans don't do that."

"Men do strange things when their lives are in danger. I'm afraid this is the beginning of a whole new war, and not a pretty one, Sandy."

"It makes me sick."

"As I said many times, events can change but the beast remains the same."

"It's weird, isn't it?"

"What?"

"That I can hang out with all these fighter pilots and not think about what their real job is. They talk about it like it's fun and games, but in the end it's bombs dropped, missiles fired, and guns killing people."

He nodded.

"Why doesn't anyone talk about that?" she asked.

"Because if they talked about it, they might never be able to do the job. If you don't see it, it isn't real."

"But how can they protect us and not hurt others?"

"Aha! Now that's the conundrum. Men will always fight more fiercely to protect their turf than those who want to take it away. That's why we can't win this. We're seeing more atrocities and inhumanity because the guys who are in control are the ones with the need and greed. Your average Joe will be lost over there."

"This once I hope you're wrong."

He pulled into the drive. "I hope I am too."

He left her at her door. A few minutes later she heard his typewriter begin.

∽

Penny came back from Kansas City two days later and knocked on Sandy's door. She had married Bob.

"You said you were going to be fair to Dave. Is this what you call fair?" Sandy shouted.

"I planned poorly, I admit. But I had no choice."

"How is that?"

"I want Bob to have a chance at a normal life."

"By marrying him when you're sleeping with another guy?"

"I don't plan to sleep with Bob."

"What?"

"I married him so I could have a say in his care. They have to listen to me now."

"And what does Bob think of you taking over his life?"

"Damn it, Sandy, I don't have to explain myself to you or anyone else. He needs me, so I married him."

"Are you going to live without sex?"

"Are you?"

"Hey, I'm not married. I'm still free to come and go as I please."

"But you don't. You're a one-man woman, Sandy. You'll never change that."

"So, will Bob's wife come home and sleep with Dave?"

"That's my business."

"Everyone is bound to ask."

"Everyone can go to hell."

"Everyone but Bob?"

"Bob's already in hell."

Sandy knew it was true, and she felt sorry for him, but Dave was her friend and so she pressed on. "I'm sorry, Pen, I can't stand to see you destroying what you have."

"I plan to do just what you said. On weekends I'll be with Bob and during the week I'll be with Dave."

"And how long can that last?"

"As long as it takes for Bob to decide to live again."

"It's all too much for my Catholic brain."

"I love two men, Sandy. One needs a wife and can't have sex; the other needs sex and doesn't want a wife. Why shouldn't I get two for the price of one?"

"Because they both may end up one day needing both sex and a wife. Where will you be then?"

"Bed-bound and likely quite content," Penny quipped.

Sandy giggled. "Are we still friends?"

"I'm counting on that."

"Me too."

CHAPTER SIXTEEN

While Penny, Dave, and Bob fell into a comfortable pattern, letters from Tim stacked up in Sandy's desk drawer. She sometimes shuffled them like a deck of cards in her desire to know everything about his new life, but she dared not open even one. Her body and heart called out for him.

As the August heat built to record highs, she became testy, short of patience and, according to Jim Andersen, a real bitch.

On the anniversary of Mike's death, she found herself alone, restless, and with the entire Labor Day weekend free. On a whim, she drove to the base to watch the air show. She was early so she ordered a scotch in the nearly empty Officers' Club bar. A man in civvies took the seat next to her and ordered a beer.

"Hot out there," he said. He was fresh-faced and very tan.

"Yes," she agreed.

"Kansas always this hot?"

"From March until October," she answered.

"And I thought Florida was bad."

That explained the tan. "Is that where you're from?"

"For now."

She wasn't looking for conversation. She sipped her scotch.

"At least Florida has the ocean," he persisted. "You can get out and not fry."

"You get used to it," she said. He wasn't going to go away. "Are you here for business or pleasure?"

"Neither. I'm with the Thunderbirds. Or at least I'd like to be. I'm auditioning to fly with them."

"Shouldn't you be out there?"

"I haven't been accepted yet. They're looking me over. No shows until I'm in."

"I thought they needed hotshot pilots. Can't they watch you fly and be done with it?"

When he laughed, his brown eyes brightened to amber. "It's a public relations thing. We're supposed to be the best—level-headed in all parts of our lives, not just flying."

"Are you?"

"I'm trying."

"Doesn't it bother you to see other guys out there wowing the crowds?"

"I've never minded having a back-row seat."

"That's a refreshing change. I didn't know they made pilots who didn't eat, sleep, and drink airplanes."

"I like to eat good food, drink good beer, and sleep with good women. The flying part is icing on the cake."

He had a genuinely nice smile. He offered his hand. "I'm Ace. And you are ... ?" His hand was smooth and warm.

"Ace? Now that's a hotshot fighter pilot's name if I ever heard one."

"Don't make assumptions," he warned. "It's short for Asa. Means 'healer.' My parents had big hopes for me."

"Well, I hate to think what my parents had in mind for me. I'm Sandy, short for Sandra. It means 'defender of mankind.'"

They laughed together and finished their drinks.

She surprised herself by saying, "I'm driving out to the flight line to watch the show. Are you looking for a ride?"

"You've read my mind." When they stood he was barely taller than she. His walk was confident but not cocky. "Have you been here long?" he asked.

"Two years."

"And you're a nurse?"

"Does it show?"

"I asked the bartender. Do you plan to make this a career?"

She shrugged. "I don't know. I just re-upped."

"Reserve or regular?"

"Reserve. I'm not ready to commit to regular."

"But it's been offered?"

"Yes."

"There are officers who would die to be offered a regular commission. It's the only way to go if you're serious about the military."

"Are you serious about it?" she asked.

"I'm not sure I want to spend my entire life at it."

"What does your family think?"

"My folks? They think it's great."

"And your wife?"

"I haven't got one yet. Do you want to volunteer?"

He made it easy to laugh. "Heavens, no! I'm already all that I can be." She stopped at the car. "Do you want to drive?"

"Sure."

She flipped him the keys.

He held the passenger door open for her. "You've never thought of being a wife? Really? A girl like you should settle down, raise a family."

"Pipe dreams," she said. "I got over those long ago."

"But society says a woman isn't complete unless she's married." He backed out smoothly and headed toward the flight line.

"Society says a lot of things that don't work for everyone."

"Well, hell, isn't a woman's place in the home? Isn't that the all-American plan?"

"It's the all-American mothers' plan. The daughters these days have different ideas."

His eyes met hers with an honesty that caused her to look away. "So, not your dream?" he asked.

"Not mine. Definitely not mine."

He pulled in to a parking place and turned to her. "I'm sorry we're here," he said. "This conversation was just getting interesting. Tell me, if motherhood and wifedom don't interest you, what does?"

"That's the thing," she laughed. "I don't know. What are the alternatives?"

"If you figure it out, will you let me know? I'm kind of in the same spot."

They walked close to the hangars, where the shade protected them from the shimmering waves of heat that rose off the asphalt and the hot wind scented with the familiar mixture of jet exhaust and prairie dust. "Look," he said, and pointed into an open hangar. "There's McNamara's baby. The F-111."

"Have you flown it?"

He laughed. "Heck, no. It's a piece of junk. The test pilots say you can find their crash sites by following the trail of debris. When one of my buddies put one through its paces he radioed the ground crew and asked, 'Hey, fellas, can you tell me what I just lost?' The ground crew answered, 'From the looks of things down here, all you've got left is a seat and your controls.'" He laughed and touched his finger to his lips. "But mum's the word. For all intents and political purposes, it flies like a dream."

He placed one hand lightly on her back. She didn't move away.

"There's my crew." He pointed to a group of white flight suits lined up beside one of the Thunderbird jets.

"Why are they in white?" she asked.

"They wear a different color every day of the week. That's one of the perks, along with first-class accommodations and lots of sweet young things drooling nearby. See?" He pointed to a bevy of young girls standing behind ropes. "They're like groupies around rock stars."

"Do you like that?"

"Wouldn't any man? But here's the secret: There's a golden rule. Look, but do not touch. We are emissaries of peace, officers and gentlemen."

As they watched, the Thunderbird pilots, helmets in hand, climbed the ladders to their planes. "It looks like they're ready to start," he said. "Let's find a place to sit."

By the time they climbed the berm by the runway, the planes had moved though waves of melted glass to the end of the field. Shivers traveled up her spine as they screamed vertically into the blue bowl of sky.

"Watch," he said. "Here comes a cloverleaf."

The aircraft shot skyward, four abreast, until they reached the top of an invisible cliff and fell over backwards. Their jet streams drew a perfect clover. Screeching earthward, they ended up flying on two collision courses. She held her breath until they skimmed safely by one another.

"How do they fly so close and stay in sync?" she asked.

"The leader uses voice control. He speaks with precise cadence the entire time we fly. It has a hypnotic quality that makes it second nature to follow his commands."

"Wow. You have to have a lot of trust to rely on one person like that. One mistake and you've bought the farm."

"Expectation is we'll follow him into the ground if that's where he goes."

"So being lead in the Thunderbirds is a pretty cool thing?"

"A unique experience. If I stay in, that's my goal."

"And I bet you'll do just that," she said.

As they watched the show, he explained each maneuver. When the last plane landed he said, "There's a reception in the city at 1800 hours. Dinner, drinks, and some dancing. Would you like to go?"

She didn't answer immediately. I'm so easily charmed, she thought. He's a fighter pilot and I should say no. But home was too lonely, and the empty feeling that had plagued her for the past month settled into her center.

"I can't go to a party dressed like this," she answered. "I'll need to run home first and change."

"Great. Drop me by the VOQ. I'll wait for you."

Traffic exiting the event, blocked every base road. By the time they made it to the VOQ, it was 1735 hours. "I think we should just go on to my place," she said. "It's on the way and will save time."

"Fine," he said.

The traffic didn't lessen, and it was almost six when they pulled up to her apartment.

Dave was on the porch with his suitcase. He smiled as they came up the walk.

"Hi, stranger," Sandy said. "Are you coming or going?"

"On my way again. Meeting in Detroit. I had to stop by for some notes."

She introduced the two men. Dave shoved his papers under his arm and shook Ace's offered hand.

"Do you have to run right off, or do you have time for a beer?" Sandy asked.

"I was perusing the traffic and trying to decide what to do. I'll take you up on the beer."

The three of them entered her apartment. She pulled a couple of beers from the fridge. Déjà vu, she thought as she watched the two men settle on the couch.

She showered and pulled on a white sundress with spaghetti straps and a thin belt that accented her small waist. She studied her face as she pulled her hair back into a loose knot. Her sunburned cheeks and nose made her appear younger and more tender than she felt. When she returned to the living room, both men whistled their approval.

They had turned on the television and were watching a ball game.

"If I'm going to make my flight, I'll have to be going." Dave stood and opened the door. "You guys have fun."

Ace stood and shook his hand again. "It's been great talking to you, Dave," he said. "I'd like to hear more about your book project. I hope we get to meet again."

"Drop in anytime."

"I think I might."

Sandy walked onto the porch and kissed Dave's cheek. "I'm glad summer's done," she said. "I sure miss having you around."

"I was worried about you," he said. "I'm relieved to see you out and about. You okay?"

She nodded. "I started the day thinking I would have a hard time getting through, but it's been okay."

"Looks like you're in good hands. I won't worry now."

She laughed. "Another fighter pilot. Maybe we both should worry."

He glanced back at Ace. "You could do worse," he said.

She stepped back into the room. "Traffic is still slow. We may as well be comfortable here rather than get caught in the heat. How about another beer?"

"Sure," he said. "Do you like baseball?"

"Love it. Are you hungry?"

"How long will it take to drive from here to the reception?"

"Twenty minutes."

"We're going to miss dinner, but the dancing won't start until nine. I saw a chicken place on the corner."

In the end, she made soup and sandwiches. They both drank another beer as they cheered for the Red Sox.

"God, this is the life," he said. "Beer, sandwiches, and a pretty girl who loves ball games. I haven't been this relaxed in months."

"Me either," she said. "It is nice."

She turned to check the traffic out the window. They had lost track of time. The sun was setting. She sat back as a player hit a ball out of the park and Ace jumped to his feet, cheering.

When he sat back down, he rested his arm across her shoulders, turned, and pulled her closer.

She felt his lips brush her temple. Why not, she thought. He was a nice guy and just passing through. She turned and tasted the flavor of his kiss. There was no bitterness, no aggression, and no dominance.

They melded together. His warm hands caressed her bare shoulders. She pulled away and leaned back on the couch.

"That was nice," he said. "Can I do it again?"

She smiled and nodded.

"You're going to make this an absolutely perfect day, aren't you?"

"I can try," she answered, "but I don't want you to miss the end of the game."

"What game?" he whispered as his lips found hers again.

She slid her hands to his hair as he nuzzled the sensitive line along her jaw. This time when his lips met hers they were slightly open.

He was a perfect kisser. She told him she wanted him with her tongue.

He answered the same way. His fingers moved to the straps of her dress and untied one side. "If you want to go to the party, say so now," he said. "If you wait one more minute, we won't be going at all."

"Give me a minute," she whispered.

"Oh, woman," he murmured, "I'll give you all night."

She slid her hands beneath his shirt and pulled it over his head. He undid the other strap of her dress and freed her breasts. His hands met behind her back, lifted her to his kiss. His touch sent shivers of desire through her. They lay together, skin to skin. He found the edge of her skirt and pushed it to her waist.

"Do you want to go into the bedroom?" she asked.

"No," he said. "I can't wait that long."

His fingers found the edge of her panties and pulled them over her thighs. When she raised her knees to help him, he entered her. She moaned with unexpected pleasure.

"You don't even have your pants off," she whispered.

"Do you want me to stop and take them off?" he asked.

"No," she answered. "I can't wait that long either."

She had not expected to have another man so soon, but she found her first one-night stand to be as exciting and good as sex with Tim had been. In some ways it was even better, because she had no guilt.

When morning came and she awoke with a man who had given her great pleasure, she wasn't too shy to ask for more.

∽

When they pulled into the parking lot of the VOQ in broad daylight, she didn't care who might see them. "You sure you won't be in trouble for missing the reception?" she asked.

"Nah. It wasn't mandatory." He glanced toward the entrance, where flight bags were lined up on the concrete walk, then pulled her close enough to slide his hand under her uniform skirt.

"What time do you fly out?"

"Around 1000 hrs. I'm flying one of the birds. I'll buzz the hospital." He stroked her thigh absentmindedly.

"You do and the general will haul your ass to Port Barrow, Alaska where he'll leave you to rot for the rest of your career."

He laughed. "If I make the squad, I'll be flying through now and then. Can I call you?"

"I'd like that."

"I won't be interfering or anything?"

"Interfering with what?"

"I can't help thinking a girl like you has to have a steady."

"I'm too independent for a steady."

"I like your independence."

He moved his hand to the small notepad in her breast pocket and pulled a pen from his pocket. "O'Connell," he said as he wrote. "Got that from your name tag. So what's your telephone number?"

She giggled. In the past ten hours they had shared more intimacy than many would in a lifetime, yet they hadn't exchanged last names.

She gave him her number. He tore off the sheet, slowly tucked the pad back into her pocket, and kissed her. "I'll be back one day," he said.

"Ace?" she asked as he opened the door.

"What?"

"How did you get a tan all over your body?"

"I have a sailboat," he answered. "When I have time to get away, I take it out, anchor it up, and sunbathe in the nude. You should try it sometime."

"Maybe I will."

He leaned back into the car and kissed her again. "I can only hope," he said.

෴

She was having coffee in the cafeteria when the first flight flew over, so low the windows rattled and the floor shook.

"What the hell?" the hospital commander shouted, before the second set roared over with air brakes squealing and engines roaring.

"A tribute to the hospital," Major Roberts said. "Someone laid a nurse last night."

"Must have been a good lay," Jim Andersen said.

Sandy smiled into her cup.

∽

At the end of the month, when Dave got back, he asked about Ace.

"He was a nice guy passing through. Don't get your hopes up, Dave. He's a fighter pilot, remember?"

"You'll have to get over that," he said.

"I don't want to get over it."

That night Tim called. "I'm sorry. I know I promised, but I had to hear your voice. I have to see you, Sandy."

"No."

"Tell me you still love me."

"I do. You know I do."

"My cross-county flight will be between Christmas and New Year's. I plan to come through Kansas. That's all I ask. A few days before we leave for Europe."

"No."

"You haven't read my letters, have you? I'm dying for you, Sandy. I need to see you."

"No, Tim. No."

When she was finally able to end the conversation, she sat quietly on the couch, stunned his voice could still fill her with desire.

She decided then to go to Kansas City with Penny in mid-October and meet with Pete Kennedy.

∽

As they waited in the conference room of the V.A., Penny raved about Bob's new caregiver. "You won't believe this guy," she said. "He's a former medic, big and brawny, but so gentle. He treats Bob like an equal, and he won't let him feel sorry for himself."

"Does this mean you won't have to drive up so often?" Sandy asked.

"Leave Dave by himself, you mean?"

"Exactly."

Penny smiled. "I won't have to come up again for at least a month. Bob says he needs time to get acclimated. It's wonderful to have some responsibility off my back."

"I think Dave's feeling discouraged."

"Because of me?"

"No. It's the whole antiwar campaign. He needs some buoying up."

Pete Kennedy came into the room. Penny took his hand.

"Our last conference for a while, Penny. Sandy, I'm glad you could make it."

He became serious and professional when they sat down. "We've had a few minor incidents this past week."

Penny was instantly alert. "Something wrong?"

"Bob had a fall."

"Is he okay? He didn't say a thing on the phone."

"He's fine. He had two days in the hospital to patch some skin grafts."

"How'd he fall?"

"Carl took him out for a few beers. On the way home, Bob insisted on walking into the house. Said he was tired of being carried across the threshold. Carl let him try."

"Carl knows better."

"It's not as bad as it sounds. Fact is, he made it into the house before he fell. He bumped a table in the dark and lost his balance. Carl broke his fall. Minor damage and a major breakthrough. He's now walking independently."

"You're kidding."

"He's slow, but he's on his feet."

"So Carl's working out fine?"

"They seem pretty much attuned to one another. No big adjustment problems, no personality clashes. But you can see for yourself this weekend. They've prepared space for you and have a big dinner in the works. I'm not invited."

"Shall I wrangle you an invitation?"

"Well, I was hoping Sandy and I could feast on hot dogs at a football game tonight." He looked to Sandy.

"Depends on who's playing," she teased.

"Kansas State against Iowa State."

"Sure, why not? I haven't been to a college game in years."

"Make sure you get her home at a reasonable hour," Penny warned as she handed Sandy their motel room key.

The game was a rout. Kansas State won 34 to 7. They had a beer at a rowdy bar and then stopped by Pete's, a few blocks away, so he could check his answering service. "I have a lot of guys in crises at the moment and I don't like to be out of contact for very long. Do you mind?"

"Not at all," she said. "I have a tendency to get pretty involved in work too."

"It's not like a job to me," he said. "It's young guys with problems they didn't cause and never expected."

"I'm sorry. I didn't mean to suggest you didn't care."

"Uh-oh," he said. "I jumped onto the serious side again."

"I think you're working too hard at this."

"I'm out of practice."

He called his answering service and began jotting down names and numbers.

She sat in a chair opposite and watched as his face recorded each call, sometimes registering pain, other times matter-of-fact business or anxious dismay.

"Looks crazy, doesn't it?" he asked with his hand over the mouthpiece. He hung up and looked to her again. "I'll have to follow up on some of these. Do you mind?"

"No," she said.

She browsed through several *Field and Stream* and *Time* magazines and tried not to listen as he cajoled, reassured, and made referrals.

"This is going to take some time," he said again, between calls.

"It's okay," she said. "Maybe I can make some sandwiches or something?"

"I'm afraid the fridge is empty, but there's an all-night market next door." He pulled out his wallet and handed her a twenty. "Would you mind? Maybe some beer and cold cuts?"

The store was stocked with good-quality groceries. She felt better as she carried her full bag back into the apartment.

He was asleep on the couch with his feet folded over the armrest and his pad full of scribbled notes lying on the carpet. She set about making sandwiches, but he was still sleeping soundly when she finished, so she found plastic wrap and put them in the refrigerator. She carried a beer onto the balcony that overlooked the busy city street.

When the traffic began to slow and the wind picked up, she stepped back into the living room. She slammed the sliding door firmly enough to make a noise. He didn't awaken. It was past midnight.

She went into his bedroom. The bed was unmade. A stack of case histories lay scattered on the shag carpet. She kicked off her shoes, undressed, and carefully folded her clothing onto a chair against the wall. If she could have a one-night stand with a complete stranger like Ace, why not with someone she at least had a fleeting relationship with? She turned on the small lamp so he would see her lacy underwear on top of the stack of clothing, before she slid between cool sheets.

His weight pressing down on the bed awakened her. She squinted into the light of the lamp. His shirt was wrinkled, his eyes still heavy with sleep.

"Did you plan to take over my bed completely or to share?" he asked.

"Share," she answered.

"I hoped that's what you'd say." She liked the way he undressed, unguarded and without embarrassment.

When he was ready, she lifted the covers so he could slide in beside her. "I didn't expect this at all," he said.

"Neither did I."

"I'm sorry I fell asleep on you."

"Are you really?"

"No," he said as he reached for her. "I'm not sorry at all."

෧෨

They had sandwiches and beer for breakfast and were on their way by seven. "You're a workaholic," she said as he dropped her at the motel.

"Can't be helped. But you've made me realize that I need to get a life."

"You need to get away from that phone."

"I'll come to Wichita. How would that be?"

"I'd like that."

"Good. I'll call as soon as I get a break and we can pick a date."

As Pete drove away, she sighed contentedly. Her second one-night stand and she felt wonderful.

When Penny arrived to pick her up, she took in the unused bed and raised her eyebrows. "And where did you sleep last night?" she asked.

"You know how I said Pete seemed to be a man with a big heart and a good brain but possibly not much in the boys' department?"

"Yes?"

"He had it strapped to his leg."

That was the only time Penny laughed during the entire drive back, but when Sandy asked, Penny assured her all was fine—Bob was perfect and the weekend had been everything she had hoped for. When they arrived home, Penny didn't stop in. Sandy pulled several envelopes from her mailbox and sat on the porch to sort through the letters. A note from Tim, but this time he had written on the envelope, "Last week of December, no excuses."

A pink envelope, addressed in sprawling handwriting and stamped with the Federal Post Office she had seen on Kate's letters, caught Sandy's attention. She tore the top fold.

> *14 October 1969*
>
> *Dear Sandy,*
>
> *My name is Dee Karter and I was lucky enough to consider myself a good friend of Kate Kiley. I'm sorry I haven't answered your letter sooner, but I wasn't sure how well you knew her. Then when I packed up her things to send them home, I found many letters from you and decided I had better write.*
>
> *You probably knew Kate as well as anyone, so I don't think I need to explain a lot, but I do want to tell you how she died and maybe why.*
>
> *She was a unique person and very complicated, so I don't think anyone will ever totally answer the whys of her death. But*

I believe it was pretty simple. For the first time in her life, and pretty much absolutely head-over-heels, Kate was in love. He was a Warrant Officer, Army type, flying helicopters for the 101st airborne. He was also married. Please don't judge her on that. There are a lot of couples in that situation over here, probably because we are so isolated and in the middle of this hostile place.

You would need to experience it to understand what this can do to people, especially to someone as fragile as Kate. Her boyfriend swore when his time was up and he went home, he would divorce his wife and marry her. But when he got stateside he wrote for a bit and then stopped. Don't get me wrong, he was a really nice guy, but I think things looked a little different when he got back to his family and he wasn't flirting with death every day.

At any rate, as the time went on without letters, Kate started partying again. She was using quite a bit of grass and, I think, maybe some heavier stuff. Not too much and not too often, but the stuff is available and many of us indulge. We talked about it, but you know Kate, she laughed and said, 'hey, I'm a big girl. I'm not dumb enough to get into anything I can't handle.'

She told me she had a hot date in Bangkok. She packed a bag of her favorite things and hopped a flight. I should have suspected something when I got off duty and found our hooch spotlessly clean and all of Kate's stuff neatly stacked in one corner, but I thought our girl had done it.

They found her in a deluxe hotel in Bangkok. She had overdosed on pills. They said it looked like she had taken an entire bottle of Seconal and went to sleep. Typical of Kate, she left only a short note, and said no good-byes. She would not have tolerated any crying scenes. I guess she knew what she wanted. I have to think she went as any free spirit might, with free will and at her own hand, but her death will haunt me for the rest of my life. I blame

*myself for not seeing the signs and for not understanding how much
she truly loved that guy.*

*I knew you would have questions, and I hope I haven't been a
totally grim messenger. Kate would not have liked that.*

Sincerely,

Dee Karter

Sandy folded the letter carefully. She wasn't sure she would tell
Dave or Penny. If Kate wanted others to know, she wouldn't have
listed only Sandy to be notified of her death. Dee said her death was
typical, but Sandy didn't believe there was anything typical about
Kate. She remembered how she had come back from her brother's
funeral, clutching that damned flag and pretending she was fine.

The phone ringing inside Sandy's apartment caused her to stand
and collect her things before any tears could form. She unlocked the
door, dropped everything on the couch, and picked up the phone.

"Is this Sandy?"

"Yes."

"Hey, this is Ace Martin. Remember me?"

"How could I forget?"

"Guess what? I made it. I'm the newest member of the Thunderbirds."

"Wow! That's great!"

"I'm on top of the world."

"You should be."

"Well, listen, the reason I'm calling. I'm planning a celebration.
What are you doing Thanksgiving?"

"Working," she lied.

"Can you get out of it? I'm planning one heck of a party and
hoped you'd play hostess for me."

Celebrating successes was too intimate for any relationship
she planned to have. She would never become that involved with

one man again. She had to think fast. "Oh, Ace, I'd love to, but I've scheduled myself for the whole weekend. There's nobody I could ask to do the holiday."

"Ah, shoot. I couldn't think of anyone I'd rather celebrate with. I'm really disappointed. Maybe another time?"

"Sure."

"How about this? Can you get some time off for New Year's?"

"Are you planning a trip up this way?"

"No. I thought maybe you could come down. We could spend a week on the boat, sail around the Florida coast?"

"Sorry. I might be able to get the time, but I'm not sure I can afford the airfare."

"Would you feel prostituted if I sent you a ticket? One of my sisters works for the airlines. She can get me tickets dirt cheap."

"Are you trying to corrupt me again?"

"Most definitely. I loved corrupting you."

She had plenty of leave saved, and flying to Florida would get her out of town for Tim's visit. Besides, hadn't she told Penny she had decided to stop looking for the perfect man and to enjoy every man perfectly?

"It's a deal," she said.

"You won't change your mind?"

"No."

"I mean about the party. It's going to be one heck of an event."

"Can't, Ace. But congrats. They couldn't have picked a better guy."

"Hey, don't get all gushy on me."

"Fat chance," she said.

"I'll be in touch. I'll look forward to New Year's. Later."

"See you later."

∽

Major Roberts summoned her on Tuesday. "Tell me what's up with Penny Patterson."

"Is something wrong?"

"She had a run-in with Dr. Fox in the O.R. Chewed him out for a minor break in technique in front of the staff. This is the second time in a week he's been in to complain."

Sandy had heard a fight between Penny and Dave in the night. "I think she's having some problems."

"Somebody needs to talk to her."

"With all respect, ma'am, shouldn't that someone be you?"

"I'm not a counselor, Lieutenant. According to my shrink, I have no empathy."

"I'll have to agree with him on that."

To her relief, her commander laughed.

"Penny and her husband have been working with a social worker," Sandy said. "He may know what's going on. I'll call him."

"Today?"

"Yes, ma'am."

She used the hospital line to call Pete Kennedy.

"I assumed things were going well with Bob and Penny," he said. "If you think it will help, I'll sound him out and see if there's a problem."

"Thanks, Pete. Hey, do you have plans for Thanksgiving weekend?"

"I have to work Thanksgiving Day, but I have the rest of the weekend off. Would you like to do something?"

"I have an invitation for Thanksgiving dinner, but I'm free until Sunday. Why don't you come down?"

"When?"

"Friday or Saturday?"

"I'd like that. I'll drive down Friday morning."

❧

Dave was washing his car on the drive when Sandy arrived home.

"The Andersens invited you, Penny, and me for Thanksgiving dinner," she said. "Shall I tell them yes?"

"Yes for me. I can't speak for Penny."

She sat on the stairs. "You two have a spat?"

"Did we disturb you?"

"You worry me."

"We both got a little carried away. If she wants to continue that relationship in Kansas City, that's her choice."

"She's having a bad time at work."

"And that's her problem."

"But, Dave ..." she started.

He flung his rag against the car. "Look, Sandy. If you want to lobby for Penny's interests, take it somewhere else. I've got things to do. I don't have time for her foolishness."

"Or mine?"

"Or yours."

"Gotcha." Her cheeks burned from his unexpected outburst. They had always been able to talk.

He turned away. She went into her place.

CHAPTER SEVENTEEN

When Sandy saw Penny's car behind Dave's on Thanksgiving morning, she hoped things were better with the couple. But when she joined them for drinks at noon, Dave tapped away on his typewriter while Penny paced in the kitchen.

"He's driving me nuts," Penny railed. "He's been working on that speech all morning because of a massacre in some Vietnamese village."

"It's a big thing," Dave shouted.

"It can wait. We need to get going," Penny urged.

"This is important. A bloody massacre and Nixon aware of it since spring."

Penny raised her eyes to the ceiling.

"You two are a real pair," Sandy tried. "Always running after a new cause. When are you going to settle down like us mortal folk?" She stretched out on the couch. They could arrive at the Andersens anytime between twelve and one. Sometimes Dave's minutes turned into hours.

"Come on, Dave, let it go." Penny moved toward him.

He rolled a clean sheet of paper into the machine. "You can wait for me this once. I wait for you every damned Sunday night!"

"No one asked you to!"

"Okay, so I won't."

Penny pulled on her coat. "Don't bother to, ever again!" She opened the door and ran out.

"Better go after her, Dave," Sandy said.

"To hell with her. She can be a patient saint with Bob, then she turns on me." He tapped the sheaf of papers into a neat stack and placed them in his briefcase. "Come on, let's go. No need to make the Andersens wait."

"Let's get Penny first."

"No." He grabbed his jacket. "If she wants to come, she knows the way."

Penny didn't show up at the Andersens.

 ∾

The next morning Sandy opened her door to Pete Kennedy.

"Now I get to see how the other half lives," he joked as he walked through her apartment.

"Frugally."

"But nicely." He pulled her into his arms. "I like the mural in your bedroom."

"Thank you," she murmured. "My friend Dave had it done."

He pulled away. "Do I get to meet him?"

"You would have, but he left this morning."

"Well, darn. I'm disappointed."

"Oh?"

"Penny talks about Dave and you all the time. I hoped I'd meet my competition."

"What?"

His face reddened.

"Pete, Dave and Penny are a pair."

"Well, that lowers my stress level. Has Penny told you about Bob?"

She shook her head.

"Then maybe I shouldn't either."

"Maybe you should."

"Bob wants her out of his life."

"Why?"

"He's in love with Carl."

"Oh, come on," she said. "This is the Bible Belt. Things like that don't happen here."

"They happen everywhere."

"It's impossible. Penny and Bob were engaged before his accident."

"Some guys don't want to acknowledge they're gay and so they try to have a normal life."

"No wonder she's upset."

"I'm glad she has Dave."

"Their relationship is going as badly as her job."

"I want to help, but she isn't very receptive." He pulled Sandy back into his arms. "I'm stupid, you know that? I really thought it was you and Dave."

She shook her head against his chest.

"Sandy?"

"What?"

"I can't put aside the feeling you're holding back."

She nodded. "I am."

"Why?"

"Because I want to stand on my own. I want to make my own mistakes and not have to worry about hurting someone else. I don't want to be half of any pair. I want to be free."

He laughed and brushed her hair back from her face. "I think I can handle that."

"Can you? Even if it means I won't be faithful to one man? That's the kind of freedom I'm talking about."

"Are you sure that's freedom?"

"I'm not sure of anything. But I want to find out. Maybe it's a phase, maybe I'm cracking up, maybe there's something wrong with me. I just know I want to make my own decisions and try everything, no holds barred, no old inhibitions holding me back." Her voice broke. "It all sounds so dumb when I say it out loud."

"It's not dumb. And there's nothing wrong with you. We all feel like you at times."

"But you're a man. Men are allowed to try everything. Girls aren't."

"But they do."

"And they're called tramps."

His laugh was a deep baritone as he pressed her against him. "If making me feel like this makes you a tramp, who the hell cares what anybody calls you?"

⤬

After Pete left on Sunday afternoon, Penny pounded on her door.

"Jesus, Penny, what are you doing?" Sandy asked.

"Have you seen Dave?"

"He flew out to a peace moratorium. Remember? He told us."

"He was supposed to be back last night."

"He probably got hung up somewhere."

"He always calls if he's delayed."

"If I remember correctly, you guys parted in a bit of a huff."

"But we talked. I thought I'd made everything okay. Oh, God, Sandy, I've really screwed everything up. What a fool I am."

Sandy made hot toddies and they settled at the kitchen table. "Tell me," she said.

"Bob's asked to have our marriage annulled."

She was grateful Pete had warned her and they'd had time to seriously discuss Penny and Bob and Carl.

Penny looked away. "He and Carl are having 'a relationship.'"

"Pete told me."

"Did he tell you he believes it would be best if I stepped away?"

"You said yourself you'd only stay until Bob got himself together."

"But being gay isn't getting himself together. This is a bigger mess."

"Maybe from your viewpoint, but what about from his? You have to admit, he isn't exactly physically appealing in his present state."

"But he's still Bob."

"You see him differently because you knew him before the accident. But think how he must feel. Here's this big attractive guy who sees him without blinders on and loves him. Don't you think that would be good for him? Look at the progress he's made in a few weeks."

Penny followed the pattern of the tablecloth with one finger. "It won't last."

"You don't know that."

"How could it?"

"Does that matter? You didn't plan on your relationship with him lasting, did you? Didn't you say something about two months, three at the most?"

"Yes."

"Hobbies last longer."

"I'm so ashamed. Oh, God!" Penny lowered her voice to a whisper. "That first weekend I stayed in his place? I tried to seduce him. He tried to tell me then, but I wouldn't listen. He was so embarrassed and I felt so damn rejected and unfeminine."

"I probably would have done the same thing."

"I thought after all he'd been through, he would appreciate the thought."

Sandy couldn't hold back her giggle, and when Penny heard it she began to laugh too.

Sandy touched her hand. "I'm sorry. It's just so damned like you, me, or Kate to get into this kind of a mess."

"I know." Her laughter became tears.

"Penny, it will all work out."

"I can't help it. I just keep crying."

"It's all too much for you."

The doorbell rang at that moment. She opened the door to Dave, who had a small blond woman tucked under his arm.

"Sandy," he said, "I wanted you to meet Shelly."

"Penny's here."

"See you another time," he said.

She shut the door and turned. Penny stood in the living room.

"Did you know, Sandy?" she demanded. "Did you know about her?"

Sandy hadn't known and couldn't answer.

"You let me cry and tell you everything, and all the time you knew about her? I hate you. I hate both of you." She grabbed her coat and opened the door.

"Penny, wait."

ᕯ

There had been no way to stop her, and although she called and searched all evening, Sandy couldn't find her friend. When Penny didn't show up for work the next morning, Sandy went to Major Roberts's office.

"I'm aware she isn't here, Lieutenant. She hasn't unlocked the O.R. and Dr. Fox is having a fit."

"She was pretty upset when she left last evening. I checked her place and her car is gone."

"I'll give her another hour before I call the A.P.s."

"Would you call me if she shows up?"

"I'm not an information service, Lieutenant."

"Yes, ma'am."

She telephoned Dave at the university. He wasn't in. She telephoned Penny at home and received no answer. She gave up on sleep and went out to collect her mail: a few bills, one card covered with Christmas stamps, and a manila envelope with a Florida postmark. She opened the card first. It was from the Schneiders.

December 1969

Dear Sandy,

We know we'll be too busy over the holidays to keep up, so we're sending our cards out early. We have tons of good news. First, Tim has completed his transition into F-4s and has received orders for England. We will be spending the holidays with his family and the New Year with mine. The change is exciting and good for us. Things are so much better than when we left Meridian. And the best news? We are expecting number three in July! Can you believe it? We never expected to have another. Tim was speechless when I told him. We are filled with joy. Will write more when we get settled again. For now, we want to wish you the merriest of Christmases and much, much happiness in the upcoming year.

Love,

Ann, Tim, Reggie, and John.

Did she know, or was she honestly sharing good news? Because Sandy never wanted the answer to that question, she was doubly grateful when she opened the large envelope and shook out a thick packet of airline tickets from Ace.

Tim's path and hers would not cross again. She pulled the curtains wide and studied the greenish cast of the winter sky. Mike's eyes had been that color when he stood beside the window and nearly destroyed her. Penny must be feeling the way Sandy had felt at that moment. She decided to call Pete Kennedy.

"Penny's here," he said.

"Thank God."

"I found her waiting at my office this morning. She drove up alone. I don't know how she made it."

"Did she hurt herself?"

"No, but I was afraid she might. She's severely depressed. She won't tell us what happened. We've admitted her to the hospital."

"Oh, Pete, things are such a mess."

"Because of Bob?"

"Because of Dave. Everything has blown up."

"I think this may go farther back. I think her martyrdom about Bob and the way she's been overtaxing herself is a way of compensating for other things."

"But Penny's so stable and so practical. At O.T. she was the one who—"

He cut her off. "I've been seeing quite a few veterans who are working themselves to death in demanding jobs or, worse, withdrawing by hiding out in the woods. We think it may be a coping mechanism to deal with the stress and slaughter of combat. She's in desperate straits at the moment."

"Do you think she'll see me if I come up?"

"It's worth a try."

"I'll drive up Saturday."

"You can stay with me."

"I'd like that."

༄

On Saturday she and Dave made the trip together. "I've been an ass," he said as they pulled into the hospital lot. "I've been over there. I should have seen this coming."

"We've both let her down."

"If we're assigning blame, I deserve the brunt of it." He held the elevator for her.

"Pete said she's severely depressed."

"And I may have pushed her into that."

Sandy remembered the white walls, the feeling of being somewhere else, the desire to be left alone. "Pete said to call him. He'll fill us in."

"You seem to know this guy pretty well."

"You've been gone a lot. You don't see everything I do."

"Obviously. It's a good thing. I worry about you enough as it is."

They walked together into the green-walled hospital room. Penny was very small in the white bed.

"Penny?" Sandy whispered.

Her eyelids fluttered.

Dave stepped forward. "Pen, I'm sorry."

She rolled away from him.

He moved to that side of the bed and lifted her hair away from her face. "Pen? I'm truly sorry," he said. "I'll never let you down again."

She mumbled something.

"I've been a fool," Dave said.

Penny opened her eyes. "Me too."

He reached over the rails and took her small hands in his big ones. "Let's agree on that," he smiled. "We're both fools. Can we start over again?"

"Yes." She closed her eyes and dozed.

Dave looked across the bed to Sandy. "She'll be all right," he said. "She'll be fine."

Sandy nodded. How could she not be, with him looking after her?

"Go find that guy Pete," he said. "I'll stay here until she wakes up again."

❦

She gazed out the airplane window as it taxied to the runway. She could see Penny and Dave walking hand in hand toward his car. She hadn't told them everything about this Florida trip—that she needed to be away from Meridian when Tim arrived or that she planned to spend the holiday with a near stranger because he had no expectations of her.

Leaving relieved her of the persistent sense of unworthiness that had plagued her for months. She tried to remember what Ace Martin looked like, but all she could recall was brown hair, brown eyes, and a wiry, sexy body.

In Miami, she recognized him at once.

"You won't need this for a long time," he laughed as he slung her coat over one shoulder. "I heard there was snow in Kansas."

"And record low temperatures."

He tossed her bag into the open back of a red MG. "Is this all you brought?"

"You said I wouldn't need more than a bathing suit."

"You always take men at their word?" He held the door for her.

"Rarely."

"Hungry?" He placed one arm over her shoulder.

"Starving."

"That seems to be a common state for you."

"Look who's calling the kettle black," she said. "If I remember correctly, you ate three times in twelve hours."

"If I remember correctly, you were the one who worked up my appetite."

Before she could think of a retort, he pulled her to him and kissed her. She might have been offended, but he was so unassuming and relaxed she laughed and returned his kiss.

"And I can tell you are going to do it again," he said.

He pulled onto a busy highway. "Now, the big decision. Shall we stop at a fast food place on the way to the boat or go to a nice restaurant, stay at my place for the night, and drive to the boat in the morning?"

"How long will it take us to drive to the boat?"

"About an hour and a half."

She surprised herself again when she said, "I think we should get takeout, go back to your place, and have dinner in bed."

His smile was huge as he abruptly turned the car into a drive-in hamburger place.

೦〜೦

The moment he closed his apartment door she was in his arms. She had the fleeting thought that she was out of control and far too easy, but his kisses ignited passion and his hands filled her with desire. They were naked on the bed in minutes.

At three in the morning, they ate cold hamburgers, showered together, made love once more, and took to the road.

೦〜೦

Polished teak and shining brass greeted her at the marina. The hatchway of the thirty-foot sloop opened into a galley with a tiny kitchen and red seats. The forward bedroom was filled with a wide bed and lit with four portholes. He showed her the smaller storage room and the bath with a shower over the head. It was all spotlessly clean. He pulled her onto the bed.

"It must be the water," she said, "or maybe the sun."

"What?"

"That's making me so horny."

"Are you?"

"Yes. Are you?"

It was afternoon before they pushed off.

As he maneuvered through the maze of boats and headed out of the bay, Sandy sat beside him and listened to his explanations of turning and stopping.

"You aren't going to expect me to drive this thing, are you?" she said. "I've never been on a boat before. I've never been on the ocean."

"You haven't? I thought all Maine gals were born on the ocean." He cut the engine, leaped up on one side, and began loosening ropes. One sail unfurled and caught the wind, and then another. "Don't worry," he said. "I've been doing this for years."

"I'm not worried."

He took the wheel with one hand, adjusted the sails, and soon had the boat cutting effortlessly through the water.

The feeling of freedom was better than flying. "This is wonderful," she said.

"Ah, wait until you see the sunset."

❦

Three days later she decided the sea was her reward for giving up Tim. Maybe, just maybe, she was finally making the right decisions.

A peaceful interlude of cool, damp dawns under steel gray skies that warmed to a golden glow of sun and surf then faded away in a haze of pink, red, purple, and blue refreshed her.

They swam at night under a canopy of twinkling stars, carefully watching the deck lights to be sure their bobbing home didn't drift too far away. They sunbathed without suits or shame: he, whenever they were clear of other craft; she, for shorter times as her skin adjusted to the sun. One day, when rain forced them to anchor up, they tried all afternoon to match their lovemaking to the rhythm of the rolling sea. They laughed each time the ocean changed its mood. Mornings they faced each other over steaming cups of coffee and debated important major decisions: eggs or cereal, shore or open sea, sun or sex.

On the morning of the fourth day, he smiled over a shared bowl of cold cereal and milk and asked, "Who are you?"

"How do you mean?"

"Who are you? Where did you come from besides Maine? How did you get to be who you are?"

She laughed.

"Start from the beginning and tell me everything. Where were you born? Who are your parents? Where did you go to school?"

"That would take all day and isn't all that interesting." She took a spoonful of cereal from the bowl.

"I've got all day." He leaned back in his chair and rested one elbow on its back. "Come on. We've bared everything else."

She laughed self-consciously under his honest gaze and realized she didn't want to tell, didn't want to share her inner self with anyone again. "Good walls, good neighbors make," she said.

"Ah! You're a Frost fan. That's a start." He seemed content.

On the last morning they fished, setting out the blue-lined poles rigged with red flashers and the smelly baitfish he kept on a cardboard tray in a cooler. They placed their poles in holders and sat back, legs crossed, hats low over their eyes, waiting for fish to strike.

"I never catch anything," he confessed. "I don't bother to check the charts and don't like to follow the charter boats to the good spots. It's either fish or solitude. I like peace."

"Do you ever sail alone?"

"Always. This trip is the exception."

"Really?"

"Really."

"Don't you get lonely out here by yourself?"

"I never have before." He leaned toward her and touched her face with one slim finger. "But I have a feeling it may seem lonely from now on."

She broke away from his gaze and scanned the horizon for something else to talk about. The silence lengthened until she had to speak. "It has been fun," she started. Her line pulled her pole down in an arc. "Hey, your luck may have changed." She reeled in too easily. A chunk of seaweed dangled from the hook.

"We're drifting into shallow water," he said and hurried to start the engine and steer away from the reef.

It was over all too soon. He tied up the boat and drove her to the airport. She traded shorts and halter for Kansas wool, folded her coat over her arm, and walked with him to the boarding area, where she kissed him warmly and without regret. It had been a great adventure and it was done. He smiled and waved as she exited the door.

⟳

In Kansas, a hoarfrost crunched beneath her shoes as she found a standing cab. She shivered, despite her coat, and breathed in the cabbie's scent of cheap aftershave, cigarettes, and wet suede coat.

"Been to California," he said.

"How did you know?"

"The tan. A dead giveaway."

She smiled. "I guess you could call it that."

⟳

Dave's place was dark and his car was gone. Her place was cold. She turned on the gas heater and curled under her afghan for a quick nap.

Her supervisory shift began at midnight.

"You aren't going to tell me you got that tan in Maine, are you?" Jim Andersen asked as she passed the Medical Officer's night room.

"No," she answered.

He followed her into the office.

"And you aren't going to tell me where you got it, are you?" he asked.

"Only if you ask."

"Where'd you get the tan, Sandy?"

"Florida." She retrieved the supervisor's report and began scanning for problems.

"And what, may I ask, were you doing there?"

"Getting a tan," she said with a giggle. "Who's this on the Seriously Ill list?"

"Sergeant. Heart attack. He's doing fine. I'll take him off the list by morning."

"Have you seen Penny?"

"She ran over to check the heart guy. She said she'd be right back." He sat on her desk and folded his arms across his chest. "Come on. Out with it. Who did you visit in Florida?"

"Nobody you know." She began logging in the night shift time cards.

"You're as closed-mouthed as the Sphinx," he said.

"Yes, I know. You've told me many times."

Penny came breezing in. "How was your Thunderbird?"

Jim stood and stomped his foot. "You vamp, Sandy! Wait until I tell Connie this one."

Penny waved her left hand in front of Sandy's face. A bright gold band shone from her ring finger.

"You're kidding," Sandy said. "You went back to Bob?"

"Nope." Her eyes were shining. "I got the annulment, got the license, went to the courthouse yesterday, and married Dave."

Sandy screamed. "Who else could manage that? Only crazy you could get married, divorced, and married again in half a year!"

Jim waved his hands in the air in mock submission. "I'm going to check on recovery room. You gals are too much for me."

CHAPTER EIGHTEEN

April 1970.

Penny and Dave's marriage meant they moved into a real house. Sandy's neighbor became a cranky old man with fierce eyes and nothing more to say than a short "Humpff" in response to her greetings. When she visited the couple's new house, she felt more like a guest than a welcome neighbor. At those times Penny's involvement in the protest movement dominated the conversation.

When several of the docs became short-timers, Sandy organized a hello/good-bye celebration. She posted an open invitation on the hospital bulletin board. On the evening of the party, her small apartment filled with officers, enlisted men, and civilians.

Pete drove down and placed his suitcase in her bedroom.

Near midnight, with the party in full swing, Jim raised the telephone over the heads of the crowd and shouted, "Sandy! Telephone."

She made her way to him.

Ace was on the line. "Hey, Sandy, I happened to be flying over and decided to cheat a little and refuel at Meridian. I'm stuck for the night and thought I'd stop by, but it sounds like you've got a party going."

She could not have Pete meet Ace. "I do. I'm sorry."

There was a long silence, and then, "Maybe tomorrow?"

"Ace, the truth is I'll be busy all weekend."

"Oh. Well, maybe next time."

"I'd like that."

"I can't say I'm not disappointed."

"I have to go."

"Later then."

When he rang off, she too had a pang of disappointment, but Dave was hailing her from across the room and she could see her neighbor in the doorway. Before she could move to him, Dave had invited the guy in. He headed to the bar.

An hour later General Magnem showed up. Ace was standing by his side.

"I picked this guy up at the club," the general said. "Ordered him to come along. Didn't think you'd mind."

Sandy looked for Pete. He was deep in conversation with Penny. She had no recourse but to smile and say, "Hey, Ace."

He stepped forward, hugged her quickly, and whispered. "I promise, I'll be good. I couldn't say no."

"I have a date," she whispered back.

She wasn't sure he'd heard, because he suddenly moved away and laughed.

"Okay, woman!" he said. "Show me the bar!"

He and the general moved into the room.

A couple began to dance to a slow tune, pushing the crowd out onto the back lawn. Sandy looked for Pete. He had disappeared.

The general hadn't gone on to the bar but instead had pulled one of the base ops secretaries into his embrace. The way they melded together said they knew each other very well. Sandy watched as their faces softened. How long had that been going on, she wondered. Funny how a word or smile could give lovers away. Had she and Tim been as obvious? Only to the initiated, she decided.

Couples separated. A new lieutenant claimed the secretary for the next dance. The woman smiled and shook her head but the tall boy persisted. When the general intervened, the lieutenant, having no idea who he was, cocked his long neck and held on.

In a way, she was in the same position as the secretary. She was not committed to either Pete or Ace but she had allowed them both to mark some territory. The music ended.

"Quite a party," Ace said from behind her. "We almost had to park downtown." He reached over her shoulder and placed a cold rum and Coke near her breast.

She turned and accepted the glass. "Cheers," she said.

Loud voices rose above the din of the next song. The crowd moved back as General Magnem stepped between the new lieutenant and the secretary.

"Excuse me, Ace," Sandy said. She moved across the room. "General." She touched his arm. "I think it's my turn to dance with you."

His muscles were taut as he took her in his arms. "You need to relax, General," she said. "Parties usually bring out the best in you."

"Smart girl," he said. "You're absolutely right."

When the dance was done, she led him back to Ace.

Before she could turn to look for Pete again, Jim and Connie Andersen were at her side. "Introduce me to your Florida friend," Jim said loudly. "I've never met a Thunderbird before." He shook Ace's hand and added, "Stole our best babysitter away for Christmas, but I'll forgive you, since she came back so much sweeter."

Pete was standing directly behind Connie. Sandy recognized the flash of pain that crossed his face. He turned and headed toward her bedroom. She followed.

His back was to her. She closed the door. "Pete?"

"Did you go to Florida to be with him?" he asked.

"Yes," she answered.

He turned. "How could you do this?"

"What?"

"Invite him here."

"I didn't. The general brought him."

"Maybe we should all do that."

"What?"

"Just drop in when we need a good screw."

"It's not like that."

"Oh? What is it like? How many others out there have shared this bed?"

"That's a lousy thing to say."

"But it's okay to do it? Have you slept with Dave, and Jim, and the General?"

Her head came up defiantly. "I don't have to answer to you," she said. "I was honest from the start."

"I didn't know this is what you meant, Sandy. I didn't know you were such a whore!"

Cold anger filled her. He had no right to call her names. "I have guests," she said. "Friends who like and accept me the way I am. I won't stand here and listen to this." She opened the door and walked out to the crowded living room.

A few minutes later Pete threaded his way through the living room and out the door. He was carrying his suitcase. Penny called out to him but he kept on walking.

"Where's he going?" she called to Sandy.

Sandy shrugged. She didn't care where he went.

Ace and the general disappeared while she was saying good night to Jim and Connie at the back door. Penny and Dave were the last to leave.

"Sorry about Pete," Penny said. "I'm sure he'll be back."

"I doubt that," Sandy said as she closed the door after them.

She sank onto the couch, snuggled under her afghan, and closed her eyes. She had lost both Pete and Ace, she was sure of it. They had each professed to understand her, but neither did.

The doorbell startled her. Ace pushed through the unlocked door and glanced from left to right. "All alone?" he asked.

"Obviously."

"I saw your date leave. Nice-looking guy. Too bad."

She wasn't sure how she should respond.

"I figured your place would be a mess. I hooked a ride back to help you clean up," he teased.

She laughed. "Sure you did."

"Honest," he said with a smile. "Watch." He quickly stacked several cups and napkins. "See." He strode into the kitchen.

"Ace?"

"Huh?" He leaned on one hand in the doorway and opened his eyes wide.

"Let it go until morning."

"Really?" His smile grew.

"Really."

He came to her and slid beneath the afghan. "You know that guy Pete is a fool."

"Why do you say that?"

"He already had his suitcase holding his spot, but he gave it up and left room in your bed for me."

She laughed. "What makes you think you can fill that spot?"

He pulled her to her feet and moved her toward the bedroom. "Come on," he whispered huskily into her ear, "and I'll show you."

⚭

The next morning she stood on the flight line and watched his small jet take to the air.

⚭

A few weeks later Penny stopped for coffee. "I'm thinking of leaving the military," she said.

"Penny! You? I thought you were a lifer!"

"I can't accept the fact that our own National Guard shot those kids protesting at Kent State. I can't support our mission any longer."

"What will you do?" Sandy asked.

"Use my G.I. benefits and continue on to my doctorate. Maybe teach at the university level."

"That will make Dave happy."

"I already make Dave quite happy," she quipped. "Sandy?"

"What?"

"We stopped by Kansas City last week and ran into Pete."

"Oh?"

"He asked about you. He says he feels like a fool and knows he was wrong to act the way he did."

"He is a fool."

"He said he'd like to call and apologize."

"He needn't bother. I don't want to hear from him."

"He's such a nice guy."

"I have no interest in the man. I'm not even mad any longer."

"Is it because of Ace?"

"No. It's about me. I don't want to be tied down with strings or words. I just want it like it is. I'm quite happy this way."

"You're afraid."

"No, I'm not."

"Afraid."

Sandy began to clear the table. "I have none of those emotions left. I want to be left alone."

"Ace sure seems to like you."

"Ace is a fighter pilot. He likes all women. We're not serious now and we never will be."

"Will you come with us to Stillwater? I'm going to give my first speech."

"When?"

"Next weekend."

"Sure."

❦

The cornflowers on the roadsides dipped their heads in anticipation of rain. In an ancient barn several hundred protesters sang songs until Penny climbed onto an old wagon and began to speak.

"It was the horror of those boys—tanned, muscled, young, missing arms or legs, yet talking about how great it would be to get home. As if everything would be okay once they'd returned.

"They didn't know how hard life would be without two legs.

"At Clark I passed this boy. He was all wrapped in gauze and pressure dressings. No arms. No legs. He spoke as I passed. 'Hey, lady!' he said. 'Come here.' I leaned close. He was crying. 'Don't let them take me home like this. Please,' he begged. 'Help me die here. Please.'

"I tried to comfort him, but he kept insisting. When he turned his head and closed his eyes, I ran away.

"The question isn't why we brought them home like that but rather why we sent them over in the first place. None of us should have been there. It isn't our war. But I went. And some of you went. Why? For the glory of our country? To save those poor people from communism? I can't believe I was so young and stupid."

Dave nudged Sandy's arm. "She's beautiful, isn't she? You can almost touch her pain."

Displaying pain is never beautiful, Sandy wanted to say, but she knew he wouldn't hear. The crowd applauded wildly.

Penny climbed off the wagon and walked toward them. She was pale, her cheeks and brow were moist, and her body was visibly shaking.

"Do you think she really should be doing this?" Sandy asked.

"Best thing for her," Dave answered.

"Glad that's done," Penny said.

"You were great, Pen. So real I could almost see the blood, smell the burnt flesh. Just great." Dave took her hand.

Nausea crept into Sandy's throat. She took Penny's free hand. "You don't have to do this, Pen," she said. "You could let it go."

Penny pulled away. "They have to know. I have to tell them. It might help if you got closer to it too. The war has got to stop."

Sandy didn't want to get any closer. They drove back and stopped at the Officers' Club for a drink. The bar was filled with new student pilots who were even younger than the last group, and much noisier. They didn't seem to share the easy camaraderie of those who passed before. In a back corner some began a beer fight, behavior usually reserved for squadron parties and never allowed in the club. As General Magnem stepped into the group to quell the disturbance, several of the boys stood and walked out.

The younger and older groups moved farther apart. The gathering became more subdued.

Ace was suddenly at her shoulder. "Come dance," he whispered. Completely surprised, she stood and moved with him to the dance floor.

"What a nice surprise," she said.

"Surprise, hell. I've been calling you all evening. I'm flying out in an hour."

"I drove to Oklahoma with Dave and Penny."

He smiled as he took her in his arms. She melted against him. Over his shoulder she caught sight of Dave watching. He had a most peculiar look on his face. What was it? When she tried to catch his eye, he turned away. He probably senses the melancholy as much as I, she thought, then gave a mental shrug and slid her arms around Ace's neck so he could press her closer.

After only two dances he had to leave. She walked with him to the base ops car.

"You bum," she said. "Surprising me like this. Next time call and I'll be sure to be here."

"Going on summer tour," he said. "Won't be back this way until Labor Day. Our anniversary of sorts."

"Of sorts," she said, and broke away. She felt a pang of loneliness when the car drove off.

 ∽

For the entire summer the pool at the club was full of young guys barreling off the board and having water fights. They bored her with their transparency. She found few men now that interested her. The humorous cards and short notes that arrived regularly in her mailbox from Ace brightened her days.

She began to look forward to his Labor Day visit and scheduled her night shifts to end before he arrived, so they would have uninterrupted time together.

One night as she walked between the supervisory office and the emergency room she thought of him and felt a small thrill pulse through her body. She laughed softly. She hadn't felt like this since she had been with Tim more than a year ago. She hadn't loved since Tim. Her smile slowly faded. Not since Tim.

Oh, God, that's what Dave had seen. Good old Dave knew her better than she knew herself. She had fallen in love with Ace the fighter pilot.

Jim Andersen caught her as she staggered into the emergency room. "Sandy! What's wrong? You look horrible."

"I don't know. I suddenly feel sick."

He reached out and took her wrist, counted her pulse. "Your heart is racing. Sit down for a minute."

She sat on the nearest chair.

"Are your fingers numb?"

"Yes."

"You're hyperventilating. This isn't like you." He found a paper sack and had her breathe into it.

After a few minutes the trembling stopped. She lowered the sack and tried to smile. "I'm fine now. I just felt weak for a minute. Must be something I ate."

She needed to be alone. She had to clear her head and think about this logically. "I'll go to the office," she said. "I honestly feel okay now."

He took her pulse again and nodded his head. "It's down. Go ahead. I'll check on you in a few minutes."

She closed the door of the office, sank into the chair, and lowered her head on the desk. Dry sobs shook her body as wave after wave of fear passed over her.

There was no need to panic, she told herself. Hadn't she handled the separation from Tim without curling up and dying? Hadn't she snuffed out the love she had with him? She had nothing to fear. She could kill this love too. It would be easy, if she remained calm.

She gathered her paperwork and made a round of the hospital. She was a big girl. Big girls were always in control. She studied the scheduling board. There was an unfilled third-shift spot on the night he would arrive. She wrote her name in the space.

When her shift was done she drove to Personnel, put in her volunteer statement, and continued on to the Headquarters building, where she left a note for General Magnem. She asked for his assistance in moving her away quickly.

On the day Ace was to arrive she left a note in the hands of the duty officer.

Welcome back! Sorry I can't meet you. I'm not feeling well and I'm on the schedule to work tonight. I'm off to bed. I'm really feeling rotten. Maybe next time? As ever, Sandy.

Once home she tried to ignore the ringing phone. When it began to drive her crazy she drove to the river park, but she found it too full of memories. She would have to talk to him sometime, she decided, and drove home. The phone was silent. In desperation she did something her O.B. patients often told her they had done before beginning labor: She filled a bucket with hot, sudsy water and began to scrub her kitchen floor on hands and knees. I'm scrubbing you out of my heart, Ace Martin, she chanted as she moved the brush across the linoleum. I do not love you. I do not. I do not love you. I do not.

Satisfied he had gone on his way, she climbed into bed and slept.

It was dark when the phone rang. Thinking it was the hospital, she answered it.

"Hi, Sandy?" Ace said.

"Yes."

"Were you sleeping?"

"Yes."

"I'm sorry. I thought I'd give you a call and see how you're feeling."

"What time is it?"

"Almost ten."

"Already?"

He laughed. "Already. How are you?"

"I'm feeling better, but I have to be at work in less than an hour."

"Listen, girl, I have to see you. Can I come by?"

"No. I have to put a uniform together. Polish my shoes. Shower. I overslept. I've got to run."

"I can't travel all this way and not see you."

"Maybe next time."

"I'll bring you something light to eat so you won't have to go to work hungry."

"Honest, Ace. I'm not feeling my best. I have to go." I will not love you. I will not. I will not love you. I will not.

"I'll come by and polish your shoes," he insisted.

"I don't need your help," she said and hung up the phone. She would put him off with a thousand excuses until he believed she had other loves. Good-bye, Ace Martin. Good-bye.

She moved into her room and began to prepare her starched whites. I'm here for the good times, she chanted. Here for the good times. She moved through the apartment and turned on every light, as if the glaring brightness might blot out the truth. She was a good-time girl, nothing more.

She turned the shower on hot and allowed the stinging spray to superheat her skin. When she could stand no more she turned on the cold and gasped as icy shocks shook her. She was a physical being. She would feel only physical pleasure. No more emotions for her. No more intrusions into her heart.

As she stepped from the bathroom, the doorbell rang. She wrapped her terry robe tightly over her damp body and padded barefoot to the door.

Ace, darkly tanned and smiling, stood on her porch. His presence sent her heart racing, caused her hands to tremble as she opened the door.

"Ace?"

"I know. I know. I shouldn't be here. Even the most beautiful women in the world need time to make themselves more so, but I couldn't resist." His banter was guarded.

"Come in," she said.

"I thought you'd never ask." He stepped through the door, tried to take her in his arms. She stiffened and pulled away.

His smile didn't fade, but he stepped back one pace. "You look terrible. You have been sick. I was afraid you were making excuses to keep me away."

She didn't answer.

"Were you?" he asked.

Oh, why pussyfoot around? Get rid of him. Make him go. She looked directly into his brown eyes. "Why are you here, Ace? I've got too much to do to waste time."

His eyes narrowed and became golden. He held her gaze. "I came to do your shoes. Where are they?"

"I'll get them," she said. She went into her room and pulled out her oldest, most soiled pair of duty shoes, liquid white polish, and a rag. Let him polish the damned things, Lord, but then make him go away.

"Here you go," she said as she pushed the shoes at him. "I've got to dress."

She shut her bedroom door and dressed slowly. When she came out she could hear him humming softly in the living room. She padded down the hall in her stocking feet.

"Nice job?" he asked with a smile. "Do I get a tip?"

"No tip tonight," she said as coldly as she could. "Fresh out of cash. Catch me next time."

"Sandy?" he said in a voice that made her knees weak. "What's wrong? Have I done something? Have I said something to offend you? Tell me." He moved closer.

She backed away. "I'm tired, Ace. I'm tired and bored. I'm tired of this base, this job, and most friends."

"Including me?"

She nodded but didn't meet his eyes.

He walked toward the door. Good, he was leaving. A sliver of pain touched each nerve along the length of her spine.

He turned and smiled sadly. "Well, we all reach that point, I guess. Nothing lasts forever."

"No. But it has been fun."

"It has." He didn't move.

She had to get away. She sat on the couch and pulled on her shoes. "I've got to go, I'm late." When she stood, he still hadn't moved.

She turned at the door. "Thanks, Ace. Thanks for everything. Lock up for me, will you?"

He raised his hand in a mock salute. In her car, she stared back at her apartment. He was silhouetted in the open doorway, watching her drive away.

"Bye, Ace," she whispered. "Bye, my love." Tears blurred the road as she headed toward the base.

∽

Jim Andersen was Medical Officer of the Day again. He waited in her office. "It's going to be one of those nights," he said. "Full moon, all the nuts and weirdoes out, and O.B. overcrowded."

She had to pull herself together. She was having difficulty concentrating on his words.

"And there's a fourteen-year-old in the E.R. in the second stage of labor. Her mother called me a stinking liar for saying as much. Her father stormed out the door saying he was going to kill some son of a bitch. I sent the A.P.s after him but as far as I know they haven't found him. The clinic waiting room is full of flu or food poisoning patients—I haven't decided which. Penny's gathering histories as we speak. And the ambulance crew is on its way to a car accident near Hays."

She felt at a loss. She couldn't think.

"Sandy?"

She shook herself and looked fully on him.

"Are you all right?" he asked.

"Why wouldn't I be?"

"You still look a little sick."

"I've got a touch of that flu. It will pass."

They walked down the deserted back corridor together. As they came into view of a woman standing with a handkerchief pressed over her face, he murmured, "The mama of the pregnant girl. I'll take care of her while you move her daughter to the unit, okay?"

She pulled the patient chart from the holder, quickly scanned her name, and moved into the E.R. The girl was small, dark-eyed, and frightened. "Help me," she pleaded.

"We will, Mandy," Sandy forced herself to speak. "I'm going to take you to another room and get you some medicine to make the pain a little better."

"I can't," she wailed. "I need to go home."

Sandy released the brakes on the cart and moved Mandy down the back hall. The girl began to scream before they reached the unit. Sandy had to bite her lip to stop from screaming with her. She handed Jim's orders to the labor unit nurse and hurried back to the clinic.

The waiting area was a mess of full emesis basins and stainless steel buckets. The sour air caused Sandy to pause and catch her breath before she hurried to the med room, where she found a note and several vials of medication.

> Compazine. I pulled these vials from the pharmacy. Each to receive 10mg. The common denominator is chocolate éclairs from the PX. Sorry to leave a mess like this. I've talked to Jim. He said give Compazine and then admit all eleven. I'll stay until you get them settled. Be in the O.R. Thanks, Penny

Dependable Penny, Sandy thought. Willing to do overtime to catch them up. She began to fill syringes.

She helped the medical unit nurse start I.V.s on some of the admissions before she learned that the young girl was undergoing a C-section. Sandy was on her way to the O.R. to check on her progress when the ambulance returned with the man from the car accident. Knowing Jim and Penny were tied up in the O.R., she hurried to the E.R. The man was in tough shape.

"Almost a goner when we picked him up," the corpsman said. "We got a line in and stopped the bleeding but he hasn't responded."

Sandy did a quick assessment and called the O.R. "Tell Jim not to start the C-section, Penny," she said. "Something's not right with this guy. He got whacked in the chest by the steering wheel. He's unconscious and barely breathing. I'm bringing him directly over there."

She and two corpsmen pushed the gurney to the O.R. doors. Jim came out, did a quick exam, and inserted an endotracheal tube. Another corpsman brought in a pint of blood and Sandy began to pump it in.

Jim shook his head. "He's a goner," he said. "Nothing more we can do." He pulled off his gown and began to scrub his hands.

Through the glass of Room 1, Sandy could see the O.R. crew waiting around the bulging belly of the young girl.

A life for a life, she thought. She and a corpsman continued on to the morgue. Her heart and body were weary with defeat.

"Sorry," she said to her dead patient. "I'm just so sorry."

"You can't apologize to them all, Lieutenant," the corpsman said.

"No," she agreed.

She put together a chart for the man, finished as much documentation as she could, and began a records search for his family. She had to awaken a personal affairs officer and a chaplain to make the trip into the city to notify the next of kin. One more swing through the medical unit, another food poisoning victim at the main door, one more shot, and one more admission before she saw the O.R. crew heading into the parking area. She hurried to the O.B. recovery area to check on Mandy and found her sleeping soundly as her mother sobbed at her bedside.

When she returned to the supervisor's office, she found that Penny had left a written report and Jim was dozing in a chair. He opened his eyes. "One in and one out. Barely breaking even," he said.

"I brought you some coffee." She sank gratefully into her chair.

"Thanks. I ordered a postmortem on the accident guy. Did you find his family?"

"Personal Affairs did. They're notifying them now."

"He went fast," Jim said. "Must have had a big internal bleed."

She leaned back and rocked her chair gently. "What was the kid?"

"A boy. Catholic Services will pick him up tomorrow."

"Find out who the father was?"

"An uncle. Been living with the family. Girl was too scared to tell."

"A.P.s find her dad?"

"Yes, thank God. He would have killed the uncle if he'd been able to get to him."

"Can't blame him."

"No." He sipped his coffee and moved to the couch where he lay down and closed his eyes. "The uncle is military too. The A.P.s picked him up. That'll keep him out of the dad's way."

"No need to have a murder hung on her dad." She turned back to her desk and began to sort through reports. "That's what I like about you, Jim," she said. "You're a true humanitarian. Always taking care of people."

He laughed. "And it's wearing the hell out of me."

"Me too." She leaned her head onto her arms and closed her eyes. She tucked her knees together and crossed her feet beneath her chair.

Jim began to laugh.

She turned around and studied him. "You're losing it, Jim," she said.

"No, you are. You have a new love."

"What are you talking about?"

He pointed to her shoes and continued to laugh. "Who is he, Sandy? You can tell old Jim."

His laughter was contagious. "Stop it, Jim, and tell me what's so funny."

"Your shoes, Sandy." He pointed to her feet again. "It's on the bottom of your shoes."

She turned her feet inward. "I love you" was printed on her soles. A strange mixture of elation and despondency filled her.

"I caught you again, didn't I? Who is he? Come on, spill the beans."

She had to get it off. She went to the hallway sink, wetted a paper towel, and began to scrub. The words remained.

Jim followed her out and persisted. "Tell me. Come on."

"It's none of your business! Just none of your goddamned business!" she hissed.

His head came up sharply. He stopped laughing. He took her by the shoulders. "Sand. I'm so sorry. I shouldn't tease you. I thought it was a joke."

She wouldn't look at him. "It's no joke, Jim."

"Can I help?"

She shook her head, moved away, and stared into the empty lobby. "It's something I have to work out for myself."

"You love him?"

She nodded.

"Ace Martin?"

She nodded again.

He came up and stood beside her. "When God blesses us with real love, it's not a good idea to turn our backs on it."

The forever physician, she thought, telling a mother her daughter would give birth, telling a wife her husband couldn't be helped, telling a young girl that to love couldn't be wrong.

"He's a fighter pilot, Jim. I can't put myself out there again. Can you understand?"

He took a deep breath and turned her gently to face him. "I do understand. But maybe you should give him a chance. If he loves you and you love him, you can't let fear keep you apart."

She shook her head.

"Tell me what you're afraid of," he said.

"I'm afraid of those smoking holes and bloody, booted feet. Don't you see? It's better to do it now than to wait until the odds catch up with him and he leaves me a widow. I'm not strong enough for that."

"Maybe he is," Jim said. "Maybe you should give him a chance to prove it."

She shook her head. "I've already decided. I've said my good-byes."

When her shift was done, she drove home slowly. Her terror, lack of sleep, and the dark sadness of the night's events made everything seem blurred and unreal. She knew that, like the breath of that dying man, his love would pass away—and peace be with you, and with your spirit, amen. She would plan a trip, go somewhere exotic, and find more anonymous lovers who would dull the pain. No need to see him ever again.

She began to work out each step so she would have solutions to every problem that came up. She arrived at the duplex, dragged her feet up the stairs, and pushed open the door.

Ace was sitting on the couch, his hands clasped on his chest, his face ghostly grim in the uneven light.

A million words might be spoken, but she could say only one. "Ace?"

"Who did you expect? The pope?"

His voice brought sanity. Confusion melted away. Here was the enemy. Enemies were mortal too. Enemies could be conquered. It was the faceless unknown that was to be feared.

He didn't move but sat stubbornly in front of her, a willful, persistent, and determined child.

"Did you get my message?" he asked.

"Yes."

"And?"

She walked past him and threw the words over her shoulder. "And what?"

He stood and took two steps toward her. "And it made you angry, or it made you sad, or just maybe it made you happy. Tell me what it made you."

"Nothing. It made me nothing."

"You're lying, Sand," he said softly. "For the first time since I've met you, you're telling a big, fat lie."

Anger welled up like a sudden storm, furious and unexpected. "I've lied to you lots of times, Ace. Lots of times! My whole damned life is one big lie."

He moved a step closer and laughed. "Bullshit. You've never lied to me. You've only lied to yourself."

He was touching her now, his hands on her arms, his body too, too close. She lashed out with one hand, caught her clawing fingers on his soft and yielding face. He grabbed her wrists.

She began to fight him, to beat his chest with frail, weakening hands, lashing out in a frantic effort to keep him away, to prevent him from touching her heart, prevent him from seeing the thing he had brought so near to the surface.

She was no match for him. He wasn't afraid. He forced her hands to her sides, reached out and encircled her in his arms, held her to him, and snuffed out the wild, hated thing that stood between them.

She remained rigid in his arms.

"I do love you, Sandy."

She tried to push him away.

"I won't hurt you, Sandy. I promise you. I won't ever hurt you. Don't fight me. Don't push me away."

She stood stiffly with her face averted so she wouldn't have to look at the gashes on his face or the softness in his eyes. She would drown if she looked into those eyes.

"You don't know me," she said. "You know nothing about me."

"I don't need to know." He pulled slightly away. "Look at me."

She couldn't.

"Look at me."

She turned her eyes to his bleeding cheek, but not to his eyes.

"Really look at me."

Their eyes locked. Misery poured from hers. Love from his.

"I know all I'll ever need to know about you, Sandy. I know that I love you. That I'll always love you. That I'll never need anyone else but you. Do you believe me?"

"How could you? I've done so many bad things."

"So have I."

"You've never killed a man."

"Yes I have, in numbers more than you or I will ever know."

"You've never truly hated anyone."

"I do now. I hate all the people who've hurt you."

"I've hurt myself. It's no one else's fault."

"Dave dropped by last night. He explained some things I might not have understood."

"Even Dave couldn't tell you things about me. Even he doesn't know the real me." She was stunned to feel tears trickling down her cheeks.

He reached up and gently wiped them away with the fingers of one hand. She reached out and smeared the seeping blood on his face. "I've hurt you," she said.

"Only a scratch."

She leaned forward and touched her face against the crimson stain. He wrapped his arms more tightly around her. She began to sob. Her tears mixed with his blood and dropped onto her white uniform. Gasping sobs, so filled with emotion she felt she would burst in her effort to hold them back, escaped from deep within. A dam was breaking, and all the forces in the universe wouldn't hold it back.

She laid her face against his chest and allowed her pent-up pain to flow freely onto his zippered pockets.

"I love you," he whispered into her hair. "I'm thankful for every person and every experience that you've known because they made you the you I'm holding now—the one who feels so deeply and so much. I need to hold you and to love you, now and always."

Her knees would no longer support her. He lowered her gently to the floor and pulled her to him, cradled her as racking sobs shook her. She willed the sobs to stop so she could speak, but they would not.

Ace wiped her face with his neck scarf until it was too wet to absorb another tear, and still she cried. He moved her to the couch, went into the bathroom and brought out a soft towel, used it until it was too damp to be of any further use.

And still she cried. For Meyer and Colonel Hart and Gramps and Randy and B.B. and Kate and Cindy and for the tiny baby Broward. She sobbed for the war widows and for her high school sweetheart who she had not understood. She cried for the new boys who threw beer and played roughly, never knowing if their futures would end in a rice paddy or a tiny airless pit. She cried for their ignorance and for her innocence and for the lost joy of her youth that she had spent so lavishly. And she cried for Bob and Penny and Dave and all the others whose voices rose above the crowds but might never be heard. And she cried for Mike, who had known so much but never truly learned.

When at last her sobs subsided, she lay against Ace's sodden chest, beside a small stack of bathroom towels, too spent to move.

He laid her head on a last rolled towel. She curled her knees against her chest and dozed. She awoke to the sound of running water. He loosened her missive shoes and helped her sit up. "You're exhausted, Sand," he whispered. "I've run a tub for you."

She watched his competent fingers undo every white button on her uniform, sat passively as he removed her underclothes, allowed him to guide her to the misty bathroom and help her into the tub. She sank gratefully into the warm, deep water. She felt a summer breeze of home, a soothing river bottom where the mud oozed thickly through her toes. She lay back and allowed him to care for her.

When the water began to cool, he urged her to stand and soothed her with a warm towel. He laughed as he pulled a flannel nightgown over her head. She recognized the scent of lemon soap and knew he had dug deep into her bottom drawer to find this friend. He led her to her bed and pulled the sheet over her. She felt his body settle next to hers, his warm arms encircle her, and his breath against her ear before she fell into a deep redemptive sleep.

She dreamed of something frightening and began to wake. "Shh," he whispered. "It's just a dream."

She slept again.

When she awoke, the room was dark and strangely silent. She sat upright. Was he gone? Oh, he couldn't be. She pushed the sheet aside. A beam of light cut the darkness and he was standing in the doorway wearing only jockey shorts and holding a spatula in his hand. The scent of bacon and coffee followed him into the room.

Shyness overtook her.

"Hi," he said.

"Hi."

"Hungry?"

"Starved."

"Come on, then. Your love slave has made breakfast."

She padded after him.

"What time is it?"

"Near morning," he said. You've slept a day away."

The table was set with candles, silverware, and plates.

"I have to go to work."

He shook his head. "I called in for you."

"Oh, Ace." She blushed at the thought of what Major Roberts might have said.

"I talked to Jim Andersen. I told him you had some darned flu."

"What did he say?"

"He said, 'Well fine, that's fine,' and then he laughed and said, 'Good luck, Ace.'"

She smiled and looked into his eyes, more than willing to drown if that's what he wished for her.

He reached across the table and took her hands. "Come on," he said. "Tell me. Say it out loud."

"I love you," she whispered.

His eyes became warm and overwhelming. He grinned. "I knew it. I knew it all along. Now say one more thing."

"What?"

"Yes."

"Yes?"

He nodded. "It's easy. It goes like this. "Yes, Ace, I love you so much I'll have to marry you."

"Oh, Ace, I ..."

He pressed a finger to her lips. "Just one small yes. That's all it takes."

She touched his face, his hair, his ears, and his lips in the way a blind person touches when they want to know the soul of the one they love.

She looked into his eyes and saw everything she needed to see. "Yes," she said as firmly as she could. "Yes. Yes. Yes."